HIS BLACK SHEEP BRIDE

BY
ANNA DePALO

AND

THE BILLIONAIRE BABY BOMBSHELL

BY
PAULA ROE

"Your father wants a dynastic marriage. Real but—"

"Loveless," she finished for him before he could spell it out for her.

He nodded. "It's been done for centuries."

Of course, it was centuries of ruthless breeding that had produced Sawyer Langsford—a man's man, a captain of industry, a guy who seemed capable of impregnating a woman just by looking at her.

"I'm suggesting a short-term arrangement for our mutual benefit," Sawyer stated.

"Well, I know what you would get out of the arrangement," she shot back.

"Do you?" he said smoothly.

HIS BLACK SHEEP BRIDE

BY
ANNA DePALO

Published in Great Britain 2011
by Mills & Boon, an imprint of Harlequin (UK) Limited,
Eton House, 18-24 Paradise Road, Richmond, Surrey TW9 1SR

© Anna DePalo 2010

ISBN: 978 0 263 88229 2

51-0611

Harlequin (UK) policy is to use papers that are natural, renewable and recyclable products and made from wood grown in sustainable forests. The logging and manufacturing processes conform to the legal environmental regulations of the country of origin.

Printed and bound in Spain
by Blackprint CPI, Barcelona

For Olivia

A former intellectual property attorney, **Anna DePalo** lives with her husband, son and daughter in New York City. Her books have consistently hit the Waldenbooks bestseller list and Nielsen BookScan's list of top 100 bestselling romances. Her books have won an *RT Book Reviews* Reviewers' Choice Award for Best First Series Romance and have been published in over a dozen countries. Readers are invited to surf to www.annadepalo.com, where they can join Anna's mailing list.

Dear Reader,

I've always wanted to write a series with aristocratic grooms. This one draws upon my wonderful New York City as well as the English countryside, which I grew to love while studying abroad after college.

I hope you're entertained (and have a laugh or two) while reading Tamara and Sawyer's romance. It was fun watching my tart-tongued, nonconformist heroine loosen up the conservative (or so she thinks) hero. Tamara may have made a devil's bargain, but Sawyer may wind up losing his heart!

I also hope you enjoy reading about Tamara and Sawyer's friends—Pia and Belinda, and Hawk and Colin. Watch for their stories, coming soon from Desire!

Warmly,

Anna

One

Serving as maid of honor at a wedding was hard enough. If you were trying to avoid someone—such as your intended fiancé—it could be unbearable.

From across The Plaza's crowded reception room, Tamara eyed Sawyer Langsford—or as he was more grandly known in some quarters, the Twelfth Earl of Melton.

She reflected that some things—say, an uncaged lion—were best considered at a distance. Sawyer was an unpleasant reminder of the match her father and his had given voice to making for years. And then, Sawyer had never vocalized *his* thoughts about marrying her, leaving her in a perpetual state of unease.

If she was wary and even hostile, it was also because her personality and Sawyer's were so different—he being so much like her tradition-bound but ambitious, aristocratic father.

Damn Sawyer for being here today. Didn't he have a drafty English castle somewhere that needed his attention? Or at least a moldering dungeon where he could sit and brood?

What was he doing playing the part of one of Tod Dillingham's debonair groomsmen?

If only he looked like a dark, unhappy aristocrat fighting private demons. Instead, he was all golden leonine prowess, owning his domain and topping most people in the room.

If she were being fair, she'd say a society wedding wasn't all that surprising a place for her to run into Sawyer. Almost unavoidable, really, since Sawyer spent a great deal of time in New York for his media business.

But she wasn't in the mood to be fair. Today, as Belinda Wentworth's maid of honor, she'd had to stand at the altar, a smile pasted on her face, aware of Sawyer mere feet away among the other groomsmen.

As the Episcopal priest had intoned the words that would join Belinda and Tod in wedlock, Sawyer's gaze had come to rest on her. He'd looked every inch the aristocrat in white tie and tails, his black tuxedo accentuating his masculinity and air of command. His light-brown hair had reflected gold, caught in a beam of light filtering through one of the church's stained-glass windows, as if some deity in a whimsical mood had decided to spotlight a naughty angel.

Shortly after that moment, the Wentworth-Dillingham nuptials had gone hopelessly awry.

Tamara would have been consoling Belinda at the moment, if the bride were anywhere to be found. But Belinda had disappeared along with Colin Granville, Marquess of Easterbridge—the man who had interrupted the wedding ceremony with the shocking news that his Las Vegas marriage to Belinda two years earlier had never been annulled.

Now, from across the room, Tamara watched with a sinking heart as her father, Viscount Kincaid, approached Sawyer and the two men began to chat.

After a moment, Sawyer looked across the room, and his gaze locked with hers.

His face was handsome but unyielding—the stamp of

generations of conquerors and rulers on his face. His physique was lean and solid, like a soccer star in his prime.

Just then, the side of Sawyer's mouth lifted in silent amusement, and Tamara felt her pulse pick up.

Disconcerted, she quickly looked away. She told herself her reaction had nothing to do with physical attraction, and everything to do with annoyance.

To bolster that thought, she wondered whether Sawyer had had advance notice of what Colin had intended—and perhaps more, had been feeding Colin inside information. She hadn't seen Sawyer near Colin earlier at St. Bartholomew's Church. But she'd seen them speaking at social functions in the past, so she knew them to be friendly.

Tamara's lips compressed.

Trust Sawyer to be friends with a villain like Colin Granville, Marquess of Easterbridge, who'd just acquired another title: wedding crasher extraordinaire.

She looked around, careful not to glance in Sawyer's direction. She couldn't find Pia Lumley, either. She wondered whether the wedding planner—part of her and Belinda's trio of girlfriends—had managed to catch up with the bride after encouraging all the guests to repair to a show-must-go-on reception at The Plaza. Or whether Pia was closeted somewhere, in fits over the nuptial disaster that had befallen them all today.

The last time she'd seen Pia, the pixie blonde had been walking away from James Carsdale, Duke of Hawkshire, another friend of Sawyer's, and toward the swinging doors that admitted the waitstaff. Perhaps right now someone in the kitchen was waving smelling salts under her friend's nose, trying to revive her from a dead faint.

Tamara sighed, but then her gaze landed on Sawyer again, and their eyes connected.

His mouth lifted sardonically, and then he turned his head

to exchange a few words with her father before both men glanced at her.

A moment later, she realized with horror that Sawyer and her father were heading in her direction.

For a split second, she thought about trying to get away. *Run! Duck! Disappear!*

But Sawyer was advancing on her with a mocking look in his brown eyes, and her spine straightened.

If the media baron was searching for a story, she'd give him one.

Of course, a delicious scandal had just landed in his lap with the Wentworth-Dillingham almost-wedding, but she could always add icing to the cake for him.

After all, didn't a number of his newspapers publish the pseudonymously-authored Pink Pages of Mrs. Jane Hollings— bane of society hostesses and tart-tongued nemesis of social climbers everywhere?

Tamara pressed her lips into a thin line.

"Tamara, my dear," her father said, his expression hearty, "you remember Sawyer, don't you?" He chuckled. "No introductions are necessary, I assume."

Tamara felt her face stiffen until it resembled a frozen tundra. "Quite."

Sawyer inclined his head. "Tamara…it's a pleasure. It's been a long time."

Not nearly long enough, she thought, before gesturing around them. "It looks as if you'll be the subject of your own newspapers after the wedding debacle today." She arched a brow. "Mrs. Jane Hollings is one of your columnists, isn't she?"

A ghost of a smile crossed Sawyer's lips. "I believe so."

She smiled back thinly. "I can't imagine being the topic of your own gossip would sit well with you."

His lips curved easily this time. "I don't believe in press censorship."

"How practically democratic of you."

Rather than looking offended by her jab, he seemed amused. "The earldom is hereditary, but the title of media baron was acquired in the court of public opinion."

It was on the tip of her tongue to ask what else was hereditary—his arrogance, perhaps?

Her father cleared his throat. "Let's turn to a more pleasant subject, shall we?"

"Yes, let's," she agreed.

Her father's gaze swung between her and Sawyer. "It seems like only yesterday the previous earl and I were sitting in his library, sipping fine bourbon and speculating over the happy possibility our children might one day unite our families through marriage."

There it was again. As far as hints went, it was about as subtle as a sledgehammer.

She resisted the urge to close her eyes and groan, and she was careful not to look at Sawyer.

Apparently, just as she'd feared, seeing her and Sawyer as part of the bridal party had been giving her father ideas—or rather, bringing back old ideas. *Very* old ideas.

She'd grown up hearing the story told and retold. Years ago, before Sawyer's father had passed away, her father and the Eleventh Earl of Melton had already been chummy enough to talk about a dynastic marriage between their two families—one that would unite their respective media empires, as well.

Unfortunately for her, as the eldest of three female half siblings—each the product of one of the viscount's successively brief marriages—she was the logical selection to fulfill dynastic aspirations.

And, likewise, Sawyer, as the successor to the earldom, since his father had died five years ago, was the natural choice on the other side.

Fortunately, both her younger sisters weren't in attendance

today, but instead were tucked away at their respective universities. She knew she could withstand Sawyer Langsford. She didn't want to worry about her younger and more impressionable sisters.

After all, she conceded somewhat grudgingly, Sawyer had massive appeal for the opposite sex. She'd seen evidence of that herself over the years, which served as yet another on her very long list of reasons to dislike Sawyer.

"Not that silly story again," she said, attempting to laugh off her father's words.

She looked at Sawyer for confirmation, but realized he was regarding her thoughtfully.

He nodded toward the band, which was playing a romantic tune. "Would you like to dance?"

"Are you joking?" she blurted.

He arched a brow. "Isn't it our job as members of the wedding party to make sure the show goes on?"

Well, he had her there, she admitted. She certainly had some obligations as the maid of honor. And assuming he wasn't a double agent for Colin Granville, erstwhile wedding interloper, she supposed he did, too.

"Splendid idea!" her father said. "I'm sure Tamara would be delighted."

She shot Sawyer a speaking look, but he just gestured pleasantly, as if to say, after you.

She preceded him to the dance floor.

She held herself stiffly in his arms, and the side of Sawyer's mouth quirked up in acknowledgment.

Her smooth, upswept red hair contrasted with her peaches-and-cream complexion, and the difference hinted at the dual sides of her personality: fiery, but poised.

She reminded him of the American actress with the fairy-tale role—what was her name? Amy Adams.

But with attitude. A lot of attitude. And he had a feeling

this Cinderella or Snow White wasn't waiting for a prince on a white steed to come save her.

Tamara had always marched to the beat of her own drummer. Viscount Kincaid's wild child. The bohemian jewelry designer with an apartment in Manhattan's SoHo neighborhood.

In fact, today she looked about as demure as he could ever remember her appearing. She wore a formfitting strapless ivory gown with a black satin sash.

But instead of the Kincaid family jewels, she wore a starburst necklace accented with black onyx, along with similarly styled drop earrings. He'd guess the jewelry was one of her own designs.

As she moved, a small rose tattoo peeked and disappeared above the bodice of her gown, right over the outside slope of her left breast—beckoning him, tantalizing him...reminding him why the two of them were like oil and water.

Her eyelashes swept upward, and she pinned him with a crystal-clear green gaze.

"What game are you playing?" she asked without preamble.

"Game?" he responded, his expression mild.

She looked annoyed. "My father refers to an arranged marriage, and in response, you ask me to dance?"

"Ah, that."

"I'd call that stoking the fire."

"I guess I should be relieved you aren't accusing me of a more sinister deed than asking you to dance."

She didn't seem to find his response the least bit amusing.

"Since you mention it," she said crossly, "I wouldn't be surprised if you had advance notice of Colin Granville's wedding escapade."

"Wouldn't you?" Interesting.

Their movements sent them skirting past another couple.

"Everyone knows you and the Marquess of Easterbridge are friends." She wrinkled her nose. "The aristocratic secret handshake, and all that."

He raised his eyebrows. "Colin is his own agent. And for the record, there's no secret handshake. It's a blood covenant—knives, thumbs, a full moon. You understand."

She didn't even bat an eyelash at his attempt at humor. "Your friendship doesn't extend to plotting society scandals?"

"No."

"It would help sell newspapers," she pointed out.

What would help him sell newspapers would be getting his hands on her father's media empire, he thought.

"Let's get back to the subject of my so-called game," he said smoothly. He exerted subtle pressure at the small of her back to guide them in a different direction.

"You're feeding the beast," she said emphatically.

By tacit agreement, over the years they'd avoided each other as much as possible whenever they'd had occasion to be at the same social function. The expectation of marriage had been like the white elephant in the room.

Until now.

"Maybe I want to feed the beast." He'd always tolerated the older generation's wedding machinations, but lately things had taken a different turn.

She looked startled. "You can't be serious."

He shrugged. "Why not? We'll probably both marry someday, so why not to each other? A dynastic marriage is likely to be as good as any other."

"I have a boyfriend."

He scanned the crowd. "Really? Where's the lucky man?"

Her chin jutted out. "He could not attend today."

"Tell me you're not dating another sad sack." *What a waste.*

She gave him a withering look.

"So that's why you're attending the wedding without a date," he continued, knowing he proceeded at the risk of incurring her wrath.

"It hasn't escaped my notice you're here alone, as well," she shot back.

"Ah, but there's a reason."

Her eyes narrowed. "Which is…?"

"I'm interested in merging Kincaid News into Melton Media. Your father is happy to oblige…if I marry his daughter." He cocked his head, and then echoed Viscount Kincaid's words with mock seriousness. "'Keep everything in the family, you see.'"

Her eyes widened, and then she said something under her breath.

"Exactly," Sawyer agreed, and then his lips quirked up. "After all, look at all the trouble you and your sisters have given him so far. You've all refused to fall in line. Your father's pinning his hopes on the third generation."

The song ended, and she made to pull away from him, but he tightened his arm around her waist. He sensed her resistance for a moment, but then he swung her deftly in a semicircle as the band moved into the next song.

He wasn't ready to let her end their conversation just yet.

And then, she felt good in his arms, he admitted, as delicious curves pressed against him.

If she were anyone else, he'd have been charming her into giving him her phone number—and maybe more. He'd have looked forward to sleeping with her.

He'd have to play his cards more carefully with Tamara, but the end reward would be infinitely greater.

Tamara gave him an artificial smile. "You sound like my father. Are you sure you're not the same person?"

Sawyer returned her smile with a feral one of his own. Tamara's father was fit and trim for a man of seventy, but that's where the physical similarity between the two of them ended. However, the viscount's salt-and-pepper hair and grandfatherly visage disguised a sharp mind and cutthroat business instincts.

"We've both got the stomach for high stakes," Sawyer responded finally.

"Yes, how can I forget?" she retorted. "Business before pleasure and family."

He shook his head. "So bitter for someone whose lifestyle has been bankrolled by the family fortune."

"It's been at least a decade since I was young enough to be bankrolled, as you put it," she countered. "I support myself these days—by choice."

He raised his eyebrows. So Tamara's image of an independent woman was more than mere show.

"I think the word *bitter* applies to different circumstances— like going through three divorces," she said pointedly.

"And yet, the viscount strikes me as someone who's far from unhappy with life. In fact, he's such a romantic, he's trying to get you to walk down the aisle."

"With you?" she scoffed. "I think not."

His eyes crinkled with reluctant admiration, even if it was at his expense. "You're a blunt-spoken New Yorker."

She arched a brow. "A woman after your own heart, you mean? Don't you wish!"

"My first marriage proposal, and turned down flat."

"I'm sure it'll do no damage to your reputation," she replied. "You media tycoons do know how to spin a story."

After a moment, he gave a bark of laughter. "For the record, what makes me an undesirable marriage partner?"

"Where do I begin? Let me count the ways…"

"Give me the five-second news bite."

"I understand why my father would want a son-in-law like you…"

He looked at her inquiringly.

"You're both peers of the realm and press barons," she elaborated.

"And those are bad characteristics?"

"But I also know why I don't want a husband like you," she went on without answering him. "You're too much like my father."

Back to that topic, were they? "Would it help to point out I don't have three ex-wives?"

She shook her head. "You're wedded to your media empire. The news business is your first love. You live and breathe for wheeling and dealing."

"I suppose the existence of ex-girlfriends isn't enough proof to the contrary?" he asked wryly.

"And what reduced them to ex status?" she probed.

He cocked a brow. "Maybe things just didn't work out."

"The key word there being *work,*" she returned. "Namely yours, I assume. My father lives and breathes the media business, even at the expense of people who love him."

He let the conversation lapse then, since it was clear they were at loggerheads. She hadn't said it, but it was clear she included herself among the victims who'd fallen by the wayside on the road of her father's ambition.

They danced in silence, but from time to time he glanced down at her averted face as she scanned the dancing and milling guests, looking as if she was searching for some escape.

She was quite a challenge. She was obviously marked by her parents' long-ago divorce and her father's overweening ambition, and unwilling to repeat her parents' mistakes.

He might have admired her unwillingness to sell herself short in the romance department. But as it happened, in these circumstances, he was the man who was being judged as not quite up to snuff.

With little effort, Tamara evoked all his latent ambivalence. He himself was the product of an ill-fated marriage between a British lord and an American socialite. So he had firsthand experience with free-spirited women who didn't adapt well to marrying into the tradition-bound British aristocracy.

His mother had named him after Mark Twain's most famous character, for God's sake. Who'd ever heard of a British earl named for someone conjured by a quintessential American author?

For a moment, Tamara made him doubt what he needed to do in order to get his hands on Viscount Kincaid's media holdings.

Then his jaw hardened. He'd be damned if he'd worked this hard to get to where he was only to be stymied by a few inconvenient conditions—including the existence of a sad-sack boyfriend.

When the music faded away, Tamara made to pull away, and he let her break free of his hold.

"We're done," she said, a challenge in her voice.

He let one side of his mouth quirk up. "Not nearly, but it's been a pleasure so far."

He watched as her green eyes widened. Then she whirled away and stalked off.

Two

The three-way conference call might as well have been invented for the girlfriend gab fest, Tamara thought.

She'd just dialed Belinda and Pia from her office phone. After Saturday's wedding disaster, she'd held off on calling. It was somewhat uncharacteristic behavior for her after a girlfriend crisis, but the truth was she'd been nursing a proverbial hangover herself. Plus, let's face it, this wasn't any old run-of-the-mill crisis involving men, money or bad bosses. It wasn't every day a woman had a bomb land on her wedding in the form of a heretofore unknown husband.

But now it was Monday morning. It was past time, Tamara thought, that she checked in and saw how her friends were holding up.

"Well, Mrs. Hollings is all over this one," she began without preamble after putting her girlfriends on speaker phone. "I swear if I ever get my hands on that woman…"

The thought that the old dragon of gossip was in Sawyer's employ only made her more irate.

Turning her mind in a different direction, she softened her tone. "Are you okay, Belinda?"

"I'll live through this," her friend responded. "I think."

"Are you still, ah, married to Colin Granville?" Pia asked, voicing the question Tamara herself wanted to ask.

"I'm afraid so," Belinda admitted. "But not for long. Just as soon as I get the *marquess*—" she stressed Colin's title sarcastically "—to agree to a valid annulment, everything will be all right."

"A quick end to a quick marriage…" Pia said brightly before trailing off uncertainly.

None of them needed a reminder of Belinda's ill-fated run to a Las Vegas wedding chapel.

Tamara knew that the Wentworths and Granvilles had been neighbors and rivals in the Berkshire countryside for generations. It was likely why Belinda had wanted her marriage to the Marquess of Easterbridge undone quietly, and had kept mum to everyone, including even her closest girlfriends, about the apparently short-lived elopement.

"Colin isn't giving you a hard time about the annulment, is he?" Tamara asked.

"Of course not!" Belinda replied. "Why would he? After all, it's not as if we had a real marriage. We dashed into a Las Vegas wedding chapel. The next morning we regretted our mistake. Colin said he'd take care of the annulment!"

"Let's back up to the part where you went into the chapel," Tamara said drily. "How did it happen? You dash to the airport to avoid missing a flight. You dash into a supermarket for some milk."

"You might even dash into Louis Vuitton to grab their latest it bag," Pia suggested.

"Exactly," Tamara went on. "But you do not dash into a wedding chapel to get hitched on the fly."

Belinda sighed. "You do if it's Vegas, and you've just run

into someone…unexpected. And you've had a drink or two that have gone straight to your head."

Pia's groan of commiseration sounded over the phone.

Tamara wondered how much blame to place on a couple of drinks, and how much on Colin himself. Her meticulous friend wasn't the type to get tipsy, at least not without a reason.

"You didn't change your name to Granville, did you?" Tamara asked. "Because if you did—"

Pia gasped. "Oh, Belinda, tell me you didn't! Tell me you didn't legally become one of the enemy!"

"Not to mention you would have been misrepresenting yourself as Belinda Wentworth for the past two years," Tamara commented.

She cringed for her friend. It looked as if Belinda, who was always so self-possessed, had dug herself a hole.

"Don't worry, I didn't change my last name," Belinda responded drily.

"So it was okay to marry a Granville, but not to become one?" Tamara quipped. "I love the way the tipsy you thinks."

"Thanks," Belinda retorted. "And don't worry—the tipsy me is not getting out of her locked and padded cell again."

Tamara laughed, but then quickly sobered. What was it about a man with a title that made a woman lose her head? Her thoughts drifted to Sawyer, and then, annoyed with herself, she focused on the topic at hand again.

Among their trio of friends, Belinda had always been the levelheaded, responsible one. After getting her degree in the history of art from Oxford, she'd begun a respectable career working at a series of auction houses. Tamara just couldn't picture Belinda eloping in Vegas with her family's nemesis. Pia, maybe, Belinda, no.

"There wasn't an Elvis impersonator involved, by chance, was there?" she heard herself ask.

Pia stifled a giggle.

"No!" Belinda said. "And I just want this headache to disappear!"

"Not likely," Tamara remarked. "I don't see Colin going away quietly."

"He will," Belinda replied adamantly. "What would make him want to stay in this ridiculous marriage?"

Now there was the million-dollar question, Tamara thought. Belinda sounded as if she was trying to convince herself as much as anyone else.

Tamara decided to turn the conversation in a different direction, to take the pressure off Belinda.

"Pia, I saw you stalking off to the kitchen at one point," she said. "You looked upset."

"I wasn't upset about Colin crashing the wedding," Pia responded. "Well, I was upset for Belinda. But I had s-someone—ah, other things on my mind."

Pia's slight stutter was in evidence, and Tamara knew it only came out these days when her friend was agitated about something.

Tamara decided to probe delicately. "Ah, Pia…these other things wouldn't have anything to do with a certain very toff British duke-turned-financier, would it?"

Pia gasped. "That didn't make Mrs. Hollings's column, too, did it?"

"I'm afraid so, sweetie."

Pia moaned. "I'm doomed."

According to the Jane Hollings column that had appeared in Sawyer's newspaper that morning, there had been an argument at Belinda's wedding reception between Pia and the Duke of Hawkshire. Reportedly, Pia had discovered at the reception that the duke was none other than the man she'd known only as Mr. James Fielding when she'd been involved with him a few years before. Upon the discovery of how she'd been mislead, Pia had apparently smashed some hors d'oeuvres into the duke's face.

"Pia, please," Belinda said, obviously trying to lighten the mood. "Doomed is committing bigamy."

"Which you didn't!"

"Almost."

"N-no one will want to hire a wedding planner who's a security risk to wealthy and titled guests!" Pia wailed.

"Did you really sleep with Hawkshire?" Belinda asked.

"He was Mr. Fielding at the time!"

"Oh, Pia."

"Oh, sweetie," Tamara said at the same time.

Naturally, Tamara thought darkly, Sawyer was friends with the duke as well as with Belinda's yet-to-be-annulled husband. Of course both of Sawyer's good friends would be disreputable.

"Well, it seems like we all had a *great* wedding," Tamara said. "Sorry, Belinda."

A sigh sounded over the phone. "No apologies necessary," Belinda said. "Not even the best spin doctor could put a good face on Saturday's disaster. It's not every day a bride almost acquires two husbands."

They all shared in some self-conscious laughter.

"Well, what made Saturday so bad for you, Tamara?" Belinda asked.

"In short?"

"Yes."

"Sawyer Langsford. Lord Odious himself."

Pia giggled.

"Oh, I don't think Sawyer is so terrible," Belinda remarked.

"Putting aside his friendship with Colin, you mean?" Tamara asked.

"Okay, I see your point," Belinda conceded.

"Sawyer is good-looking," Pia said. "Those topaz eyes, and all that rich, burnished hair—"

Tamara made a face. "Whose side are you on?"

"Well, yours."

"Good."

"What about Sawyer's presence put you out?" Belinda asked. "You've socialized before without any problem, as far as I could tell."

"Because we've always ignored each other," Tamara replied. "But my father seeing the both of us in the wedding procession reminded him of the cherished idea that he and the previous earl had of having their children marry each other."

Pia spluttered. "You and Sawyer?"

"Hilarious, I know," Tamara responded.

"Oh, rats," Belinda said. "If I'd known, I'd have suggested to Tod that he pick another groomsman."

Tamara grimaced. "It's not something I like to talk about. In fact, it's an idea I've been hoping was dead and buried. But then Sawyer made it clear on Saturday that he's willing to entertain the idea."

Pia and Belinda gasped.

Exactly, Tamara thought.

When she'd heard Sawyer was to be in the wedding party, she'd figured she was a big enough girl to handle it. But she hadn't foreseen Sawyer's proposal.

"You and Sawyer are so different!" Pia said. "You're the Bridget Jones to his Mr. Darcy."

Tamara closed her eyes in existential pain. "Please. Bridget and Darcy ended up together."

"Oops, sorry!"

Tamara knew Pia was a romantic. Being a wedding planner suited her friend's personality. The only surprising thing was that Pia herself wasn't married. But then, Pia had had her own experience with an odious man.

"So what's next for you two?" Tamara asked, wanting to change the subject.

"I'm flying to England for a few days on business."

"And I'll be in Atlanta to consult with a client on a wedding."

"Abandoning the field of battle?" Tamara couldn't resist joking.

"Never!" Belinda declared.

"In a sense," Pia said at the same time.

"I'm regrouping and marshalling my forces," Belinda went on, "including getting a lawyer."

"In meantime," Pia said, "I'll be coming up with some spectacular ideas for Belinda's second act as a bride." She added uncertainly, "Or should I say, third act...?"

There was a pause as everyone seemed to wince.

Then Tamara noticed a light flashing on her phone. "On that note, I think I have a call coming in."

As Tamara ended the call with Belinda and Pia, she wondered for which of the three of them Saturday would prove to be most portentous.

Her parting exchange with Sawyer came back to her.

She'd told him they were done, and he, damn him, had just replied insouciantly, "Not nearly, but it's been a pleasure so far."

One week later, Tamara wondered at her rotten luck.

Sawyer, again.

Usually she ran into him only once every few months. Maybe a couple of times a year.

But here he was—at a big fashion party taking place in a large TriBeCa loft. Minor celebrities, socialites and journalists were here to appreciate an up-and-coming designer.

But what was Sawyer doing here?

Tamara had seen a reporter for Sawyer's newspaper, *The New York Intelligencer,* at the party. Sawyer's own presence certainly was not necessary.

She knew he attended his share of parties, but this one was not the type he usually attended. Last time she checked, he didn't have a particular interest in fashion. In fact, she was sure his suits came from an old and stuffy Savile Row tailor with a warrant from the queen.

Sawyer's presence was a reason to keep up her guard, but at least she had body armor tonight in the form of a date.

She looked around. Tom hadn't yet returned with their drinks.

As she scanned the room, however, she noticed Sawyer walking toward her.

Rats.

She turned, but just as she ducked behind the heavy velvet curtain that encircled the perimeter of the room—obviously in place to hide blank walls and elevator doors from the view of the assembled guests—a familiar voice reached her.

"Leaving the field of battle?"

She halted, irritated that his words echoed her own to Belinda, but unwilling to show him any reaction.

Squaring her shoulders, she swung back toward him. "Never."

He gave a predatory smile. "Good."

She waved her hand toward the curtain to indicate the crowd on the other side. "I was simply trying to avoid getting blood on the designer labels in our latest skirmish."

"Thoughtful of you."

She tilted her lips in the semblance of a smile. "You might try it sometime."

After a moment, he had the indecency to chuckle.

"What are you doing here?" she blurted.

"I received an invitation, I accepted."

She frowned. "I've never seen you at a fashion event before."

"There's always a first time. Otherwise life would be boring."

She felt heat stain her cheeks, and shook off the feeling he was making a sexual suggestion about her...them.

"I suppose," she responded coolly, "though I also know there are certain things I don't care to try."

She tried to ignore the fact that her pulse had begun to skitter and skip the minute she'd heard his deep voice resonating behind her.

Her reaction both puzzled and annoyed her. Was it because he'd admitted to entertaining the idea of wedding her? It was only that she felt pursued, she insisted to herself. Surely she hadn't sunk so low as to feel flattered by his attention.

This was Sawyer, the man she'd spent a lifetime avoiding and disdaining. She wasn't like some medieval bride, content to be betrothed from birth.

Still, she couldn't help noticing he made his own fashion statement of sorts tonight. He looked model-perfect in a tieless tan suit and open-collar green shirt. It was about as fashion-forward as she could ever remember him looking. Had it been a long while since her recent encounters with Sawyer, or had he begun relaxing his sartorial standards and she simply hadn't noticed?

As if conducting his own wardrobe assessment, Sawyer gave her a sweeping look that ran up from her peep-toe slingbacks to her knee-length sheath dress, held up by spaghetti straps.

His eyes paused for a moment at her chest, before he raised them to her annoyed expression. "A redhead who isn't afraid to wear red. You never disappoint."

"I'm so glad you approve!" She couldn't help feeling there was an element of disapproval in his words. He was of her father's world, after all. Bohemian jewelry designers didn't fit.

In the next instant, however, he surprised her by reaching out to tuck a strand of hair behind her ear.

She stilled as he paused to finger a teardrop peridot earring. The contact was intimate—erotic, even—though he wasn't touching her directly.

"I'm interested in having some jewelry pieces designed," he said, his deep voice sending an involuntary thrill through her.

Pushing aside how very aware of him she was, she asked, making her voice sugary, "For your current love interest?"

He took his time answering. "You could say that."

She looked at him with exaggerated disbelief. "Am I to assume that's why you arranged to intercept me at a fashion event? Because you're looking for a jewelry designer?"

"Among other things."

She held on to her irritation because it was easier to deal with than how disturbing his nearness was. "Let's get back to what you're doing here. Or should I say, how you knew I'd be here?"

He gave her a level look. "One guess."

"My father," she said flatly.

"Correct."

Her lips tightened. "When I see him again..."

She castigated herself now for revealing to her father some of the details of her social and business schedule in response to his seemingly casual questions a couple of weeks ago when they'd met for lunch.

No question she and her father needed to have a serious conversation. One that included the reasons why he shouldn't interfere in her life. It apparently wasn't enough she was based in New York and he was often in London, putting the breadth of the Atlantic Ocean between them.

Sawyer regarded her with an unreadable expression. "Marriage is not such a crazy idea."

"Don't tell me you're still considering this!"

"The idea has its merits."

"And here I was thinking you sought me out to have a trinket designed for your current flame! Instead, you hauled yourself here in order to make a marriage proposal. Now there's a good, solid reason to attend a froufrou fashion event, when everyone knows you have zero interest in fashion!"

Thank goodness they were in a semiprivate area of the room, Tamara thought. The last thing she needed was for their argument to be witnessed by avid onlookers.

"Are you done?" he asked, his topaz eyes glittering.

Not by a mile. "How efficient of you. Well, you can erase the marriage proposal from your BlackBerry calendar! Good luck with the rest of your day."

She turned away, but she'd taken only two steps when he grasped her arm and swung her back toward him.

"You have to be the most prickly woman I know," Sawyer muttered.

"Yet another reason I wouldn't make a suitable wife," she flung back. "I can bring home the sarcasm, serve up your ego in a pan and never let you forget you're a—"

"Damn."

In the next moment, Sawyer's lips came down on hers.

Tamara stilled.

Sawyer's lips were soft but firm, and in the next instant, Tamara became aware that he tasted sweet but heady and carried the warm scent of man.

Sensation coursed through her, and her body hummed to life. She'd been kissed before, of course, but kissing Sawyer, she was discovering, was like doing vodka shots when she was used to beer.

Time slowed. She felt the heavy thump of her heart, and became aware of his lean, muscular strength pressed against her.

She reached up to clutch Sawyer's shoulders, and in response, he made a low, growling sound and deepened the kiss.

Her brain radioed the message that she'd been right to steer clear of him in the past. The man was pure testosterone poured into a suit—and he was sending her pheromones into chaos.

Help.

And then the sound of laughter came through the heavy, thick curtains. And just like that, she felt jolted from his sexual spell.

Tearing her lips from Sawyer's, she opened her eyes and shoved him away.

Her heart hammered as he rocked back a half step. But after a moment, his face went smooth and cool.

It was as if the hot lover of a moment ago who had caused her senses to riot had morphed back into the tycoon with an implacable facade.

"Well," Sawyer said slowly, "I guess we answered one question."

A question? She was thinking more in terms of exclamation points. Lots of them.

"Which is?" she huffed.

"We have no problem with sexual chemistry."

Her eyes widened. "Get over yourself."

He gave her a sweeping look, and muttered, "It's you I think I need to get over."

A wave of heat washed over her. An image of Sawyer, naked and looming over her in bed, flashed through her mind.

"You need to come with a warning label!" she shot back.

His smile was rather wolfish. "Isn't that what I'm proposing?" he asked. "Make the world safe for other women. Take me off the market."

"I'm a jewelry designer, not a lion tamer."

"You could be both," he said, his voice smooth as honey.

She cursed herself for finding his sexual banter seductive. Wasn't she an educated, independent woman of the twenty-first century?

Sawyer, on the other hand, was a throwback to feudal

lords—and thanks to his ancestors, he had a real, present-day title to match.

Well, he'd have to look for his countess elsewhere. She didn't know where—though she supposed a fashion event with plenty of beautiful, pedigreed women tottering around in four-inch heels wasn't a half-bad bet—but she knew she wasn't in the running.

"In any case," Sawyer said, breaking into her thoughts, "I'm not proposing what your father has in mind."

"Oh?" she asked with false smoothness. "Then what are you proposing?"

"Your father wants a dynastic marriage. Real but—"

"Loveless," she finished for him before he could spell it out for her.

He nodded. "It's been done for generations."

"This is the twenty-first century."

Of course, it was centuries of ruthless breeding that had produced Sawyer Langsford—a man's man, a captain of industry, a guy who seemed capable of impregnating a woman just by looking at her.

"I'm suggesting a short-term arrangement for our mutual benefit," Sawyer stated.

"A short-term marriage of convenience?" she asked incredulously.

"Right."

"Well, I know what you would get out of the arrangement," she shot back.

"Do you?" he said smoothly.

She ignored the subtext of sexual suggestion. "You'd get control of Kincaid News. But what in the world would be the incentive for me?"

"You'd be doing the right thing for your family," he said, unperturbed. "The majority of your father's media business is in the United Kingdom, while most of my company is in the United States. With corporate synergies, both our companies can continue to prosper. Your father needs a successor for the family firm, and I know the media business."

He added with a quirk of the lips, "Your father would stop trying to interfere in your life. He'd be forever in your debt."

She frowned. "Only because I'd be married to you!"

The price was too high.

"We'd seem to be married for a short while," Sawyer allowed. "But we'd both know the truth."

She felt an unexpected twinge, and then despite herself, she asked, "What about divorce? What happens to the companies then?"

"Once the companies have merged, I'm betting there'll be no turning back. Your father will have his money, and he'll be forced to concede the efficacy of the deal."

"How convenient for you," she responded. "You get your hands on Kincaid holdings without the long-term baggage of a Kincaid bride."

Sawyer's lips quirked again, and this time, she itched to wipe the smile off his face.

"I wouldn't call you a piece of baggage," he said.

"I'm not marrying you."

"There'd be additional benefits for you."

"Those being what?" she retorted.

"I'm in a position to help you move your jewelry business to the next level," he said. "In a way your father hasn't been."

Her spine stiffened. "There are too many strings attached," she said warily. "Anyway, what do you know about my design business?"

"I know Kincaid has refused to become an investor."

Tamara relaxed. It was apparent Sawyer's only clue about her business had come through her father.

She conceded that Sawyer's persistence was a valuable business trait. But she wasn't going to base her married life on a business deal—especially one where she had little to gain and all of her hard-won independence to lose.

"No thanks," she retorted. "I've got the situation well in hand."

"There you are!"

At the sound of a familiar voice, Tamara turned around and discovered Tom making his way toward them along the line of draped curtains, one champagne flute in each hand.

How had Tom thought to look for her here? Still, she was grateful for the rescue.

"Sorry, babe," Tom said. "I was intercepted by someone I knew. He was a guy who used to play some of the same gigs as Zero Sum."

Tom was the quintessential yet-to-make-it-big rocker. He was slightly unkempt, his brown hair curling at the neck of a black T-shirt and matching jacket. He and his band, Zero Sum, hadn't given up on looking for their big break.

Tom had been her occasional date for the past year, whenever he was in town. But right now, Tamara couldn't help contrasting him to Sawyer, who stood about half a head taller, and a world of difference away in smoothness.

Tamara considered herself tall—or at least, not short—at five-seven, but Sawyer had a considerable height advantage on her.

"Tom, you know his lordship, the Earl of Melton, don't you?" she asked, using Sawyer's title in order to strive for some emotional distance between them.

Sawyer's look said he saw right through her ploy.

She ignored him. "My lord, may I present Tom Vance?"

She watched as Sawyer and Tom shook hands and took each other's measure.

"Melton as in Melton Media?" Tom asked.

"One and the same," Sawyer replied.

Tom's face brightened. "Pleasure to meet you, ah—"

"My lord," Tamara supplied, trying not to roll her eyes.

"My lord," Tom repeated, and then shot a grateful look at her. "Thanks, Tam."

"Tam?" Sawyer queried sardonically. "Like Tom and Tam?"

"You've got it." Tom grinned, happy as a puppy.

Tamara could see the wheels turning in Tom's head. To Tom, meeting Sawyer was like hitting the networking jackpot. Sawyer's media outlets presented limitless opportunities. Free publicity! Advertising! Name recognition! In short, the kind of opportunity that Tamara's father refused to provide to Zero Sum.

Sawyer glanced at her. "Tam—Ms. Kincaid, excuse me, won't you? There's someone who's expecting me."

Tamara had no doubt Sawyer had switched from *Tam* to her surname in order to mock her. Still, she was grateful their encounter was at an end.

Unfortunately, she didn't think they'd also put an end to the subject of a dynastic merger—marital, corporate or otherwise.

Three

The bar of the Carlyle Hotel was as good a place as any for three notorious bachelors to lie low.

Or rather, two notorious bachelors and one notorious groom, Sawyer amended.

It was ironic for him to lie low, since he was the press. But these were his friends.

Like his two fellow aristocrats, he'd grown up here, there and everywhere. Still, despite their peripatetic existence, he and his bar companions had managed to become friends.

And now they had another thing in common. Ever since the wedding fiasco at St. Bart's nearly two weeks ago, they were imbrued by the scandal of the moment.

The bar, with its dark woods and mellow lighting, was masculine and clubby and the perfect atmosphere to come together and commiserate.

It was also discreet without being sequestered. Because Sawyer would be damned if he was going to tuck in his tail and hide.

"Hell of way to crash a wedding, Easterbridge," James Carsdale, Duke of Hawkshire, said, going straight to the heart of the matter.

"You could have given us some warning," Sawyer added drily.

Sawyer had to admire Colin's sangfroid. Of the three of them, the marquess was the most reserved and enigmatic. And now he'd just thrown not one, but two ancient British families into upheaval with his surprising news at the wedding—and his shock-maximizing method of delivery.

In response, Colin Granville, Marquess of Easterbridge, who'd been the last to arrive, took a swallow of his Scotch on the rocks.

They were sitting at one corner of the bar, away from the few other patrons. Since it was a hot and sunny day, and still a couple of hours from sunset, the dark bar was not even half-full.

"You're the media, Melton, and you were a groomsman," Colin finally pointed out lazily. "A double conflict of interest. You'll understand why I didn't take you into my confidence."

Sawyer took issue. "You know I was picked as a groomsman because Dillingham and I are distantly related through our mothers. We're not friendly in a true sense."

"Yes," Colin responded wryly, "but that fact, along with your role as one of the world's most famous press barons, made you dynamite for the wedding party. The expectation of glowing press coverage was likely more than Dillingham could pass up. Not to mention cementing the extended family relationship."

Sawyer shook his head. "As it turned out, the only dynamite at the wedding was you, and Dillingham got more media coverage than he bargained for."

In response, Colin raised his glass in mock salute.

"If you couldn't confide in Melton," Hawk said, resting his

elbow on the back of his chair so he could lean back in his position between his companions, "you could've at least told me."

"Spoken like a true international man of mystery, Mr. Fielding," Colin returned.

Sawyer smothered a laugh. He couldn't picture their care-free, sandy-haired friend trying to pass himself off as a mere mister. Nor did he understand why Hawk would have wanted to.

"Right, and what's going on there Hawk?" Sawyer asked. "The rumor mill, and pardon me for reading my own newspapers, has it that you were more than friendly with a certain lovely wedding planner—"

Hawk grimaced. "What's going on is a private matter."

"Precisely my point," Colin said.

"A private matter, Your Grace?" Sawyer quizzed. "You mean between you and your alias, James Fielding?"

"Put a sock in it, Melton," the duke growled.

"Yes, Melton," Colin said, siding with Hawk, "unless you'd like us to quiz you on your pursuit of the fair Ms. Kincaid."

It was Sawyer's turn to grimace. His friends knew his acquisition of Kincaid News was tied up with Tamara's hand in marriage. Fortunately, they *didn't* know the particulars about his most recent interactions with Tamara. She'd gotten under his skin—so much so that he'd kissed her. And it had been some kiss—hot and wonderful enough to leave a man thirsting for more.

"I've seen Kincaid's daughter with a date," Hawk commented, arching a brow. "Always the same one."

Sawyer shrugged. "She takes a date from time to time."

"A date who's not you," Colin pointed out.

"Just an occasional date?" Hawk probed. "And you know this how?"

Sawyer gave a Cheshire-cat grin. "From the man himself,

Mr. Tom Vance, lately of the rock band Zero Sum, and perhaps soon to be the recipient of some very good career news."

Colin quirked an eyebrow, for once betraying a hint of surprise.

Hawk started to shake his head. "Don't go there..."

Since he already had, Sawyer gave both of them a bland look. "Know of any good West Coast record producers?"

She was sunk.

Or more accurately, practically destitute.

Tamara stared at the letter in her hand. Her bid for investors had fallen flat. Financing was tight these days, and people apparently weren't lining up to give money to a lone jewelry designer with a big idea and not much else to her name.

She'd maxed out her credit cards and had already gobbled up her allotment of small business loans.

She looked around her loft from her seat at a workbench cluttered with pliers, clasps and assorted gemstones. Her business had a name, Pink Teddy Designs, and not much else these days. Yesterday, she'd received notice her rent would be increasing, so soon even the four walls around her would cease to exist—as far as she and her business went, anyway.

She'd have to find another place to live and work. There was no way she could afford a ten percent rent increase—not with things the way they were.

She'd never have admitted this to Sawyer when she'd encountered him last week at the fashion party in TriBeCa, but these days she was hanging by a thread—one that was becoming very frayed very fast, ever since she'd left her salaried position two years ago at a top jewelry design firm to strike out on her own.

Rats.

She was desperate—and Sawyer's words reverberated through her mind. *I'm in a position to help you move your jewelry business to the next level.*

No, she wouldn't let herself go there.

And with any luck, Sawyer didn't have a clue as to just how dire her current financial situation was. He hadn't seemed as if he did. In fact, his words to her that night indicated he thought she was looking to expand her business, not merely survive.

She hoped her appearance had also served to throw him off the scent. She'd dressed to project an image of success. She'd worn expensive earrings of her own design to the fashion party—as much for advertising as for anything else, though the earrings were worth much more than the typical Pink Teddy piece of semiprecious jewelry.

Yes, she dreamed of expanding her business and having her name added to the roster of top celebrity jewelry designers. But she'd also had to start small, given her financing, or rather lack thereof. And now she was nearly broke.

People assumed she had money—or at least connections—as the daughter of a millionaire Scottish viscount. In fact, she was entitled to be addressed as the Honourable Tamara Kincaid and not much else. After her parents' divorce when she was seven, she'd gone to reside in the United States with her mother, who had been able to maintain a respectable, but not settled, lifestyle. Instead, thanks to child-support payments, Tamara had been entrusted to the care of a series of babysitters, schools and summer camps while her peripatetic mother had continued to travel and move them within the United States.

Her mother resided in Houston now with husband number three, the owner of a trio of car dealerships, having finally achieved a measure of stability.

Tamara sighed. Partly because of the physical distance, she and her mother weren't very close, but a fringe benefit was that her mother didn't interfere much in her life.

Of course, she could hardly claim the same benefit with

respect to her father, who owned an apartment in New York City.

But unlike her mother, she'd thumbed her nose at her father's money. Because the strings attached had been more than she'd been able to accept. As she'd grown older, her father had made his opinions known, and her artsy tendencies, her penchant for the bohemian and her taste for the unconventional had not gone over well.

Her father's attempts to meddle had, of course, reached their zenith in his crazy plan to marry her off to Sawyer.

Really, that scheme was beyond ridiculous.

Sure, her parents' marriage had been an ill-advised union between an American and a British aristocrat—a still-naive girl from Houston on the one hand, and the young and ambitious heir to a viscountcy on the other. But her starry-eyed mother, who'd imagined herself in love, had been thrilled by the prospect of residing in a British manor house.

In contrast, Tamara prided herself on being a worldly-wise New Yorker. And much as she hated to admit it, she had her father's skeptical nature. She'd inherited her mother's coloring and features, but that's where similarities ended.

She liked her life just fine. She was bohemian with an edge.

A marriage between her and Sawyer Langsford was laughable. They barely spoke the same language, though she had been known to read his paper, *The New York Intelligencer,* and occasionally watch the Mercury News channel.

To Sawyer's credit, Tamara acknowledged, his media outlets didn't stoop to petty sensationalism. And she had to admit he'd built an international media empire from the two British radio stations and the regional newspaper he'd inherited from his father. At thirty-eight, he'd stuffed a lifetime's worth of career accomplishments into a mere fifteen years or so.

At twenty-eight, she was a decade behind Sawyer in experience and worlds away in outlook. Yes, she wanted her design business to float instead of sinking into the great abyss, and yes, she dreamed of becoming successful. But she didn't aspire to the same lofty heights of empire building that her father and Sawyer did.

She'd effectively been abandoned twice by her father—once, in a transatlantic divorce, and then again by Viscount Kincaid's devotion to his media company. She couldn't—wouldn't—risk acquiring a husband who was from the same mold.

It would be beyond foolhardy, notwithstanding the kiss the other night.

Still, the kiss had repeatedly sneaked into her thoughts over the past few days. Sawyer had made her toes curl. And embarrassingly, she'd clearly responded to him.

But she knew why Sawyer had kissed her. He'd been trying to convince her to agree to a marriage of convenience.

If Sawyer thought she was a pushover for his seduction techniques, however, he had another thing coming. So she'd had a brief and primitive response to his air of raw power and sexuality. She was still well past the age of gullibility—of being swayed by a momentary attraction into a relationship with someone who was so very wrong for her.

In contrast, she and Tom were alike. They enjoyed prowling SoHo at night, appreciated the city, and were both artistic. They were friends, first and foremost.

They weren't two people from very different backgrounds united by lust. In other words, to her relief, they were definitely *not* her parents.

As if on cue, her cell phone rang, and it was Tom.

"You'll never guess what's fallen in my lap," Tom said.

"Okay, I give up. What?" she replied.

"I'm flying out to L.A. to meet with a big music producer. He heard one of our demos and is interested in signing the band."

"Tom, that's wonderful!" Tamara exclaimed. "I didn't even know you were in touch with a producer out in L.A."

Tom laughed. "I wasn't. The guy got his hands on the demo from a friend of a friend."

"See, networking works."

Tom gave an exaggerated sigh. "Here's the thing, babe. I'll be gone. Physically, existentially and in every other way."

She picked up on his meaning.

"What?" she said with mock offense. "You'll no longer be available to be my standby date?"

It was easy for her to adopt a lighthearted tone, she realized. Tom had never been more than a casual, occasional date for her—a reliable escort when she had to attend one social function or another. He was nothing more, despite their Tom-and-Tam epithet, and that was the reason she could be happy for him without rancor.

"Afraid not," Tom responded now. "Will you ever forgive me?"

"If I don't, you could always write a song about it," she teased.

Tom laughed. "You're a pal, Tam."

Tom's words summed up their relationship, Tamara acknowledged. It had always been easy and casual. Such a contrast, she thought darkly, from her fraught interactions with—

No, she wouldn't go there.

"It was a lucky break running into your friend the Earl of Melton."

Tamara started guiltily. "He's not my friend."

"Well, friend or acquaintance—"

"And what do you mean it was a lucky break?" she asked, even as she was touched by a feeling of foreboding.

"Well, this music producer has a friend who socializes with the earl. Seems the earl had heard my music—"

She'd just *bet* Sawyer was a fan of Zero Sum.

"—and had talked it up to a friend of his, who passed along the recommendation to his music industry connection."

Tamara felt a wave of heat wash up her face. He didn't... He wouldn't...

And yet, it was all too convenient.

When she found Sawyer, she was going to let him have it, and then some.

For Tom's sake, however, she forced herself to sound cheerful. There was no reason to rain on Tom's parade by imparting her suspicions about how his lucky break was more than mere luck.

Besides, from Tom's perspective, it didn't matter how his intro to a top music producer had come about. The bottom line was that he was getting his chance to hit it big.

"I owe this all to you, Tam," Tom said gratefully. "I don't need to tell you how tough things have been in the music industry lately, so getting someone to take a chance on Zero Sum is a big deal."

If only Tom knew *exactly* what he owed to her, Tamara thought.

"I'll keep my fingers crossed for you," Tamara said. "Blow them away."

"Thanks, babe. You're the best."

When she ended her call with Tom, she set down the phone and stared at it unseeingly, her brows knitting as she contemplated Sawyer's skullduggery.

She'd barely begun to get herself worked up over Sawyer's fiendishness, however, when the intercom sounded.

After she pressed the intercom button by the front door, she jumped as she heard Sawyer's voice.

She took a deep breath. Apparently her confrontation with Sawyer would occur sooner than she'd expected.

"Come on up," she said with a semblance of serenity, and buzzed him in.

Four

Trust Tamara to name her company something ridiculous and suggestive like Pink Teddy Designs, Sawyer thought as he rode the elevator up to the third floor.

The name had been emblazoned next to the buzzer for Tamara's apartment in a cast-iron warehouse building that had long ago been converted into lofts. Located along one of SoHo's narrow side streets, the sidewalk in front of Tamara's building had nevertheless been almost as crowded with pedestrians and street vendors peddling everything from paintings to T-shirts as SoHo's main commercial strips, Broadway and Prince and Spring Streets.

It looked as if Tamara had rented one of the cheaper apartments she could find in one of Manhattan's priciest boho neighborhoods. Factories and warehouses had long since given way to high-end retailers such as Prada, Marc Jacobs and Chanel, though some artists who had bought their lofts when they were cheap still held on.

Of course, Sawyer thought, the businessman in him could

appreciate that Tamara's choice of location made sense. Any business had a certain image to project, and location was part of it. But it seemed as if Tamara had cut corners where she could, starting with choosing a side street and a lower floor, closer to street noises.

He stepped out of the elevator and found Tamara's apartment. But just as he was about to hit the bell, the door opened.

As a first impression, Tamara made quite an impact. In two seconds flat, he registered a short V-neck purple dress, black peep-toe sandals with bows and an opal pendant nestled on the pillow of her cleavage.

His body hummed to life.

"What are you doing here?" Tamara asked, her voice cool and clipped, though her eyes flashed fire.

He twisted his lips sardonically. "That makes twice. Is that the way you greet all your clients?"

"Only the ones who aren't welcome." Then belying her words, she stepped aside. "What do you mean by *client?*"

Sawyer walked into the boxy but airy loft. "I want to have a piece of jewelry designed, if you'll recall."

Tamara's face registered disbelief before her eyes flashed fire again. "You can't be serious."

"That makes twice again. I seem to have a knack for eliciting the same reactions from you." Then he added, in answer to her question, "In fact, I am serious, and I thought you'd be happy about the offer of business."

He watched as she clamped her mouth shut. *Splendid.* He'd stopped her adamancy with a tantalizing lure—a reminder of what he had to offer, and what she stood to lose.

Sawyer scanned the loft. It looked like what his prior investigation had revealed: an apartment that also served as an office and business headquarters.

Near the back, he could see a partition that appeared to section off a sleeping area. To his right, near the entry door, there was a kitchen with light wood cabinets and black appliances. In front of him, the space was dominated by a comfy work area—a deep-red velour couch and armchair, a few potted plants and a large glass-topped table cluttered with what looked, at a glance, like the tools of the jewelry-making trade. A workbench stood off to one side.

The entire space was marked by a high ceiling and accentuated by large, inverted-U-shaped windows that let in plenty of natural light—a precious commodity in Manhattan's pricey real estate market.

Hearing a click as Tamara shut the door behind him, he walked with deliberate casualness to a nearby waist-high glass display case.

He let his eyes scan the bracelets, necklaces and earrings on display, all made from some type of green gemstone.

"It's green agate, in case you're wondering," Tamara said crisply as she stopped beside him.

He looked up from the case, and she regarded him challengingly, almost defensively.

"I was reading your stare," she explained.

"You have a unique style."

"Thank you, I think."

His lips quirked up. "You're welcome."

She looked pointedly at his custom-made business suit, as if making a silent judgment about the contrast in their two styles.

Perhaps she was also wondering why he'd bothered to fit a visit with her into his busy work schedule.

He wasn't about to accommodate her unspoken question, however. Because the truth was, though it was late Wednesday afternoon and the middle of his workweek, he'd cleared his schedule in order to come downtown and find her. And if Tamara knew the importance he'd attached to his visit, she'd clam up and retreat. Or more likely, it would raise her hackles again.

"What sort of commission do you have in mind?" she asked finally, saving him from a response.

He figured it was too much to hope she'd had an abrupt change of heart about creating jewelry for him. More likely, her curiosity was simply piqued. But he'd work with that for now.

"A coordinated set," he said blandly. "Earrings and a necklace."

"Of course," she responded with a corresponding lack of inflection. "Do you prefer a particular type of stone?"

He looked into her eyes. "Emeralds."

"A popular choice—" she gave him a saccharine smile "—but I can't help you. I focus on bridge jewelry made with semiprecious stones—"

"Designing fine jewelry with precious stones can't be much different," he countered.

Tamara hesitated before conceding grudgingly, "No, it's not."

"Great, then there's no problem," he responded smoothly. "Which stones do you like?"

She frowned. "I don't see how that enters—"

"You're a professional designer," he diverted. "I'd like to know what you think. What stones do you prefer, assuming money isn't an issue?"

She clenched her jaw. "Emeralds. Dark-toned ones."

He gave a satisfied smile. "Then we're in agreement. Make them big, and surrounded by diamonds."

She pursed her lips. "Has it ever occurred to you that I simply might not like a commission from you?"

"Never." He flashed a smile. "You're in business to sell jewelry, and I'm here prepared to spend six figures."

With an oblique reference, he cast another lure for her. He was a seasoned player at the negotiation table and now he brought his skills to bear.

She looked exasperated. "You are decisive."

"Yes, I am." He hid his satisfaction in the chink in her armor. "Aren't most of your clients?"

"I don't usually do custom orders," she responded. "It's not how I operate. The people who buy my jewelry appreciate something offbeat."

He grinned. "Not your usual high-society bling bling."

At her nod, he added, "Then I hope you can…accommodate me."

It was sexual banter, but he was careful to keep his expression innocent. Nevertheless, she regarded him with suspicious displeasure for a moment.

"No request is too unusual," she replied finally.

"What a relief."

She raised her eyebrows. "I'll need a deposit, and you'll have to give me time to contact my suppliers and find the right stones. Fat emeralds are not among my usual orders."

Touché. Still, he was happy to have her think of him as gaudy and tasteless as long as it got him one step closer to his goal. "Naturally, I understand. I hope I'm not putting you out."

"Not any more than the unexpected appearance of a persistent would-be client," she shot back.

The shadow of a smile touched his lips. Tamara certainly knew how to give as good as she got. What a waste she would have been on Tom. Sawyer was not the least bit repentant about his ruthless maneuvering.

Rather than respond directly to her jab, he turned the conversation in the direction he wanted it to go. "I thought you'd be happy about an expensive order." He glanced around at their surroundings. "I understand you could use some help."

Now that he had her on the hook, he could afford to drive his point home.

Tamara hesitated. "What makes you think so?"

"I have my sources."

She scowled suddenly. "Have you been talking to my father?" She held up a hand, as if to stop him. "No, wait. Don't bother answering that question."

"For the record, it was through my own digging. But what I didn't find out on my own, your friend Tom was happy to volunteer."

She ignored the reference to Tom and braced one hand on her hip, her eyes narrowing. "You had me investigated?"

He let his lips quirk up on one side. "I like to know who I'm doing business with. Avoids nasty surprises."

"So I should be flattered?" she demanded, looking outraged. "Is it a compliment that I merited the same full-blown investigation you might accord to a prospective business partner?"

"In or out of bed," he added to get a rise out of her.

Her face flushed with color. "I see." She gave him a sweeping look. "And I suppose none of your…girlfriends were infuriated by having to pass muster? Was the privilege of sleeping with you just too great a prize?"

He gave her a slow grin designed to incense. "No complaints yet."

"Oh!"

For a moment, she looked as if she was speechless with outrage, fishing around for the right words for a proverbial clobbering.

Finally, she bit out, "I suppose that's why you're here today—to order a trinket for one of the lucky winners?"

He cocked his head to the side, and then raised his hand to slowly brush a tendril back from her face.

She stilled.

"You could characterize it that way," he said in a deep voice that held just a hint of laughter.

She brushed his hand aside. "Fine," she huffed, her voice nonetheless holding a hint of breathlessness. "It's not my business why my clients come to me—or how."

"Not too discriminating to do business with the devil?" he baited her.

She gave him a narrow-eyed look. "Let's step over to my desk to discuss what you're looking for." She paused, and then added emphatically, almost warningly, "In a necklace and earrings coordinate set, of course."

He gave a low laugh as he followed her.

This sale was costing her, but she was gritting her teeth and bearing it since she needed the money. Pink Teddy Designs meant a great deal to her, and he planned to exploit the attachment to his every advantage.

Shamelessly...ruthlessly...unrepentantly.

Because if there was one thing he knew, Sawyer acknowledged as he admired Tamara's backside and shapely legs, it was that Kincaid News was worth the effort...and so was Tamara. And certainly, it would be no hardship to bed Tamara along the way to getting what he wanted.

At her desk—which was actually the large, glass-topped table he'd seen earlier—he sat in a bar-height chair at a right angle to her.

"So describe to me what you're looking for." She set aside some metal boxes so they sat out of her way, and added belatedly, "In earrings and a necklace."

"In earrings and a necklace, of course," he murmured, echoing her words.

In fact, he'd love to describe what he was looking for—in and out of bed.

The truth was, he acknowledged to himself with some degree of surprise, if he'd ever let himself really look over the years, he'd have said Tamara wasn't too far off the mark from what he usually looked for in a woman, though he'd never dated a redhead.

She had inherited her mother's model looks and figure. She had generous breasts and hips, but still managed to look willowy and statuesque. And she had amazing bone structure.

Her lips were full, balanced by an aquiline nose and delicately arched brows over crystalline green eyes. She was good enough to grace the cover of any glamour magazine, if she chose. That she *didn't* choose said a lot about her.

Physically, she fit his type. But he'd always envisioned someone who embraced his aristocratic heritage as his bride.

Tamara pulled a white paper pad in front of her, and then reached for a pencil. "Describe to me what you're looking for. If the design isn't to your liking, we can always play around with it. Computerized design technology is an amazing thing these days, but I prefer to start with an old-fashioned sketch."

He cocked his head and regarded her. "Something unique. Something that will have people take a second look."

"That's a wide universe," she replied archly, her pencil hovering.

He shrugged. "Let your imagination run wild."

She gave him another narrow-eyed look, as if she was thinking of hitting him over the head, or wondering at his audacity—the equivalent of asking the wife to pick out a gift for the mistress.

"I'm thinking of a choker," she said sweetly.

He laughed softly, and she put down her pencil and reached for a three-ring binder.

"Here," she said. "These might give you some ideas. They're some computerized drawings I've done."

"Great," he said, taking the binder from her.

While he paged through her drawings, she occupied herself with arranging objects on her desk and pointedly ignoring his study of her designs.

Finally, he set the binder on the table with deliberate casualness. He wasn't going to let her off the hook too easily. He knew what he wanted, and he wasn't going to stop until he got it.

"These are good, but I need more," he said.

She looked nonplussed. "More?"

"Yes. It would be better if you modeled some of your designs for me."

It took a moment for his words to sink in, but then her eyes flared, and their gazes clashed.

He shrugged, a smile playing at his lips. "Call it a singular lack of imagination."

He watched as she seemed to grit her teeth. How much was she willing to do for a lucrative commission?

He could practically see the wheels turning in her head. How far would she go to indulge his whims?

"Which one?" she finally asked with exaggerated patience.

He had little doubt her use of the singular was deliberate. She had no intention of modeling any more than the bare minimum for him.

Ignoring her hint of impatience, he picked up the binder again and thumbed through it.

Her designs were good. Better than good. He'd inherited the Langsford family jewels, and in addition, he'd bought his share of pricey jewelry over the years, so he was no novice buyer. And to his practiced eye, these designs looked fresh and different.

"This one," he said, stopping at a page and showing it to her.

She shook her head. "That piece has been sold. I don't have another one here like it."

Unperturbed, he moved on to another page. "What about this one?"

"That's topaz. The yellow gold setting wouldn't be right for diamonds and emer—"

"Humor me," he said with all the assurance of someone used to calling the shots—and being right. "I'm not looking at the metal but at the design."

"Right. Of course."

He hid a smile. *The client was always right.* She couldn't argue there, much as she obviously wanted to.

Tamara pushed back her chair and marched over to a safe across the width of the loft. After opening the safe door, she removed two velvet boxes.

Sawyer watched her intently, his body stirring.

Without looking at him, she stepped over to the gilded full-length mirror mounted on the nearby wall.

From the smaller of the two boxes, she retrieved one earring and then another, putting them on one by one.

Sawyer shifted in his chair.

"You need to put your hair up in order to show them off properly," he said, his voice resonating in the quiet room.

Tamara compressed her lips, but then, with a show of impatience, as if she found all this ridiculous, and still refusing to look at him, she reached into a nearby drawer. She removed a plastic clip, and proceeded to put up her hair.

Sawyer parted his lips and sucked in a deep breath as heat shot through him.

The image in the mirror was enticing, enchanting even. When was the last time he'd seen Tamara with her hair up?

The earrings were about two inches long, the large, multifaceted topaz stones at the ends of them catching the light. They moved fluidly along with Tamara, brushing the tendrils of hair that had failed to find a home in her plastic clip.

Sawyer resisted the urge to go to her and press his lips to the tender curve of her neck. He knew he was playing a dangerous game that he was at risk of getting caught up in himself.

Tamara bent to the larger of the two velvet boxes and lifted out an exquisite and elaborate fringelike necklace with topaz stones.

Sawyer stood up abruptly. "Let me help you."

Before she could argue, he was behind her, taking the necklace from her unresisting fingers.

"I'm an expert at doing and undoing clasps," she protested weakly.

"Nevertheless, let me make the gallant gesture."

"Practicing for the real moment?" Tamara tossed out, her words belying her response of sexual awareness, her nipples outlined against the fabric of her dress.

Sawyer let his lips curve lazily. "If I were, then I'd do this next."

He didn't think. He just gave in to temptation.

Fortunately, in this case, business and pleasure were one and the same.

Five

Tamara felt a sizzle shoot through her as Sawyer nuzzled her ear, and then bit down gently on her earlobe, the large topaz stone of her earring rocking between them as he did so.

She swallowed, holding back a small gasp. Sawyer's body, hard and unyielding, brushed against hers, igniting a simmering heat in her.

Tamara was mesmerized by their image in the mirror.

Sawyer toyed with the delicate shell of her ear, and then his mouth closed over her earlobe again and gave a gentle tug. All the while, his breath sent small shivers coursing through her.

Tamara closed her eyes. It was her only defense. The image in the mirror was just too erotic.

Sawyer's hands gently kneaded her shoulders.

"Relax," he said in a low voice.

Tamara struggled against the undertow of his seduction. She already knew the power of his kiss, and a part of her couldn't believe she'd allowed him to get this close—again. What had she been thinking?

She'd reached with greedy hands when he'd offered the enticement of a hefty sale. His down payment alone would be enough to cover her monthly rent. But then what?

This was the road to ruin.

"Sawyer…"

But before she could say more, he turned her to face him, and his mouth came down on hers.

His lips were warm and supple, and he deepened the kiss before she had time to marshal her forces.

The kiss washed over her like a warm summer rain, making her feel vital and alive. In her head, she was spinning, her head thrown back with laughter, her nipples plastered to her wet clothes.

Sawyer kissed the way he did everything—confidently, decisively…persuasively. And more importantly, the effect of his kiss on her was powerful and shocking.

His hips pressed against her, making her want to rub against him. With very little effort, he had her restless and aroused.

The kiss that Sawyer had stolen at the fashion party *hadn't* been a fluke. And wasn't that the real explanation for why she'd let things progress to this point? Because the question had been dogging her?

He was in the wrong field, she thought absently. He should be hawking kisses instead of news. Then he'd be even richer than he was.

Sawyer's arms, all hard muscle, banded around her, and one hand settled on her backside, molding their bodies together. Her arms crept around his neck, drawing him to her. She wiggled closer, brushing against his arousal and eliciting a throaty growl from Sawyer.

Tamara knew if she was honest with herself, she'd admit she'd never experienced a kiss like Sawyer's. But then forbidden fruit was a powerful aphrodisiac.

Still, a shred of reason intervened. *This was her last chance.*

With a last bit of resolve, she tore her mouth from his. "Wait a minute!"

She flattened her hand on his chest, but the steady, strong beat of his heart, his warmth and solidness, seemed to brand her, and she snatched back her hand.

Sawyer's eyes glittered with golden fire.

Summoning a determination she didn't feel, Tamara opened her mouth.

"Don't lie to yourself, and don't lie to me," Sawyer said softly, his tone nevertheless conveying a note of implacability.

Her brows snapped together. Well, she wasn't going to engage in any hollow denials. But she didn't like the way he'd thrown her off balance.

"What do you want?" she said.

"I think you already know."

"You came in here for a necklace," she persisted.

"Among other things."

How could he seem so rational when she was still trying to recover from the effect of their kiss?

"Don't think you can seduce me into changing my mind about your proposal."

"Fine," he said, gimlet-eyed. "But I'm offering a way for you to save Pink Teddy Designs. I thought that would appeal to the small-business owner in you."

She hated that he knew what straits she was in. She hated that he had well-honed instincts and knew her weak spots.

"I see," she said coolly, striving to match her tone to his. "I suppose if you're going to torpedo my social life, you feel you owe it to me to at least help me professionally?"

He arched a brow. "Are you talking about Tom?"

"Yes!"

"There was no passion there."

"How do you know?" she retorted.

"The cutesy moniker says it all. 'Tam and Tom.' You sounded like pals."

"Meaning you'd never be caught dead dating someone who was worthy of a cutesy little tandem name?"

"Correct," he said, and then added bluntly, "Did you sleep with him?"

A note of belligerence had entered his tone. She knew Sawyer's purpose was to dismiss Tom as inconsequential.

"It's none of your business," she snapped.

"I'll take that as a no," Sawyer said. "Poor bastard. I thought so."

She wanted to wipe the satisfied expression off his face. "Tom is one of the good guys. He isn't after control of my father's company."

"Don't kid yourself, sweetheart. Tom isn't a saint." Sawyer's eyes swept over her. "On the other hand, since he kept his hands off of you, maybe he is."

Tamara felt a strange thrill. Had Sawyer just admitted to finding her hard to resist?

She pushed the question away. She reminded herself that Sawyer was simply trying to get his way. He'd say or do *any-thing* to sway her. He was ruthless. Just like her father.

With that thought, she scoffed, "What could you possibly have to pin on Tom?"

Sawyer looked her in the eye. "Maybe he was dating you because of your connection to Kincaid News."

Her eyes widened. "You're despicable!"

"He jumped at the opportunity to go to L.A., didn't he?"

"Only because you arranged to make him an irresistible offer!"

Tamara reluctantly recalled that Tom had asked her about Kincaid News, even after she'd explained to him that help was unlikely to come for his band from that quarter. Still, she refused to see his interest in her as less than genuine.

"He was quick to sell you out with information about your current financial situation," Sawyer pointed out ruthlessly. "When it became clear how I could help his career, he was eager as a puppy."

"And you're a puppy in need of obedience training!"

Sawyer's lips quirked with amusement. "Volunteering for the job?"

"No, thank you."

Sawyer's expression became enigmatic. "At least I've been clear about what I want."

"Yes," she retorted disdainfully. "Kincaid News."

"No, you and Kincaid News," he contradicted, and then his look softened. "I'm offering you a final chance to salvage your dream. Isn't becoming a jewelry designer what you've always wanted to do?"

She was like Eve being tempted by the apple, Tamara thought. How had he known she'd always wanted to be a designer? Even though she knew it was part of his persuasive ploy, it was refreshing to have someone at least pretend to take her dream seriously.

"I remember visiting Dunnyhead once," he mused, naming her father's estate in Scotland. "You were wearing a bead bracelet that you'd made yourself."

Tamara was surprised Sawyer remembered. Her father had given her a jewelry-making kit during her stay at Dunnyhead. She'd just turned twelve, and it had been one of the few times after her parents' divorce her father had seemed aware of her interests and hobbies.

She'd strung together translucent green beads from the kit into a fair semblance of a hippie bracelet. Her father, she recalled, hadn't been particularly impressed. Still, she'd kept her beaded creation for years afterward.

During that stay at Dunnyhead, she recalled she'd played with her younger sisters, Julia and Arabella, who'd been five and two. But until this moment, she hadn't remembered Sawyer's visit.

"Who did you want to be when you grew up?" Sawyer probed, his tone inviting. "You must have had someone you aspired to be like."

"I wanted to be an original," she replied, her defenses lowering a notch.

Sawyer gave a low laugh. "Of course. I should have guessed. Tamara Kincaid has always been unique."

Despite herself, a smile of shared amusement rose to her lips. "After the divorce," she divulged, "my mother kept some pieces from Bulgari, Cartier and Harry Winston that my father had given her."

"And I bet you loved putting them on," he guessed.

"My father wouldn't let me play in the family vault," she deadpanned.

"I'd let you play with the Melton jewels," he joked, but his eyes gleamed like polished stones. "Hell, you could wear them to your heart's content."

"Trying to bribe me?" she said lightly.

"Whatever works."

Her eyes came to rest beyond Sawyer. She saw her workbench scattered with the implements of a jeweler's trade.

All of it, however, was in danger of disappearing from her life. And suddenly, inexplicably, what Sawyer offered was so very tempting.

Would it be so bad?

"It wouldn't be terrible," he said, as if reading her mind. "A short-term marriage of convenience gets us what we both want, and then we go our separate ways."

"As opposed to my father's proposal of a real but bloodless and indefinite dynastic marriage?"

Sawyer inclined his head.

"You're proposing that we double-cross my father?"

"I wouldn't put it that way," Sawyer replied, "but one rascal deserves another, don't you think?"

The image that his words conjured brought an involuntary smile to her lips. Would it matter to her father what type of marriage she and Sawyer contracted if the bottom line was that he got what he wanted—seeing Kincaid News into capable hands?

And yet. "We'll never convince my father that we have a real marriage."

Sawyer arched a brow. "We've just proven we'll have no problem convincing people the passion is real."

She felt a rippling warmth suffuse her.

When had she turned so hot and bothered where Sawyer was concerned? Perhaps when she'd discovered their kisses had her seeing a kaleidoscope of colors.

Still, she hedged. "You said this would be a marriage of convenience."

He gave her a bland look. "Are you asking whether I'd expect you to share my bed?"

She kept her expression unchanged, but at her sides, her fingers curled into her palms. "I just want us to be clear."

He smiled lazily. "The answer is no. That is, unless you decide you'd like to be in my bed."

"Hardly," she replied tartly.

His eyes laughed at her. "A man can dream."

She felt a quiver in response to his compelling magnetism. She turned away to hide her reaction, surveying her domain, and then hugging herself. What was she willing to give up to save this?

Not too discriminating to do business with the devil.

Sawyer's words came back to her, and now she knew he was right.

"Six months," she said without looking at him. "That should be more than enough time—"

"However long it takes."

"You said it would be short-term," she countered, her tone faintly accusatory.

He settled his hands on her shoulders, warm and caressing. "I'm looking forward to it."

When he bent and nuzzled her neck, she closed her eyes. He kissed her throat, and she couldn't help thinking he was sealing the deal.

And then a moment later, he was gone, out the door.

With her fingertips, she touched the still warm and tingly spot where he'd kissed her.

What had she done by bargaining with the devil?

"I'm going to marry Sawyer Langsford."

Her statement was met with a joint gasp.

Tamara looked from one to the other of her friends. Pia's eyes had gone wide, while Belinda just looked at her in frozen silence, her coffee cup halfway to her lips.

They were sitting in Contadini having a casual Sunday brunch, but her announcement blew the relaxed atmosphere right out of the water.

Tamara glanced at Pia. "Any chance you can squeeze a small and hasty English wedding into your schedule for next month?"

"Oh, dear Lord," Belinda breathed, rolling her eyes. "Tell me you're not pregnant!"

Tamara looked at her friend in alarm. "Of course not!"

Was it her use of the word *hasty* that had made Belinda jump straight to pregnancy?

Belinda set down her cup. "Well, we can rule out drunk, since it's Sunday morning and you're sipping orange juice, so...what is going on?"

"She looks sane to me," Pia murmured to Belinda, who nodded in agreement.

Belinda and Pia were both back in New York for the moment, and Tamara had decided that now, at one of their regular brunches, was as good a time as any to spring her momentous news on them.

"Of course I haven't lost my mind," she said.

At least, she didn't think she had.

Belinda gave her a penetrating look. "Has your father strong-armed you into this? I know he saw you and Sawyer together at the wedding reception—"

"Oh, Tamara," Pia jumped in, her brow puckered, "there has to be a way out!"

"And it's easier to find a way out before the wedding than after," Belinda muttered.

Tamara took a fortifying breath. "My father hasn't pressed anything." *Sort of.* If it hadn't been for her father's conditions on the merger of Kincaid News with Melton Media, Sawyer would never have proposed. It was a humiliating way to have received her first marriage proposal, but a humiliation that brought salvation for her business. "In fact, I've hardly ever given a decision this much calculated thinking."

"Uh-oh," Pia breathed. "Calculated thinking for a wedding? Oh, Tamara!"

Tamara repressed a sigh. Of course, Pia, the eternal romantic, would be shocked and alarmed at the idea of a marriage of convenience.

"Beats the opposite," Belinda put in. "I don't recommend the impetuous elopement."

Tamara raised her hand. "Hear me out."

"I'm all ears," Belinda replied. "This I have to hear."

Tamara steadied herself. "You both know Pink Teddy Designs has been in financial difficulty for some time." It was a painful admission. Her business was everything to her—her dream, her quest for validation. "But what you don't know is that recently things have come to a head. My rent is set to increase and I've tapped out my credit."

Belinda's eyes narrowed. "So you're marrying Sawyer for financial reasons?" she guessed. "Can I just weigh in with the fact that money is on my list of bad reasons to get married?"

Pia shook her head. "It'll never last."

Tamara pushed at her breakfast plate. "I don't want it to last!"

Pia's eyes rounded. "And what about poor Tom?"

"Poor Tom is on his way to Los Angeles, hot on the trail of a record deal, thanks to Sawyer."

"Wonderful," Belinda remarked sarcastically.

"I mentioned my father had a long-cherished wish to unite the Kincaid and Langsford families," Tamara said. "But what I didn't mention is that he's made his agreement to Melton Media's merger with Kincaid News conditional on Sawyer convincing me to marry him."

Pia gasped, her hand briefly covering her mouth. "You're willing to throw away your chance to marry for love?"

Tamara was tempted to say she was a bit cynical about love after the examples set by her parents, but she stifled her reply. She supposed in Pia's business, it was helpful—maybe even necessary—to believe in true love. Why disabuse her friend?

And, truth be told, Tamara conceded, she wasn't a *hardened* cynic. Her secret indulgence was chick flicks that made her misty-eyed. She'd wonder whether it was possible to find a man who set her pulse racing *and* held her close to his heart. She'd wonder if, despite her parents' example, a happily-ever-after was attainable for her.

She pasted a smile on her face. "No, don't worry. I'm not giving up the chance of love forever. With any luck—" her lips twisted self-deprecatingly "—a second marriage will be the charm."

"Or third," Belinda muttered.

"Or third," she agreed, since it was clear her friend was hoping for a third wedding.

Thrusting aside the fact that her own father had been

married three times, Tamara quickly explained the terms of her agreement with Sawyer for a short-term marriage of convenience: Kincaid News in return for the money to save Pink Teddy Designs.

"I don't know," Pia said doubtfully when she'd finished, shaking her head.

"What could go wrong?" Tamara asked. "In six months, a year at most, we both go our separate ways."

"Famous last words," Belinda said. "It's taken me more than two years to get an annulment."

Tamara needed to know her friends were behind her. More importantly, she needed both her friends' help if she was to convince her father that she and Sawyer had succumbed to dynastic expectations rather than come up with a plan of their own.

"I need you both to act as if you believe Sawyer and I have finally decided to do our family duty," she said baldly. "Otherwise I'll never convince my father."

Pia's eyes widened, and Belinda snorted disbelievingly.

"Your father will never buy it," Belinda said.

"It's my only hope."

Her only hope, and Pink Teddy's.

Neither Belinda nor Pia had a ready reply, but Tamara could tell from their expressions that they reluctantly understood her predicament.

She sucked in a breath. "So will you do it? Will you show up when I marry—" she stumbled over the word, and Belinda looked at her keenly "—Sawyer? Even if it turns out to be in a drafty British castle?"

Belinda sighed. "I'll bring my Wellingtons."

"And I'll help coordinate," Pia chimed in.

Tamara glanced from one to the other of her friends. "Even if Colin and Hawk are almost certainly going to be there at Sawyer's invitation?"

There was a palpable pause.

Pia grimaced. "You know you can count on me. Just keep me away from the hors d'oeuvres."

"I'll bring my attorney," Belinda added grimly.

Tamara laughed.

For a moment, thanks to her friends, she could forget just how complicated a situation she was getting into.

Still, this was surely going to be some wedding.

Six

"Tell him to come in," Sawyer said into the speakerphone, and then rose from behind his desk.

Floor-to-ceiling windows revealed a spectacular view of the Hudson River. The corporate offices of Melton Media were located on the upper floors of a gleaming midtown Manhattan building.

Sawyer had taken several strides when his office door opened and Viscount Kincaid strolled in.

"Melton," the viscount acknowledged jovially as he came forward and shook hands.

Sawyer wasn't fooled for a second. Though Tamara's father was a couple of inches shorter than his own six-two, the older man had an air of prepossession and command that only someone born into authority or accustomed to it for a long time could exude.

In Kincaid, diabolically, the genial visage of a Santa Claus was joined to the shrewd mind of a Machiavelli—a trap for the unwary.

"Shall we proceed down to the executive dining room?" Sawyer asked.

It was well before the daily news deadline for East Coast newspapers going to press, but they were both busy men.

"I'm ready whenever you are," Kincaid said, nevertheless reaching into the inner pocket of his suit jacket for his buzzing BlackBerry.

Kincaid kept up his end of the phone conversation as they made their way downstairs via the suspended metal staircase that joined the executive floors of Melton Media. They were far from the chaos of the newsroom. Melton Media's corporate offices were housed in a separate building from *The New York Intelligencer.*

Sawyer listened as, apparently, Kincaid attempted to verify by phone a juicy rumor that he'd heard at a cocktail party the night before. Clearly, the viscount had the news business in his blood and wasn't averse to rolling up his sleeves and working the phones himself when necessary.

Tellingly, though, Sawyer couldn't discern from Kincaid's end of the conversation what the rumor was or whom the older man was talking to. Sawyer felt the competitive juices start to flow in his blood.

Kincaid was a worthy adversary and would be a worthy business partner.

"Rumor confirmed?" Sawyer asked with feigned idle curiosity when the viscount finished his call.

"Yes," Kincaid replied with a note of satisfaction.

"I thought we were on the same team," Sawyer said with mock reproof.

"Not yet. Not until the merger goes through."

Sawyer's chuckle held an element of respect. Viscount Kincaid might be a family friend, but he was a fierce competitor.

When Sawyer had asked for this meeting, he'd suggested he pay a call to Kincaid headquarters, but the viscount had gainsaid him. Perhaps Kincaid wanted another opportunity to take a look around the company that would soon merge with Kincaid News.

Sawyer had inherited an already significant company from his father and had built it up, branching out internationally from the British newspapers and radio station that his father and grandfather had run. His grandfather had married into the newspaper business by wedding a publishing heiress, but he'd taken to it like a natural.

Kincaid was a different animal altogether. He'd labored in the trenches of the news business, selling family real estate in Scotland to build up his company. His gamble had paid off handsomely, but Kincaid was no fool. He knew that, in order to survive, Kincaid News needed fresh blood—someone well positioned and savvy enough to take advantage of the new mediums of communication out there, from online sites and streaming to smartphones.

Namely, the viscount needed Sawyer.

And Sawyer was eager to absorb a competitor at a relative bargain.

At that thought, Sawyer paused and mentally grimaced. Correction: a relative bargain and a bargaining relative. Kincaid had turned the business into a family legacy, and he wasn't going to let it pass into other hands without a familial tie.

He and the viscount entered the executive dining room, which was one floor below Sawyer's office and had an equally impressive view of the Hudson. The long table had been set for two.

They dined on steak frites accompanied by iced tea. The conversation moved idly from politics and the upcoming elections to the doings of various business associates, until, finally, Viscount Kincaid set aside his fork and fixed Sawyer with a piercing look.

"Well, I know you didn't invite me here to discuss golf," Kincaid said gruffly, "so out with it, Melton."

Unperturbed, Sawyer took his time wiping his mouth and setting aside his napkin. Then he looked at the other man squarely.

"I'd like to ask for Tamara's hand in marriage."

Kincaid's eyebrows rose. "Bloody hell, you've done it."

Sawyer nodded.

"How?"

Sawyer gave a ghost of a smile. "I don't suppose it could be my charm and persuasiveness."

Kincaid shook his head. "Hogwash. Tamara would never fall for it."

"I have been wooing her." It wasn't far from the truth. He *had* been trying to convince Tamara to see things his way.

Kincaid's eyebrows drew together. "Since when?"

"We preferred to conduct our relationship away from prying eyes."

Sawyer thought back to his last private encounter with Tamara. She'd been so responsive in his arms, her luscious female curves pressed into him. And he—he'd wanted to tumble her backward and have hot, sweaty sex with her right there in her studio, her red hair fanning out on that damnable red velour couch.

Sawyer felt his body tighten at the memory, and shifted in his seat. "I think you'll find that Tamara isn't unaware of her familial obligations."

His last statement was met with a pause, but then Kincaid waved it away with one hand. "Certainly not in character," the viscount growled. "She's shown nothing but disregard until now." Kincaid shook his head. "Her sisters, too. Three daughters and not a one with an appreciation of what it took to built Kincaid News or how I footed the bill for those fine prep school educations."

"She does bear you some affection, you know."

Sawyer would bet that beneath Tamara's tartness and Viscount Kincaid's bluster lay a genuine—if oftentimes fraught—bond between father and daughter.

A light appeared in Viscount Kincaid's eyes, but it was quickly replaced by a look of cloaked cunning. "Is that so? Then I'll expect a grandchild to be in the cards in the not too distant future."

Sawyer schooled his expression—this was a complication that he hadn't foreseen. "Perhaps Tamara and I would like to enjoy ourselves first."

"Enjoy yourselves later." Kincaid settled back in his chair. "In fact, I like the idea of a grandchild so much I fancy I'll make it a condition of the merger."

Cagey bastard.

"My daughter *enceinte* before the merger goes through."

"That wasn't part of the agreement."

"How much do you want this merger?"

"As much as you do, I would have thought," Sawyer replied drily.

"I can wait," Kincaid returned. "I've got some life in me yet, and God knows I've long since pinned my hopes on a third generation taking over the reins of Kincaid News." Kincaid leaned forward. "The question is, will you or someone else be a worthy caretaker for Kincaid News in the meantime?"

Sawyer said nothing. He'd learned long ago that a tough bargainer didn't jump in with his next best offer right away. He stayed cool and deliberated his options.

In this case, he supposed he could call the older man's bluff. *Good luck convincing Tamara or either of her sisters to marry another newsman.*

But an image suddenly flashed through his mind of Tamara being bedded by some faceless pretender to the throne of Kincaid News, attempting to conceive the sought-for grandchild. He discovered that the thought of some other man fathering Tamara's child didn't sit well with him.

Better me than some faceless bastard, Sawyer thought.

Kincaid sat back in his seat, a smile hovering at his lips, seemingly satisfied by Sawyer's reaction, or at least lack of immediate objection. "Marrying Tamara is the first step. I'll do everything in my power to see that you actually make it to the altar, including making all the necessary public pronouncements that I'm overjoyed."

"Naturally," Sawyer said sardonically.

Kincaid leaned forward again, apparently warming to his subject. "I've done all I can up till now to help you, including—" Kincaid looked suddenly sly "—sharing all I know about Tamara's comings and goings."

Sawyer had to admit Kincaid had been helpful in that respect. Without inside knowledge, he'd have had a harder time.

"But the second step, the necessary step before I sign over Kincaid News, is getting Tamara pregnant," Kincaid went on, quirking a brow. "And for that, you're on your own."

"Of course," Sawyer said drily.

Kincaid couldn't have put it more baldly. Sawyer would have to entice Tamara into his bed.

"Naturally," Kincaid said, "I won't breathe a word to Tamara about this new condition to the merger."

"Thanks for the small favor."

Kincaid chuckled. "I wouldn't want her to lock you out of the bedroom just out of spite."

"Thwarting you has been a favorite pastime of hers," Sawyer observed with a jab.

The viscount's face darkened briefly. "Yes, but those days are past now…as long as you get her to the altar."

Kincaid's new condition on the merger presented a complication that Sawyer hadn't anticipated. He'd bargained with Tamara for a marriage of short duration. Once they both got what they wanted, they could go their separate ways. A baby had never been part of the equation.

He wasn't thrilled at the prospect of having a child with a divorce envisioned in the future. But then again, he was thirty-eight, his life was destined to become only busier after the business merger with Kincaid News, and he had a duty to the earldom to produce an heir. Sure, he could wait for a woman suitable for the duties of a countess, but right now that prospect seemed highly indeterminate.

On the other side, there was the very concrete reality of *Tamara,* who, however unsuited and averse she might be to being a countess, made his blood sizzle.

His body tightened as images flashed through his mind of just how pleasurable it could be to try to conceive an heir with Tamara.

"So, do you agree to the terms?"

Viscount Kincaid's voice brought Sawyer back from his mental calculations.

Sawyer knew without hesitation what his answer was. "Yes." He reached for his glass and raised it in mock salute. "To the merger of the Kincaid and Melton lines, corporate and otherwise."

Tamara waltzed into Balthazar at noon. It had been an easy walk from her loft. She'd been surprised when Sawyer had called and proposed that they meet at a restaurant in her area.

Now, inside the restaurant entrance, she spotted Sawyer immediately. He looked impeccable, as always, in a red tie and pinstripe suit, even if his hair was a little tousled from the wind outside.

Unconsciously, she smoothed her own hair as he approached her.

"You look fine," he said, his deep voice flowing over her like warm honey.

When she stopped in midmovement, Sawyer's mouth lifted.

"More than fine," he amended. "You look great."

The frank male appreciation that suddenly fired his gaze sent sexual awareness washing over her.

"You don't look too shabby yourself," she responded, surprised at the hint of breathlessness that crept into her voice.

She'd tried not to care when dressing this morning, but she'd given up and finally settled on a short-sleeved heather-gray sweater dress cinched by a thin purple belt and paired with magenta patent platform heels.

She was a rebel with a cause, she'd thought defiantly. She didn't care what a countess was supposed to look like. This is what she looked like.

Sawyer clasped her hand and brushed his lips across hers.

At her surprised reaction, he murmured, "We have to make it look good in public."

Of course. She steadied herself. "I'm surprised you came downtown. I'd have thought Michael's or 21 was more your taste."

Michael's was favored by the media crowd, and 21 was a clubby bastion famous for the jockey figures that adorned its facade.

"I was looking for a place that was a little off the beaten trail," Sawyer returned equably, and then winked. "And I thought I'd show you I can be flexible."

"Well, don't expect me to convene at La Grenouille with the ladies who lunch."

"Perish the thought," he said with mock solemnity, and then smiled. "But I'll turn you into an uptown girl yet."

"That's what I'm afraid of," she returned drily, even as a frisson of electricity danced across her skin at their repartee.

"It may be pleasurable, too," he murmured with a glint in his eye, and then cupped her elbow and steered her forward.

She was disconcerted by how attuned she was to Sawyer and their most casual contact. Had the sexual awareness been caused by their recent kisses, or had it always been there—the unacknowledged reason she'd always kept her distance from him?

A restaurant hostess materialized beside them, and without a word, they were guided to a quiet corner table.

This, Tamara thought, was the kind of service Sawyer was used to by virtue of his wealth, title and high profile. It was the type of service she'd likely be accorded as his wife. She was afraid she could easily become accustomed to the red-carpet treatment.

Tamara slid into her booth seat, Sawyer's lingering touch at her elbow facilitating her way, and Sawyer followed, sitting to her left.

"I'm assuming this meeting is to settle details?" she asked without preamble, settling herself more comfortably on her seat.

"You could say that."

She studied him. "I could—but would it be correct?"

Sawyer's lips twitched. "You mean your father hasn't called you to celebrate his Machiavellian victory?"

She shook her head. "Amazingly, no."

"An admirable and uncharacteristic show of restraint."

She looked at him shrewdly. "Perhaps he was afraid of undermining you."

Sawyer merely laughed, and then reached up to smooth back the hair that had fallen over her shoulder.

She stilled as he touched one of her dangling earrings, set with amethyst stones and Swarovski crystals.

"Is this another of your creations?"

She nodded, and then asked boldly, "Examining your investment?"

He caressed the line of her jaw. "Yes, and it's lovely."

Oh.

Tamara looked away in confusion, and was saved by the approach of a waiter who asked if they would like anything to drink.

After inquiring if wine was her preference, Sawyer smoothly narrowed the choices with the waiter to one, and then turned back to her and settled his hand on her thigh beneath the table. "Does that meet with your approval?"

Feeling the warm weight of Sawyer's hand moving along her thigh, she stuttered assent.

Sawyer looked at her innocently. "Is there something else you'd like, Tamara?"

"What?"

Sawyer's eyes laughed at her. "Is there something else you'd like to drink?"

She looked up at the waiter. "No—thank you."

When they were alone again, Tamara frowned at Sawyer. "What are you doing?"

"You mean this?" Underneath the table, Sawyer's hand clasped hers, and then with his other hand, he slid a ring on her finger.

Tamara felt her heart slow and beat louder.

"A gift from the family vault," Sawyer said. "I hope you like it."

She swallowed and searched Sawyer's gaze, but she read nothing but unadulterated desire there.

She knew, of course, that she and Sawyer were engaged—in a manner of speaking. But the weight of the ring brought the reality of it forcefully back to her.

Slowly, she lifted her hand and rested it on the tablecloth. A beautiful diamond ring in an open-work setting twinkled in the light. Two sapphire baguettes and two accent diamonds adorned either side.

It was a breathtaking piece of jewelry. The diamond was large and undoubtedly flawless, and the open design gave the ring a deceptively modern feel.

"It's a good complement to the earrings you're wearing," Sawyer said with studied solemnity. "It's not a modern piece, but I hope you like it."

She looked up. "Really, it isn't necessary for a pretend marriage—"

"Yes, it is," he said firmly. "The only question is whether you like the ring. I know your tastes tend to the contemporary."

"I love it," she confessed. "It's a creation that any designer would be proud of. The lattice work is timeless and beautiful."

Her response seemed to satisfy him. "I'm glad. The ring was a gift to my great-grandmother, but I had it reset. The original center stone was a sapphire."

Tamara looked down at her hand again. The ring was a tangible sign of her bargain with Sawyer.

"You'll get used to it," he said.

Startled, she glanced up.

He appeared amused for a moment. "I meant the ring. You'll get used to the weight of the ring."

Tamara rued the fact that Sawyer looked as if he'd guessed what was on her mind.

She angled her hand back and forth. "It's exquisite."

"As is its wearer."

She shifted in her seat. She was uncertain how to handle Sawyer. Was he just practicing his romantic technique for the benefit of onlookers?

She wanted to make some acerbic reply about leaving his false devotion for an occasion when they had a real audience, but somehow the words stuck in her throat. Instead, she found herself succumbing to the effect of his nearness and seductive words more than she cared to admit.

"What was the occasion for the gift originally?" she asked, striving to keep the conversation on an even keel.

Sawyer looked suddenly mischievous. "Do you really want to know?"

She raised her brows inquiringly.

"The birth of my great-grandmother's sixth and last child."

Her eyes widened. "Oh, well…"

"Quite." His eyes laughed at her. "One doesn't get to be the twelfth in a direct line of successive earls without ample fertility along the way."

"Perhaps you should be seeking a woman who will better accommodate you in the…fecundity department."

His eyes crinkled. "Perhaps you suit my needs just fine."

She was unsettled by his cryptic reply, but before she could respond, he picked up her ring hand and raised it to his mouth, kissing the pad of each finger individually.

Her eyes widened as a shiver chased through her.

"Someone I know just walked into the restaurant," he murmured, a twinkle in his eyes.

She shot him a skeptical look. "Of course."

"You doubt me?"

She extracted her hand from his loose grip. "Should I?"

Sawyer chuckled, and just then a waiter materialized with a bread basket, followed by their regular server with their wine.

When they were both sipping Pinot Grigio, Tamara attempted to put their conversation on a more businesslike footing. "Tell me about the details that you've obviously called me here to discuss."

He arched a brow. "Your patience has run out? Very well, let's start with Pink Teddy Designs. How much is your lease costing you?"

She relaxed a little, lowering her shoulders. So Sawyer had come here to make good on his promises.

"Too much," she repeated.

"It's a fashionable address—an astute business move."

"Thank you."

"I'll cosign your lease renewal."

Her eyes widened. "How did—?"

He looked at her quizzically. "How did I know the lease was your most pressing concern, you mean? A few discreet inquiries to the landlord netted information on current rents—and the fact that they were going up."

"Lovely," she said acerbically. "I didn't realize my lease was information available to the press!"

Sawyer's lips twisted wryly. "It's not, but I happen to know the head of Rockridge Management."

She made a disgruntled reply.

"You'll also need a cash infusion."

Tamara compressed her lips. Knowing it was best not to look a gift horse in the mouth, however, she forced herself to hold her tongue.

Sawyer considered her. "How does two million dollars for initial financing sound?"

Tamara swallowed. She'd only fantasized about having that kind of cash on hand.

"No strings attached?" she queried.

Sawyer inclined his head in acknowledgment.

Of course, she reminded herself, they both knew that Sawyer wouldn't expect repayment of the money. She had bargained away something else. She'd agreed to a sham marriage.

She cleared her throat. "Thank you...I think. I can promise I'll put the money to good use." And then because she didn't want him to have the impression that she was completely without resources, she added, "I just met with a client this morning, actually."

When Sawyer looked at her inquiringly, she elaborated, "It was a hedge-fund wife who recently opened her own boutique in the Hamptons. She bought a bracelet for herself and selected a few other pieces to carry in her store."

Just then their waiter reappeared, and asked if they were ready to order.

Tamara belatedly realized she hadn't even looked at the menu, but because she'd been to Balthazar before, she ordered the smoked salmon from memory. Sawyer, after a few idle inquiries of their waiter, ordered the grilled branzini.

Afterward, Tamara braced herself and looked at Sawyer squarely. "I suppose we should discuss the wedding itself."

He smiled faintly. "I'll leave the details to you. I understand many women have preconceived ideas of what their wedding should look like."

Yes, and in her case, the idea had never been a sham marriage contracted to a very proper British earl.

On top of it all, Sawyer was also a press baron in her father's mold. She could hardly get any closer to exactly what she *didn't* want.

Sawyer studied her. "It seems only fitting, though, that the marriage of the Earl and Countess of Melton occur at Gantswood Hall, the ancestral home of the earls of Melton."

Tamara resisted pointing out that it was hardly necessary to go to such trouble for what would be a short-lived marriage. But then again, she'd been half expecting Sawyer's proposition of a proper British wedding. "Very well. I suppose the sooner, the better."

Sawyer's lips quirked. "Anxious, are you?"

"The sooner we begin, the sooner the corporate merger will occur and we can be done with this."

"How about next week then?"

Tamara shook her head. "Pia would have a heart attack. I already asked her to help plan the wedding. Three weeks."

"You and Pia Lumley are close."

It wasn't a question, but a statement. Tamara nodded anyway. "Pia is a dear friend and one of the best bridal consultants around. She also needs all the help that she can get now that—" her voice darkened "—your fiendish friend the Marquess of Easterbridge ruined Belinda's wedding day."

Sawyer laughed. "'Fiendish friend'? You certainly have a way with alliteration."

"Don't change the subject," Tamara snapped back. "Your friends seem to come in one stripe only—namely, villainous."

Sawyer arched a brow.

"I suppose you're chummy with the Duke of Hawkshire, too?"

"Yes, but not with his alias, Mr. Fielding."

"Very funny."

"Since we're on the subject of our marriage," Sawyer said drily, "what have you told your friends?"

"Pia and Belinda?" Tamara responded. "They know the truth, and they've already said they'll be at any wedding to support me."

"Splendid."

"We'll need a referee if, as I assume, your titled compatriots will make an appearance, too."

Sawyer inclined his head. "I imagine Hawk and Colin will be there, schedules permitting."

"Everyone else, including my mother and sisters," Tamara said determinedly, "will believe that for reasons known only to me, I've decided that you are Mr. Right."

"Since Hawk has already claimed the moniker Mr. Fielding, I'll settle for Mr. Right without qualm," Sawyer quipped.

Tamara eyed him doubtfully. "Well, I'm glad that's all resolved—anything else?"

"Since you mention it—"

Tamara tensed. "Yes?"

"There is the small matter of where we'll reside after the wedding."

Tamara felt her stomach plummet. Why hadn't she thought of such an obvious and all too important detail?

"I'll keep my business in SoHo," she said automatically.

"Right," Sawyer agreed, "but we won't convince anyone

that we're serious about this marriage unless you move into my town house after the wedding."

Share a roof with Sawyer? They could barely share a *meal* without sparks flying.

"I suppose I can bear it for a short while," she responded in a disgruntled tone. "Will I have my own wing?"

Sawyer laughed at her sudden hopefulness. "Why don't you come see? It occurs to me you've never been to my home, and that's a detail that should be rectified as early as possible. In fact, what are you doing the rest of the afternoon?"

She wanted to lie. She wanted to say she had a slew of meetings. But if Sawyer could make time in his busy CEO schedule, her demurral would hardly ring true. And besides, he had a point about her becoming familiar with the place where she'd soon be living.

"I'm free," she disclosed reluctantly.

Sawyer smiled. "Fantastic. We'll ride up there right after lunch. My car is outside."

The waiter arrived with their food, and as the conversation turned to more mundane topics, Tamara had time at leisure to reflect on what she'd gotten herself into.

Was it too late to back out now?

Seven

Tamara wanted to hate everything about Sawyer's life, but she was finding it impossible to do so. Instead, she clung tenaciously to indifference—was it too much to ask?

It was bad enough that Sawyer himself was demonstrating remarkable skill at seduction. Must his lifestyle be an added lure?

Tamara discovered that Sawyer's town house was a four-story structure on a prime block in the East 80s. The limestone facade was set off by black wrought-iron flower boxes at the windows and a matching black front gate. Shrubbery concealed from prying eyes the garden that ran along one side of the residence.

And in an unusual setup for Manhattan, Sawyer's town house boasted its own garage, enabled by the residence's prime corner location.

Except for a few minor details, the house might have been a transplant from London's fashionable Mayfair district—just like its owner.

A middle-aged, uniformed employee came hurrying out the front door and down the front steps of the town house, and Sawyer handed his car keys to him.

"You might as well garage the car, Lloyd," Sawyer said. "I don't know how long I'll be home."

The man inclined his head. "Very well, my lord."

Sawyer glanced from Lloyd to Tamara and back. "Lloyd, this is Ms. Tamara Kincaid, my fiancée."

Without missing a beat, Lloyd said gravely, "Welcome, Ms. Kincaid. May I offer my utmost felicitations on your engagement?"

Tamara stopped herself from saying that felicitations weren't necessary. Instead, she shook Lloyd's hand and accepted his congratulations before he got into Sawyer's black Porsche Cayenne.

She turned to Sawyer. "What? No Bentley? No valet named Jeeves?"

Sawyer smiled briefly. "The Bentley is at my country estate. I sometimes prefer to drive myself, so Lloyd has time on his hands. There's also a butler, housekeeper and part-time chef, whom you'll soon meet, but no valet."

He added teasingly, "I like to keep things a little democratic when I'm stateside."

Tamara nodded at the house. "I'd have assumed a bachelor like you would prefer a penthouse co-op."

"I find it hard to completely shake the habits of an English country gentleman, even in New York," Sawyer said as his hand cupped her elbow and he guided her toward the front steps. "I hope you like the town house nevertheless."

"It has an understated elegance," she said. "It's...very attractive."

Understated elegance shouldn't appeal to her, but it did. Sawyer was obviously rich as Croesus, and it was hard to withstand the beauty that money sometimes bought.

In Sawyer's case, Tamara grudgingly admitted, generations

of wealth came with good taste that meant he didn't flaunt his money, so beauty didn't shade into gaudiness.

When had she developed an appreciation for low-key charm? Her mind went back to her meeting this morning with the hedge-fund wife. *The bigger, the better* appeared to be that client's motto. Sawyer just seemed appealing in comparison, she told herself.

When she and Sawyer stepped inside the town house's cool foyer, she took in the gilded mirror on one wall, the crystal chandelier overhead and the black-and-white tiled floor.

Sawyer's cell phone rang, and he fished it out of the inside pocket of his suit jacket. "Excuse me a moment. It's work, I'm sure."

Tamara turned away. She was grateful for the interruption actually. She needed the reminder that like her father, Sawyer was tethered to a demanding business—a business for which he was marrying her.

A middle-aged woman stepped from the back of the house, an inquiring look on her face as she took in the tableau before her.

Tamara extended her hand. "Hello, I'm Tamara, Sawyer's fiancée."

She didn't care what the proper etiquette was for a future countess. This one greeted the household help with her first name.

Tamara watched as the chestnut-haired woman briefly looked surprised before her face settled back into a pleasant expression.

Were all the members of Sawyer's household so well trained? Or perhaps, Tamara thought hopefully, they were inured to shock by his various escapades.

"Oooh, gracious!" the woman before her said with a British accent as she shook Tamara's hand. "We thought Lord Melton would never settle down. A crafty one, he is!"

"So true," Tamara responded.

Sawyer sauntered out of the foyer and into a nearby room, still with his cell phone pressed to his ear.

"I'm Beatrice, the housekeeper," the woman said. "The butler—"

"Alfred?" Tamara inquired drolly.

Beatrice hesitated, looking momentarily perplexed. "No, Richard, my husband. He's running an errand at the moment."

Tamara gave a studied sigh. No Jeeves the valet, no superhero's butler named Alfred.

Beatrice clasped her hands together in front of her chest. "I've been praying that Lord Melton would finally find happiness and settle down."

Tamara didn't know about the finding happiness part, but Sawyer had definitely decided to acquire a countess. "Lord Melton is certainly fortunate that those nearest to him have him in their prayers."

The devil.

Beatrice threw her a surprisingly perceptive look. "And why not? He's been a fair, kind and generous employer."

"Have you thought about writing ad copy, Beatrice?" Tamara quipped.

Beatrice laughed lightly. "Oh, you're simply perfect! Exactly the person I've been praying for. You'll do very well here, miss."

"It's Tamara, please."

Tamara wanted to protest that she wasn't perfect at all. And, she wouldn't be around long enough to need to worry about how she'd fare.

She wasn't the answer to Sawyer's prayers in any way but one—namely, the bride who would net him Kincaid News.

Beatrice leaned forward conspiratorially. "We use the name Sawyer when we're not around guests."

Wonderful, Tamara thought. She'd made jabs about Sawyer's loftiness, but he was turning out to have egalitarian tendencies to rival any new money Silicon Valley plutocrat. And his housekeeper *liked* him.

She grasped at any straw she could think of. "Tell me he owns a custom-built submarine and employs someone just to shine his shoes."

Beatrice shook her head, her expression sympathetic. "He's been known to toss his own clothes in the washing machine."

At that moment, Sawyer reentered the foyer, pocketing his cell phone. "Ah, Tamara, I see you've met my indomitable housekeeper."

"Yes."

Beatrice smiled. "And I've met your lovely fiancée. I'm absolutely delighted to offer my congratulations, my lord—"

"Sawyer," Tamara corrected sardonically.

"I'm going to give Tamara a tour of the house, Beatrice."

"Of course." Beatrice turned to Tamara. "I hope you'll feel readily at home here. Please don't hesitate to let me know if there's anything you need."

After Beatrice departed, Tamara discovered on her tour with Sawyer that his house was decorated in an English style, with furniture from the eighteenth and nineteenth centuries blended with more modern pieces. Lively flower patterns on the upholstery contrasted with stripes and solids.

She wanted to hate everything, but unfortunately she was too knowledgeable not to appreciate tastefulness and elegance.

And the house was intimate. Yes, she could identify several valuable objets d'art and a couple of Matisses—Belinda would love them—but the Gainsborough portraits of family ancestors and the Ming dynasty vases had obviously been kept at the historic family home set among thousands of rolling acres in the English countryside. But even with its nod to English décor, this town house was more the home of a twenty-first century entrepreneur than of an aristocrat with a centuries-old title.

After she and Sawyer had passed through the front parlor and dining room, they went downstairs to the kitchen and servants' rooms. There, she was introduced to André, the chef.

Thank goodness, Tamara thought, for the French chef. At least one person lived up to stereotype.

Afterward, she and Sawyer took a private elevator to the upper floors.

"There are six bedrooms on two floors here," Sawyer said.

"I'll take the one farthest from you," Tamara replied. "In fact, since I won't be here for long, and I'd really prefer to remain inconspicuous. What about the maid's room in the attic?"

Sawyer grinned, but Tamara didn't like his too-knowing expression.

"There is no servant's bedroom in the attic. That's only on my Gloucestershire estate," Sawyer deadpanned.

"How unfortunate."

A smile continued to play at Sawyer's lips. "Wouldn't you like to judge all the rooms and decide which one is to your liking?"

Suddenly, Tamara became acutely aware that she and Sawyer were on this floor of the house all by themselves, and Sawyer was surveying her with lazy amusement, a gleam in his eye.

She raised her chin. "Like Goldilocks, you mean? No, thank you!"

Especially since one of those rooms belonged to Sawyer himself. She didn't intend to be his latest sexual conquest—even if she was married to him.

"One bowl of porridge may be too hot, another may be too

cold," Sawyer teased. "One bed may be too big, another may be too small and another may be…just right."

His eyes laughed at her, and he murmured, "Am I remembering the story correctly?"

Damn Sawyer. He'd somehow injected sexual innuendo into a fairy tale.

"I'm not so discriminating," she said, tight-lipped.

Sawyer quirked a brow. "Really? Let's put it to the test."

His hand enveloped hers, and he gently tugged her forward as he pushed open the bedroom door closest to them.

"What are you doing?" she demanded, her voice only slightly breathless.

Peripherally, she noticed they'd stepped into a room with a four-poster queen-size bed and furniture in a gleaming walnut.

Sawyer spun her forward in a dancelike move, and she landed, sitting, on the side of the bed.

Sawyer smiled. "What about this one, Goldilocks?"

"You're ridiculous!"

"Not me, the bed. Too firm, or too soft?"

She bounced off the bed. "Neither!"

"Just right, then?" he said, irrepressibly. "Are you quite sure?"

Before Tamara could react, Sawyer sat on the bed himself, and pulled her back down to him, his mouth settling on hers.

Oh. All through lunch, she'd tried so hard *not* to think about kissing Sawyer.

He kissed, she acknowledged again, in the same way he did everything else in his life—with an intensity and lazy self-assurance that was hard to resist.

Sawyer's hands came up to either side of her face, anchoring her, his fingers threading into her hair.

He caressed her mouth with his in slow, leisurely strokes.

"Your mouth drives me crazy," he muttered, and then

stroked the pad of his thumb over her bottom lip. "It's these lush, pouty lips."

"Thanks very much! You make me sound like a stripper or a porn star."

He smiled. "Don't ever disguise them with lipstick."

She sucked in a breath, but before she could say anything, Sawyer was off the bed and pulling her with him again.

"Where are we going?" she asked on a laughing gasp.

She'd never seen Sawyer let go like this. It was so not in character.

Okay, who was she kidding? It was *thrilling,* and she couldn't help responding to it.

"There are five more bedrooms," Sawyer said as he strode across the hall, leading her by the hand. "This one is mine."

Inside his bedroom, he swung her to face him.

Tamara got a general impression of a four-poster king-size bed, more gleaming dark wood and a distinctly masculine feel.

Then her gaze landed on Sawyer again.

"Oh, no," she said breathlessly, shaking her head at the look in his eyes.

Purposely, he advanced on her, and she backed up until the bedpost stopped her retreat.

Why had she never noticed Sawyer's raw masculinity until recently? Even in a conservative business suit, his tie in place, he looked impossibly sexy. The rakish look in his eyes made her weak-kneed.

A sizzling warmth suffused her. Her breasts tightened, and a heavy ache pooled between her legs.

Maybe before she hadn't wanted to see Sawyer as he was. Maybe *this* was the real reason she'd kept him at a distance.

She itched to caress the firm line of his jaw and the strong column of his neck. She curled her fingers into the palm of her hand to stop herself from doing so.

Sawyer gave her a sexy smile. "What are you thinking?"

"What am I thinking?" she tried, thinking one of them had to hold on to sanity. "Isn't the question, what are you doing?"

He was too close. The inches between them crackled with electricity.

Sawyer's smile widened. "Perhaps I've realized that I'd enjoy having you as my wife in every way."

"Thanks very much!"

"How long has it been for you?" he murmured. "I know you and what's-his-name weren't intimate."

Her mouth dropped open, and then snapped shut. "Tom, his name is Tom. And I'm not discussing this with you."

Sawyer's smile turned lazy and knowing. "That long, then?"

He touched her, smoothing the backs of his fingers down the side of her breast in a gentle caress, and Tamara sucked in a breath.

"Damn you," she whispered.

He slid his hand up her arm, bringing her into his embrace. "Your eyes tell a different story, Goldilocks."

"Oh?" she said, cursing the catch in her voice. "Do tell!"

Sawyer searched her face, arousal stamped on his. "Your eyes are already cloudy with desire."

She tried to look bored, even as the press of his arousal sent a fresh wave of awareness shooting through her. "You're making me sleepy."

Sawyer chuckled before his expression turned seductive and intent again.

"What's the matter, Goldilocks?" he muttered, his head bending toward hers. "Are you finding that this bed is just right?"

And then his mouth met hers again.

He tasted of wine from their meal, and the scent of some expensive and finely-milled English sandalwood soap clung to his skin. The combination was strangely intoxicating. And she yielded to it, her hands running up his arms until she clung to him, her arms around his neck.

Damningly, she didn't think about whether this was *right*. It just felt *good*.

She'd passed the point of reflection and gone on to someplace more elemental.

Sawyer pressed her against the bedpost, his muscled thigh wedging between her legs.

He toyed with her lips, and she moaned with each nip and suck and gentle graze.

"That's right," he approved gutturally. "Let me know how you feel."

His mouth wandered away from hers, tracing along her jaw, and her head fell to one side, exposing her neck for their mutual pleasure.

While he kissed the column of her neck, his hands roamed and molded, running down her sides, from the curve of her breasts to the jut of her hips. In response, her fingers curled into his shoulders with pleasure.

When Sawyer's mouth came back to hers, he slid his hand up under the hem of her dress. Her head fell back, and she moaned again as his hand brushed aside her panties.

They both held still as his hand caressed her, his fingers delving into her moist heat, stroking her. From beneath her lashes, Tamara noticed Sawyer's eyes glittering down at her, his face intent with arousal.

"Ah, Tamara," he breathed. "Ah, Goldilocks…"

Sawyer's free hand went to his belt, but then he suddenly stopped, his head tilting.

A moment later, Tamara heard it, too—the unmistakable sound of footsteps.

Someone was coming up the stairs.

Just as Tamara frantically jerked away, Sawyer stepped back, his expression turning smooth and businesslike even as he took care to straighten her dress.

Sawyer was a practiced master of seduction. The thought flashed through her mind a second before she peripherally noticed someone walk past their open doorway.

"I hope you've enjoyed our tour, Tamara," Sawyer said in a voice loud enough to carry.

His eyes laughed down at her, his expression gently mocking.

"Who was that?" Tamara whispered urgently.

Sawyer bent his head toward hers.

"I believe a person sent by the weekly housecleaning service," he said with a grin, matching her low and urgent tone.

Argh. Gathering her dignity, or what remained of it, she stepped away from him so that she was no longer cornered by the bedpost.

"No need to be concerned," Sawyer said. "I'm sure she wouldn't have been too surprised to discover an engaged couple locked in an embrace. Embarrassed, maybe, surprised, no."

Sawyer had acted deftly to avoid embarrassment to an outside employee. Unfortunately, Tamara thought, her own mortification was unabated.

She should be thankful that Sawyer had again been thwarted by the unexpected arrival of a third party. Instead, she was concerned, very concerned, by her reaction and increasing susceptibility to his charms.

"We're not really an engaged couple," she responded with false composure. "Or need I remind you of our agreement?"

Sawyer's eyes narrowed a fraction, but then his lips quirked.

He reached out and smoothed her hair. "What's the harm in a little pleasure along the way?"

What indeed. She took another step back, and he dropped his hand back to his side.

"We don't suit," Tamara said firmly, "and we never will."

His expression turned mocking. "We suited just fine a minute ago—"

She made a sweeping movement with her arm, gesturing to the room around them.

"This is not my world," she said, putting aside her earlier charmed reaction to his town house. "And I'm not going to trade away who I am in exchange for it."

He arched a brow.

"We may need to put on a convincing show that our marriage won't be a complete sham," she continued stubbornly, "but we don't need to be too convincing. And you don't need practice!"

Sawyer gazed at her thoughtfully for a second, and then laughed throatily.

She turned on her heel.

Unfortunately, *this* Goldilocks had made her bed, but she wasn't sure whether she wanted to lie in it.

Eight

Tamara stood at the base of the steps of Gantswood Hall and surveyed the picturesque hills in the distance. From her vantage point, she could see the white dots of grazing sheep on the hillsides under the July sun. The stately home that was Sawyer's ancestral family seat sat amid the Cotswolds, and like most of the neighboring architecture, was made of an inviting honey-colored limestone, worlds away from the bleak, drafty castle she used to imagine him in.

A car that Sawyer had sent to pick her up from the airport stood parked near the front entrance of the Tudor mansion, its driver unloading her luggage.

Tamara breathed in the crisp country air, fragrant with the smell of grass and leaves and fresh streams.

The truth was she hadn't ventured to a stately British country estate since reaching adulthood. Not even to her father's family seat, Dunnyhead. She had been expecting to be put off by the whole experience. She was surprised to find herself…enchanted.

Gantswood Hall lay farther south than Dunnyhead, and its landscape was less bracing, more pastoral. It was the Gloucestershire countryside at its best.

But it was more than the landscape that drew her. A part of her, she acknowledged now, would always remain attached to the British countryside, no matter how many miles and how much time she stayed away. And soon she'd have a new—if temporary—tie to bind her there.

She'd arrived today as Tamara Kincaid, but she would leave as Tamara, Countess of Melton, and she would be addressed as Lady Melton or simply, my lady.

In deference to the mantle she'd opted to assume, she'd dressed conservatively in fawn-colored pants and a sky-blue shirt. She could have, she thought, walked out of an ad for Ralph Lauren.

Absently, she ran her finger over the spot on her shirt that covered the small rose tattoo she'd acquired in an East Village salon a few years ago.

She might have donned the uniform of a British aristocrat, but, she reminded herself, inside she was still the free-spirited designer with a SoHo loft.

Of course, she'd retained possession of said loft only thanks to Sawyer's timely intervention. He'd cosigned her lease renewal and assumed payment of the monthly rent. He'd also deposited a generous sum in Pink Teddy's commercial bank account.

"The first installment," he'd said, acting as if the amount were of little consequence.

The recollection should have made her happy. Instead, she wanted to cringe.

She felt bought.

She shook her head. Why shy away from the truth?

She *had* been bought. She'd had a price and Sawyer had met it.

She surveyed the hills before her, where all matter of

wildlife still roamed. All of it was the domain of the earls of Melton, no doubt at least partially acquired through various dynastic marriages over the centuries.

And now she was about to become the latest Langsford bride. In two days, she'd wear an embroidered lace wedding dress and Kincaid jewels to wed Sawyer in the village chapel. Pia would help make sure everything went off without a hitch.

Though the wedding was to be small, all the immediate family would be in attendance, including her mother and stepfather, Mr. and Mrs. Ward George, her sisters and, of course, her father. On Sawyer's side, his mother, Mrs. Peter Beauregard, and her teenage daughter from her second marriage, Jessica, would be present. And then, of course, there would be Belinda and Pia, and the Marquess of Easterbridge and the Duke of Hawkshire. Adding some buffer to the mix, a number of extended family, a few other friends, some neighbors and Sawyer's closest business associates would also be in attendance.

Tamara tamped down the well of turbulent anticipation. Since she'd never eloped in a Las Vegas wedding chapel, at least they wouldn't have to worry about any former husbands making an appearance.

No, the only concern this time would be the possibility of a runaway bride, Tamara thought with a barely suppressed hysterical laugh.

She replayed her mother's reaction on the phone when she'd announced she was getting married.

Honey, no.

You'll find life as Sawyer's wife absolutely stifling. What has possessed you to even think…?

I hope your father hasn't pressured you.

And then, once it had become apparent Tamara was determined to go through with the marriage, remaining steadily mum about her reasons for doing so other than that she'd fallen for Sawyer Langsford, Susan George had sighed heavily.

I never imagined you'd aspire to status, Tamara. But, darling, I can't fault you if you do. Certainly having married wealth and position has benefited me.

It was Sawyer's wealth she was counting on, Tamara thought now. It was his financial support that had made her agree to this farce of a marriage at all. So why did standing on the steps of his ancestral estate, expecting him to come and greet her at any moment, feel so strangely like coming home?

Tamara heard footsteps behind her, and turned.

Sawyer.

Her heart skipped a beat.

He trotted down the front steps of the house, looking virile in riding boots, form-fitting trousers and an open-collared shirt. A thin sheen of sweat glazed his throat and brow, giving him an air of healthy vibrancy.

Her pulse thrummed in her veins, and she swallowed. *Don't be silly,* she told herself. Sawyer was a cool-headed businessman. And they had made a heartless bargain. *Best remember that.*

There would *not* be a repeat of their romantic interlude at his town house—at least if she could help it.

When Sawyer reached her, he gave her a quick kiss on the lips before she could react.

"Do you ride?" he asked.

"Horses?"

Sawyer's mouth quirked up. "No, taxis." He gestured in the direction of the house. "The stables are beyond the gardens."

"I haven't ridden in ages."

He surveyed her, his topaz eyes missing nothing. "Then tomorrow morning we should see about ending the drought. I'll have riding attire bought for you."

"No need," she responded. "I brought along riding boots and appropriate clothing."

It was a grudging admission. She'd hoped to hold him off with her comment that she didn't ride any longer. But just in case, before she'd left New York, she'd made sure she bought some riding boots and clothes. She'd felt duty-bound to do so by her bargain to play the role of the happy fiancée.

When Sawyer arched a brow, she added somewhat defensively, "I've come prepared to play my part, if nothing else."

Their eyes held for a moment, unspoken meaning stretching the silence between them while her driver walked past with her bags.

"Your belongings will be put in our private set of rooms," Sawyer said.

When Tamara opened her mouth to argue, he added, "We have to maintain the pretense that this marriage is real."

"Yes, after the wedding!"

Sawyer looked amused. "Don't tell me you want to act the role of the blushing bride."

With unfortunate timing, she felt herself flush.

Damn him.

And it didn't help that right now he looked as virile a male specimen as could possibly stride over Gloucestershire's green grass.

"Why not play the role to the hilt?" she flung back.

Especially since in this case it gave her an excuse to maintain some distance from Sawyer.

"You don't need to worry," he said sardonically, though a teasing glint remained in his eyes. "The private rooms are two adjoining suites. The countesses of Melton have all traditionally had their own suites—including a separate bed."

She raised her chin. "How clever of them."

The corners of Sawyer's eyes crinkled. He stepped closer

and habitually tucked back a strand of her hair that had caught the breeze.

"I'm glad you've arrived," he murmured.

She searched his expression, but all she saw was appreciation—and the promise of something more.

Sawyer bent and brushed his lips across hers again.

He tasted of leather and sweat and clean country air, and she involuntarily felt herself sway into him.

When he straightened, his expression was enigmatic. "We might as well start practicing now if we're going to convince our guests this marriage isn't just a brief arrangement."

"Of course," she managed.

His eyes glinted. "Follow me," he said, turning. "I'll show you the house."

They walked up the front steps together and into the cool, dark front hall, where Sawyer hailed an older woman who appeared to be Beatrice's counterpart in England—the housekeeper.

"Ah, Eleanor," Sawyer said. "May I present Ms. Tamara Kincaid, my fiancée?"

As she shook hands with Eleanor, Tamara was careful to disguise her inner turmoil.

Sawyer's greeting had left her unsure of her footing.

Not good. Not good at all.

Early the next morning, Tamara knocked on the partially open door of Sawyer's study before walking inside.

Sawyer looked up at her knock.

He stood, hands braced on hips, behind a massive wood desk at the other end of the room. Sunlight shafted in from the windows, bathing him in a beam of radiance. He looked like a historical lord plotting his next conquest. She quelled the feeling that in this case that might be *her.*

Breathing in deeply, she sauntered farther into the room.

They had missed his study on their tour of the house the day before, though they'd skipped very little else.

As she'd suspected, Gantswood Hall was heavy with the weight of history. The walls of the reception rooms were mounted with Gainsboroughs, van Dycks and other priceless works of art, including portraits of Sawyer's ancestors. Busts and other valuable sculptures dating back hundreds of years were showcased in the halls and entry. Beautiful molded-plaster ceilings added to the ambience of centuries of genteel wealth.

"Do you always stand behind your desk?" she asked now, half expecting to see Sawyer contemplating a battle map—no doubt like ancestors of yore.

"Not always, but sometimes," Sawyer responded, lips curving. "It helps with the restless energy when I'm deliberating something."

"And what would that be?" she asked.

"Some architectural improvements to a set of outlying buildings on the estate," he responded.

While he pushed together papers on his desk, she scanned the room.

Sawyer's study was more or less what she expected it would be. It had beautiful built-in bookshelves and old and valuable artwork. All that was missing, she thought wryly, was a pipe and smoking jacket and the late Alistair Cooke announcing the beginning of *Masterpiece Theatre*.

Interestingly, however, the room displayed what looked like a variety of travel memorabilia, including various framed photos.

She stopped before a bookshelf and examined a wood mask that appeared to be painted with gold and bronze.

"Nepal," Sawyer said.

She glanced at him. "I didn't realize you'd ever been."

"Five years ago. But I did not attempt to scale to the top of Mount Everest, in case you're wondering."

"Of course," she quipped. "You're too busy climbing to various corporate pinnacles."

At his chuckle, she glided on along the line of bookshelves until her eyes landed on a mahogany frame. Bending toward it, she realized it was a photo of a helmeted Sawyer emerging from a tank.

"Embedded with an army unit at the front lines," he elaborated, sauntering toward her.

She arched a brow as she turned to look at him. "Working as a war correspondent is part of your job as head of a news corporation?"

"Only occasionally. Don't tell."

"Far be it for me to ruin your reputation as a stuffy aristocrat."

"After my studies at Cambridge," he said, "I did a brief military service."

"Couldn't escape the family tradition?" She knew many upper-class families still looked upon a military career as a gentleman's calling.

"Didn't want to," he responded, refusing to be drawn in.

She turned away, and seeking a more neutral topic, pointed to a framed photo of him and three people dressed in traditional African garb standing in front of a nondescript building.

"As I recall," Sawyer said, answering her unspoken question, "we had just arrived at the medical station with vaccines after dodging a handful of armed rebels in a Jeep."

"Oh."

She hid her surprise and confusion. Sawyer wasn't supposed to be Indiana Jones disguised as a staid British earl. He might live the news business, but it was clear it went beyond empire-building and down to the trenches. He helped people, and he found and told their stories.

To her chagrin, Sawyer made her occasional volunteer work

serving food in a New York City homeless shelter seem rather insignificant.

"Are you ready to ride?" Sawyer asked.

Why, oh, why, did she have to see sexual suggestion in his words?

He was so close she only had to reach out a hand to feel the hard planes of his chest, or the outline of a muscular thigh beneath form-fitting riding pants.

Sawyer's topaz gaze traveled over her, from her hair caught in a ponytail to her white shirt, snug-fitting pants and polished black boots.

She wet her lips.

Sawyer's eyes came back to hers, too knowing. "You didn't answer my question."

Had they been talking about something?

"Are you ready to ride?" he repeated, his eyes holding a telltale glint.

"Of course."

He took a half step closer. "Good…then there's just one more thing."

"What's that?" she asked with a touch of breathlessness.

He bent his head, and she watched his mouth curve…right before he settled his lips on hers.

Her hand came up to his chest, but before she could use it to keep some physical separation, he captured it in his, drew it aside and laced his fingers with hers.

His mouth moved over hers, and when she would have made to pull away, he pressed her back against the bookcases, settling his body against hers.

He coaxed her into a soul-searching kiss even as his free hand roamed her curves.

Her hand curled around his, and he held her firmly.

He fit against her curves, his hard planes pressing her, molding her, and she could feel his growing arousal. She picked up the faint scent of sandalwood soap underneath that of freshly polished leather.

She didn't want to desire *this*. Desire *him*. But pure need fueled her response.

She responded to his kiss with a growing urgency, her hand plowing through the hair at the back of his head.

As if seizing upon her response, he moved his mouth from hers to trail kisses along her jaw. With an impatient hand, he undid the upper buttons of her shirt, exposing the lace of her bra, and then pressed small, warm kisses against the soft flesh of her throat.

When he moved up to claim her mouth again, his hand molded and squeezed her breast, and she met him greedily.

Sawyer made her feel. She was almost afraid of how much and *what* he made her feel.

It wasn't supposed to be like this. This wasn't part of their agreement.

She made a monumental effort to summon the will to resist.

At that very moment, however, as if Sawyer could read her mind, he drew back.

Sawyer's eyes glittered down at her, and she swallowed, clutching her open blouse with one hand.

He rubbed her lower lip with his thumb. "You look as if you've been thoroughly kissed."

"Thanks to you," she replied.

She had meant it as an accusation, but Sawyer just gave her a slow, satisfied smile.

"Thanks to me," he agreed, his voice still rough with arousal. "No one will doubt we're anything but lovers on the eve of being newlyweds."

The reminder of the status of their *relationship*—if it indeed could be called that—was the last jolt she needed to free herself from their sexual interlude.

"I'll meet you outside," she said tightly.

As she stalked from the room, she could feel Sawyer's gaze on her.

Damn him. How could she call him on his game of seduction when he kept claiming it was no more than that—a game?

Nine

Sawyer stood at the altar waiting for the bride.

He'd started on this road as a means to acquiring Kincaid News. But somewhere along the way, acquiring—no, possessing—Tamara had begun to consume his thoughts.

He wanted her. In his bed. Under him. Moaning, just as she had in his study yesterday before they'd gone horseback riding.

He'd discovered she rode a horse well. *Like a bike,* she'd said. *You never forget.* These days, he was finding her fairly unforgettable, too.

Damn.

His cutaway morning coat wasn't structured to conceal an arousal. If he wasn't careful, he'd be giving the guests in the pews an eyeful.

So far, he had been able to use the excuse of acting like an engaged, albeit not necessarily in love, couple as cover for his real and increasing need to seduce her—a need, he admitted, that he had increasing trouble remembering was tied to his bargain with Kincaid.

The church organ struck up, and a hushed silence fell over the guests. All eyes went to the doors at the back, which swung open to reveal Tamara on the arm of her father.

Sawyer drew in a breath at the sight of her as she started toward him.

She looked magnificent. Her vivid hair was piled up in an elaborate knot, and a delicate diamond tiara, one of the Kincaid family heirlooms, nestled there, matching the diamonds at her ears. Her dress was a strapless ivory lace confection with a full skirt. Gauzy material wrapped around her shoulders like a shrug and tucked into her bodice.

But it was her face that enthralled him. Classical beauty defined her features, her green eyes captivating beneath arched brows, her lips pink and glossy, inviting his kiss.

Sawyer sent a silent apology to the minister standing next to him, because all he wanted at that moment was to pick Tamara up, stride back down the aisle and ravish her.

Instead, he waited patiently until Tamara reached him and Viscount Kincaid kissed her cheek.

Once she put aside her bouquet of tightly-packed roses, he took her hand, claiming her.

He felt a tremor go through her and glanced her way, but her alabaster profile remained composed.

He barely registered the voice of the minister. "We are gathered together…"

He kept Tamara's hand in his, feeling the vital flow of life between them.

The minister led them in their vows, the same ones used in royal weddings. Sawyer felt his eyes crinkle when Tamara delicately repeated "to love and to cherish" and omitted "obey."

For his part, he intended to love and cherish her—in the

full physical sense and as soon as possible. In that way, his vows couldn't be more real.

When it was time for the exchange of rings, he produced a filigreed wedding band of platinum and diamonds and slipped it on her finger. There it joined the diamond engagement ring that he'd given her.

He was glad to see Tamara's lips curve into a faint smile as she looked at the new ring on her finger. He'd debated long and hard before selecting the wedding ring at longstanding Langsford family jewelers Boodle & Dunthorne. He'd wanted a ring that fit Tamara's fashion-forward sense and was impressive enough for the new Countess of Melton. From the look on Tamara's face, he'd made the right choice.

Moments later, Tamara slipped a wedding ring on his finger—the plain platinum band with small grooved edges that he'd ordered.

When it was time to kiss the bride, he settled his lips on hers with satisfaction, letting her glimpse his simmering passion and feel the promise of more.

He was joined to Tamara now, and somehow it didn't feel just like a means to an end. Except, of course, if that end was the wedding night.

Tamara sipped her champagne, adjusting to the weight of two magnificent rings on her finger—and adjusting to the enormity of what she'd just done.

Married to Sawyer. She was now the Countess of Melton.

She was seated among the seventy-odd invited guests in the main dining room of Gantswood Hall, where the traditional wedding breakfast was taking place.

Thankfully, she thought, glancing around, this whole affair would soon be over. Pia was ignoring the Duke of Hawkshire, and Belinda and Colin sat like two combatants at an impasse.

The remaining wedding guests and a roving photographer were convenient buffers.

In fact, the only person who appeared in the best of spirits was her father.

As if on a cue from her thoughts, Viscount Kincaid pushed back his chair and stood.

"A toast," her father announced, raising his glass.

Tamara nearly groaned aloud, and everyone else dutifully reached for their glasses.

This, Tamara thought, was destined to be her life if she stayed married to Sawyer. There were all sorts of issues of protocol, precedence and etiquette that she would need to be aware of. She would need to conform to certain rules after years of priding herself on being a nonconformist.

True, she'd enjoyed her horseback ride yesterday. True, she found Sawyer's kisses more potent than any other man's. But they were all wrong for each other.

She pulled her mind back, realizing her father was looking at her, for once in her life, with approval.

"To Tamara, my dear daughter, and Sawyer, whom I proudly welcome as my son-in-law," her father said. "May your marriage be long and fruitful."

Tamara refused to glance at Sawyer. *If only her father knew*. This time he'd met his match in ruthlessness.

"And may you find a lasting happiness together."

Tamara hid her surprise. She wasn't expecting *that* toast. Looking at her father's face, though, she realized he meant it.

"To Tamara and Sawyer," the other guests said in unison, saluting them before sipping their champagne.

Tamara set down her glass, and then before she could react, Sawyer picked up her hand and raised it to his lips.

"I shall endeavor to use my very best efforts to make Tamara happy," he announced, gazing into her eyes.

She could almost read the end of his sentence in his tawny gaze. *In bed.*

Extricating her hand, she gave a fixed smile. "Sawyer, you've already made me happy."

She thought of her loft back in New York and her dreams for Pink Teddy, and banished all thoughts of Sawyer's seductiveness.

Sawyer's amused expression was all too knowing, and she angled her chin up stubbornly.

She refused to be vanquished over plates of salmon in a delicate cream sauce with a side of asparagus spears.

A door connected the master's and mistress's private quarters at Gantswood Hall.

Sawyer contemplated the door now. He'd just showered, his hair still damp as he pulled on a pair of cotton pajama bottoms.

In centuries past, the door, which connected the earl's and countess's sitting rooms, had been the gateway through which the lord and lady of the house were expected to meet to do their sacred duty—namely, to beget heirs.

It was how his father had been conceived, and his father's father and so on down the line.

He himself, on the other hand, had by all reports been conceived in one of the luxury hotel suites at Claridge's, soon after his parents had embarked on their impetuous and tempestuous union.

His aristocratic father had married a free-spirited American socialite and heiress, and the marriage had been a—thankfully brief—disaster.

The thought gave him a brief moment's pause. He was well-versed in the pitfalls of marrying a woman unsuited to the role of countess.

But he'd struck his bargain with Viscount Kincaid. And even in this day and age, he had a duty to secure the earldom by producing a successor to the responsibilities of his hereditary peerage.

And the truth was he was as impatient to consummate his marriage as any bridegroom. He'd been suffering the pangs of frustrated desire for his bride for too long.

Tonight, God help him, there'd be no untimely interruptions by sad-sack boyfriends or unsuspecting household help.

Tonight, he'd seduce Tamara.

With that thought, he strode to the door and tapped lightly. After a moment, trying again and receiving no answer, he turned the knob and entered.

Tamara's sitting room was empty, and so, for that matter, was what he could see of her bedroom through the doorway.

Where was she?

It was nearing midnight, and they'd both had a long day. After the wedding breakfast, they'd continued to socialize with various guests, until they'd seen a number of their visitors depart.

Sawyer walked farther into Tamara's bedroom.

Her personal belongings lay about, and his eyes came to rest on the wedding dress that was draped on a rose-and-gold-striped armchair.

Walking over, he picked up the dress and brought it up to his face, closing his eyes and inhaling deeply.

A hint of jasmine.

A little exotic, a lot erotic.

His body tightened.

Allowing the lacy gown to drop back onto the chair, he let his eyes follow a path of strewn clothing from where he was standing to the bathroom door.

A pair of red panties, a white garter…

His blood began to hum.

He could hear the shower running now, and his feet took him to the bathroom door.

He didn't even think. He opened the door and walked inside, and immediately focused on Tamara's silhouette visible through the fogging shower door, her dark-red hair partly wet.

Her face was turned up to the shower jet, her eyes closed as soapy water ran in rivulets over her shoulders and disappeared beneath the steam that partially concealed her from his avid gaze.

Sawyer felt his blood pound harder in his veins. His body was revved, ready on a hair trigger to seek mind-blowing pleasure with her.

At that moment, Tamara turned her head and saw him.

He watched her eyes go wide with shocked surprise.

They stared at each other while the steam continued to rise between them.

Then she slapped her hand on the handle of the shower and shut off the water.

"What are you doing here?" she demanded as she turned to face him again.

"I live here, if you'll recall."

He wanted to enjoy the show. *Step out of the stall slowly.*

He reached for one of the plush beige towels hanging nearby and moved toward the shower door.

Her green eyes flashed, as bright as any fine emeralds. But despite the performance, he could read her nervousness.

"You haven't answered my question," she said.

"We need to discuss what we're doing tomorrow," he replied. "This is the only time we'll have to speak privately. We still have guests—including your father—who'll expect us to act like content, if not lovestruck, newlyweds."

It wasn't a complete lie. They did need to talk.

But his body damned conversation. It wanted something more elemental from her.

"Out," she demanded.

"Precisely what I was thinking." He held the towel before him. "I won't look."

She hesitated, and then chin held high, opened the stall door and stepped out.

He lowered the towel, and she sucked in a breath.

He drank in the sight. Her shoulders and arms were sculpted, her waist tiny. And her breasts...

He swallowed. *Beautiful.* Her nipples were erect and rosy, beckoning to him in their tightness.

And that damned rose tattoo...

"You said you wouldn't look!"

His lips twitched. "The sight proved irresistible."

Her eyes rounded, the sexual current oscillating between them.

"Tamara, all grown-up," he said roughly. "You do make an exquisite countess."

Her lips parted, her eyes moving from his bare chest and down to his arousal.

The part of his brain still functioning was a bit amused by her loss for words. The other part took satisfaction in the evidence that she was just as affected as he was.

He let the towel fall from his grasp to the floor.

The curls at the apex of her thighs were just as dark and lushly red as her hair.

Heaven.

He reached out and drew the pad of his forefinger over her nipple.

She gasped, and he hoped the sensation was as exquisite as she gave every evidence of it being.

Her eyes flashed. "Looking for some novelty, Sawyer? A shag with someone who's not your usual type?"

"With someone who's my wife."

"In name only!"

"Labels are only as meaningful as we allow them to be."

She bent to snatch up the towel, but he was just as fast... bending with her and dragging her into the shelter of his arms as his mouth fastened on hers.

Lips locked together, they rose slowly.

He folded her close, and her arms inched around his neck. The wetness that still clung to her skin dampened them both, joining them, as his arousal settled against her.

Ever since their first kiss, the attraction between them had been combustible, and now it seemed they were both powerless as it flamed to life again.

His hand slipped down her back, rubbed over her derriere and back up again. *She felt so good.*

He moved his mouth from hers, trailing kisses across her cheek and down to her throat.

"You're a moth to the flame, aren't you, Sawyer?" she taunted softly.

He lifted his head, and looked into her green eyes, bright with desire and provocation.

"Does it get boring for you buttoned-down types?" Tamara asked.

"Never when you're around."

A hint of vulnerability flashed across her face, but it was quickly gone. "Is that a compliment?"

"A promise."

She opened her mouth, but he swallowed her response with his, breathing in the scent of jasmine that lingered lightly on her skin.

He slid his hand over her thigh, lifting it and wrapping it around him.

He let his hands dance over her body, plying her with pleasure until he felt her relax. Only then did he bend over her, cupping and nuzzling her breasts.

He laved one nipple and then the other, heard her moan, and then fastened his mouth over one breast.

Her hands tangled in his hair, and her moan fueled his ardor.

He lifted his mouth to move to the other breast. "You're so responsive."

"We unconventional types usually are."

Her reply made him smile.

"Show me," he urged, planting a quick nip on the rose tattoo that always drew him.

She was obviously set on reminding him how different she was from his usual type, because she thought he was after a quick coupling with novelty value.

Instead he… Well, he would love to demonstrate to her just how *novel* an experience theirs could be. There was so much passion between them that he couldn't wait to explore.

But then he thought unexpectedly of that hint of vulnerability he'd seen earlier.

Damnation.

He wanted her. But if he took her, she'd think it was because she was the flavor of the day.

The movement of her hand cut into his thoughts. He felt the flutter of a caress along his arousal, and then another, and bit back a groan.

Her hand slid up and down along the length of him through his pajama bottoms, again and again.

Hot and heady sensation coursed through him. His breath became more labored and he felt his muscles bunch, readying his body for release. He needed to be inside her. Except he couldn't.

Hell and damn.

He turned his head and growled next to her ear, "You, too."

Then he cupped her intimately, his hand delving into the damp curls at the juncture of her thighs, interrupting her hand in its steady motion on him.

After a moment, he slipped a finger inside her and felt her body clasp around him, pulling tight as a bow.

They both groaned with satisfaction.

He moved his thumb, finding the nub hidden in her curls with unerring accuracy, and pressed.

She gasped, and then her hand reached up to grasp his arm. "Sawyer…"

"Yes, say my name," he replied thickly.

He pressed forward, feeling her tremble with anticipation.

And in the next instant, she shattered, shaking and crying out, her body racked with waves of pleasure that seeped from her skin to his.

He held her, and moments later, feeling her heart still pounding, he moved damp hair back from her face and brushed his lips across hers.

A promise.

"Sawyer," she said scratchily.

But he wasn't done.

He knelt and cupped her bottom, bringing her against his mouth. He gave her an intimate kiss, one that had her body rising up to meet him while the breath seemed to leave her lungs in a whoosh.

Soon, she came apart again, this time against his mouth, and his palms smoothed down her legs, easing the tremor that signaled her release.

When he finally rose, his eyes locked on hers. Her face was flushed, her lips full and red, and her eyes wide and glazed.

He stifled an oath. His body still hurt with his unspent release. But in her eyes, there was still that vulnerability, reminding him how easily she could be hurt by what he did.

He bent and handed her the fallen towel, though many of the droplets that had clung to her skin had evaporated—no doubt due to their steamy encounter.

Then silently, he turned and walked from the room before he gave in to temptation.

Ten

With experienced precision, Tamara used the tweezers to set the opal in place, and then sat back and sighed.

She removed her visor, whose attached magnifying glass she had previously turned up, and rubbed the back of her neck.

She stared out at the majestic English countryside beckoning to her from between the damask drapes of her sitting room. It was early, before eight, but soon she'd have no choice but to face Sawyer again.

After having slept badly, she'd resorted to one of her better relaxation techniques. There was something soothing, almost tranquilizing, about jewelry-making. Like knitting, it kept the hands busy while allowing the mind to wander.

She always traveled with a jewelry project or two, just so she'd have something to turn to if necessary—and with Sawyer around, it was proving *very* necessary.

Methodically, she put away her implements, placing pliers and tweezers back in their carrying cases. She closed the box holding semiprecious gemstones, and put away her portable metal-working kit.

She hadn't heard any movement in the earl's suite next door, so Sawyer was either sleeping soundly or had woken up before she'd gotten out of bed.

For her part, she had tossed and turned last night, willing herself to sleep.

Despite having had not one, but two, orgasms in Sawyer's arms, she'd gone to bed alone and feeling frustrated and out of sorts.

How dare Sawyer surprise her while she was in the shower? How dare he bring her sexual fulfillment—not once but twice? How dare he leave without explanation?

She was so confounded by his behavior she didn't know what she was most upset about.

How dare Sawyer twist her in knots.

Of course, she'd been an active participant in their romantic interlude. She'd told herself she was going to remind him just how incompatible they were—the bohemian, wayward daughter and the aristocratic lord. But events hadn't unfolded in the way she'd expected.

Her cheeks flamed as she replayed the scene from last night. Sawyer had shown a greater mastery of her body and all its pleasure points than any man she'd ever known.

And then he'd left abruptly.

Was it because he'd come to his senses and realized the two of them were, in fact, a crazy pairing?

She felt an unexpected squeeze around her heart.

Her cell phone beeped, indicating she'd just received a text message, and she got up to retrieve it from where it was recharging on a nearby table.

When she reached her phone, she realized the message was from Sawyer.

Tour the Cotswolds with me at eleven. The guests will expect it.

Before she could reply to the text, however, she heard a discreet knock on her sitting room door and went to answer it.

When she opened her door, she discovered Sage, one of the maids she'd been introduced to, standing in the hall.

"My lady," Sage said, "his lordship sent me to attend to you."

"Thank you," she replied, wondering what Sage thought of the lord and lady of the house communicating at arm's length on the morning after their wedding. "However, I do not require anything at the moment."

She looked down at herself. She was wearing an oversized T-shirt and well-worn pajama bottoms. She hadn't even bothered with a robe. No doubt about it. She was hardly countess material.

For Sage's benefit, though, she added, "But please tell his lordship I will meet him for our tour as planned."

Sage hesitated for a moment, as if perplexed, but then nodded and retreated.

As Tamara closed the door, she thought about how Sawyer was a blend of the modern and archaic. He'd sent a text message *and* a lady's maid within moments of each other. He had a Manhattan town house suited to a media baron *and* an English country estate worthy of an earl.

But, she reminded herself, they were still hardly compatible. Sure, he'd surprised her on several fronts, but just because Sawyer had shown signs of being less buttoned-down than she'd dismissed him as being, it didn't mean they weren't oil and water.

She was thoroughly modern. More than slightly bohemian. Independent and American.

She and Sawyer were proving compatible in the bedroom, but as she well knew, much more was involved in a successful marriage.

* * *

As Tamara walked alongside Sawyer through the nearest village, she couldn't help but be impressed again with the natural beauty of this part of Britain.

Traditional thatched-roof cottages clung together in little groups under the late-morning sun, and everywhere the local golden limestone was in evidence, from low-lying walls to the exterior of homes and businesses.

The setting was picturesque, and it fired her imagination. She wanted to go home—no, sit in the fields—with her sketchbook and design something inspired by the local landscape.

The locals all hailed Sawyer by name, and he introduced her as his new countess.

This meet-and-greet, she thought, had been Sawyer's purpose in proposing a walking tour of the local village.

Fortunately, she'd dressed for the role of the new mistress of Gantswood Hall. Before she'd left New York, she'd made sure to buy clothes that would be more appropriate to wear during her trip than her usual attire. Her flowered blouse, A-line blue skirt and ballerina flats complemented Sawyer's blue shirt and beige pants.

Yet she'd refused to disguise herself completely. Her favorite self-designed earrings completed her outfit.

She'd expected Sawyer to frown at the sight of such loud accent pieces. Instead, strangely enough, he'd smiled.

She and Sawyer left the baker's shop and sauntered down the street, and Sawyer picked up her hand, lacing his fingers with hers.

At the moment, there was no one approaching them, so she had a brief window during which to speak her mind.

"I'm hardly going to be the Countess of Melton long enough for all these introductions," she protested in a low voice.

Sawyer shot her a sidelong look. "Nevertheless, the locals

expect it. There would be raised eyebrows, and likely some degree of affront, if I didn't introduce you."

"I see."

Of course, she did. Sawyer was simply performing his duties as earl. And as his countess, she now had her obligations, as well.

"The villagers have all been friendly and welcoming," she added. "And everyone appears to like you."

Sawyer looked amused. "You're surprised?"

She'd heard tales from the locals of his do-good nature, from his initiatives in local eco-friendly improvements to his charitable endeavors.

Aloud, she said, "Perhaps they're seeing only one side of you. The beneficent one."

Sawyer stopped and laughed, swinging her to face him. "And you, I suppose," he said in a low voice, "have seen others?"

She searched his face and remembered last night—seeing him nearly naked and clearly aroused.

"Did you like my other side?" he asked, his voice a caress.

"Why did you leave so abruptly?" she countered.

"Why do you think?" he responded. "If we'd continued, I would have fulfilled your expectation that I wanted to bed you as a novelty."

She was surprised by his forthright answer. "And that isn't what you were looking for when you appeared during my shower?"

His lips quirked. "I'm thinking you're a lot more complex than a novel shag—"

Her eyes widened.

"—and the earl is only one part of who I am."

He held her gaze for a moment longer, and then looked up the street.

She turned, too, and noticed a passerby was approaching. Their private conversation was at an end.

"This is ridiculous."

"Humor me," Sawyer responded, capturing her hand from where he lay on the picnic blanket set near a small duck pond.

It was a glorious summer day, with the occasional puffy cloud drifting overhead, and they had a basket of wine and cheese and French bread with them.

Timing was everything, he thought, and he planned to use this interlude to his advantage.

Tamara looked down at him from her sitting position, her brow puckering. "Everyone thinks this isn't a love match, but a dynastic marriage for mutual advantage—"

"Yes, except they don't know exactly what mutual advantage." He waggled his brows as he rested her hand on his chest. "They think you married me for my money and title—"

"Well, for your money," she conceded.

"—and I've married you to secure Kincaid News."

"Which you all but have."

"True."

Legal due diligence was being performed, and the merger documents were being drawn up. Soon Kincaid News and Melton Media would be one company—if all went according to plan.

"So," Tamara argued, "people are hardly expecting us to act lovey-dovey. Not that Pia and Belinda, or the Marquess of Easterbridge and the Duke of Hawkshire, for that matter, ever had that expectation. And in any case, they've departed."

"Your father and most of the rest of our families remain," he was obliged to point out solemnly. "One can never have too much assurance when you're the father of the bride and are on the verge of parting with your business."

"Then I wonder why my father did it," Tamara countered.

Sawyer shrugged. "He's getting older, and consolidation is the name of the game in the media business these days. In any case, he'll retain a title in the new organization. He'll have power over what remains under the name Kincaid News."

Tamara studied him. "And how do you feel about having my father around?"

Sawyer smiled. "I plan to observe and learn all his tricks."

She shook her head with mock resignation, and Sawyer played with her hand on his chest.

She looked enticing, staring down at him from her position on the blanket. Her dark-red hair caught the summer breeze. An off-the-shoulder crocheted top and short, layered skirt gave her the look of a latter-day peasant girl and accentuated her sensuality.

Sawyer felt his body stir in response.

She didn't look as if she was immune to him, either, dressed as he was in an open-collared white shirt and dark trousers.

But first he knew he had to break down some of her resistance. Due to some perverse streak of nobility, he'd resisted taking her to bed two nights ago. Her hint of vulnerability had done him in. But now he vowed to rectify the matter.

"You're enjoying the English countryside," he remarked.

She nodded. "It's pretty. I've never been to Gloucestershire before. It's inspiring."

He hoped it would inspire her right into his bed, but he settled for arching a brow.

"Not for your jewelry, surely?" he inquired.

She nodded her assent. "The natural beauty is arresting."

"I see." And he did. There was natural beauty right in front of him.

"There's some British in you yet," he joked.

"Scottish," she amended. "Way up north. A different landscape from this."

She slipped her hand from his grasp, and he shifted to his side, propping his head on his bent arm.

"We haven't spoken much about your jewelry business," he said, realizing he was curious. "I know about the hedge-fund wife, but apart from her, who are your clients?"

"You mean, what is my business plan? What are my marketing and promotion efforts?" she joked. "Are you afraid you'll never recover your investment?"

"I already have," he replied glibly, "and in any case, I could afford the loss."

Tamara looked into the distance, at the hills visible beyond where they sat on an expanse of ground within sight of Gantswood Hall.

"I'm an artist, not a businessperson," she said, and shrugged. "I produce what I can by myself, and then exhibit at art shows and specialty boutiques."

She gave a half smile as she gazed back down at him. "You could say my clientele is rich individuals, or at least they're whom I aim for."

"Then you're in luck, since I happen to know a lot of wealthy people."

At her raised eyebrows, he added jokingly, "Of course, if you changed the name of your company to Countess of Melton Designs, you'd add a certain panache."

"I couldn't," she protested. "We'll only be married a short time."

He quirked a brow. "Diane von Furstenberg kept the *von* long after her divorce from the prince."

Tamara laughed. "Okay, yes."

He liked her laugh. She didn't do it very often around him, so it was like catching sight of a shooting star.

"As soon as we return to New York," he said, "we'll hire someone to manage the numbers side of Pink Teddy. And

I'll introduce you to people who'll be curious about your collection."

For a moment, she seemed both surprised and pleased, but then she shrugged. "New York seems a world away right now."

He searched her expression. "Don't we both know it."

A noise came from the direction of the house, and she looked up and shaded her eyes. "My father is heading to the tennis court with your mother, Julia and Jessica."

Sawyer followed her gaze. Everyone, he saw, carried a tennis racket.

"Kincaid is up for a challenge," he remarked. "My mother still plays a superior game of tennis."

"My father's determined to remain in the game, in more ways than one," Tamara countered.

Sawyer looked back at her. "The tennis court was added to the grounds during my father's day, at my mother's insistence."

"Was it part of her plan to deal with her new surroundings?" Tamara asked, dropping the hand that shaded her eyes.

"That and running down to Wimbledon every year," he replied half-jokingly.

"How long did your parents' marriage last?"

"Too long." He trailed a hand along her arm. "But the divorce became final the day before my fifth birthday. I recall the birthday party at Gantswood Hall being a huge affair with ponies, clowns and fireworks. But, of course, no mother. Looking back, I wonder whether the party was as much a celebration of the divorce decree as anything else."

Tamara arched a brow.

"Of course, as the heir," he said, reading her look, "I remained with my father after the separation. My mother was the bolter."

Tamara grimaced. "And your father never remarried."

"There was no need to. He had his heir."

Tamara tilted her head. "You seem to bear no ill will toward your mother."

He gave a brief nod. "I eventually understood my parents' complete incompatibility. My mother was twelve years younger than my father and a rich American debutante impressed by a title. After I was born, she began to long for a jet-set life, while my father was busy with his properties and his newspapers, and remained attached to the traditions set by generations before him."

"But she wed again, obviously," Tamara remarked.

"Once she'd tired of being a divorcée, she married Peter, a widowed Wall Street investment banker." Sawyer's lips twisted ironically. "She then unexpectedly found herself pregnant again at forty-one."

"It's quite a story," Tamara commented.

"There were unexpected benefits from the divorce for me," he said. "If it wasn't for my mother, I would never have received my business degree in the States after finishing up at Cambridge. Her contacts, and those of my stepfather before he died, proved invaluable for expanding my business in New York and beyond."

"You're practically American."

"A dual British and American citizen by birth," he confirmed, though he understood Tamara to be joking about his temperament and disposition rather than his nationality. "You have a lot of curiosity."

Tamara flushed.

"Care to compare notes?" he prompted, smoothing his fingers down her arm in a light caress.

She focused on the movement, and he said innocently, "We're in view of the tennis court."

She hesitated, but then said finally, "My parents divorced when I was seven. I left for New York with my mother. But surely you know that part."

He nodded. He remembered hearing of Viscount Kincaid's divorce when it had occurred.

Tamara's lips lifted with dry humor. "Unlike you, I wasn't the male heir, so I could be spared. My father made two more attempts at marriage and obtaining an heir, but I think he finally gave up."

"I'm surprised he stopped at two more," Sawyer commented with gentle humor.

Tamara lifted her shoulder. "You'd have to ask him why, though I believe three ex-wives and the attendant children began to constitute enough of a burden."

Sawyer chuckled, but then queried softly, "Is that what you were? A burden?"

She looked at him with that amazing crystal-green gaze. "I was never called it, but my father and I don't see eye-to-eye on many issues."

"As the Countess of Melton, you have a title that takes precedence over that of your father's, you know," he pointed out sportingly.

She gave a brief laugh. "I hardly care."

"And yet, here you are enjoying country living, and married to me, fulfilling paternal expectations."

"Only for the short term," she protested.

His eyes crinkled. "Then we should make the most of the time we have."

He tugged her down to him, and caught by surprise, she fell against him.

"What are you doing?" she said breathlessly.

"Tut-tut," he admonished. "We're in full view of the tennis court."

"You do make your antecedents proud," she retorted on a half laugh. "Such capacity for trickery…such an unerring sense of duplicity…"

"Mmm," he agreed. "You forgot 'such a skill for seizing the moment.'"

Then his mouth came down on hers.

Tamara studied the partially finished necklace.

Diamonds and emeralds. She'd pressed her suppliers in the Diamond District until she'd found what she was looking for for Sawyer's commission.

Sawyer was helping her business by giving her a large and lucrative order for jewels…for another woman.

At the thought, Tamara felt a twist in her stomach.

From her seat at her workbench, Tamara looked out the loft window of her former and current place of business and thought about picnicking with Sawyer by the pond.

She and Sawyer had left his Gloucestershire estate for his town house in New York two days ago, the day after their picnic on the grounds of Gantswood Hall.

Remarkably, she'd managed to stay out of his bed. She'd moved into the bedroom adjoining his at the town house, and there she'd stayed.

There hadn't been an attempt at seduction since their idyll by the duck pond.

Of course, the picnic had been all for show—for the benefit of her father and other guests—but the kiss hadn't been.

Tamara touched her fingers to her lips. Sawyer had kissed her thoroughly, as usual making her body hum, and she'd sunk deeper and deeper into their embrace. When she'd finally looked up, it had been to notice they had attracted the attention of their family at the tennis court and of three ducks from the nearby pond.

She'd half expected Sawyer to make an appearance in her bedroom on their last night at Gantswood Hall, but though she'd tossed restlessly until the early hours, he hadn't appeared.

He'd surprised her. Again.

Was he bent on being unpredictable?

Not another novelty shag.

She almost laughed at the thought that Sawyer could have been *her* novelty shag. Certainly, aristocratic media moguls weren't her type. She'd steered clear of Sawyer for years.

But then she'd enjoyed her stay at Gantswood Hall more than she expected. She'd enjoyed Sawyer more than she'd expected, especially now that she'd allowed herself to really talk to him.

They were alike in ways she'd just discovered and previously hadn't permitted herself to admit. They were both the offspring of trans-Atlantic marriages that had ended badly. And they were both connected to two different worlds. She'd been charmed by Gantswood Hall, while Sawyer, she allowed herself to acknowledge, was a New Yorker in his own way. He had a business to run—a very twenty-first century one that wasn't just newspapers and television and radio, but online social networking sites, as well.

And then, on top of it all, she'd been stunned to discover the daredevil that lurked inside the serious and proper aristocratic. His adventures dodging bullets had surprised—no, shocked her. Her own claim to being unconventional—a bit bohemian and with slightly flamboyant fashion sense—just seemed… insignificant in comparison.

And, of course, Sawyer attracted her sexually as no man ever had.

She was afraid she was falling for h—

No, she wouldn't let her mind go there.

L— No, *infatuation* wasn't part of the program.

And yet…

Here they were, *married.* And she had another couple of months at least to try to stay out of Sawyer's bed while the dust settled on the merger of Kincaid News and Melton Media.

Help. She knew all about how oxytocin flooded a woman's

head during sex, bonding her to her sexual partner. Making her think she was in l—

It could only be more so when the sexual partner was already your husband.

Still, she also knew the pitfalls of someone of her background and disposition marrying someone like Sawyer. Didn't she?

Tomorrow, Sawyer would expect her to appear on his arm for a reception and dinner at an Upper East Side consulate to honor visiting European royalty. It was to be their New York debut as a couple.

Did she dare make her first public appearance in a role she'd spent her life avoiding—that of the new Countess of Melton?

Eleven

She came down the town house stairs in a draped strapless emerald dress—folds of fabric crisscrossed her bodice before cascading down in a chiffon skirt. She'd paired the dress with—in a nod to her more unconventional side—peep-toe green satin pumps with feathery bow confections over the vamp. She hadn't had much time to shop for this evening, but fortunately she'd found the perfect dress at the second designer boutique she'd visited.

Sawyer stood at the foot of the stairs, looking every inch the wealthy and powerful aristocrat and media baron.

Frank male appreciation was stamped on his features, and she breathed in deeply to quell the sudden butterflies in her stomach.

Sawyer had knocked on her bedroom door moments before and, when she'd told him she was almost done getting ready, he'd insisted there was something she had to see downstairs.

Stifling a sigh, she'd complied. Her hair had already been

done, thanks to the salon she'd visited earlier in the day, and her makeup had been carefully applied. There really hadn't been much else to do, except dither until the appointed time.

"You look fantastic," Sawyer said now.

"Thank you," she responded.

She wet her lips, and his eyes focused on her mouth.

Sexual tension crackled between them.

She told herself she'd dressed the part of a proper countess in order to convince the world that theirs was a real marriage, and not to please Sawyer. But she knew she was playing a dangerous game.

Sawyer slid a velvet case off a nearby console table. "I wasn't sure how you'd be dressed tonight, but I believe I chose well."

He held the box in front of her, and she swallowed.

He looked amused. "Don't be afraid to open it."

"I thought you'd choose a Pink Teddy creation," she tried gamely.

"And I thought you'd make another exception for the Melton family jewels," he teased, opening the box for her.

She caught sight of the jewelry inside, and her mouth opened in silent surprise.

Nestled on an ivory satin surface was a simple but exquisite tiara made of diamonds and emeralds.

She touched the tip of one tiara point. "It's beautiful."

"Only as beautiful as the intended wearer."

She searched his expression.

The corner of Sawyer's mouth lifted. "After all," he said with a tinge of humor, "if we're going to convince the world we're really married, we might as well play the part to the hilt."

She felt let down at his words, and broke eye contact before he could read her expression.

Of course, this wasn't real. She knew that.

The tiara was real, but the countess wasn't.

She retreated to safe territory. "It reminds me of the Queen Victoria Emerald and Diamond Tiara."

Sawyer smiled. "You're familiar with it? One of my nineteenth-century ancestors liked it so much, she commissioned a tiara in a similar style."

"Well, the Queen Victoria tiara was very famous in its time," she responded, and then touched one of the points on the tiara resting in Sawyer's hands. "It's in what's known as the Gothic Revival style."

"If one tiara gets you this excited," Sawyer teased, "I really should let you play in the family vault."

The sexual suggestion in his comment, accompanied by the look in his eyes, made her heat. And just like that, the air between them became charged again.

"I'm not excited."

"I am," he murmured.

He set the box down and removed the tiara. Carefully, he nestled the jewelry in her hair.

"There," Sawyer murmured.

He admired his handiwork for a moment before his topaz gaze traveled to meet hers.

He bent and brushed a kiss across her lips.

She felt the tingle down to her toes. "I'll be right back," she said, her voice breathless. "I'll have to go anchor it with pins."

Somehow she found her way back upstairs, and with shaky legs, sat down in front of her vanity. How was she going to survive tonight?

Was it gauche to be unable to take your eyes off your wife on your first public appearance as a couple?

If so, Sawyer thought self-deprecatingly, he was as un-sophisticated as they came.

But he didn't give a damn. He was impatient to get Tamara home—alone.

Around him, assorted dignitaries and politicians mingled in the reception rooms on the ground floor of the consulate. Later, they'd all ascend to the second floor for a sit-down dinner.

And unfortunately, Tamara seemed to be having a marvelous time and appeared in no hurry to leave. He'd seen her chatting and laughing with two older women whom he knew to be old money pillars of New York society. Then a little while later, he'd seen her fall into conversation with a junior royal as if the two of them had been acquainted for some time.

Already a couple of other guests had stopped to congratulate him on his recent marriage and remark on how charming his wife was and how much they'd enjoyed talking with her and how lucky *he* was.

He'd have dismissed the remarks as idle cocktail party conversation and meaningless flattery, but he'd witnessed Tamara entertaining one conversation partner after another.

It was August in New York, so a sizable portion of the fashionable crowd had decamped to their summer homes in the Hamptons. The crowd tonight was made up mostly of those from the aristocratic and political spheres, with a strong concentration of foreigners. And despite any apprehensions on her part, Tamara was fitting just fine into his social circle.

Sawyer listened with one ear to the two gentlemen with him discussing the economic legislation being debated by the European Union Parliament in Brussels. The rest of his attention was on Tamara across the room, as she chatted amiably with Count de Lyndon, a portly, white-haired gentleman wearing an impressive number of medals and other recognitions on a red sash.

From his vantage point in the consulate's impressive entry, at the foot of the imperial staircase leading to the banquet rooms, Sawyer could easily survey the guests circulating among the various rooms *and* keep an eye on Tamara, her profile to him.

How convenient.

He wondered idly whether Tamara's gown had a zipper at the back or side. He itched to find out.

Damn it.

The bodice of Tamara's gown had fallen a fraction of an inch by the time they'd stepped inside the consulate more than an hour ago, and he'd just been able to make out the top of her rose tattoo.

Now, with laser-sharp vision, he zeroed in on the tattoo again from across the room. The faint outline that he could discern was driving him crazy.

"I say, don't you agree, Melton?"

"Yes, certainly," he responded absently.

"Oh?"

Sawyer's gaze swung back to his companions. The man who'd expressed surprise was the holder of a defunct Eastern European dukedom, as Sawyer recalled.

"You agree that the legislation is a good idea?" the duke asked.

Sawyer glanced at the other man in their circle, a career foreign service officer, who'd posed the original question.

"Any controversy is good for the news business," he hedged.

The duke's face relaxed. "Ah, of course. Rightly said!"

"Will you excuse me, gentlemen?" Sawyer asked. "I've discovered someone I wish to speak with across the room."

His wife.

As he strode toward her, he watched her laugh at something her companion said.

Ever since their wedding day, his desire for Tamara had seemed to grow exponentially. If only there hadn't been that hint of vulnerability that had stopped him on that first night. And then misguided chivalry had taken over. It had somehow seemed *crass* to wed and bed her immediately. He was regretting those scruples now.

Tamara glanced up at him when he joined her and Count de Lyndon. A small smile hovered at her lips.

He longed to kiss her smile, steal it and keep it for his own.

He mentally shrugged at his bit of whimsy.

Lyndon inclined his head, and Sawyer shook the man's hand as they exchanged greetings.

"I wasn't sure you'd be here tonight," Lyndon said heartily. "I half expected you and your lovely bride to be on a honeymoon voyage."

Sawyer threw a quick glance at Tamara. "The honeymoon has been postponed for a more convenient time."

With any luck, he and Tamara would start their honeymoon in earnest in bed later that night.

Sawyer had seen a number of men tonight allow their gazes to linger on her appreciatively. It had made him unaccustomedly possessive, and now he staked his claim.

He rested his hand on the small of Tamara's back as he stepped closer to her. "What have you and Lyndon been discussing, sweetheart?"

From the corner of his eyes, Sawyer noticed Lyndon catch the endearment and smile with knowing amusement.

Good. Let everyone think he was the enamored bridegroom. After all, he had a role to play. That's *all* this was—that and his unfettered lust for his new wife.

"Your wife was enlightening me about the fine art of pottery," Lyndon said.

Sawyer shot Tamara a look of mild surprise.

She lifted a shoulder in a half shrug. "It was a hobby of mine in past years."

"One that I've recently taken up," Lyndon chimed in.

Sawyer looked from Tamara to the older man. "And did she also tell you she is a talented jewelry designer?"

Lyndon chuckled. "Are you, my dear?"

"It's a small business," Tamara allowed.

Sawyer addressed Lyndon. "Your wife may be interested in Tamara's designs. Tamara is making quite a name for herself with her colored gemstone jewelry."

"I shall certainly mention it to Yvonne," the count declared, a twinkle in his eyes. "She does love to be one step ahead of the other ladies."

"As a newsman, I can empathize with the desire to keep ahead of one's competitors," Sawyer said smoothly. "Tamara's studio is located right here in the city—down in SoHo."

"Splendid," the count responded. "Yvonne and I won't be heading to Strasbourg until the end of next week."

From the corner of his eyes, Sawyer noticed Tamara looking at him speculatively, as if she was both astonished and impressed by his seamless plug for her business.

"Your bride is charming, Melton," Lyndon said. "A breath of fresh air in contrast to these women—" he gestured around them dismissively "—who are afraid to get their hands dirty."

The count leaned toward Sawyer as if about to share some confidential information. "She—" he looked at Tamara approvingly "—works with her hands. She even likes gardening!"

"Does she?" Sawyer said, amusement crinkling his eyes. "I'll have to put her to work at Gantswood Hall, then."

Tamara raised her eyebrows. "Really? How much does the gardener earn?"

The count laughed heartily, and clapped Sawyer on the shoulder. "There you go, Melton. Any other woman here would have been decidedly not amused."

"But I am not amused," Tamara protested halfheartedly.

At that moment, another man approached to engage the count, and Sawyer said smoothly, "You don't mind if I steal my wife away, do you, Lyndon?"

"Not at all, not at all," the count responded, waving them away even as Sawyer guided their retreat with his hand at the small of Tamara's back.

When they'd gone a few feet, Tamara asked with slight exasperation, "Do you know everyone? It does seem as if everyone that I've spoken with here knows you."

Sawyer nodded at an acquaintance. "Yes," he acknowledged without vanity, "but the Count de Lyndon is a fifth cousin once removed on my father's side. A female ancestor married into the Belgian aristocracy."

"How charming," Tamara returned, not looking at him either, but smiling as they glided passed a couple of guests and into an adjoining reception room. "You Langsfords have infiltrated bloodlines far and wide."

Sawyer chuckled. "Why not? Queen Victoria and her progeny did it. We had a royal model."

"And you've since been multiplying like bunnies, apparently," Tamara muttered.

Sawyer leaned close and murmured, "Your tattoo is showing above the bodice of your dress."

He caught Tamara's small gasp just before her hand slapped over the spot on her bodice where the tattoo was daring to show itself.

"Are you worried your aristocratic friends will be offended?" she asked tartly, nevertheless matching her low tone to his.

"No," he murmured. "I'm worried they'll want to bed you as much as I do."

Sawyer watched with satisfaction as her skin tinged pink.

Good.

He'd been suffering the temptations of the damned ever since their wedding night, thanks to her. Let her feel some of the heat.

"Are you concerned that I'm being perceived as sexually

available?" Tamara demanded, still refusing to look at him. "Because I can assure you that my behavior tonight has been beyond reproach."

"I see you've misunderstood me," he replied. "You couldn't possibly be more sexually promiscuous than some of the women here."

"Speaking from personal knowledge?"

"I'm in the news business."

"I understand."

"Do you?" he inquired, letting his hand slip to cover her backside and leaning down again so that his mouth was close to her ear. "I wonder."

Her lips parted.

"I'm afraid some here will be consumed by the same inescapable desire I am," he said. "The desire to strip you out of that emerald dress, for example, and make slow and sweet love to you until you cry out my name again and again."

Sawyer watched as Tamara's eyes, focused on the room in front of them, went wide with shock and, yes, a mirroring desire.

She wanted him, too.

She swallowed. "It's hot in here."

"Quite."

She finally looked at him, and her eyes conveyed the same message that was in his. *Let's leave.*

"Tell me you feel faint," he said thickly.

He'd seize *any* excuse she gave him.

"I—"

Unfortunately, they were joined at that moment by the Consulate General.

Sawyer managed to school his expression into a pleasant one as he exchanged greetings and shook hands with the other man.

Damn it. Were he and Tamara destined to be forever interrupted?

* * *

Hours later, Sawyer drove them home in his Mercedes and parked in the private garage next to the town house. Tamara alighted from the car, but before she could take more than a couple of steps, Sawyer came around and took her hand.

Together they walked from the garage directly into the garden and toward the town house itself.

"Did you have a good time?" Sawyer asked, his voice deep.

"Yes," she responded.

She realized with some surprise that she *had* enjoyed herself, despite how unsettled she'd felt thinking about this evening ahead of time.

Tonight, she'd smiled and chatted even as she knew she was comporting herself flawlessly. In fact, she hadn't been sure where Tamara Kincaid had ended and the Countess of Melton had begun. One had blended seamlessly into the other.

On top of it all, a couple of female guests had expressed interest in Pink Teddy creations, and it was only belatedly she'd discovered it had been Sawyer who had extolled her work to them.

His support of her work was oddly touching. Of course, he was probably just looking out for his investment, but still, his encouragement was more than she'd gotten from any man in her life before.

And all along tonight, it was Sawyer's eyes she'd felt. His appreciative gaze had made her acutely aware of her femininity as she'd sipped champagne and tried to concentrate on the conversation around her.

Sawyer stopped in the garden now, and raising their linked hands, placed a kiss on the back of hers. "I'm glad you enjoyed yourself." He bent and brushed a kiss across her lips. "You make a lovely countess."

"Mmm," she responded just before he kissed her again.

When they broke apart, she breathed against his mouth, "What are we doing?"

It had been a magical evening, but she wasn't so far gone on champagne and tiaras not to be lucid enough to ask the question.

Since when, she mused, had *starchy* ceased to be a turnoff for her and started being a powerful aphrodisiac?

Tonight, Sawyer had looked every inch the titled aristocrat born to wealth and privilege—one who, she acknowledged, by dint of his own intelligence and hard work, had expanded the family business to make himself one of the most powerful media tycoons on either side of the Atlantic.

Once upon a time, she would have disdained the aristocrat and not appreciated the executive. But tonight, she'd thrilled to his barest touch and trembled at his heated gaze.

She hadn't been able to help herself.

"I'm giving in to the pull between us," Sawyer said, adding with a note of self-mockery, "We are married, after all."

"An arrangement," she felt compelled to point out.

"One for which we can change the rules at any time."

He kissed the corner of her mouth, and then flattened her hand on his tuxedo shirt, right over his heart.

She felt a flutter, and then another. He was vital and uncompromisingly male.

It was a warm night, the heat of the day fading only a little. Beyond the high wall of the garden, traffic along the nearby avenue stirred the air.

Sawyer eased down the zipper at the back of her dress, and she did nothing to stop him. As her dress sagged against her, and her small satin handbag dropped to the ground, he surveyed her with golden eyes.

She shivered and her nipples hardened further.

"You're irresistible," Sawyer breathed.

She wet her lips. "I didn't think you were paying attention."

"Oh, I was paying attention, all right," he responded, tracing the tattoo that had been exposed near her breast. "This rose has been driving me crazy ever since I first saw it."

At her inquiring look, he added, "While we were dancing at Belinda's wedding reception." He nodded at her now crumpled dress. "Where did this emerald concoction come from?"

"A lucky last-minute find."

"An inspired choice," he modified. "I couldn't keep my eyes off of you all evening."

He bent and covered her nipple with his mouth—a kiss that had her body rising up to meet him as the breath left her lungs.

She held on to his shoulders for support as her head swam. The hard bulge of his arousal pressed against her, exciting her further.

This was *Sawyer. Sawyer.* Her longstanding nemesis. And yet, he made her blood sing, and it was all so delicious. It was a forbidden melding of the proper and the naughty. The oh-so-respectable Earl and Countess of Melton well on their way to coupling outside, unable to keep their hands off each other.

"Sawyer, no. Not here," she said throatily when he finally raised his head to steal a kiss. "Someone at a window might see us."

Her concern was not unfounded. Sawyer's town house sat near several tony white-glove apartment buildings.

"It's dark," he responded gruffly. "And the trees here provide plenty of cover."

"If the media ever get wind of this, you'll never live it down." She added after he stole another kiss, "I can see the headline—'Media Baron Victim of His Own Press.'"

"They wouldn't dare," Sawyer said, but he nevertheless swung her into his arms. "Where to, your ladyship?"

She linked her arms around his neck. "If we're going to be respectable, then I suppose a bed."

Sawyer nodded, and then strode with her toward the house. Minutes later, he kicked open the door to his bedroom.

But instead of laying her on the bed, he set her on her feet and backed her against one of the bedposts. "Let's finish where we were unfortunately interrupted the last time."

Tamara shivered as a vivid image flashed through her mind of their last romantic interlude in his bedroom.

Sawyer undressed her swiftly, following every inch of exposed skin with kisses, and she thrilled with excitement.

Tamara's mind whirled. Familial expectations and everything else receded into the background, and all that mattered was her and Sawyer and what was happening between them in this room.

When he knelt before her and gave her an intimate kiss, the breath left her lungs.

"Oh." She grasped the wood behind her for support, and then as he continued to move his mouth against her, she slid against the cool, notched bedpost pressing against her.

Her climax hit her suddenly and unexpectedly, her back arching, her mouth falling open.

Seconds later, Sawyer straightened, his eyes glittering.

She belatedly realized she was naked while only Sawyer's tie was undone.

He quickly rectified the situation, however, by stripping, and she watched with hooded eyes as he revealed an impressive physique. His erection sprang free of his underwear, and he was finally completely and gloriously naked.

She wet her lips. "I didn't think you buttoned-down types were so..."

He gave her a slow, sexy smile.

Instead of taking her then and there, however, he surprised her by removing the pins from her hair and setting aside the tiara he'd given her earlier in the evening.

She hadn't worn it with any other jewelry, wanting to showcase her one special piece. It had been an unorthodox move, but one that had felt right.

"Hair down this time, Goldilocks," he said.

"I thought you hated the fact that I always let my hair down," she quipped.

He smiled, obviously catching her double meaning. "Maybe I'm loosening up, or maybe I'm a fan of your hair."

Deliberately, he arranged the flowing waves of her hair over her breasts, and then drew the pad of his forefinger over a nipple.

She gasped at the exquisite sensation.

And then he kissed her again. He linked his hands with hers and raised her arms above her head, and guided her instinctively until they both fell on top of the bed.

Sliding his hand down her thigh, he pulled her leg up over his hip, spreading her.

She kissed him hungrily, her fingers flexing on his back.

"I've been told you work well with your hands," Sawyer teased gutturally between kisses. "Show me."

And she did, drawing her palms over him and tangling her fingers in his hair, all the while making love to his mouth until they were both moaning and panting for more.

When Sawyer finally slid inside her, expanding and filling her, she sighed into his mouth with sweet relief.

"Ah, Tamara," he breathed.

She urged him forward, heedless of everything but the primordial urge to copulate.

And he satisfied her, tirelessly, until a sheen of sweat covered his skin, and his unadulterated male scent filled her nostrils.

She gasped, climaxing as he pressed her in just the right spot, and calling his name again and again.

And still he kept going.

She came once more, and then with a shout, Sawyer threw back his head and took his own peak.

Spent, he rolled to the side, taking her with him, and she nestled against him.

Her last thought, before she drifted off to sleep, was that sex with Sawyer had been strangely like finally coming home.

Twelve

He felt great.

He couldn't remember the last time he'd woken so relaxed and...*satisfied*.

Sawyer grinned to himself as he came down the town house steps dressed in black pants and a crisp white shirt left open at the collar. His hair was still damp from his shower.

He would have suggested to Tamara that they shower together, but she'd already been in one of the adjoining bathrooms when he'd woken, and then she'd slipped downstairs while he'd been dressing.

Fortunately, it was Sunday, so he wasn't expected at the office or a meeting. Instead, he knew his chef would have laid out a traditional English breakfast.

He could begin the day in a relatively leisurely manner, though he'd still consulted his BlackBerry upon rising, and his laptop would be waiting for him within easy reach at the dining-room table.

When Sawyer encountered Richard on his way to the dining

room, the butler said with his occasional formality, "Good morning, my lord."

Sawyer smiled easily. "Good morning, Richard. Another hot day, won't you say?"

"Indeed." The butler added, "Her ladyship is already taking brunch in the dining room."

"Excellent. By strange coincidence, it happens to be exactly where I'm headed."

Sawyer was careful to keep his expression bland, but he nevertheless thought he detected a knowing glimmer in the butler's eyes.

When he stepped inside the formal dining room, his eyes immediately connected with Tamara's.

Though the dining room was done in yellow and blue, with brightly striped wallpaper above the wainscoting, Tamara added light to the room.

She was wearing a shimmery sleeveless top, in a coppery color that played off the red of her hair.

"Good morning," he said.

She'd taken a seat near his usual one at the end of the table, and had already helped herself to eggs, toast and coffee.

"Good morning." She seemed to hesitate.

He looked at her thoughtfully. Perhaps she was feeling her way past any uncertainty on the morning after?

Well, he'd have to rectify matters. Before taking his own seat, he bent toward her, and when she looked up automatically, he brushed his lips across hers.

At that moment, André, the chef, brought in a dish of eggs and bacon for him, still warm from the kitchen, saving them from further conversation.

Sawyer helped himself to a scone from a plate already on the table. He was famished, and he smiled to himself when he thought about why.

"Tea?" Tamara inquired.

"Yes, thanks."

Usually, André poured his tea for him. He liked it strong, with a little sugar and no milk.

"Thank you for bringing in breakfast, André," Tamara said as she reached for Sawyer's cup and then a tea bag. "It is delicious. You'll have to share your recipe for these lovely scones."

André smiled. "Thank you, madam."

Sawyer lifted his eyebrows. Of all his household help, his chef was the most reserved and formal. The fact that Tamara had quickly developed a rapport with him spoke volumes.

Sawyer couldn't remember the last time he'd complimented his chef. He paid the man well to prepare his food, and had come to expect as a matter of course that André would perform to his usual high standards.

Seemingly oblivious to his surprise, Tamara poured hot water and added just the right amount of sugar to his tea, and then placed Sawyer's cup and saucer on the table next to his plate.

After Sawyer had taken a bite of his eggs, she nodded at his laptop. "I'm surprised you haven't surfed the news sites already."

"I checked my BlackBerry before coming down," he responded, and then felt his lips twitch. "But thank you for your concern that I not neglect my work."

Normally, he would be engrossed by his laptop, Sawyer admitted to himself, but this morning, he had more enticing distractions. Namely, his wife.

He could think of many pleasurable ways to spend the day with her, but he acknowledged that at least some of those should involve something other than a bed.

Nevertheless, he let his eyes caress her face.

Tamara cleared her throat. "Speaking of your work, I suppose we should talk about where we're heading from here."

There was no need for her to elaborate. His quest to control

Kincaid News had been the motivation behind their marriage of convenience, but they'd arrived at a new status after last night.

"Perhaps we should take things as they come," he hedged with care.

His motivation was becoming tangled, he knew, but he didn't want to examine it. He wasn't clear anymore on how much he was pretending.

He knew the terms of his handshake agreement with Kincaid, but truth be told, last night he hadn't been thinking about the possibility of a pregnancy. Instead, he'd been ruled solely by his desire for Tamara, and the pleasure of making love with her.

Want was merging with need and leaving obligation behind.

Tamara regarded him carefully. "We didn't use any protection."

He raised his eyebrows. "You aren't on the pill or any other contraception?"

She shook her head. "There was no reason to be. Tom and I—"

"—weren't intimate," he finished for her. "Yes, I know."

Sawyer was glad he'd gotten rid of the sad-sack musician. He wasn't Tamara's equal. Sawyer thought that instead she needed someone that was—well, *him*.

More importantly, last night he could have made Tamara pregnant. The thought of a child—his and Tamara's—filled him with profound feeling. He discovered he wasn't averse to the idea at all—far from it—and not only because of his pact with Kincaid.

Still, he knew that for now he had to focus only on overcoming Tamara's trepidations. He'd accomplished the first step of getting Tamara into his bed. He could concern himself later with getting her to agree to dispense with contraception altogether.

"We'll use something from now on," Sawyer said, and then shrugged. "It isn't likely that last night will have...consequences."

"And if there are consequences?" Tamara asked after a pause.

He reached out and ran his hand along Tamara's forearm in a reassuring caress. "We'll work it out." He tried to lighten the mood. "You know, newlyweds have children all the time."

"We aren't like other newlyweds," she disavowed. "We have a business arrangement."

Sawyer felt an unaccustomed prick. "It certainly felt as if we were newlyweds last night."

She looked away, and a pink flush tinged her skin. But when her eyes came back to his, her chin rose. "I spent my life avoiding you—this."

"Likewise," he teased, "but I found that sleeping with the enemy was fantastic."

She arched a brow. "Recharged your batteries, did I?"

Sawyer laughed, glad to see the spirited Tamara back. "Face it, sweetheart. Our charged relationship makes us fantastic in bed."

"Fishing for a compliment?"

He flashed a grin. "For acknowledgment."

He watched her eyes flash, but when she opened her mouth to respond, he laughed and stole a kiss before she could say anything.

Still, when he straightened, she said doubtfully, "This is a bad idea."

He arched a brow.

"Us, as lovers."

Actually, he thought that being Tamara's lover was one of his most outstanding ideas ever.

"Our parents made poor matches."

Too true, he thought with a grimace. Still. "That doesn't have to apply to us."

"How can it not? We've talked about this. Our parents' marriages failed because of incompatibility. The only difference was that my mother wasn't a wealthy American heiress, but a starry-eyed girl from Texas who'd just begun to model."

Sawyer's lips tilted upward. "After last night, I can certainly relate to the urge to give in to desire."

"Exactly, and I'm afraid we'll let—" she waved one hand around "—physical attraction cloud our judgment."

"What a delightful prospect." He looked at her with hooded eyes. "Let's retire upstairs right now and put that proposition to the test."

"Really," she insisted meaningfully.

He sighed and sat back in his chair. "I've met your mother, Tamara, and you two are hardly alike, except—" he paused meaningfully and swept her a look "—you've certainly inherited her model looks and figure."

"Is that my appeal?"

He caught Tamara's guarded expression, which belied her flippant words.

She was afraid of getting hurt.

There it was again—that damned vulnerability that had done him in last time.

Still, he felt strangely tender and protective. "You're beautiful."

And she was. Her green eyes were very expressive of her feelings, and her dark-red hair reflected her firecracker personality.

He'd been around many beautiful women in his life, but there was something special about Tamara.

There'd always been something special about Tamara, he thought, if he'd cared to acknowledge it.

Tamara looked at him, wide-eyed, her eyes like glistening pools. "Oh…"

"Do you want me to show you?" he asked, her emotional

response making him want to push aside his laptop and breakfast, lay her down on the table and demonstrate how beautiful he found her. "You can look as artsy and antiestablishment as you want, but it won't change that you're a beautiful woman."

The air between them became charged with meaning.

"It won't change that you're the daughter of a model from Texas who married a British viscount and media mogul," he went on. "You've also inherited your mother's features and there's nothing you can do about it."

Tamara looked startled at his insight, almost as if she'd never admitted as much to herself.

But she recovered quickly. "Just like your title and hereditary obligations don't change the fact that you're in many ways as American as your name? You're passionate as much as any headstrong American heiress."

He nodded in self-deprecating acknowledgment. "Well said."

She smiled reluctantly, sharing in his humor. "Thank you."

He pushed back his chair and stood. "We're mutts, you and I. Both British and American. In that way, we're more alike than our parents ever were."

"Where are you going?" she asked.

He walked to the door and flipped the lock, and then turned back to survey her.

"Since we're done with breakfast," he said, though neither of them had eaten much, "I thought I'd demonstrate my passionate side again—strictly for the purpose of confirming your assessment, of course."

She looked startled, and then laughed. "Of course."

He moved toward her, undoing the buttons at the top of his shirt.

Tamara pushed back her chair and stood, a small laugh escaping her. "Someone could—"

"—interrupt," he finished for her. "Splendid. Let's start the gossip mill going about what a wonderfully intimate relationship the Earl and Countess of Melton have. After all, that's been the plan all along, hasn't it?"

Frankly, he didn't give a damn about the plan. His only thought right now was what they could do with a dining-room table.

The look he gave her was full of promise before he trapped her against the table, pushed a couple of dishes away with one arm, and bent her backward...

Tamara looked at the stick in her hand, trying to comprehend it.

Two little pink lines should be simple enough to interpret. And yet, her mind refused to grasp what her senses were telling her.

Fortunately, her test kit came with two more sticks. She tried them both, her hand betraying a slight tremor.

Minutes later, there was no mistaking the matter. There were two pink lines of equal intensity.

Emotions chased themselves through her and looped around again. Elation was followed by panic and both were pursued by uncertainty.

She stared at herself in the bathroom mirror.

Five weeks. It had been five weeks since her last period. She had always been regular.

Oh.

She'd only been intimate with Sawyer for three weeks, and this had happened.

Her hand covered her abdomen, over her brown floral print dress cinched by a wide belt.

She'd bought a pregnancy test kit on the way home from work at her SoHo loft. She'd meant to take the test tomorrow morning, after Sawyer departed for work. But once she'd arrived back at the town house, nervous curiosity had over-whelmed her.

She was stunned to realize she was thrilled at the thought of a child...hers and Sawyer's.

These past three weeks had been idyllic. It had been a honeymoon without an official honeymoon. She and Sawyer had laughed, had fun together and grown closer than she'd ever expected. They'd fallen into some of the daily rituals of a married couple, waking together, getting ready for work and attending social functions in the evening.

Unsurprisingly, as the Earl of Melton and a high-profile media mogul, Sawyer received numerous invitations to galas, premieres and parties. And of course, since they were putting themselves forth as the newlywed earl and countess, they accepted many of the invites.

Stepping out as Sawyer's wife had not been a hardship, and, in fact, if she was honest, had served her well. Sawyer's social introductions had already brought more business to Pink Teddy than she would have ever expected.

Sawyer had repeatedly voiced an admiration for her artistic talent in a way that no one—and certainly no man—ever had before. And he'd acted as a sage business advisor—a sounding board who'd offered the services of his own hand-picked accountant. For someone who always prided herself on her independence, she was amazed to discover how pleasant it was to face challenges as a team.

And yet...and yet a part of her was terrified.

What would Sawyer's reaction to her pregnancy be? Surprise? Shock? Withdrawal?

Her arrangement with Sawyer was supposed to get her business off the ground. A baby wasn't part of the deal. She knew the reason why Sawyer had married her, and it wasn't so the two of them could have a happily-ever-after.

These past weeks as Sawyer's wife had been pleasurable—she couldn't deny it. But Sawyer had never so much as hinted their sleeping together was anything more than a nice little dividend to their arrangement. He'd never said he loved her.

She felt a pang.

We'll work it out.

Sawyer's words came back to her.

Unexpectedly, he had a chance to make good on his promise. She prayed that his reaction would be all she hoped for and more.

But first, she had to tell him her news.

Tamara checked her watch. It was six in the evening, but she knew Sawyer would still be at his office. He'd told her that he had a late meeting.

Tamara wandered out of the bathroom and into the bedroom that she and Sawyer shared. First, she called her ob-gyn's office to schedule an appointment.

Then she paced. She could wait until Sawyer arrived home, trying to tame her restlessness until then, or she could try to intercept him at work. With any luck, she'd arrive at Melton Media when his meeting was over, or just a little before.

Impulsively, she grabbed her purse from where she'd dropped it on a nearby chair and hurried out of the bedroom. When she reached the town house foyer, she asked Lloyd, who happened to be around to drive her to Melton Media.

Within the hour, she was at Sawyer's offices. Building security recognized her as the new Countess of Melton and waved her by without the need to check in.

She rode the elevator up, and when she reached Sawyer's executive floor, she crossed the reception area, her footsteps muffled by carpeting.

Sawyer's office door was half-open, but just as she was about to peek inside, she froze at the sound of her father's voice coming from within.

"I'm glad to hear most of the due diligence has been completed," her father said.

"My attorneys have said the merger documents will be

ready for our review in the next couple of weeks," Sawyer responded. "Then we can pick a closing date."

Tamara could see neither man from her vantage point, but their words reached her distinctly.

"Splendid," her father replied. "Of course, the deal won't close until I know that you've upheld your part of the bargain and gotten Tamara pregnant."

Tamara sucked in a breath.

"Naturally," Sawyer responded, his tone dry but easy.

She was suspended by shock and disbelief for several moments before realization sunk in, followed by hurt and anger.

She felt as if a boulder had come crashing down on her spirit…and her heart.

The villain.

The double-dealing toad.

She flattened one hand against the office door, pushed and walked inside.

Sawyer's gaze immediately connected with hers from where he sat behind his desk. He rose at the same time that her father swung around in his chair.

Tamara could tell from Sawyer's expression that he'd understood everything about her sudden appearance.

"Tamara—"

"I see I've come at an inconvenient time," she announced, ignoring Sawyer's warning tone.

How dare he warn her. If anything, he was the one who needed to be cautious given how she was feeling at the moment.

Her father belatedly stood, too. "Now, Tamara, I don't know what you heard…"

She held up a silencing hand. "Enough to know that you'll never change. It's Kincaid News you're concerned about first and foremost, isn't it? And it always will be."

Her tone was bitter, but her true rancor was directed at Sawyer, whose face was inscrutable.

"Tell me," she said, willing her voice not to waver as she lowered her hand to clench it at her side, "was any of it real? Or were you faking the emotion even when you slept with me?"

You're beautiful.

He'd seduced her. And she'd fallen for it. *For him.*

Her heart squeezed.

She might not be an ingénue like her mother had been, but she'd nevertheless let herself be swept away by flattery and pretty words.

Her father cleared his throat, his expression grim. "I will leave you and Sawyer to discuss this matter between yourselves."

"Isn't it a little late to decide to stop meddling?" she tossed out as her father made his way to the door.

"Where I come from," her father responded, turning back, "it's called looking out for one's interests, and it's gotten me to where I am, though you and your sisters stubbornly refuse to recognize it."

"I hardly have a choice about recognizing it in this case, do I?" she retorted. "You and your—" she glared at Sawyer "—ilk have seen to it."

Silence reigned then as her father exited the office.

When she heard the office door click, she swung back to face Sawyer.

"All this time I thought you were deceiving my father," she charged, "but I was the one that you were keeping in the dark about the truth, wasn't I?"

Sawyer looked implacable, his eyes flinty. "I was above-board with you that day at your loft when I suggested a marriage of convenience. It was only later that Kincaid attached another condition to the merger—"

"And you agreed!"

She took his silence for an admission of the truth.

"I thought you forgot to think about contraception because you were swept up in the moment," she accused. "But you didn't forget, did you? You intentionally didn't ask!"

She'd been swept up in the moment, while *he'd* been planning his next move with the deliberation of a chess master.

The realization stung.

"I was nothing more than a pawn in your game," Tamara said. "All of it was a lie."

Sawyer's jaw set. "Is that what you think?"

"What else can I think? Are you going to deny you deliberately set out to sleep with me?"

"No, I'm not going to deny it."

Tamara lowered her shoulders. *So.*

"I'm not going to deny that I did everything in my power to get you into my bed because I desired you," Sawyer said. "Because whenever I was around you, all I could think about was repeating that first kiss and then some. Because I couldn't get you out of my mind, and I didn't want to."

She shivered, but then steeled herself against his words. Sawyer was an expert at seduction, she reminded herself.

"Why should I believe you?" she demanded. "Why shouldn't I think this is just another ploy to win? You'll do anything to get your hands on Kincaid News, won't you? You'd even seduce your rival's daughter. You're just as ruthless as my father."

"These past few weeks, I'd do anything to get my hands on you," Sawyer shot back, "and as far as I can tell, you felt likewise."

"Yes," she admitted, "and more fool me."

Sawyer stepped toward her, but she raised a hand to ward him off. "Don't, please. There's nothing you can say to make this better for me."

"Tamara—"

"It's over."

Sawyer's tawny eyes kindled, and his stony facade finally cracked. "The devil it is."

"Are you worried about your precious merger falling through?" she demanded accusingly.

"No, damn it," Sawyer said with quiet force.

"I guess this is what they call a Pyrrhic victory," she tossed back, and then spun on her heel and made for the door.

Sawyer didn't attempt to stop her, though some tiny irrational part of her hoped he would.

We'll work it out.

As she hurried to the elevator, she knew there wasn't any way to fix this situation.

Or her heart, either.

Thirteen

Tamara knew that returning to the town house wasn't an option. Instead, telling Lloyd, who was waiting for her outside Sawyer's offices, that she wouldn't need to be chauffeured, she hailed a cab and went straight from Sawyer's building to her SoHo loft.

Once there, she loosened the reins on her hurt and humiliation. Tears pricked her eyes.

What was she going to do?

She stared at the four walls around her. What had she given up to keep this? She'd made a devil's bargain, and now she was alone and pregnant.

She dropped her purse on the glass-topped table and covered her face with her hands.

She took several deep, steadying breaths.

She could handle this. *She could handle Sawyer*. She'd forged her own path in the world.

Dropping her hands, she waited a moment and then picked

up the phone. Pia and Belinda had always been there for her, and she knew they'd lend moral support now.

She tried Pia's number first, and felt some of her tension ebb when her friend picked up.

"Are you in Atlanta?" she asked after an exchange of greetings.

"No, back in New York," Pia responded. "The Atlanta wedding was last weekend."

"Well, I have some news to tell you, but first I'm going to conference in Belinda."

"Okay," Pia said, her tone suddenly curious.

When Tamara reached Belinda, she asked, "Where are you?"

"I'm at the airport. Newark, to be precise. I'm flying out to appraise some artwork."

"I hope you and Pia are sitting down, because I have some news." She paused and took a deep breath. "I'm pregnant."

Pia and Belinda gasped.

"I knew this marriage of convenience with Sawyer was a bad idea!" Belinda said.

Tamara could only silently second that judgment.

"I should have known," Belinda said darkly. "Sawyer is Colin's friend. Those aristocratic types make a woman do what she never dreamed of doing."

Tamara wasn't sure which situation Belinda was talking about—hers or Tamara's own. Maybe both.

"At least I got off with an ill-advised elopement. But pregnancy!" Belinda sighed. "Oh, Tamara."

Tamara imagined her friend chewing her lip, her brow puckered with concern—though Belinda was always warning that frowning caused wrinkles.

"What does Sawyer think?" Pia asked.

"I haven't told him."

"You haven't told him?" Pia repeated.

"It's a good thing I don't often cross paths with Sawyer,"

Belinda said. "I'd hate to be in the position of keeping this from him."

"Are you going to tell Sawyer?" Pia asked, going to the point. "Or should I say, when are you going to tell Sawyer?"

"I'd like to keep this news under wraps until there's no denying the obvious," Tamara announced. "Aren't there celebrities who've hidden their pregnancies until the ninth month?"

She knew that despite everything, she was going to raise this baby. Her hurt and anger right now hadn't altered her feelings about the pregnancy.

"Wow," Pia remarked. "How are you going to keep this, uh, development from Sawyer while you live with him?"

"Simple. I won't have to because I've left him."

"What? *Why?*"

"Apparently, our marriage of convenience wasn't merely convenient," she elaborated. "I was kept in the dark about the fact that Sawyer agreed to my father's condition of a grandchild, or at least a pregnancy, before the merger of Melton Media and Kincaid went through."

For her friends benefit, she quickly outlined what had happened when she'd unexpectedly arrived at Sawyer's offices. Humiliating though it was, she divulged her discovery that Sawyer had agreed to seduce her for his own gain.

"You should have his head on a platter," Belinda declared unequivocally when Tamara was done recounting what had happened.

Tamara couldn't agree more. "If only."

"Maybe you and Sawyer can work it out," Pia surprised her by saying. "You know, for the sake of the baby."

"Stay married, you mean?" Tamara asked incredulously. "Are you joking?"

"I've see you two socialize since you've been married. You glow when you're around him."

Pia's bald statement gave Tamara momentary pause, but everything inside her right now—anger, hurt, pain—made her rebel against it.

"Of course I glow," Tamara responded. "It's what happens when my temper has been lit."

"He can't take his eyes off you," Pia said with quiet certainty. "Trust me. I've observed many couples."

Pia was a romantic, Tamara reminded herself. "Sexual attraction, nothing more," she said succinctly. "Where did I read about how much men think about sex?"

"Probably *Cosmo*."

"Well, on at least one occasion, Sawyer more than thought about it," Belinda quipped.

Tamara felt herself flush. "Yes, well...I'm swearing you both to secrecy."

"Of course," Belinda said. "And if there's anything I can do to help, all you have to do is ask. You know I'd help you and the baby any way I can."

"I second that," Pia said. "But Tamara, what are you going to do?"

It was, Tamara thought, the question of the hour. "Well, for starters, I refuse to be under the same roof as Sawyer," she said. "I'm at the loft, and I'll be staying here for the time being."

"And then?" Pia prompted.

And then...

She hadn't let herself think about it. Though after Sawyer's betrayal, they obviously couldn't continue on together.

Her heart constricted.

"I haven't thought through a plan yet," Tamara admitted, "but Sawyer and I will go our separate ways. It's what we planned all along."

Tamara knew the pain she felt was only a fraction of what she'd feel in the coming days, weeks...years even.

"I don't know," Pia said doubtfully. "What is it you told Belinda recently—I don't see him going away quietly?"

It was closing in on nine in the evening when Sawyer let himself into the town house. Richard, his butler, had the evening off.

It was dark. Quiet. Unaccustomedly so.

He'd grown used to coming home to someone.

Tamara. His wife.

Except now she was gone.

He loosened his tie with one hand.

Tamara hadn't said anything about where she was going when she'd left his office. In New York, she could be any number of places. Hotels, sublets and short-term rentals abounded. She could also be staying with Belinda or Pia.

Damn.

Lloyd had phoned him soon after Tamara had left Sawyer's building, wanting to know if he should wait to drive Sawyer back to the town house.

After some questioning, Sawyer discovered Tamara had waved off the chauffeur as she'd exited his offices, stating that she preferred to take a cab to her next destination.

Sawyer could tell from Lloyd's tone that he was concerned something was amiss between his employers. Nevertheless, not caring that he'd be feeding Lloyd's suspicions, he'd instructed his chauffeur that he'd find his own way home.

Now he faced a house and a future without Tamara.

What a mess.

And most damningly of all, he'd had a hand in creating it.

He wasn't usually one to imbibe, but tonight he felt like drinking himself into a stupor.

His arrangement with Tamara had been for their mutual convenience, but it had become one for their mutual pleasure and enjoyment, as well.

At least, he'd thought so.

In fact, he'd begun to think he and Tamara should stay married. Things were working out well. It had been surprisingly easy to share a bed and a roof with her, which he'd never done with any other woman.

Why rush into a divorce? Instead, he'd begun to think they should take their time and see where things led.

But now, there'd be no wife and no baby.

Paradoxically, he felt the sting of loss for a child that had never come into being. His child and Tamara's.

Quite apart from his deal with Kincaid, Sawyer realized he'd been looking forward to having a child with Tamara—a little girl with her red hair and green eyes, or a child that blended both their features.

An image flashed through his mind of Tamara's face when she'd stepped into his office and interrupted his meeting with Kincaid.

Despite her charged words, she'd looked crushed.

Sawyer cursed under his breath.

He should never have agreed to Kincaid's secret condition. The only reason he had, he admitted to himself now, was because the idea of bedding Tamara had already begun to have irresistible appeal.

When he reached the library, he went straight to the wet bar and mixed himself a Manhattan. Maybe after a couple of drinks, he'd forget Tamara's devastated look in his office.

Sure enough, a couple of hours later, he was slumped in an armchair, sitting in the dark, his tie hanging loose around his neck. He was right where he wanted to be—well on the way to oblivion.

He felt a low, steady throb at his temples, and his gaze came to rest on the blinking light of his phone.

He stared unseeingly at it. He'd noticed the message signal earlier, but had ignored it. He didn't care who it was if it wasn't Tamara—and he knew the message wouldn't be from her.

Now, though, he was far gone enough, and idle enough, he just might believe in a snowball's chance in hell.

So languidly, he picked up the receiver.

After the standard automated voice intoned that the first message had been received at seven o'clock, Sawyer listened to the call.

"Mrs. Langsford, this is Alexis from Dr. Ellis's office," a woman's voice said. "I'm sorry for the confusion, but I inadvertently scheduled you for a day that Dr. Ellis will not be in the office. Please call us to reschedule your obstetrical appointment."

Even through his current haze, Sawyer stiffened, his senses going on alert.

If Tamara had an obstetrical appointment, then that meant...

Pregnant.

The call was either a mistake—had the woman meant to say gynecological appointment?—or Tamara was pregnant.

Sawyer grasped the arm of his leather chair as a mix of emotions roiled him. Shock was followed by exploding joy.

He was going to be a father.

And then his gut tightened and his next thought was, *Hell.* An unholy mess had just deepened into a life-altering event.

Tamara had known she was pregnant, and she hadn't told him. Had she meant to tell him tonight? Instead, she'd left him.

It's over.

His jaw tightened. Like hell.

In the process of fishing her keys out of her purse, Tamara looked up, saw him and froze.

Despite herself, longing and a sweet piercing pain shot through her.

Sawyer looked grim and uncompromising as he dropped

his folded arms and straightened from his position lounging against his car.

Rather than being dressed in a business suit, he was casual in a blue shirt and pants. He was unshaven, and pronounced creases bracketed his mouth.

Why hadn't she noticed him and the car before?

Her only excuse was that the sidewalk had been crowded with lunchtime traffic. People still walked rapidly in both directions, and the curb was congested with street peddlers.

But now, as if the crowd were parting before a mighty personage, he came toward her.

She muttered under her breath, and then fumbled and dropped her keys. She bent to retrieve them, but somehow he was there first.

"Allow me," he said smoothly.

Sawyer picked up the keys from the ground and inserted the correct one in the front door of her building.

"After you," Sawyer said, as he pushed the door open with one hand.

"What are you doing here?" she demanded.

She was the one who'd been wronged, she reminded herself, and yet he was turning the tables on her.

Sawyer quirked a brow and nodded around them. "Do you really want to have this conversation on a busy street?"

"You helm a media company. The last thing you'd want is a public scene."

He smiled mirthlessly. "Try me. There's always a first time. And you'll find different rules apply to the boss."

Her chin jutted out. "Pulling rank?"

"Pulling strings, if I have to," he replied.

"Charming."

"I'm glad you're still impressed by my charm, among my other sterling qualities."

Abruptly, she turned, leaving him to follow her into the vestibule of her building.

"Pressing your case?" she tossed out as they crossed to the elevator and she jabbed a button. "I think we've said all there is to say."

"Hardly," he contradicted, his voice too close for comfort.

Out on the busy street, at least the forcefulness of Sawyer's presence had been muted by the crowd. Here in her building, though, she felt its full, unmitigated effect.

He was big and overpoweringly male, and despite herself, she felt a primitive awareness.

They rode up in the elevator in silence, and then he let them into her loft with her keys.

She should have bristled at his presumption, but the truth was, she admitted to herself with disheartening frankness, if not for Sawyer, Pink Teddy Designs would no longer even exist.

And yet, he didn't own *her*.

She dropped her purse on her desk and turned to face him.

"I have to admit," he said with unreassuring calm, "it didn't occur to me initially to look for you in the most obvious of places. You've surprised me."

She felt her pulse thrum through her veins. "I'm not hiding, Sawyer. I just chose to leave you. Unlike you, I have nothing to hide."

"Don't you?" he said, his facial features tightening, and anger lacing his soft words.

Her chin came up, but she didn't answer him. She wasn't sure she trusted herself to repeat the lie.

Instead, she walked over to her safe and used the combination she'd committed to memory to open it. She kept Pink Teddy's more precious pieces inside.

Since he'd presented her with an opportunity, she thought she'd hand over his purchases to him—perhaps that would convince him that the two of them were really finished.

She retrieved two green felt boxes and walked back toward him. "I've finished the pieces you commissioned."

As she opened the bigger box, her gut twisted. All this time, she'd been working on this project—*his gift to another woman*—and he'd been deceiving her.

She watched now as Sawyer stared at the glittering gems.

She knew what he was seeing. Initially by chance, and then by design, she'd fashioned a necklace with alternating emeralds and diamonds that complemented the Langsford tiara.

She knew she'd outdone herself, though pleasure had mixed with pain as she'd worked, so that the project had become a sweet torment. Presumably, Sawyer's mistress would get the emerald necklace, and in all likelihood, sometime in the future, another woman would wear the Langsford tiara as Sawyer's wife.

The creation of the necklace had been an act of self-flagellation, she admitted to herself. It had perhaps started as a reminder not to fall for Sawyer, but it had evolved from there. Had she been half hoping to foster feelings in him for her? Had she begun to hope she'd be the owner of the jewelry she fashioned?

Except she hadn't counted on becoming pregnant. Except she hadn't known of his ultimate treachery.

His face inscrutable, Sawyer lifted the necklace with one hand, letting the jewels run over his fingers like a waterfall.

Tamara placed the now-empty jewelry box on her work table, and then opened the smaller velvet case.

Emerald earrings immediately caught the light.

In her opinion, the earrings were just as breathtaking as the necklace.

She glanced at Sawyer's face and noticed his eyes had narrowed. Did he see the similarities to the Langsford emerald tiara here, too?

His face unreadable, Sawyer took the case from her. "They're exactly what I was looking for."

A fresh stab of pain shot through her, and she called herself all kinds of fool. "You know what they say. Give the client what they don't know they want."

"Is that what you do?" he asked, setting aside the case with the earrings with what seemed like deceptive calm.

Tamara raised her chin. "Now you can leave."

"I disagree." He quirked a brow. "When were you planning to tell me you're pregnant?"

He said it so quietly she looked at him blankly for a second. He couldn't possibly—

Then she froze. "What makes you ask that?"

"Don't bother to deny it," he said with sudden and quiet force.

She searched his gaze, holding her ground. "And what if I am?"

His eyes locked with hers. "Then a divorce is bloody well off the table. There is no way I'll let anyone call into question the legitimacy of the heir to the earldom."

Of course, Tamara thought with a sinking heart. Even apart from his agreement with her father, Sawyer's concern was with his potential future heir, not with *her.*

"It could be a girl," she pointed out challengingly.

"Regardless." His eyes traveled down her dress, intimate and probing, reminding her all too forcefully of all they'd been to one another.

"How did you find out?" she asked.

His eyes flashed. "A phone message left by the doctor's office. You need to reschedule your appointment."

Tamara closed her eyes briefly. She'd had her home number transferred from the SoHo loft to Sawyer's town house after the wedding. In her turmoil, she couldn't believe she'd forgotten to do something so basic as to call her doctor's office and update her contact information.

So Sawyer knew all, and much earlier than she'd anticipated and hoped. *So much for keeping a secret.* She hadn't even had time to marshal her forces.

She looked at Sawyer challengingly. "This pregnancy doesn't change anything."

"Permit me to disagree. It changes everything."

"All right, it changes everything," she retorted. "I'll never forget that this baby was conceived to fulfill some—" she waved her hand "—deal with my father."

They were too close, furious with each other.

"All those pretty words," she scoffed, "when you were just deceiv—"

He cut her off with a hard kiss, reaching deep into her soul.

She breathed in his musky male scent and sensed the leashed power in him. He caressed her mouth, demanding a response from her that she unwittingly gave.

When he raised his head, he demanded, "Does this feel real to you?"

She stared at him.

He looked uncompromising. "We're not getting a divorce."

She turned away. "I'm not sure the law will let you stop me."

He grasped her arm and swung her back toward him. "I'm not concerned with the letter of the law."

"Oh?" she asked, bracing herself. "Then with what precisely?"

His expression remained implacable. "Try to walk away, and I pull the plug on this—" he glanced around them "—and fight you all the way on custody. Stay married and all this stays yours, along with the title, position and social standing that comes with being my wife."

She gasped at his bluntness.

This wasn't the man who'd made love to her—the man

she'd thought she was coming to know. This was the ruthless media baron who'd grown an empire—a man that her father could admire.

She knew Sawyer could very well follow through on his demands. He paid the rent on her SoHo loft. Moreover, he'd invested in her jewelry business, and had commissioned her most expensive order to date. He'd breathed new life into her company.

While the law might ultimately prove to be on her side, she didn't have many resources to fight him.

"A contested divorce will be long and expensive," he said, as if reading her mind. "And it'll be messy. I can tie you up in court on procedural issues alone. And then you'll still need grounds for a divorce."

"Oh?" she queried, her tone sarcastic. "You don't think your behavior qualifies as unreasonable?"

He smiled without humor. "I see you're familiar with the legal grounds for a divorce."

"Of course," she retorted, her eyes snapping. "My father has been divorced three times!"

"If you insist on going through with a divorce, then the score will be three to one."

She refused to respond to the taunt. She was nothing like her father. True, she'd be a divorcée, but that was a far cry from being a serial groom who let business trump love and family every time.

"The divorce can still happen after the baby is born," she tried. "With this baby, you can lay claim to having fulfilled the terms of your agreement with my father. Kincaid News will be yours. Why contest a divorce?"

"It's simple," he said, his eyes all golden fire. "I want you back in my house. In my bed."

"We don't always get what we want."

Their gazes clashed, the standoff drawing out the tension between them.

Then unexpectedly, he looked down at the necklace he was still holding in his hand.

She'd toiled over it these past weeks, wanting it to be perfect. Thinking about him. What a fool she'd been.

"Here," he said, holding it out to her. "This was always meant for you."

Automatically, she stretched out her hand and took the necklace from him.

"Thank you," she said flippantly, unthinkingly disguising her hurt. "My lawyer will be in touch."

Sawyer's face tightened, and then he turned and strode to the front door. Seconds later, the door slammed shut behind him, the noise reverberating through the loft.

Her confrontation with Sawyer over, energy ebbed out of her like a receding wave.

She sat down heavily on the bar-height chair behind her.

Outside, a car honked. The busy city went on with its life.

She focused unseeingly on the necklace in her grasp, her hand pressing against the cool stones.

This was always meant for you.

She couldn't let herself believe him. She knew better than to trust him.

Fourteen

"Tamara is pregnant."

Sawyer's announcement fell into a lull in his conversation with Hawk and Colin.

It wasn't quite the sudden and unexpected announcement it seemed. They had all been sitting in Colin's majestic penthouse living room for an hour already.

But after a snifter or two of brandy, even the most tightly buttoned of men couldn't be faulted for opening up.

It was a Friday evening, and each of them was still dressed in work attire—though ties had already been loosened or shed.

"Surprising," Hawk finally remarked with a surfeit of understatement.

Colin lifted his tumbler in salute. "Congratulations on your impending fatherhood, Melton."

"Thank you."

There was a pause as all three of them took a swallow from their drinks, toasting the impending arrival.

"You've bested me, Sawyer," Colin remarked. "I eloped. You've made the wife *enceinte*."

Colin's face was inscrutable despite his levity, and Sawyer wondered again at the basis for his friend's incomplete annulment. It was unlike Colin to leave any loose ends.

Sawyer leaned back in his leather chair. "Still, you may discover I'll be following your path to a matrimonial lawyer. If you have a recommendation for a good one, pass it along."

At his position beside the mantel, Hawk raised his eyebrows in surprise.

Colin—seated nearby on a camel-colored leather couch—as usual didn't give anything away with so much as the slightest change of expression.

"Surely you don't mean to divorce Tamara now," Hawk remarked.

"No, but she may intend to divorce me."

"You mean to let this go?"

Sawyer grunted. The hell he did. He'd pushed his way back into Tamara's loft, into her *life,* and demanded she come back to him, backing up his words with the threat of stripping her business from her and an ugly divorce and custody fight.

He pushed aside any misgivings at his heavy-handedness. She'd meant to leave him, and who knew when she would have seen fit to inform him of his impending fatherhood?

Yes, he'd made a mistake by agreeing to Kincaid's secret condition, but two wrongs didn't make a right.

He pushed back the encroaching thought that his actions had smacked of desperation.

"I can suggest an excellent lawyer who will deliver a protracted fight, if necessary," Colin said. "On the other hand, I can't guarantee he'll actually complete the divorce—though, on second thought, isn't that what you want?"

Hawk's eyebrows lifted. "Are you admitting, Colin, that you purposely didn't finalize the annulment of your Vegas wedding?"

"I admit nothing," Colin replied. "Except, of course, for the end result."

Hawk laughed shortly. "You're an enigma, Easterbridge."

Colin merely tipped his head in acknowledgment.

Sawyer's mouth twisted with dry humor, but the smile faded when he thought of his own recent dealings with Tamara.

Were his actions those of a desperate man? After discovering Tamara was pregnant, he'd acted reflexively. He'd tracked her down the next day and given her an ultimatum.

Well done, Melton.

He realized suddenly that Colin and Hawk were looking at him and waiting.

He looked from one to the other of his companions. "Have I missed something?"

"Should we expect to read news of your protracted divorce battle in the *Intelligencer?*" Hawk countered with a question of his own.

"I bloody well hope not," Sawyer responded grimly.

"You're going to persuade Tamara not to divorce you, then?"

Persuade wasn't exactly the right word, Sawyer thought. *Threaten* and *coerce* were more accurate.

"I've talked to her," he responded shortly.

It had been two days since his confrontation with Tamara at the loft, and since then, he'd stubbornly embraced his righteous anger.

"Talked?" Hawk queried now.

"I laid the alternatives out for her." Sawyer's lips thinned. "The ball's in her court."

Hawk said nothing for a moment, and then gave a short bark of laughter. "In other words, you went in all hotheaded." He shook his head slowly, ruefully. "I never thought I'd see the day."

"What?" Sawyer asked irritably.

Hawk traded a glance with Colin. "I never thought I'd see the day you'd lose your head over a woman."

Sawyer gave a grunt.

Was Hawk right? Had he lost his head? Tamara had a way of firing his blood, in more ways than one. He'd never had a woman get under his skin that way.

But he'd lived too long, had borne too much witness to his own parents' divorce, and was too aware of his and Tamara's differences to believe he was in l—

Hell and damn.

The realization hit him like a punch to the stomach.

"I don't see what you know about it, Hawkshire," he nevertheless responded with aristocratic hauteur. "Isn't there a wedding planner somewhere who'd dispute your understanding of women?"

Hawk surprised him by refusing to take the bait, and instead, shrugged. "I've learned a few things since. Or maybe it's just easier to see someone else's situation clearly."

Sawyer remained silent.

Had he lost his grip on reasonable behavior where Tamara was concerned? But then, when had he ever been reasonable about Tamara?

And more importantly, Sawyer thought, what was he going to do about it now that she refused to believe or trust him?

When the loft buzzer sounded, Tamara was expecting a delivery person or perhaps an unexpected client.

It was a Friday evening, but people had been dropping by regularly to visit her studio ever since her engagement and subsequent quick marriage.

She knew she had Sawyer to thank for the buzz.

Sawyer.

No, she wouldn't let her mind go there.

But when she went to the intercom, she discovered it

wasn't a delivery or client. Instead, her father asked to gain entrance.

Without acknowledgment, she hit the button to unlock the building door downstairs, left her front door ajar and then wandered back deeper into the apartment, her arms wrapping around herself.

She turned around only when she heard her father's footsteps and then the loft door closing. She knew she looked peaked from her latest crying jag and lack of sleep, but she didn't care. It was only pregnancy hormones, she told herself.

She eyed her father warily. "What are you doing here?"

As usual, he was dressed in a business suit for the office.

She wasn't sure why she hadn't turned him away. Perhaps because she thought he hadn't truly received his comeuppance. She'd left her ire for Sawyer three days ago, and her father had, advisedly and rather uncharacteristically, beaten a hasty retreat from the field of battle.

Rather than respond directly, her father surveyed her. "You look awful."

"Thank you," she retorted.

"In fact, you remind me of myself during one of my divorces."

"I'm surprised that disposing of a wife affected you that much."

Her father sighed. "I suppose in your eyes I bear a passing resemblance to Henry VIII."

"My only quibble is with the word *passing*."

Her father's lips lifted in barest acknowledgment as he stepped farther into the loft and took a seat in her armchair.

She remained standing.

"I suppose there's much we can quibble about, including the particulars of my divorces, some known, some not."

"I've witnessed enough."

"Perhaps." Her father looked around, his eyes coming to

rest on a nearby display case before looking back at her. "It's quite an inviting space that you have here."

"Thank you. I managed to hold on to it with a devil's bargain."

Her father raised his eyebrows mildly. "Sawyer?"

She nodded. "He covered my rent and then some in return for a short marriage of convenience until the merger went through. Of course, I didn't know you had attached a very significant additional condition." She glared. "How could you?"

Her father sighed. "You never asked me why I wanted this match between you and Sawyer."

"Kincaid News," she responded succinctly.

"True, but the old earl and I also thought you and Sawyer would suit."

She arched a brow. "After the failed marriages that you both experienced?"

Her father shrugged. "Every marriage is different. Your mother's inability to adapt to being a viscountess was just one of the reasons that our marriage didn't work, though it was a major one."

"The other being that your heart belonged to Kincaid News?"

Her father grimaced. "I did do my best to make you appreciate your heritage, both with Kincaid News and the title."

"Yes, you did," she allowed. "But anyone can see that Sawyer and I are—"

"—meant to be together."

She shook her head stubbornly. "Will you do anything to succeed? Sawyer has been *pretending*."

"Then he's a damned fine actor." Her father sighed again. "I've had three wives. Allow me to boast some discernment when it comes to a man being ruled by his passion for a particular woman against all reason."

Tamara almost laughed. True, Sawyer had a surprisingly

passionate side, but he was also a ruthless and calculating operator of the first order.

Much like her father.

"You always accused me of putting Kincaid News first, and that may be so. But Sawyer is a different breed, or at least he's become different." Her father shot her a piercing look. "This isn't about business. Quite clearly he values something else more these days."

"All the evidence is to the contrary," she replied bitterly. "Especially now that victory is in his grasp. In a few short months, he'll be a father."

The minute the words were out of her mouth, Tamara clamped her lips shut.

"Ah, I see," her father said, a twinkle in his eyes. "May I extend my heartiest felicitations?"

"Sawyer didn't tell you?"

Her father shook his head. "No. I imagine he wanted to protect you from further upset."

Her gut twisted. "I suppose making me pregnant is quite enough."

"Sawyer is refusing to go ahead with the merger," her father announced. "Only you can get him to see sense and change his mind."

Tamara's heart clenched. Sawyer was refusing to proceed with the merger? She couldn't fathom it, even as her heart whispered that it was because of her. Because he cared.

Still, she steeled herself—she'd been hurt and betrayed too much already. "Do you really expect me to care?"

Her father scrutinized her face. "I believe you do care, whether you want to or not."

She sniffed. "It'll pass."

Her father grasped the arms of his chair and rose. "If you felt that way about him, you wouldn't be pregnant in the first place."

Tamara opened and closed her mouth.

Her father gave her a little smile. "Perhaps you've met your match." Then he leaned over and peered at the jewelry she had on display inside a glass case. "Your craftsmanship is quite superb. I imagine that with someone at your side handling the business angle, you'll have no problem becoming exactly who you want to be."

"Oh? And who would that be?" she asked challengingly.

Her father surprised her by straightening, and then walking over to her and giving her a quick peck on the cheek. "You'll figure it out. You can keep holding on to bitterness at a perceived wrong, or you can leap with your heart. I may be a serial divorcé, but I also never stopped believing in the leap of faith."

He tapped her nose. "In fact, I made another leap of faith with you and Sawyer. Don't try to prove me wrong for the sake of making a point."

After her father had departed, Tamara was left to ponder his words as she absently moved things about in the loft.

Today had been the closest she and her father had ever come to an honest and forthright conversation. And it was all due to Sawyer, strangely enough.

And Sawyer was calling off the merger.

She supposed she should thank him.

Or stay mad at him.

Or…take a leap of faith.

Tamara stared at the pouring rain beating against her loft windows from her position looking out over the back of her couch. As soon as the thunderstorm let up, she promised herself she'd leave.

She nervously fingered one of the emeralds on the necklace that encircled her neck.

She was going to make the biggest leap of faith of her life today.

She looked down at herself. She'd carefully chosen the

scoop-neck beige knit dress to show off her necklace to its greatest advantage.

A rap sounded at her front door, startling her. She wondered who it might be. Her buzzer hadn't sounded from downstairs.

She crossed the room and checked the peephole. She stilled, but then in the next moment, she opened the door.

Sawyer stood there, wetness clinging to the shoulders of his open trench coat and to his trouser legs.

She hungrily took in the sight of him.

"May I come in?" he asked. "One of your neighbors was kind enough to allow me to follow him into the building."

Silently, she stepped aside, and then shut the door once Sawyer was inside.

Then they stood facing each other. Neither spoke, though the air between them was fraught with tense energy.

She studied his face. It had the same smooth, uncompromising planes as always, but droplets of rain clung to his tawny hair, and his eyes...

The expression in his golden eyes was pure, undisguised longing, and she caught her breath.

He held out some papers in his hand. "These are the documents so far for the proposed merger. Tear them up if you want."

She swallowed hard as she took them from him and placed them aside. "Why?"

He raked his free hand through his damp hair. "Because I can do without Kincaid News, but I can't live without you. Because I've searched for a way to have you trust me, and this is the only way I have left to try to convince you that you matter more."

She sucked in a breath. "Oh, Sawyer."

"I took the wrong tack when I came here the other day," he went on. "But for the record, you still have something that belongs to me."

"What's that?"

He took her hand and guided it until it lay flat against his heart.

Her eyes widened. And then, all of a sudden, her heart began to thud loudly.

Time slowed. From outside, the dim noise of the roaring city could be heard.

Her lips parted, and then closed again.

Emotion clogged her throat. "I—"

"Help me out," Sawyer joked, his voice nevertheless carrying an undercurrent of need.

Instead of replying, she went on tiptoes, pulled his head down to hers and pressed her lips against his mouth.

In response, he banded his arms around her, and opened his mouth over hers.

They kissed in a hot press of need, unable to get enough of each other.

When they came up for air, he looked into her eyes. "I love you."

"Oh, Sawyer." She felt the prick of tears. "I love you, too."

Tenderly, he cupped her face and stroked his thumbs over the dampness near her eyes. "What's this? Tears for me?"

She nodded. "I've been shedding buckets for the past several days." She took a tremulous breath. "In fact, I was coming to see you just as soon as the rain let up."

He looked at her inquiringly.

"My father came here yesterday to tell me you were refusing to go through with the merger, and he had some surprisingly sage advice to deliver with the news."

"Shocking."

She gave a smile at his dry humor. "I thought so, too. Apparently, it was clear to others much sooner than it was to us that we'd suit, quite apart from Kincaid News or Melton Media. He made me begin to think...to hope..."

"Sweetheart." Sawyer lowered his hands as his eyes traveled down to her throat. "Is that why you're wearing the necklace?"

She nodded. "I thought you'd take it as a sign when I showed up on your doorstep. Did you mean it when you said the necklace was always meant for me?"

Her heart squeezed because his answer still mattered.

"Yes," he said, lifting his shoulders with obvious mock regret. "There was no past girlfriend. The jewelry was a ploy to get close to you."

Relief washed over her even as she swatted him. "Oh, you…"

He chuckled as he caught her hand, but then sobered. "I promise, no more deception."

"Yes," she agreed. "I was so hurt and angry when I discovered you had to sleep with me in order to gain control of Kincaid News."

"There was no *had to* about it," he countered. "It was pure want all the way. I may have told myself in the beginning that it was at least partly for the sake of the company, but ever since our first kiss, I'd been fighting my growing desire for you."

"Do you think we'll be able to make it work?"

"What? Our marriage?"

She nodded.

"We have so far."

She gave a small smile. "Do you think the world is ready for a Countess of Melton who sports a tattoo?"

"They already are," he replied, his hand inching up her dress and caressing her thigh. "And they're going to love your jewelry."

She searched his face. "You really want me to continue designing jewelry?"

"Yes, without a doubt. You have a wealth of talent. And on top of it all—" he smiled with secret promise "—I have some jewelry I'd like to commission for a certain woman."

"Oh?" she asked, even as he lowered the zipper on her dress and let it drop to the ground—in the process, doing delicious things to her insides.

"There's a necklace I have in mind for a certain flame-haired, green-eyed entrepreneur."

"Mmm?"

"Yes," he said huskily, trailing a finger down her cleavage. "I have an idea in mind for a large ruby pendant that will come to rest right here."

"Do tell," she said. "I see the beginnings of a wonderful collaboration."

"One of many," he responded.

And then he proceeded to demonstrate exactly how pleasurable their latest collaboration could be.

Epilogue

"This is fast becoming your favorite spot."

Tamara looked up and smiled at Sawyer. She nodded toward the ducks nearby as he sat down next to her on the picnic blanket. "We have to keep up appearances for the ducks. Kiss me."

Sawyer arched a brow, but amusement lurked in his eyes. "I doubt they're expecting us to act all lovey-dovey."

She nodded seriously. "Their sense of well-being depends on it."

"In that case…"

He obliged her with one of his heart-hammering kisses. Afterward, he tucked her into his embrace and nuzzled her temple.

Tamara sighed. She and Sawyer had decided to make as many trips back and forth across the Atlantic as they could until it was no longer possible for her to travel during her pregnancy.

And Gantswood Hall was fast becoming her favorite

retreat. She looked forward to raising children here—and in New York.

She was still finding her way in her role as the Countess of Melton. She trod the line between expectation and her own temperament. But in the way that mattered most, she knew she filled her role exceptionally well—she had Sawyer's love.

"Your father has arrived," Sawyer remarked.

"Oh?"

"Business matters," Sawyer replied shortly.

She nodded. Of course, her father had been thrilled with the news that Tamara and Sawyer had reconciled.

"Not come to gloat again, has he?" she asked, turning her head.

Sawyer laughed. "Maybe that, too."

With a baby on the way, and Sawyer and Tamara so obviously devoted to each other, Viscount Kincaid had declared himself completely satisfied.

Tamara sighed. "Oh, well. Gantswood Hall is a large estate. Let him gloat in the east wing."

Sawyer laughed. "We could have warring factions under the same roof, and it would hardly register in a home the size of Gantswood Hall."

Tamara smiled wistfully. "Speaking of warring factions, I wish Belinda and Pia would resolve their differences with Colin and Hawk. It would be nice to invite our friends here at the same time."

"They'll work out matters," Sawyer said with conviction. "Now kiss me—there's a duck eyeing us."

Tamara laughed and turned for Sawyer's kiss.

Some things were worth more than the most precious gems.

* * * * *

A Child. Yelena's child.

How had he missed *that?*

A deathly calm swept in to cleave his entire body, slicing at his control and reopening past wounds all over again.

"How old?" he finally asked.

She actually had the audacity to lift that proud chin of hers, to meet his glare with one of her own. "Five months."

As his mind did the math then double-checked, a thin film of rage clouded his vision, choking him into silence. If he'd had any smidgen of doubt about his plans, any tiny attack of conscience, she'd well and truly obliterated them.

The night Yelena had declared she loved him, she'd been pregnant with another man's child.

THE BILLIONAIRE
BABY BOMBSHELL

BY
PAULA ROE

All the characters in this book have no existence outside the imagination of
the author, and have no relation whatsoever to anyone bearing the same name
or names. They are not even distantly inspired by any individual known or
unknown to the author, and all the incidents are pure invention.

Published in Great Britain 2011
by Mills & Boon, an imprint of Harlequin (UK) Limited,
Eton House, 18-24 Paradise Road, Richmond, Surrey TW9 1SR

© Paula Roe 2010

ISBN: 978 0 263 88229 2

51-0611

Harlequin (UK) policy is to use papers that are natural, renewable and
recyclable products and made from wood grown in sustainable forests. The
logging and manufacturing processes conform to the legal environmental
regulations of the country of origin.

Printed and bound in Spain
by Blackprint CPI, Barcelona

My deepest thanks to all who've helped me with this book, in particular Lis Hoorweg for her knowledge of Canberra and its surrounds, Monique Wood for her insights into the mysterious world of public relations and Linley for her always awesome brainstorming skills. And Dad, for explaining the complexities of shares, partnerships and business practices (and no, this doesn't mean you have to read the book!). Special mention goes to Maxine Sullivan and Robyn Grady—your support and encouragement always lift my heart. And lastly, to my fabulous editor, Charles—here's to our first book together and the many more to follow!

Despite wanting to be a vet, choreographer, card shark, hairdresser and an interior designer (although not simultaneously!) British-born, Aussie-bred **Paula Roe** ended up as a personal assistant, office manager, software trainer and aerobics instructor for thirteen interesting years.

Paula lives in western New South Wales, Australia, with her family, two opinionated cats and a garden full of dependent native birds. She still retains a deep love of filing systems, stationery and traveling, even though the latter doesn't happen nearly as often as she'd like. She loves to hear from her readers—you can visit her at her website at www.paularoe.com.

Dear Reader,

What a crazy year it's been! Writing Alex and Yelena's story has been anything but a smooth road—among other things I've been quarantined, slammed with flu, chickenpoxed (not mine!) and crashed via computer... not to mention those crazy school holidays when nothing seems to get done. Such speed bumps are a good reminder of where your priorities lie. And in their own way, my hero and heroine hold family above all else—a value I'm sure many of you can agree with!

I'm especially pleased to bring you a story that features two major Australian contrasts—our capital city, Canberra, and iconic Ayers Rock (or Uluru, as we Aussies call it). Rest assured I spent many hours researching to make Diamond Falls a uniquely breathtaking place that sets the scene for Alex and Yelena's romance. I hope you're drawn in to their world as much as I was.

As a bonus, you can drop by www.outbackbillionaire-sandbabies.wordpress.com where Robyn Grady, Maxine Sullivan and I have set up home for our three special billionaires and babies books.

With love,

Paula x

www.paularoe.com

One

"You didn't say yes?" Yelena Valero whirled from the unrestrained twentieth-floor view of Canberra's Lake Burley Griffin to her boss's inscrutable countenance. "Tell me you didn't say Bennett & Harper PR would take on Alexander Rush as a client."

"No." Behind his desk Jonathon Harper's bushy eyebrows took a dive as he reclined in the leather chair. "*You* said yes. Rush made it perfectly clear it's you or no account."

The air sped from her lungs, momentarily disorienting her. In the next instant her heart kicked in, an insistent thump-thump against her ribs. "Jon...you know we had history—he was involved with my sister—"

"And I really don't care. You've known him since, what—tenth grade?"

"Yes, but I really don't think—"

"Here are his clippings." Jon tossed a file on his desk. "This is non-negotiable, Yelena," he added pointedly before she could say another word. "I gave you six months off, no questions. You want to be considered for partner now? You clear your schedule. What Alex Rush wants, you give him."

With a final wave of his hand, he turned back to his computer, dismissing her.

Yelena glared at his perfectly groomed head for a few seconds before sweeping up the file and turning on her heel.

By the time she'd stalked down the hall, her high heels clicking out her fury on the cool slate floor, reality had swept in to douse every irrational thought.

She ground to a stop, staring at her closed office door at the end of the silent hallway. If she was Jonathon's partner, his equal, he'd never have played her. But the man obviously thought her and Alex's tenacious past was an advantage, not the major train wreck Yelena knew it was.

She closed her eyes and took a deep breath.

One, two, three. Her stomach tossed with shock, fear—and…

Four, five, six.

—a queasy sense of exhilaration. *Wait, what?*

She frowned, scrunching up her face.

Eight, nine.

Ten.

After a slow exhale she breathed in again. The relaxation technique finally began to kick in, calming her pulse, regulating her breathing.

Slowly she opened her eyes and focused on her door. Alex Rush represented the unknown. He'd always been a threat to her control, yet time and again she'd ignored the warnings.

But she desperately needed this promotion. The freedom it would give far outweighed any monetary compensation—freedom to set her own hours, to work from home. To pick and choose her own clients. To prove to her very traditional parents that she didn't need a rich husband to keep her in dresses and spa treatments. And above all, it meant she could be a proper mother instead of an absent one.

As she pulled her back straight and gently rolled her neck for good measure, she felt the familiar pop of muscles through her shoulders. Then she stalked the rest of the way to her office with more decisiveness than she felt.

Alex Rush stood alone in Yelena's simple, almost austere office, his back deliberately to the door. He knew the huge window, one that took in Canberra's Parliament House in its commanding August morning glory, haloed his height to strategic effect. He needed all the power and authority his size projected, needed to put her at a mental disadvantage, to show he was in control and calling the shots.

His confidence had briefly bowed to uncharacteristic hesitation before he'd determinedly swept the doubts aside. *No time for second thoughts.* Yelena and her brother Carlos had dug their hole so they only had themselves to blame.

The swift click of heels against tiles broke through his subconscious and in the next instant the door whooshed open with an efficient shove.

Game on.

To his irritation, his heart rate rocketed, bathing his body in anticipatory warmth.

"Jonathon tells me you asked for me personally, Alex. Mind telling me why?"

He slowly turned, bracing for battle. Yet for all his mental preparation, he was woefully unprepared for the breathless impact that seeing Yelena Valero always evoked. The solid, pounding heat, the thud his blood made as it sped through his veins—hot, arousing—as if he were a teenager again and seeing her for the first time.

Yelena was drop-dead gorgeous. Sure, the fashionistas would declare her too curvy, her hair too wild, her jaw too square, her lips too full compared with her younger sister's sleekly polished looks. Yet the sight of her always managed to stop his breath.

You're not seventeen anymore. Yelena dumped and betrayed you, siding with Carlos—the man who's hell-bent on destroying you. She's nothing more than a way to make her lying bastard of a brother pay.

A thread of intense fury whipped out, blinding him to everything else. He let it sit there for a heartbeat, tasting the bitterness, almost relishing it, before efficiently stuffing it back into that special place in his mind. Compartmentalizing, his attorney had declared, as if the revelation had deserved a standing ovation.

No one knew he'd spent years perfecting an airtight mask of composure. And by God, he wouldn't lose it now, even though the reckless temptation to reach out and kiss Yelena senseless snaked through his body, forcing his muscles into a tight clench.

"Who let you in my office?" she asked suddenly.

"Jonathan."

She fell silent, the stillness lengthening as she blinked slowly, a small furrow creasing her brows.

"It's been a while, Yelena."

Her eyes narrowed at his inane comment, as if they were seeking the hidden meaning behind his smooth words.

"I hadn't noticed." She stared at her desk then pointedly at him as he remained still, blocking her way.

Not noticed? Fury burnt away the residual lust that had pooled in his brain. He'd done nothing *but* notice the passage of time since his nightmare had begun. His entire world had crashed on Christmas Eve and Yelena…well, she'd simply moved on as if he'd been a temporary pit stop on her journey to the top.

Sharp pain shot through his hands and he glanced down. He'd tightened them into fists.

With an inward curse he forced himself to relax, sweeping

his gaze down her body, knowing she'd take umbrage with his perusal. From her black high heels, the snug grey skirt and matching jacket loosely tied at the waist to the fire-engine red shirt that looked so soft his fingers briefly retightened, she was business personified. Her wild hair was smoothly tied back, makeup subdued. Even her jewelry—small gold hoop earrings and a simple chain with the familiar blue eye of Horus—signaled restraint. So unlike the Yelena he knew, the woman with the wild kisses and hot skin, the sultry take-hold-of-your-groin-and-squeeze laugh.

The one who'd dropped him like a ten-ton millstone when he'd been accused of murdering his father.

She scowled and crossed her arms, dragging him back to the present. "Have you quite finished?"

He allowed himself a smile. "Oh, not by a long shot."

Before she could say anything he stepped aside, leaving her to her personal space. With slow deliberation, he lowered himself into one of her guest chairs.

She settled behind that titanic desk, her eyes on him, a wary cat assessing a potential threat. The privileged, spoilt daughter of Ambassador Juan Ramerez Valero, wary? The thought astonished even as it empowered.

"Nice office." He flicked his gaze over the room. "Nice desk. Must've cost a bit."

"Of all the experienced reps in Bennett & Harper, why did you ask for me? Wouldn't our history bother you?"

"Still as blunt as always, I see," Alex murmured, unsurprised.

She crossed her arms and awaited his answer in loaded silence.

"You're one of the best," he stated, deliberately playing to her vanity. "I've been watching your campaign for that singer—Kyle Davis, right? Getting the public to do a one-eighty on a tax cheat was impressive. What you can do for me completely outweighs any—" he paused, his gaze feathering across her mouth before going back to her eyes "—past history."

He knew his subtle ego stroking fell way short when she met his eyes head on, unblinking. He'd never been subjected to her "Queen of Silence" look but he'd seen it focused on others. It was a look meant to fluster and embarrass, usually given after an improper or rude comment. It was all in the steady stare, the slight curve of her eyebrow. And the expectant stillness as cool as the steel from the ancient swords that adorned her father's study.

Yet he easily held her gaze until she was the one forced to break the silence.

"And what exactly would you be hiring me to do?"

"What you're renowned for—positive spin. And, of course, discretion."

"Spin for you?"

"And my mother and sister."

"I see."

Yelena remained calm as, with one fluid movement, he crossed his ankles, then his arms. A perfect image of untouchable male confidence and control, one that ran roughshod over their furtive weeks of intense pre-Christmas passion as if it'd just been something she'd dreamt up.

The guilt-ridden ghosts of her past reared up under his silent inspection, astounding her. Alex Rush had been completely off-limits. Yet that hadn't stopped her from falling for her sister's boyfriend.

She swallowed heavily. *Get a grip.* He was here for business, nothing more. Whatever they'd shared was temporary. Dead and buried.

"You owe me, Yelena."

She stared at him, the startling cut stabbing deep. Damn him for going there and putting a voice to her guilt. As she warred with her conscience, he added, "And you know my family, which will make your job easier."

"Not very well."

"More than most," he countered. "And *we're* familiar with each other."

He made the word *familiar* sound much dirtier than it should. Those arresting, come-to-bed azure eyes, combined with the subtle dip in his voice, did something terrible to her body. Terrible in a wonderful way.

"So your silence means you're taking my account?" he finally said.

She wrenched her gaze from his and picked up her pen to give her nervous hands something to do.

"B&H would be crazy to turn down the son of William Rush, the founder of Australia's leading airline company," she returned calmly. No reason to elaborate, to confirm that her boss had used her partnership application as leverage.

Instinctively her hand sought out her necklace, to rub the Horus pendant dangling there. And just like a magnet, that small movement commanded Alex's eyes.

She abruptly stilled. Fiddling with that pendant was a nervous tic, Alex had laughingly pointed out years ago. *Words can lie but your body can't.* The tic said she was unsure, out of her depth. Conflicted.

His knowing eyes shot to her face and suddenly the memories streamed in, flushing her skin and warming her body in places she'd closed off these last eight months.

"Did you discuss any details with Jonathon?" She said firmly pulling her diary across the desk.

"No."

"Okay." She flicked open the diary and scribbled a few notes, then looked up. "I'll need a few days to get a team together then I can schedule you in for next week—"

"No." He leaned forward and Yelena only just managed to resist scooting back. Even with her huge desk between them, she still felt...vulnerable somehow. As if there was nothing to stop him from leaning across the oak expanse and kissing her.

Her pulse leapt to life, her breath stuttering for one brief second. Ridiculous. Alex Rush was here as a client. She would put his feather in her professional cap, get her promotion and move on. It wasn't personal. Not anymore.

"You can't make next week?" she asked, squelching her body's disturbing reactions.

"We need to start now. Jonathon assured me I would be your only priority."

Yelena tightened her jaw. *Damn you, Jonathon.* "Fine. So let's start."

"Good." He rested his elbows on his knees, snaring her in his gaze. "As you know, the Rush name has had some adverse press these last few months."

Understatement of the year. "I understand you were questioned, suspected but never formally charged for your father's death. It was finally ruled as accidental."

His bright eyes narrowed. "Many people, including a few media outlets, still believe I got away with murder."

I don't. The automatic reply lay on the tip of her tongue but she quickly swallowed it. They both knew the answer. "I'm sorry, Alex."

"What?" His eyebrows went up, cynicism creasing his brow. "You're not going to ask?"

She blinked. "I don't need to."

"Oh, that's right. You were my alibi. Or at least, you would've been if you hadn't suddenly left the country that night."

"Alex…" She leaned back in her chair as his harsh accusation tore into the half-healed wound. "I tried to…I—"

"By the way, how was your holiday? Europe, wasn't it?" His words, although polite, were tinged with barely hidden disdain, sending her heart clunking against her ribcage.

"My…?" *He didn't know.* Well, how could he? Her father

had never issued a press release, though not through Yelena's lack of pleading. To anyone interested enough to inquire, Gabriela was backpacking in blissful anonymity through Asia, absent from the headlines.

Just as they'd always wanted.

"What?" He raised one derisive eyebrow. "You had some sudden life-or-death situation overseas so you just left without even the courtesy of a phone call?"

She clamped down on a dozen furious comebacks, testing the words on her tongue. "I was with Gabriela."

"I see. And how is my footloose ex-girlfriend? I'm assuming she found someone else to be her handbag because I've heard nothing." His mouth thinned, as if barely able to contain his scorn.

You have to stop this. Now. She slapped her hands on the desk, stared at the polished wooden surface and took a deep breath.

"Don't go there, Alex." She managed to rip her eyes away from his piercing blue ones and snap her diary shut with firm finality. "You hired me to do a job. If I'm to do it, we need to leave our personal lives out of it—including whatever issues you and Carlos have."

His gaze turned sharp. "What issues would they be?"

"I have no idea. The last time I saw him was two months ago."

Did he know how much that wounded her, having Carlos lock her out of his life? Apart from a few throwaway comments, she had no idea what her brother's relationship with Alex was since Alex's return to Canberra. Which was a good thing, she decided. She'd grown up this past year—becoming a mother and moving out of the Valero home had not only provided the independence she craved: it had also put a stop to Carlos's stifling "big brother" routine. And she'd banned Alex from her mind, preferring not to know what he was doing or whom he was seeing.

As he considered her with intense scrutiny, the atmosphere slowly disintegrated. It was like…expectancy. As if he wanted to ask a million questions but something held him back. Definitely not the Alex she knew.

"I'll need to speak with your family," she said abruptly.

And just like that, their moment was gone.

"Of course." His expression smoothed and he stood, startling her. "I've arranged an 11:00 a.m. flight." He glanced at his watch. "I'll have a car pick you up from your apartment at ten."

She blinked. "I'm sorry? I thought—"

"You. Me. Flight at eleven," he repeated succinctly. "You need to meet my family—your clients. They're at Diamond Bay."

"Your outback resort?" she asked faintly.

"The same. Don't be late."

"What…" She shook her head, frowning. "What about my team?"

"I need to get back to the resort. Plus my staff is fielding a million calls, so right now, I need one hundred percent discretion. At this moment, *you* are the team."

Of all the—! She shot to her feet. "I can't do everything myself! I need an assistant, an event planner…"

He waved away her protest with a regal hand. "I have ample staff for that. And once we have a firm schedule, you can delegate."

She stared at him. "I have a *life,* a—"

"I thought your work was your life." His chilly appraisal brushed over her almost insultingly.

She crossed her arms. "You don't know anything about me anymore."

"That's true."

The sudden drop in temperature did nothing to cool the slow burn creeping up her neck. Yet before she could form a retort, he reached into his jacket and removed his mobile phone. "Pack for a week. I'll see you at the airport."

Then he was gone, the only evidence of his presence the very male notes of a lingering aftershave.

Yelena was left staring at her open door, stuck in a deep frown that sent tiny aching shards into her temples.

Stop scowling, Yelena. You'll give yourself wrinkles.

Her mother's familiar command cut into her thoughts like diamonds on glass and she automatically smoothed out her features.

How on earth could she leave the past behind and concentrate on her job when this was the result of their proximity?

She'd packed a lifetime of living into the last year. She'd lost a sister and Alex. Even Carlos had drifted away; he'd become so publicity conscious, and the only time they talked these days was to argue. She'd disappointed her family, her life had shattered then been fused back together in irregular mismatched pieces. Like an expensive vase outwardly displaying a flawless façade, only to reveal the hairline cracks on the inside.

Yet Yelena had finally gained control. And she'd become a mother. Through it all, Bella had been worth everything she'd suffered.

She had to do this for Bella.

As she tidied her desk, grabbed her iPhone and locked up, she remained focused on that one honest truth.

Alex Rush was the Holy Grail of clients. His campaign would cement her career and her promotion. And despite his unspoken yet obvious falling out with Carlos, despite their torrid history, he'd chosen her. If he could make this just about business, then so could she. She wasn't about to blow her future on the mistakes of her past.

Two

"I'm just about to feed Bella," Melanie, her neighbor and babysitter, announced from the kitchen as Yelena walked in her front door. "You want?"

Yelena dropped her bag on the counter then took the warm formula from her neighbor with a smile. "Of course. Did my mum call in?"

"She phoned just after you left this morning…" Mel trailed off as she followed Yelena down the quiet hallway and into Bella's room.

"And? Hello, gorgeous girl—how's my *bella* Bella today?" Yelena reached into the crib, scooping up the gurgling five-month-old baby with a theatrical gasp. "You are so big! How did you get to be so big? What did she say, Mel?"

The woman pulled a thread from her tank top's hem, giving the task entirely too much attention. "She said she was coming down with a cold and didn't want to give it to Bella."

"I see." Despite knowing exactly what her mother was like, Yelena's heart still squeezed painfully. Maria Valero played tennis and had a personal fitness trainer. She'd been a three-step-skin-care woman since her teens, she took vitamins, ate just enough to stay healthy, eschewed caffeine, chocolate and other skin-destroying addictions. The woman was going to outlive everyone including, she suspected, Bella.

The lie still had the power to hurt, which meant it still mattered.

"Better to be on the safe side," Melanie added diplomatically as she handed Yelena a cotton towel. "Babies can pick up things so easily."

"That's true." Yelena settled in the huge rocker, gently placing the squirming baby on the nursing pillow that Mel arranged under her arm. When Bella's tiny rosebud mouth latched onto the bottle, something deep and primeval sucker-punched her low.

Fierce and total adoration engulfed her as she gazed down at the feeding baby. She'd do anything for Bella. Her world began and ended with this little girl.

"So what's this business trip you're taking?"

Yelena's gaze remained riveted on Bella, smiling at the baby's gentle slurp. "Just a new client."

"For how long?"

"I should be back next Monday."

"So…" Melanie frowned. "Who's going to look after Bella for a week? Your mum?"

Yelena shook her head. "Can you honestly see her coping with a baby?" *And I wouldn't dream of leaving Bella with a woman who rarely had time for her own children.* "No, Bella's coming with me."

"Wow." Melanie crossed her arms and perched her bottom on the arm of the one-seater. "I didn't know B&H had a nanny service. I'm so in the wrong profession."

"They don't—the resort we're staying at has. And as it's extended travel, B&H foot the bill. Anyway," Yelena said, grinning and gently wiping drool from the baby's mouth, "don't tell me you'd rather work in my frivolous, soulless profession than go back to your thankless, underpaid teaching career."

Melanie's grin matched her friend's at their shared joke. "Nah. And it's not like Matt can't afford to keep me, being head of oncology and all. Plus I get to be a hands-on mum and pick Ben up from kindy. Best of both worlds."

"Well, after this client, I'm expecting that promotion to kick in."

"And about time, too. You work twice as hard as anyone in that firm. But I will miss Bella—she's adorable." She gently stroked the infant's downy head before winking at Yelena. "Even if she does look like her mother."

Deep protectiveness surged, and Yelena answered with a smile. "Hey, can you do me a favor and pack a few things for her while I finish up here?"

While Melanie gathered up clothes and feeding equipment, Yelena burped Bella. Sitting here in the comfort of her daughter's girly lemon-and-white bedroom, it was so very easy to ignore the world. Bella *was* her whole world, from the moment she'd been born. She'd made a promise to that squirming little bundle, wrapped warmly in a birthing blanket.

I'll protect you, keep you safe from harm. And I will always, always be there whenever you need me.

She'd been doing fine until Alex Rush had waltzed back into her life and demanded her complete attention.

Bella sneezed and Yelena gently turned her, bringing the chubby face in line with hers. The baby's thickly lashed brown eyes stared right at her, the tiny mouth working an invisible pacifier.

Yelena studied Bella as she gurgled, her gummy grin stretching. Yet she couldn't squash the trepidation fluttering around in her belly.

Alex was a smart man: once he saw Bella he'd do the math.

There'd be no going back. Yet leaving Bella at home was not an option. Her childhood, all those years of emotional neglect, had seen to that.

"If Alex Rush wants me, then he'll have to deal with you too, sweetheart."

You can do this. She put entirely too much emphasis on what she'd meant to Alex. He'd moved on from what they'd been to each other, just as she had. He didn't care enough to hate her. What mattered now—what had always mattered—was doing her job. Turning the tide of public opinion was his sole purpose. Whatever he felt about her would only be temporary, just as this campaign was.

Alex settled into the luxurious comfort of Rush Airline's private Cessna, trying to focus on the work spread in front of him but failing.

His grievances against Yelena's brother had been gathering momentum ever since his father's accidental-death ruling. Alex had left the sanctuary of Diamond Bay in June, returning to Canberra to discover the huge ripple effect William Rush's death had wrought. The speculation, the unrelenting police interrogation and the intense press scrutiny paled in comparison to discovering Carlos's true colors.

He muttered a foul oath, the blade of betrayal still sharp. Carlos had been a casual acquaintance from university, one who'd mixed in the same elite social circles. On a whim he'd considered Carlos's business proposal, encouraged by the prospect of escaping from the shadow of Australia's favorite son, William Rush.

Two short years later and he and Carlos had set up a partnership, developing a handful of franchised travel agencies under the name of Sprint Travel.

He wasn't so blind to ignore the fact that Yelena's approval had played a part in his decision. Hell, he could still hear her glowing endorsement of her brother as partner material.

That woman could tempt the Lord himself...even if she were sister to the Devil.

He dragged a hand over his jaw and absently rubbed the whisper of stubble, its familiar rasp an empty echo in the cabin.

You were an idiot. A stupid, bloody idiot, thinking with your libido, not your head.

All his life he'd had this unnerving ability to know when people weren't telling the whole truth—his father had crudely dubbed it "Alex's crap detector" with a certain amount of pride. But with Carlos he hadn't seen it coming...and yeah, he thought grudgingly, not *wanted* to see it because the brother of Gabriela and Yelena Valero couldn't possibly be a lying snake...right?

He snorted. Wrong on all counts. A week after he'd been cleared of his father's death, he'd been served with the breach of contract documents. He'd read them through, choking back his shock at the neatly typed legalese. If the courts sided with Carlos and the partnership was dissolved, all Alex's shares would go to Carlos. Technically it was legal, but morally?

Before he had time to wrap his head around that, the next blow fell. A loyal agency manager with friends at the Federal Police and the Canberra Times had voiced concerns about Carlos's creative accountancy practices.

And that's when things had turned ugly.

The betrayal wounded him deep, much deeper than any financial loss. With fury in his blood, fueling every waking hour, he'd dug for the truth. And as the articles about his family steadily grew worse, so, too, did his desire for vengeance. He'd used every contact, every favor at his disposal to uncover something, anything solid to wield as his sword of justice, but until recently Carlos had been clever. No paper trail and no one willing to go on record.

And then, suddenly, two breakthroughs. Last week he'd contacted three potential victims of Carlos's rip-off schemes who hadn't automatically slammed the door in his face. And, more importantly, Alex had discovered Carlos was the one who'd been feeding infidelity stories of his dead father to the press since March.

Everything had clicked into horrible focus. Yelena was the only person who could've overheard that shameful, ugly confrontation with his father in his office. The only one who could've blabbed to Carlos about it.

It wasn't about business anymore. This was personal.

Damn them. Damn *her*.

His fist tightened on his pen until a tiny cracking noise forced him to release it with a hollow clatter. The marks across his palm rose quickly.

Soon they would be on their way to Diamond Bay, where he'd have Yelena completely to himself. He'd make sure Carlos Valero knew his perfect, respectable sister had willingly fallen into his bed then he'd hand all his evidence about Carlos's wrongdoing over to the authorities. Only complete and utter humiliation would vindicate him.

Wasn't one sister enough for you? Keep your hands off Yelena or God help you, I'll bring you down. His mouth slashed into a grim smile as he remembered Carlos's hollow phone threat, now securely saved on his message bank.

Anger meant mistakes and Alex was counting on Carlos to make one.

Alex glanced at his shiny Tag Hauer. What if she didn't show? He tossed away that thought as quickly as it formed. He knew Yelena, knew how hard she worked to control her world, how she craved independence and respect. A successful campaign with the Rush name behind it would send her career into orbit.

Yet relief still surprised him when he finally heard her voice in the alcove.

Then she rounded the corner carrying a strangely shaped bundle and he frowned.

"What's that?" he asked over the sudden roar of the plane's engines.

"'That' is my daughter."

Oblivious to Alex's stunned silence, she smiled at the attendant who'd flipped down the bulkhead's portable cot then gently placed the bundle inside.

"You don't have a baby," he said sharply as she eased into the seat opposite.

"I do." She shrugged off her jacket then buckled up, keeping her eyes firmly on her task. "Her name is Bella."

"You adopted."

His tight statement snapped her eyes to his. "That's none of your business, Alex."

"It is if you're bringing your private life to work."

Her icy gaze matched his. "You of all people can understand why she's here. I will not hand her over to my family while I run off for a week, no matter how badly I need your account."

Her steady glare, her steely posture, all spoke of complete and utter control.

He paused, recalling her proud, dry-eyed confession that the Valero children had been raised by nannies and boarding schools while Maria Valero had played the part of the foreign diplomat's wife to perfectly coiffed perfection.

It had been the first time he'd been aware of something more than just physical desire for Yelena.

His teeth ground together with an inward growl. "So she's yours?"

In her infinitesimal pause he had his answer. He didn't need to see the quickly suppressed anxiety in her eyes that accompanied the curt nod.

A child. Yelena's child.

How had he missed *that?*

A deathly calm swept in to cleave his entire body, slicing at his control and reopening past wounds all over again.

"How old?" he got out.

She actually had the audacity to lift that proud chin of hers, to meet his glare with one of her own. "Five months."

As he did the math then double-checked, a thin film of rage clouded his vision, choking him into silence. If he'd had any smidgen of doubt about his plans, any tiny attack of conscience, she'd well and truly obliterated them.

The night Yelena had declared she'd loved him, the night of his father's death, she'd been pregnant with another man's child.

Three

The plane banked high in the air then slowly eased off. For the next hour, Yelena tried to bury herself in Alex's clippings, but time and again she caught herself staring out the window, into the painfully bright clouds and searing blue sky.

Bella finally stirred and she gave up any pretense of working. Instead she rummaged in her bag for a bottle of formula. But even as she fed Bella, she was acutely aware of the man seated directly opposite...and his complete and utter lack of interest in her. When Bella began to fidget—obviously sensing her mother's tension—Yelena glanced over.

The dark scowl as he focused on the papers on the table was so oddly out of place that her eyes lingered. She'd never seen Alex so angry, so untouchable. Her memories of him were scattered with flirtatious banter and unspoken attraction.

Don't forget kisses. Treacherous kisses that promised as much as they cajoled her to forget.

She glanced down at Bella, at those large half-mast eyes,

her mouth hanging slack on the bottle. With a tender smile, she put a towel on her shoulder then placed the baby over.

Ten minutes later, she moved her sleeping daughter back to the cot, packed away the forgotten paperwork then focused on the land spread out below.

Mile upon mile of red sand, punctuated by a hint of scrub. With most of Australia still in the throes of waning winter, August in outback Northern Territory meant rolling hot sand dunes, coupled with freezing cold nights.

She'd looked up the National Bureau of Meteorology on the Internet while waiting for Alex's car service and stumbled across a real-time Web site that beamed Ayers Rock, Diamond Bay Resort and the Yandurruh community to the entire world.

Gabriela had mentioned the resort once but her bare-bones description didn't do the stunning Internet feed justice. And now, looming in the distance, Yelena could just make out the shiny, curved dips and arches of Australia's most exclusive resort.

Perched on the edge of sacred Aboriginal land that included distinctive Ayers Rock, she'd expected Diamond Bay to be a towering eyesore in comparison to the Outback's raw beauty. But instead of a monstrosity, the resort was more like an undulating oasis. As the plane took a pass then looped back around to the small airstrip, Yelena unashamedly pressed her nose up against the cold glass. The structure flowed across the land, shimmering in the midday sun, the elegant, curving roofs rolling gently like an enormous albatross flying low across the stark red desert that stretched far into the distance.

Tension momentarily forgotten, she turned to Alex.

"What made your father build such a lavish resort way out here?"

Slowly, almost reluctantly, he raised his gaze from his papers to meet her eyes. "For privacy. And solitude." Then he turned back to his work, dismissing her.

Yelena inwardly cringed at his polite response, stripped of any inflection.

Was it so difficult to look at her, to talk to her? An unwelcome tangle of regret stuck in her throat and Yelena swallowed, forcing it down.

Thankfully, the awful silence was drowned out by the mechanics of the landing plane, then the clunk of doors and whirr of steps.

As she grabbed her jacket then reached for Bella, she felt Alex's presence close behind. When she turned, she saw her briefcase in his hand. With a spare silent nod, he indicated she should precede him.

Murmuring her thanks, she took the metal steps one slow clink at a time, keenly aware of Alex following, watching her every step.

A long, black limousine met them at the airstrip, and as Alex silently held the door open for her, Yelena noticed the baby capsule in the backseat.

She strapped a gurgling Bella down and got in, leaving Alex the window. When the door closed with a solid thunk, sealing them off in air-conditioned comfort sudden claustrophobia from the familiar spacious luxury made her breath catch. It had everything to do with the man who sat broodingly beside her, giving her the cold shoulder as if she'd committed an unforgivable sin.

With a sad sigh, she tilted her body away from him and murmured soft nothings at her daughter, making smiley faces as she quickly glanced at her watch.

Six days, twelve hours to go.

She placed a hand on Bella's little kicking feet, tension sending her stomach into a hundred fluttery butterflies.

This was ridiculous. Resolutely she pulled her back straight and turned in her seat, giving Alex her full attention.

"What do you want to achieve from this campaign?"

Visibly startled, he turned from the window, his expression dark as thunder. Yet he remained silent.

"Alex?" She prompted. "Your goals?"

"Who's the father?"

She recoiled. "That's none of your business!"

"Like hell it's not."

"Like hell it is!" Fury boiled up, singeing her control. "We are over, Alex. You and I have a business relationship, nothing more. I don't discuss my private life with clients and I don't intend to start now."

"And yet you bring your daughter on a business trip."

Her eyes narrowed. "This is the first time a client has made unreasonable demands. You left me no choice."

"Everyone always has a choice, Yelena."

She stiffened but refused to bite. "If you're concerned about not having my full attention, I can assure you Bella will in no way inhibit my ability to do my job."

"I see." His stare felt like smoldering flames on Yelena's skin. Fury, yes, but also a sliver of something else. Pride? Pain?

No. Alex Rush would never show that type of vulnerability.

A hard knot twisted inside her. For a second, she thought she'd seen something more beneath that hostile surface. The way he held his body, the tight line of his jaw, the flinty eyes, all convinced her of that.

Once upon a time they'd been friends. She should be relieved he'd managed to clamp a lid on his emotions, yet all she felt was cheated somehow.

"I can't offer you anything, Alex, except my full and utter focus on your campaign. Please respect that." *I can't erase what you see as a painful betrayal.* Instead she gathered up her self-control and forged on. "Now. Tell me about your goals for this campaign."

He glared at her, almost disbelieving, until suddenly, something cold and distant swept over him.

He glanced away, too nonchalant to be convincing. "For months the papers have been peddling lies and gossip about my father having an affair."

Yelena nodded. "I read the clippings. How's that affected your mother and sister?"

"My mother was politely asked to leave two of her charity boards. Instead of the usual phone calls, invitations and appearance requests, there's been a thunderous silence. And Chelsea's tennis trials sponsor pulled out which, before you ask, isn't about the money—it's about the stamp of approval being withdrawn on the basis of a bunch of lies."

"And, of course, your father isn't around to defend himself."

He gave her a sharp, unreadable look. "Of course," he echoed.

"Alex…" She chewed on the inside of her cheek for a second. "*Was* your father cheating?"

A sudden scowl creased his forehead. "No."

He paused as if about to add more, but when silence followed she asked slowly, "Can you be a hundred percent sure?"

"Of course I can't—no one can!"

"Okay." She ignored his hot glare and continued. "So we need to refocus, attract positive attention. An effective campaign is about subtlety—we want to create a slow but steady groundswell of public support without being blatant."

"If you're thinking of going down that clichéd, 'bring out the loving family for the press conference' route—"

Her mouth twisted. "No, I'll leave that to our next disgraced politician. It's a well-used tactic but it does evoke remorse and sympathy—you know, the whole 'he loves his family so he must be a good guy' thing. But it has to be done right. Tell me, while we're on the topic of your father, did you ever issue a public statement declaring your innocence in his death?"

"My solicitor did."

"But did *you,* personally?"

"No."

"Why not?"

"Because…" He frowned. "I was never charged. The police investigation was a complete farce, based on anonymous tips and half-baked rumors. I didn't want to give it more attention."

"I see."

"No, you don't." He met her gaze stonily. "After my father died, there was an almighty outpouring of public sympathy. The great and brilliant William Rush, taken in his prime. It went on for weeks—his brutal childhood and meteoric rise from poverty, his business dealings, influential friends. Then when I was dragged in for questioning, his fondness for gambling and drinking started making headlines."

"That's when it turned."

"Exactly. The cheating rumors were the last straw. My mother doesn't deserve that kind of smear. Nor does Chelsea." His eyes suddenly sparked, burning with purpose. "You asked me what I want from this campaign? I want my family to be accepted on their own achievements, not judged based on malicious gossip. I want you to woo the press, the public and their peers. And I want you to do it with subtlety."

"I'm always discreet."

"No. I mean, as far as everyone is concerned, I am not your client. And you are not running my PR campaign. I don't want to give the press any cynical 'stage-managed spin' headlines."

"I see," she said, frowning, not seeing at all. "So how do you intend to explain my presence?"

Alex's brief scrutiny said much more than his casual shrug. "Old friends catching up?"

Yelena's stomach pitched as the car pulled smoothly to a stop. Flustered, she shoved her bag strap over her shoulder and began to unclip Bella. "Who's going to believe that?"

"They believed all that crap about my father, didn't they?"

Yelena gently lifted the sleeping baby then got out of the limo. "Why on earth would I—" The words died on her tongue as she straightened, her cursory glance transforming into a wide-eyed stare.

She gulped. This place wasn't five-star—it was a hundred. From the ground, the resort's magnificence couldn't be more obvious. The frontage was old-style Grecian villa, with twin marble entry columns, sky-blue tiles and sky-high ceilings. Yet the apartments that rose on either side screamed sleek sophistication. The unusual rolling-roof design was stunning, the white-and-blue tiles complementing the stark desert surroundings.

"Takes your breath away, doesn't it?"

Yelena turned back to Alex, who was leaning against the car door with crossed arms and ankles, a powerful, commanding figure in brooding silence.

Ouch. The snapshot moment tightened her chest in painful remembrance. Last year, the same man but with a come-hither smile. She'd been leaving work, only to find him leaning nonchalantly on her car. Then he'd reached out and kissed her until her knees gave way...

All she could do was nod and slip her sunglasses up her nose. "Gabriela said the place was huge but..."

His blink-and-you'd-miss-it frown forced her words back down her throat.

"It was designed by Tom Wright, the guy who did Dubai's Burj Al Arab." His response was cool and impersonal, setting her teeth on edge. "I'll show you to your room." He nodded to the steward, who had their bags in hand, then strode into the marble-columned entrance without waiting to see if she would follow.

Before his long-legged strides took him to the far wall of his suite, Alex spun around and resumed pacing, raking a hand through his hair. He scrubbed at the roots, recalling that brief conversation in the car.

He'd known Yelena for nearly fifteen years, a good part of those spent lusting after her in typical adolescent fantasy. But he'd never, ever thought her capable of deliberate deceit. Until now.

Was your father cheating?

Why had she asked when she damn well knew the answer? She'd overheard his argument with his father, and hadn't hesitated to share what she knew with Carlos.

He reached the wall again and with a curse and a growl, turned.

She was trying to throw him, to make out she was innocent. That had to be it. Yet...

There'd been a small hesitancy in her question, a flush to her cheeks. The way her dark eyes briefly met his then flitted away.

He ground to a halt, a foot away from the sleek, monochrome writing desk. Carlos's betrayal had seriously screwed up his mind, made him doubt himself for the first time since...

He snapped his head up, glaring at his reflection in the golden mirror above the desk. Thanks to that one mistake, he'd spent the past months revisiting every deal, every business choice he'd made. More bloody time wasted on second-guessing perfectly legitimate decisions.

With an angry sigh he yanked his tie loose and undid the top buttons of his shirt.

It would drive him crazy if he let it. He'd already allowed

sentiment to seep in, putting him two steps back with Yelena.

Way to start the big seduction, mate. Yet he couldn't stop the questions from tumbling out, the need to know overriding all common sense. Yelena always had that effect on him. Twice he'd let anger rule the moment and twice she'd slammed up the shield, using their business relationship as defense. If he kept pissing her off, he'd have a better chance of harnessing a bushfire than getting her into bed. It was time to refocus on his plan.

Just like that his brain emptied, Yelena's features charging into the void to hijack his senses. *Finally,* his body seemed to groan. *You've caught up.*

It'd been too long since her subtle, exotic scent had sent him into meltdown, since he'd felt the silken slide of that wild chocolate hair against his skin.

And another man had claimed that right.

No. A bolt of fury jerked his jaw into a clench, unable to stop his mind from going there.

It could have been your child. Yours and Yelena's.

With gritted teeth he forced himself to let it go. And if his father hadn't been drunk and drowned in their pool, this alternate reality would cease to exist. But he *had* and now Alex had to deal with everything stemming from that one life-changing event.

If he couldn't get a grip, then his plans were history. Which left his family with nothing but a legacy of scandal and lies, terrible reminders of a past that he'd vowed would be buried with his tyrant father.

He glared out the large glass doors, out onto the wild beauty of the Australian Outback. To his far left, the distinctive ochre of Ayers Rock loomed, a sharp contrast to the overt lushness of Diamond Bay.

He loved the peace and isolation of this place. It was the only one of William's creations that didn't scream his autocratic presence in every brick and line, the only place untainted by his violence.

Alex absently rubbed a palm across his shoulder, recalling old wounds. He'd regularly endured the man's fists and his "fight for what you want—no one else will" dictum, a dictum that had surprisingly stuck. The only thing of value he'd gotten from that son of a bitch.

It was time to get his head straight and see this thing through.

The memory of soft eyes and a sinful laugh washed over him, making him groan. That thought carried him out the door, down the heavily carpeted gold-and-cream hallway to the end of the corridor where he'd deliberately placed Yelena.

He knocked and after a muffled "Hang on!" Yelena opened the door with a rushed smile. Her expression faded when she saw him standing there.

She'd removed her business suit. Instead, she was dressed in jeans and a stark white T-shirt, the dark denim a perfect frame for her long legs, the soft cotton shirt clinging demurely to her curves and prodding his imagination into overdrive. Extreme womanly curves.

He offered a thousand colorful curses to his growing libido before she silently stepped aside to let him enter.

"Did Jasmine come and see you?" he asked by way of greeting before striding into the room.

Yelena's mind blanked as an unexpected tingle flushed her skin, his warm body and familiar scent brushing fleetingly past.

"The babysitter," he reminded her.

She gave herself a mental shake. "Yes, she's in the bedroom with Bella. Thank you for arranging that."

He shrugged then paused in the middle of the room, surveying it. "The resort provides an exceptional nanny service. Is the room to your liking?"

"Perfect—if a bit large."

"All our suites come with a living area, two bedrooms, separate bathroom. And of course, a view."

He picked up a remote control from the coffee table and thumbed a button.

Slowly, the curtains began to whir apart.

"Your curtains are electronic?" she asked.

"Yeah." Her surprise amused him: the small grin he gave had her cool resolve thawing an inch. "Can't have our guests *manually* opening their curtains."

She shook her head, reluctantly matching his smile. "Of course not. They might—oh."

It was a fantasy view. Dead ahead, a huge cliff face loomed, a waterfall glinting in the sun as it crashed over the edge into a massive lagoon. A veritable forest of native flora gathered at the base, creating a protective canopy that shaded a paved walkway. Yelena could barely pick out the private cabanas Diamond Bay provided for all its pool goers.

It was like something from a big-budget movie set where the characters stumbled upon a fertile, ancient land miles below the earth's surface. Yet Yelena knew it was the real thing. Diamond Bay—the only man-made body of water in the state.

And surrounding it all, the shiny curves of the resort gently undulated, forming a completely decadent—and totally private—haven.

"That's…"

"Amazing?"

Yelena took one step towards the view, then another. "Breathtaking."

He crossed his arms. "William Rush did have a taste for the spectacular."

She slowly swung her gaze to him, studying his profile as he stared out at the view.

Something was off. There was tension, yes. She'd expected

that—even disgust, considering what she'd dumped on him in the plane. But there was something more... She grazed her eyes over his face. The almost imperceptible frown creasing his brow. The strong, fixed jaw. The aquiline slope of his nose that led down to a mouth that she remembered was way too warm, way too tempting.

He shifted, those azure eyes snaring her. "I had a feeling you'd like it," he murmured, almost to himself.

A spark of something deep within flared her senses for one second, but in the next he glanced away and she wondered if she'd just imagined it.

It left her breathless. And irritated.

"I'll show you where you'll be working," he said shortly, completely unaware of his effect on her heart rate.

She nodded, disappeared into the bedroom then returned with her briefcase and a thick notepad.

"Your sister's fourteen, correct?" Yelena began as they made their way from the suite and down the hushed hall.

"Fifteen in March." His eyes suddenly relaxed. "You've never met her, have you?"

"Once. Gabriela invited her to a thing at the embassy last year."

"Ah, that's right... the Christmas in July Ball." They turned left and stopped at the elevator bay. "She was stoked. Couldn't stop flashing that 'special guest' invitation under everyone's nose." His mouth quirked as he punched the button.

"Your mother couldn't come that night—she was sick, right?"

"Yeah." His eyelids suddenly came down as he crossed his arms, angling his body towards the elevators.

Odd. Yelena frowned but before she could add anything more, Alex spoke, his gaze still on the closed elevator doors.

"That was the night you kissed me for the first time. In the kitchen, remember?"

She snapped her eyes up, cheeks warm. "*You* kissed *me*."

His mouth slanted. "And you told me to take a hike afterwards."

"You were Gabriela's boyfriend."

"Only one of many."

"Are you accusing my sister of—"

"Oh, come off it, Yelena." She just caught his eye roll before the doors pinged open. "You and I both know Gabriela's a good-time girl in every sense of the word. I served as her designated arm decoration when she was in town but I certainly wasn't her only love interest."

I can't talk about this. Yelena tightened her grip on her bag, steadfastly focusing on the closing elevator doors as the memories flushed over her skin, making her tingle.

"Tell me more about Chelsea."

He paused, letting her know he knew she was changing the subject. Finally, he said, "She's an amazing kid—a promising tennis player, too. Brash and tough on the outside but inside…"

"A typical teenager—vulnerable and unsure."

"Yeah." He looked at Yelena then, his small smile startling her. "What would you know about that?"

"Everything." Alex watched her mouth twitch as they both left the elevator and headed across the marble lobby. "I was the new kid at school, remember? And a foreigner."

"I remember your first day." How could he forget? She'd been every male senior's wet dream—a stunning, dark-haired beauty driving up to Radford College in a sleek black BMW, hair blowing, fashionably impassive behind flashy Dior sunglasses.

"I was nervous as hell," she said, snapping him from his fantasy as they kept walking past the reception area.

"Couldn't tell. You glided through that car park like you owned the place."

Yelena gave a short laugh as he held open a set of glass doors for her. "'Glided'? Hardly."

"Yeah. Gabriela bounces through life. You glide like a perfectly groomed ship on smooth water." Palm down, he cut his hand through the air, a visual to back up his statement.

"Is that how you see me—perfect? Untouchable?"

He paused, his hand on the door that proclaimed, simply, Alexander Rush. She watched his sensual mouth curve, his piercing blue eyes creasing in sudden humor.

"Never untouchable, Yelena."

Her breath caught as she remained trapped in the steady knowledge of his gaze. *This* was the Alex she knew—the teasing charmer who threw out little double entendres just to see her fluster. Not the bitter man flinging accusations in her office. And certainly not the Alex of the dark moments, the hidden secrets and brooding silences she'd thought Gabriela had exaggerated for dramatic effect.

"Coffee?"

"What?"

"I said, do you want coffee?" His mouth tweaked into a delicious grin. "We can have it out by the pool."

Guiltily she nodded. She'd known her sister and Alex were a mismatch the instant Gabriela had told her...when? May. Over a year ago. A lifetime. Yet she'd loved him in her own way. Didn't he deserve to know what had happened?

As she stood in the still expanse of Alex's office, pretending to take in her surroundings while he made a phone call, she wrestled with the promise her parents had wrenched from her. Finally he hung up.

"My mother and Chelsea will meet us at Ruby's—one of our many coffee bars—at four."

"Alex..."

"Yes?" He placed his hands on his hips, head tilted in familiar awareness.

Gabriela's dead. It was right on the tip of her tongue, sitting there all ready to come out, but with one gulp she swallowed it. She'd been clear with Alex from the start—she was here for business. Disturbed at how easy her control had slipped in less than a day, she quickly grabbed for the reins.

"Do your mother and sister know why I'm here?" she asked.

Slowly he leaned against his desk, bracing his palms on the rich, dark wood.

"No. And I don't want them to, at least not yet. My mother will think it's unnecessary…that British stiff-upper-lip reserve thing. She'd say I was wasting my money and your time, that everything would eventually blow over—" He stopped midsentence, his jaw tightening. Then he cleared his throat, crossed his arms and said, "They've been here two weeks and only just started to relax—I want to keep it that way."

His pointed look stung. "I know how to do my job."

"Good." He nodded to the huge aerial shot of Diamond Bay on the wall opposite. "People pay for a media-free zone here. No papers, TV, phone, Internet—unless by request. I've given you a conference room next door with everything you need. Only guests are allowed into the resort, and only then by private plane, so no reporters. You'll have complete privacy to work."

Complete privacy. In a stunning resort that radiated Alex's presence and family power from every floor, every wall. Yet despite the tension rumbling between them like an ominous earthquake warning, she'd felt a connection to this place from the moment she'd set foot on the rich red soil. As if the sole purpose of her stay was to help her relax.

"Do you get to stay here often?"

He paused. "Not as much as I'd like. I travel between Sydney, Canberra, L.A. and London, mostly."

Yelena tipped her head. "London? So Sprint Travel is thinking of franchising to the U.K.? Carlos…"

Yelena let her words peter out at Alex's tight face. "Carlos what?"

"He...he just mentioned it in passing."

"I see," he said smoothly, before straightening to his full six-foot-three height. "But to answer—no. Rush Airlines has investments in the U.K. and the States. Do you want to see your work space?"

He quickly left the office and walked down the hall, leaving Yelena no choice but to follow.

Four

"Welcome to Diamond Falls, Yelena." Pamela Rush's handshake might have been hesitant but her smile was sincerely warm. A pair of flowing beige pants and a floral shirt tied low around her middle emphasized a trim figure, with a large broad-brimmed sun hat completing the ensemble.

"My gardening clothes," Pam said with a smile, then swept off her hat and gave her short, choppy hair a ruffle. "I have a greenhouse extended onto my suite. We try to be as self-sufficient as we can."

Yelena noticed the loving smile Pam gave Alex as he sat down. Then she glanced over at the lanky girl—Alex's sister—who was lounging unceremoniously in the comfy sofa chair opposite.

"I already ordered coffee for us—I hope you don't mind." A tinge of worry lit Pam's eyes. "Unless you drink tea, Yelena…?"

Yelena smiled reassuringly. "Couldn't function without my coffee."

"You're Gabriela's sister, right?" Chelsea asked as she swung her legs around, her feet landing with a small thunk on the slate floor. The teenager was all long limbs and coltish grace in cutoff denim shorts and black T-shirt declaring Vampire Princess in blood red. Familiar white iPod headphones dangled from her neck, her brown hair pulled up into a ponytail, revealing a makeup-free face. She looked all of ten years old.

"I am," Yelena said. "You and I met last year."

"At the Christmas in July Ball." Chelsea grinned and nodded. "You were dressed in black Colette Dinnigan—from her *next* season winter collection."

Yelena smiled. "I have friends in high places. And you have a good memory. Are you interested in fashion?"

Chelsea shrugged. "Sort of."

"One of her many interests," Pamela Rush said with a gentle smile at her daughter. Chelsea blinked and shrugged, trying to carry off teenage blasé but losing. The intelligence in her blue eyes, so like Alex's, indicated much more depth than Yelena suspected people knew. "Chelsea's going to be the next Martina," Pam added proudly.

"Mum!" Chelsea rolled her eyes as she wrapped her headphones around the iPod. "Don't—"

"Excuse me, Mr. Rush. Drinks?"

The waiter placed three coffees and a thick chocolate shake before them with a flourish. Yelena caught Chelsea's flushed gaze as it flitted up to the cute waiter then back to the tabletop.

Smothering a smile, she turned her attention to Alex's mother.

She'd seen photos of Pamela Rush in the gossip magazines and society pages. The former airline hostess had aged well, with hardly a wrinkle on her striking face, no visible grey hairs in her rich, brown pixie cut.

"Didn't you have long hair at one point?" Yelena asked curiously.

If she hadn't been studying the woman so closely, she would've missed the slight waver on Pam's lips just before they stretched into a smile.

"Sometimes you just need a change."

Yelena nodded, glancing away to cover up her embarrassment. Of course. The woman had lost a husband, her son had been accused of murder. Some people ran away, some drank. Some simply went to pieces. Pamela Rush cut her hair.

"So what brings you to Diamond Bay, Yelena?" Pam asked.

Yelena gave Alex a fleeting glance. He raised one eyebrow, inviting her to continue.

"Distraction-free work—"

"And a little relaxation, too." Alex added evenly, his smile sending a quiver of warmth into her limbs.

"Well, this is the place for it," Pam said with a nod.

As Pam poured milk into her coffee, Yelena made a few observations. *Genuine smile. Polite. Poised.* Her fingers twitched, eager to make notes, but knew she'd have to wait until later. Instead she picked up a packet of sugar, gave it a flick then ripped open the top and dumped the contents into her black coffee.

She lowered her eyes to furtively study Alex. He appeared calm, the muscles in his face relaxed, his brow smooth. She even caught a small twitch of approval lingering at the corner of his mouth.

A frisson of pleasure jetted through her body, startling her. *This isn't your first campaign. You can't let a client's stamp of approval go to your head.*

"Is Gabriela overseas?" Chelsea said suddenly, leaning forward with her elbows on her knees.

Thrown, Yelena slowly took her cup and raised it to her lips before focusing her attention on the teenager. "Um… yes."

"For the fashion season? It starts in September, right, with New York, then London, Milan and Paris?"

It was only after Yelena had taken a sip of scalding coffee and returned the cup to the saucer that she realized her other hand had been halfway up to her necklace. Instinctively her eyes met Alex's. At his frown, she lowered her hand then clasped them together on the table.

"How do you know?" She gave Chelsea a small, curious smile. "Gabriela wasn't—" she paused to swallow, then finished faintly "—she hasn't modeled for years."

"I know—she's a booker for Cat Walker Models in Sydney, right? I've been following their blog. They said they were going to send staff to cover the shows and I just figured she'd be the obvious choice."

The dull pain squeezed her heart but she managed to return Chelsea's smile. "I think you're more than 'sort of' interested in fashion."

"Yeah," she muttered and glanced away with a barely hidden grimace. When she returned her gaze to Yelena's, it was…different. Hard. As if she'd aged ten years in the space of two seconds. "But Dad reckoned it was a waste of time."

Then she reached for her shake and began to vigorously stir it with the straw.

What on earth was that? Yelena chanced another look at Alex while everyone drank but failed to glean anything from his controlled blue stare.

Too controlled. Yelena dropped her eyes as her thoughts began to snowball. What was going on here? She cast her mind back to this morning, rehashing their conversations. Yet she couldn't pin down anything tangible, any dead giveaway that would assuage her concerns. It was more a gut feeling, something instinctive that told her Alex wasn't telling her everything. After months—years—of covert flirting and casual chat during endless social functions they'd been thrown into, she could sense it. She could sense it every time the topic of conversation turned to his family. And she could sense it after three clandestine moments when they'd shared fevered kisses and whispers of hot passion.

She knew it now.

In one of Gabriela's rare moments of insight, her sister had likened Alex Rush to a dormant volcano—beautiful and calm on the outside, but inside a raging mass of hot, bubbling conflict.

Take care of him, Yelena. He's one of the good guys.

Yelena glared at her cup. Damn it. She'd been trying to erase Gabriela's gentle command from her memory, just as she'd been forcing herself not to think about Alex and all the complexities that made him tick. But she was involved again—and it didn't only include him now.

With sudden inspiration, Yelena placed her spoon on her saucer and leaned forward. "I tell you what, Chelsea. I know a few people in Sydney—if you're interested, I can get us front-row tickets to David Jones's fashion show next month."

Chelsea's rounded eyes snapped up to hers. "Really?"

When she glanced over at Pam, Yelena quickly added, "Of course, your mum would have to approve."

"Mum? Please? Please, please, pleeeeeease?"

But it was Alex who butted in with, "What about your training? And school?"

The spark of defiance in the teenager's eyes was hard to miss. "What about it?"

Pam began awkwardly, "I thought you were focusing on the Perth trials next year?"

Chelsea glared at the tabletop, muttering something under her breath.

"What?" Alex said with a frown.

"I said, 'I doubt I'd get in, anyway.'"

"So you want to just drop it? Is—" Alex paused then

leaned forward in his chair, irritation evident "—is that what you want? After you've spent so much time and effort on training?"

Chelsea's expression turned sullen. "Why don't you start yelling about how you've spent thousands on my tennis career? Then you'd *really* sound like Dad."

If Chelsea had picked up her soda spoon and stabbed him with it, Alex couldn't have looked more hurt.

"Sweetheart…" Pam said slowly before Chelsea cut her off with a venomous look.

Wow. Anger like that didn't come from just a little family disagreement. Fascinated yet discomfited, Yelena watched the scenario play out before her, unable to look away.

"If you want something that badly—" Pam began.

Chelsea leaped to her feet, face flushed. "Don't you *dare* quote Dad to me, not now, not after—"

"Chelsea!" Alex said roughly.

She scowled at him. "And you shouldn't be defending him! This whole thing sucks! Everything sucks!"

And with that, she stormed across the café and out the glass doors.

Alex scraped his chair back but Pam put a hand on his arm, shaking her head. He sat, his face turbulent, as an awkward silence fell.

Yelena looked over to Pam, who was making short work of the napkin in her lap, eyes staring at her half-empty coffee. And Alex, well, that gaze would end up burning a hole in the table pretty soon.

"You know what?" Yelena said firmly, turning to Pam. "I'd love to see your greenhouse if you have the time."

The older woman glanced up, blinking rapidly. "Now?"

"Sure." She tempered her request with a smile. "Work can wait. And I love plants even though I have a black thumb."

"Black thumb?"

"They always end up withering away, despite my best efforts."

Pam's shaky smile told Yelena she was grateful for the attention shift, yet Alex's expression remained closed.

Yelena stood and casually linked her arm through the older woman's. But then, suddenly, she paused with a confused blink. Had Pamela Rush *flinched?* Her eyes sought Pam's but their crystal-blue depths reflected nothing but gentle politeness.

She shook herself, dismissing the moment.

"I'll see you for dinner, darling?" Pam said, glancing back to Alex.

Yelena didn't want to look at him but she managed to force her gaze to where he still sat, silent and thoughtful.

When he looked first at his mother, then her, she could see the wheels of his mind working overtime. With one raised eyebrow, she met his eyes steadily.

He glanced back to Pam. "I'll probably be working. I'll let you know." Slowly he added, "What about Chelsea?"

Pam shook her head. "She's been angry for the last two weeks. I've been giving her some space, so please don't chase her down. She needs to—" she paused, as if rethinking the words "—figure out who she is and what she wants. You know what it's like at that age."

"Yeah."

Yelena couldn't fail to notice Alex's parting scowl, dark with something she couldn't quite put her finger on. It lingered in her mind long after Pam led her from the café, across the foyer and towards the private suites.

Alex was neck-deep in numbers with only half his mind on the task when Yelena breezed into his office an hour later. "You have to tell your mother."

He slowly placed his Montblanc pen on the sheaf of

notes and leaned back. The leather chair gently groaned in protest.

"What have you said to her?"

"Nothing." She put her hands on her hips, obviously unaware how that emphasized the generous flare of her curves. "But I've never worked on a campaign that didn't have the full support of the client."

"*I'm* your client."

She shifted her weight, one long leg thrust forward aggressively, tilting those hips in one slow, suggestive motion. Alex's breath caught in sharp appreciation.

"Tell me, if it weren't for Pam and Chelsea, would you have hired me?" Yelena said.

If it weren't for Carlos they both wouldn't be here. "No," he said curtly, arousal doused as resentment began to bubble up inside. He swiftly stood. "What have you two been talking about?"

"Well, naturally she asked what I did for a living so pretty soon she'll put two and two together." She paused, shaking her head. Alex watched a small strand of hair escape her ponytail and settle on her shoulder. With an impatient sweep, she shoved it back.

"I also get the feeling she thinks you and I are—" she paused, her hand fluttering up to her necklace "—conducting some kind of secret liaison."

"I see."

When he moved out from behind his desk, Alex noticed the way she put weight onto her back foot, unsure and unsteady. As if poised for a quick exit.

Yelena never backed down from an argument. Which meant something else had unnerved her, something that went beyond mere discomfort at his mother's assumptions. Was he finally getting to her? Just as satisfaction curled his mouth into a grin, a dark alternate thought thinned it.

"Being romantically linked with a suspected murderer embarrasses you."

Yelena eyes widened at the hint of disgust peppering his flat statement. "No! How could you possibly think that?"

"So what's the problem?"

"You have to stop lying to her."

His eyes narrowed. "I am not lying."

She snorted, unperturbed by his mounting irritation. "Lying by omission is still lying. I get enough of that from my bro—"

Appalled, she snapped her mouth shut…not quick enough.

"What's Carlos done?" He growled.

What on earth was she thinking? Their eyes deadlocked, both unwilling to back down until Yelena finally conceded.

"Nothing. He's said absolutely nothing to me for months. This whole silent treatment you're giving him isn't going to solve the problem, you know."

"What makes you think there's a problem?"

"Do not treat me like an idiot, Alex. There's a problem."

Instantly, the temperature dropped. "That's none of your business."

"Rubbish. Not only will this impact on Sprint Travel and this campaign, but he's my brother—your business partner."

He shot her a look. "What happened to your 'no personal questions' rule?" He slowly crossed his arms. "Can't have it both ways. Or—" he let the words trail off, one eyebrow raised "—are you deliberately trying to pick a fight?"

His voice dipped into a shockingly intimate timbre. Immediately her body started to tingle with anticipation, heart rate thumping.

His mouth tweaked. "You always loved a good, long—"

"Alex!"

"Argument." Now he was grinning at her outright. They were having a serious discussion and he was *amused?*

Infuriated, she tried to pull herself together. "Maybe I'm getting sick and tired of all your weird looks."

"What weird looks?"

"As if you can't stand me one moment but the next, you want to…"

"Kiss you?"

He crossed the room too quickly for her to register his intent and when his hand snaked out and grabbed her arm, surprise rendered her immobile.

She pointedly stared at his hand then coolly met his eyes. "Do not touch me."

"Why not?"

Her heart accelerated as her cheeks became warm. "Because you're being unprofessional."

He gave a mocking snort. "So you can feel it."

"Feel what?"

He slowly ran his palm up, curling long fingers around the soft part of her forearm to gently hold her prisoner. "How it is between us. How it's always been—even when I was off-limits and dating your sister."

She yanked away, severing the moment. "Don't you dare bring that up!"

"It's true."

Yelena took a step back, then another. "But it didn't make it right." She stuck her hands on her hips, guilt and desire now burning her face. "Do you know how many times I wanted to tell Gabriela about us? And every time I psyched myself up to it, she'd bounce in with a stupid grin on her face, telling me how happy she was. I hated myself for lusting after my sister's boyfriend. What we were doing was wrong."

His eyes darkened. "All you and I did was share a few kisses—we did nothing immoral."

"Maybe not in your mind. But every time I was with you—" *I was so damn happy, yet so miserable because* you *made her happy.* "Oh, forget it," she bit off and whirled away, stalking to the door.

Yet just as her hand slapped on the cold wood, she paused. Her feet itched to storm out that door, her fingers falling to clench the polished handle as if it were a lifeline. But the damage was done. She'd not only flung open the gate to their past, she'd blithely charged on through.

With reluctance dogging every second, she turned back. "Alex...about Gabriela."

"What?" He'd grabbed his mobile phone from the desk and was absently checking his messages. "Did she ever manage to sign Jennifer Hawkins to her agency? I knew she was angling for her."

At Yelena's silence he glanced up. "What? She's returning to modeling? She's back in town? She's getting married?" At this last one he gave a snort, part amusement, part skepticism.

"No."

That small word had a truckload of seriousness behind it. His smile faltered, then froze. "What?"

Yelena fingered her necklace and swallowed, the huge lump passing under her skin and down her throat. "Gabriela's dead."

Seconds passed like a yawning chasm, deathly silent yet loaded with meaning.

His entire face tightened into incredulity. "You're kidding."

"Would I lie about something like that? It was never officially announced so there's no way you could've known."

"When?"

"In March. She called me from Spain on Christmas Eve, right after we...you and I..." She trailed off guiltily. Parked in his father's driveway, making out like two teenagers. Half-clothed, his hot mouth on her body, frantic kisses full of hope and promise for the future before she'd breathlessly begged him to stop. *We have to tell Gabriela—she deserves to know.*

"She called me on my way home, desperate for help," Yelena continued. "I tried calling you at the airport but you'd switched your phone off. Then when I landed in Madrid, I kept calling—your mobile, your house. Finally I got some security guy but he wouldn't let me speak to you."

"So you stopped trying."

It wasn't an accusation, just a statement of fact. The truth of it hacked off a little piece of her heart. She *had* just given up.

"I called for a week," she admitted, "but you'd imposed a complete communication blackout. I even told them I was from Bennett & Harper PR, but nothing. I thought you'd…" To her embarrassment, her voice wavered.

Alex's hands went to his hips. "You thought I was breaking up with you?"

"Wouldn't you?" she countered. "I'd left without warning and ended up with Gabriela in a bunch of tiny, off-the-grid towns, some with barely enough sanitation, let alone phone towers. When we finally got to Germany in early March, I found out about your father—a few weeks after you'd been cleared. Then Gabriela's issues, her death, overshadowed everything else."

She held his gaze until he finally glanced away, dragging a hand over his eyes.

"I didn't know. My life has been—" He stopped, dropped his gaze and exhaled forcefully. "I'm sorry about your sister. How did she…?"

"Car crash. She was…" *Impulsive. Reckless. Selfish.* "Gabriela," Yelena finished lamely with a small smile and a shrug.

"And your parents haven't issued a statement?"

"Not through my lack of trying." At his look, her breath caught in her throat, the past and the present mingling to form a heavy mantle of resentment that threatened her composure.

"That's not right, Yelena."

"Yes, well. Gabriela's always been the crazy one—she was the reason we immigrated in the first place. This is just another example of my parents trying to avoid scandalizing the sacred Valero name at any cost."

Her phone went off, intruding on the moment. Quickly she glanced at it. "It's late. I have to go." Ignoring his frown, she pocketed the phone. "I have to feed Bella at six."

She shoved the door open but paused with her hand on the knob. Slowly she turned, fixing him with a steady look. "I'd appreciate you keeping this news to yourself."

At his silent nod she gave him a grateful, fleeting smile. "Thanks. And could you talk with your mother? Let her know why I'm here?"

Again, another nod.

"I'll see you tomorrow."

"Yes."

Then she turned and walked out the door.

Five

Yelena keyed open her suite door and shuffled inside. The cool air hit her face, a wonderful relief against her hot, burning cheeks.

"Jasmine?"

The nanny popped out from the kitchen with a smile, a clean baby bottle in one hand. "Bella's been up for a few minutes. She's a precious little thing, that one."

"She is." She smiled, and the cloying pressure slowly released like a steamer set from boil to off.

"She looks exactly like her mummy, too, all curly dark hair and beautiful skin. I'll bet those gorgeous brown eyes will steal a few hearts."

"I'm counting on it." Yelena grinned as she laid her bag on the glass-topped table. "Before I forget, Jasmine—do you have an invoice for me?"

Jasmine looked confused. "Mr. Rush didn't mention anything about billing you."

Oh. Another revelation in this great, surprise-filled tsunami.

Telling Alex about Gabriela's death had been the right thing to do. And now that guilt no longer weighed on her mind, she could focus more clearly on other things.

Like this campaign.

The pleasant yet confusing hour she'd spent with Pam had only exacerbated her curiosity. Oh, it wasn't anything obvious: Pam was a passionate gardener, encouraging her to smell and touch at every opportunity. But every so often Yelena got that odd, uncomfortable feeling. It wasn't anything Pam said, but rather what she *didn't* say.

It happened every time William Rush's name was mentioned.

For the second time today, a terrible thought surged up but she quickly squashed it down. From one who'd spent years keeping a lid on her emotions, she recognized the same in Pamela Rush. Yet, she acknowledged slowly, some secrets should be kept at all costs.

As the nanny tidied up the last of the dishes, Yelena checked her phone for messages. One from Melanie, wishing her good luck. One from Jonathon, reminding her to check in tomorrow morning. And curiously, one from Carlos—a curt directive to call him back.

He sounded angry.

Yelena placed her phone on the table. She wasn't in the mood for angry, not after the day she'd had.

Pulling the tie from her hair, she ran her fingers through the heavy mass then vigorously rubbed her scalp. She not only had to deal with Alex and all the anxiety his presence entailed, but now there was this strange family tension, something obviously personal that floated below the surface.

Normally she'd question everyone involved, uncover the truth, work out their needs then provide the best possible spin. But something about this situation grated. She'd handled her share of contentious people and their issues but it had never felt quite so personal before.

That ruffled her normally cool composure. Could she be impartial when she still remembered how it felt to have Alex's mouth on hers, his hot breath sending shivers of desire across her skin?

"I'm off." The nanny was at the door, one hand on the knob. "I'll see you tomorrow at seven."

Yelena managed a genuine thank-you but when the door clicked shut, the smile she'd been holding quickly slid away.

With a sigh she padded into the bedroom, her eyes fixed on the crib in the corner. She peered over the edge, holding her breath, but what she saw took the last of it away.

Her baby, her gorgeous girl, blinking sleepily. She'd made a fist and was gently sucking on it with tiny baby grunts, her other hand tightly grasping the rubber end of her brightly colored pacifier.

That's right, bella. *Whatever makes you comfortable in this strange sounding, strange smelling place. You hold on to it.*

She sifted through her work priorities as she changed and fed Bella then settled her back down. As she backed from the room, leaving the door open a bare inch, she glanced back to the living area, to the pile of files on the table, to her iMac ready and waiting to boot up. In the bedroom, she could just hear Bella's tiny settling sounds before she got herself off to sleep.

Her heart wrenched, no less painfully than it had a thousand other times before. Bella, the love of her life, in one room. In the other, her work, the tangible result of her achievements and symbol of her independence. Two opposites, yin and yang tied together to make a whole.

I need a hot shower. The desire was sudden and immediate and she stripped off, leaving the clothes where they fell, then stepped into the enormous bathroom.

She'd checked out the room before, but the opulence of this piece of interior design still took her breath away.

The bathroom dwarfed her bedroom at home, the large sink big enough to bath Bella in. Above, the last rays of the sun streamed in through the huge skylight. The shower on the left boasted plain glass doors, twin showerheads and a half wall of frosted glass bricks.

But it was the spa bath that held her attention. Fashioned like a miniature eternity pool, the blue marble spa ended at the amazing view of Ayers Rock and the red desert soil. One-way, tempered double-glazed glass, she recalled from the brochure in the sitting room.

On the bright-blue marble counter sat a dozen top-end beauty products—creams, lotions, cleansers. Next to it, a golden basket of bath items. With a grin, she selected a green bath bomb and sniffed.

The gorgeous smell of lemongrass and orange sent her toes curling in pleasure and she glanced up to catch her reflection in the large mirror. All these beautiful things, these amazing smells were a temporary distraction. She stared at herself, tilting her head left, then right.

You're twenty-eight. You're successful, you're driven, you're direct. Yet would she have the guts to approach Alex with her concerns about Pam?

It would take timing and subtlety. She'd have to be nonthreatening and put him at ease, something she guessed would be a monumental task.

A flash of apprehension slithered across her face, settling in her dark-brown eyes fringed with long lashes. They were Valero eyes—her father's, Carlos's. And Gabriela's.

The door's tinkling chime shattered the moment and she quickly grabbed a robe before turning from the mirror, leaving the wisps of dread clinging to the ornate bathroom tiles.

Chelsea Rush stood at the door, eyeing the corridor nervously over her shoulder. "Can I come in?"

"Uh...sure."

As Chelsea scuttled past, Yelena gently closed the door. She gave the girl a few moments to fiddle with the decorations, to murmur appreciatively at her iMac then gracefully fall into the huge cream leather sofa.

"I see Alex put you in the Big-Shot Room," the girl finally ventured.

Yelena perched on the sofa arm and smiled. "Really?"

"Yeah. It's our superspecial executive suite for visiting sheikhs, rock stars, prime ministers. I heard one of the Rolling Stones trashed it once and Dad sent him the bill. The bathroom's awesome. And you get freebies."

"So I saw." Yelena moved to the seat. "Must be great living in a place like this."

"Alex and Mum love it."

"And you?"

Chelsea shrugged. "It's better than Canberra. Our house felt like a mausoleum."

The house William Rush died in. "What about school? Your friends?"

She watched the teenager's mouth thin. "I've had tutors since January."

"Ahh." Not exactly a full answer but Yelena let it go. "Can I get you a drink? Soda?"

"No, thank you." Chelsea continued to look around the room, avoiding Yelena's eyes until she lit upon Bella's empty bottle on the dining table. "You have a baby? Here?"

"I do. Her name's Bella."

"Cool. Mum loves babies—she'll probably offer to baby-sit, so watch out." Chelsea grinned. "How old?"

"Five months. She was born on the eighteenth of March."

"I'm a Pisces, too! March fourth. That's funny." She paused then said casually, "Can I ask you a question?"

Despite Chelsea's nonchalance, Yelena knew it wasn't going

to be any ordinary question. Still, she tucked her legs beneath her and sat back, deliberately casual. "Sure."

"Did you mean it about those fashion show tickets?"

Yelena nodded. "Absolutely."

"Why?"

Yelena looked her straight in the eye, smiling. "You remembered my favorite designer. That tells me you're pretty hooked."

"But you don't know me." When Chelsea's brow furrowed, her confusion clear, Yelena swallowed. What could she say that wouldn't break Alex's request for confidentiality? "I mean…you're Gabriela's sister and all—"

"Exactly." Yelena thankfully grasped the straw. "And I know what it's like when no one else gets what you love. It'll be a fun way to get to know each other. Believe it or not, it's been a while since I got out." At the teenager's continued silence, Yelena said softly, "But if you think your mum won't approve…"

"No, it's not that," Chelsea said, her gaze skittering away. "I just… well… Alex told me and Mum he's hired you to handle the press. So why would you want to…why are you—?" She scowled, as if annoyed by her lack of eloquence.

Yelena almost sighed in relief. "Why am I offering to socialize on private time?"

"Yeah. All that stuff they're printing about my dad. About him cheating on Mum—"

"Chelsea. You can't take any notice of that. The press make stuff up all the time. I'm here to help take the focus off that."

"But that's the thing…" When she lifted her chin, the tortured look in those shimmering blue pools stunned Yelena. "I think it *is* true."

Six

The firm knock on the door made them both jump. For a second they both sat there, staring at each other, until Yelena finally found her voice.

"Who is it?"

"Alex."

Chelsea leapt to her feet, shaking her head.

"Just a minute," Yelena called then turned to the panicky girl.

"We had a row... I'm supposed to be in my room... I have to go!"

"Chelsea—"

"Shh!" Chelsea hurried over to the patio doors and swept them open. Cold night air swirled in. "I can get back through the lagoon walk. I'll talk to you later."

And then she was gone.

Mind racing, Yelena slowly closed the glass doors, crossed the living room and opened the door.

Alex stood there in his shirt-sleeves, tie and top buttons askew.

She pulled the robe tight around her waist as her stomach gave a weird little flip. "I was just about to have a shower."

"Okay."

He remained there, silent, until she said slowly, "Did you need me for something?"

A minuscule smile pulled the corner of his mouth for a second before it disappeared. "We need to talk about a few things."

Could she handle any more today? With an inward sigh, Yelena pulled the door wider. "If you want to wait, you can come in."

"Sure."

Alex was not a patient man. While she was in the shower he sat on the couch for all of twenty seconds. He knew because he counted every single one. When he realized what he was doing, he shot to his feet and grabbed the remote, flicking on the huge plasma television. Pretty soon he clicked that off and started to pace but eventually ended up staring out at the night lights through the window. Another five minutes and his patience felt as if it had been put through a shredder. Twice.

Normally, once he'd dismissed something from his mind, it stayed gone. Yet his second thoughts about Yelena's involvement in Carlos's scheme had bizarrely festered, chewing away at his thoughts until he realized he had to take action. It had only increased in urgency after his one-sided conversation with Chelsea thirty minutes before.

Yet as the minutes ticked by his thoughts were not on his sister's sullen countenance but on Yelena. Yelena in the shower. Naked. Hot water running over her silky skin, making it slick and slippery—

"What did you want to talk about?"

He whirled, swallowing a groan. She stood in the entry

wrapped in a Diamond Bay robe, her long hair tousled and damp, curling down her back.

The urgent craving to kiss her—hard—engulfed him.

Almost as if he'd voiced the desire, she rocked onto her back foot. "Alex? Has something happened?"

His groin tightened as he bit off a bitter laugh. *Yeah, something's happened.* With a deep breath, he forced his mouth into a smile.

"I ordered room service."

She blinked then grabbed her clothes where she'd tossed them on the floor. "Thank you. But that wasn't necessary."

"I thought we could discuss this campaign over dinner." When she paused in her folding he smiled again, this time a sincere one. "You have to eat."

The silence stood for a few seconds until she nodded. "I'll get dressed."

Yelena whirled on her heel, forcing herself not to run into the bedroom and slam the door. *It's business. Remember that.* Yet everything she remembered of Alex contradicted that hollow statement.

After vigorously rubbing her still-damp hair, she quickly stepped into underwear then shoved on a pair of soft pink cashmere track pants and a plain black T-shirt, securing her hair into a high ponytail. A quick check of Bella deep in sleep and she was ready to face Alex. One deep, fortifying breath—okay, two—and she finally walked out into the lounge room.

The sight of him made that last breath shudder in her chest. Even with his back to her, he still commanded her focus. Tall and muscular, that was Alex. He always made her feel feminine, even delicate, which was no mean feat given her height. His wide shoulders were capable of taking on a hundred worries, weathering any crisis. He was like a house built on iron-clad foundations.

She'd once overheard Carlos describe him as "entitled and

arrogant" but she knew all too well strength and conviction could be misinterpreted as arrogance by some.

As he shifted, her eyes went to the curve of his neck, to the tanned exposed skin just above his collar.

Her body tightened as a bolt of desire shot through every womanly part. She knew how he felt beneath those clothes, that solid chest, those sweetly curved biceps, the delicious way his muscles bunched and rippled beneath hot, touchable skin.

As her senses prickled with remembrance, she watched Alex shuffle through the press clippings she'd left open on the table. It took a few moments to recognize his expression but when she did it sent her back a step.

Every muscle in his face, every line had contracted into something so blatantly raw and painful that it made her throat constrict. This whole situation affected him more than he'd ever admit. As she watched him flick through the clippings, a soft curse crossed his lips.

Her heart ached for him at that moment, compassion propelling her forward.

"It's a weird paradox, isn't it?" she said softly.

He turned, the shutters descending as he placed a hand on the stack. "What? Being eviscerated by the press?"

"Having people think you've gotten away with murder, yet being hounded by every news outlet for your exclusive story."

"You get used to it."

"No, you don't." She went to the table and shuffled the clippings back into their folder, determinedly ignoring the minuscule distance separating them. Yet she couldn't ignore the way her entire body tingled under his scrutiny. "No one could."

"And you know what it's been like for me."

She snapped her chin up, barely catching the tail end of his look—a mixture of derision and irritation.

Something inside her gave way. "I've been there, Alex. It may have been on a small scale, I may have only been fifteen but I remember every single humiliating detail." She shoved her hands on her hips, back rigid. "It's all the Spanish press covered for weeks—'Gabriela, the wild twelve-year-old druggie daughter of Senator Juan Valero.' They'd follow us to school, bribe our friends for an exclusive. One even broke into our summer house. We couldn't function, couldn't *breathe* without causing a headline. We moved to Australia to get away from that." She paused for a breath, her face hot. "So don't tell me I don't know what it's like. I've lived it."

Alex stared at her, at the tightly controlled, elegant fury beneath that icy demeanor.

She frowned. "Gabriela never told you?"

"No. She just said your father was appointed to the Spanish embassy."

"He chased that appointment, much to my mother's horror. In her opinion, Australia was an uncultured backwater. My father spent a lot of time and money—not to mention kissing up—to ensure our past faded away."

"So that's why…" At her raised eyebrow, he finished off with, "You're a peacemaker. You always have been."

She shrugged, dropping her eyes. "Am I?"

"Yes. I've never seen you deliberately start an argument."

"Oh, I've started a few," she said dryly.

"Not in public. And I reckon that's why you're in PR. It's why you're so good at it. You know, creating calm in the face of public frenzy."

She blinked, faintly chagrined. "Maybe."

"Definitely." It didn't take a genius to figure that out. Before now he'd never fully recognized Yelena's obsession for calming waves. Yet it was hardly surprising, given what she'd been through. And, he realized, if one person could drag the Rush name out of the gutter, someone who was passionate, compelled and committed, it was Yelena.

Something must have given him away, something he'd let slip that showed on his face, because she was smiling at him, her first honest-to-goodness smile since she'd walked into her office at Bennett & Harper.

"Alex, I need to ask you about—"

"Mmm?"

Yelena swallowed as a familiar look passed over his features. It was his frankly provocative "I want to taste you" look—*that look*—that made her blood zing, exciting all her womanly bits, making her wish for one insane second that he'd do exactly what his eyes promised and kiss her.

The fight-or-flight response snaked low in her gut, her brain commanding her to run. Her leg muscles tingled in preparation, waiting for the signal.

Then the doorbell chimed and she nearly jumped a foot in the air. A fact Alex didn't miss, judging by his grin. She shot him a glare and went to answer the door, unsure if relief or annoyance tossed in her stomach. Both felt dissatisfying.

The waiter swept in and began to set up the meal. By the time he'd left, it was as if their little exchange had never happened. Which was fine considering she'd other things to focus on right now: her stomach began to rumble as Alex removed the warming lids with a flourish.

He'd ordered a large platter of assorted seafood—barbequed calamari, beer-batter fish and delicately crumbed scallops. To one side, there was a bowl of fresh salad with three separate dressings. Next to that, a bowl of crisp chips accompanied by a dish of dressing and crumbly sea salt.

He watched her closely. "You approve?"

"You know I do." Seafood and chips were her favorite—he knew that. A reluctant smile tugged at her mouth. A peace offering?

Then he was pulling out her chair. "Shall we eat?"

Despite Alex's declaration that they needed to discuss business, they filled their plates in silence, two people resolutely focused on that small act of polite domesticity. Yet after Yelena had taken a bite of her food her taste buds exploded, clearing her brain of all else.

"This is amazing!" She savored the delicate flavor of calamari.

Alex smiled, chewing away. "All credit goes to Franco. I stole him from Icebergs in Sydney. Try the chips with the aioli."

She speared a chunky golden chip with her fork, obediently dipping it into the creamy white dressing.

Luxury burst over her tongue and she gave another appreciative groan. But what did her in was Alex's sensual mouth, curved up in amusement. It brought back a moment of pure unadulterated desire so powerful that it staggered her.

"Told you," he murmured before shoving another forkful in his mouth, chewing slowly without taking his eyes from her.

That all-knowing gaze recorded her every movement, from the faltering breath she drew, to the gradual exhale. It was keenly familiar, that almost promissory glint in his eyes, as if the past few months had ceased to exist and he was once again all hers.

Her skin felt so warm she was sure her temperature had risen a few degrees, the air so thick she had trouble clearing her throat. But finally she did.

"I've had a few ideas for your campaign."

A brief flicker of surprise shadowed his eyes. "That was quick."

"That's what you hired me for."

She'd deliberately steered their conversation into neutral waters. So what prompted her tiny pang of disappointment when his eyes suddenly turned serious?

"Go on."

"I think we should start with something local. Some kind of party or celebration that includes the community and Diamond Bay employees." She placed her cutlery on the table and leaned forward. "This resort employs thousands and generates some major tourist dollars. Your tenth anniversary is next year, right?" At his nod, she continued. "So as a lead-up, you could host a party—say the first of September for the first day of spring. It could be a showcase for local talent, too. Chefs, musicians. Artists. Decorators. We can have a main marquee for the art and decorations, then a separate one for the music. And outside we can set up long tables for the food, with Diamond Bay covering any shortfall. It'd be a social and practical event rolled into one."

She paused for a breath, looking at Alex expectantly. But when he remained silent, her broad smile faltered. "Well? What do you think?"

"The first is two weeks away," he finally said.

"I've organized other events in less time. And because we'd be using a lot of external resources and labor, Diamond Falls' workload will be less."

"I see."

"We'd need one of your legal people to take care of the insurance. We'd also need a supplier liaison and a press person. I checked your staff directory—you have a dedicated press office and a banquets division, yes?"

"Yes." He gave his attention to his plate, where he proceeded to cut into a piece of fish with one clean slice. "You've given this some thought."

"I have. Actually, the idea came from your mother."

He looked up, capturing her eyes as he slowly placed the food in his mouth. Yelena nodded. "She was talking about the local talent—musicians, artists—and how she wanted to get involved with them, promote their work to a wider audience."

"I see," was all he said as he chewed. *How could he not*

know this? Finally swallowing, he added, "Do you have some figures, details?"

"I'll need to speak with one of your accounts people... tomorrow?"

He reached for his wineglass and cradled it gently in his hand. "I'll arrange it."

"Great!" Yelena felt relief shade the edges of her satisfied smile and with a nod she refocused on her meal.

Thankfully, discussing local businesses and the physical logistics of arranging the event kept them talking until after coffee. But when Alex called room service to clear the table, Yelena's good mood shattered with her ringing phone.

It was Carlos.

"Where are you?"

"Why?" With a glance at Alex, she quickly walked down the hall and into the bathroom.

"Are you with—" he paused, then almost spat out the words "—Alex Rush?"

"Again, why?" She gently closed the door.

"Dammit, Yelena! I told you to stay away from him."

"You've told me nothing of the sort."

"I would've thought my silence on the subject didn't need elaboration."

She glared at her reflection in the mirror. "I'm not a mind reader, Carlos."

His huff of impatience cranked up her irritation. "What's gotten into you? You used to be so..."

"Compliant?"

"Sensible. People have been talking."

Something in his tone bothered her. A lot. "So what's new?" At his aggrieved sigh, she narrowed her eyes and leaned back on the door. "What? Can't I go about my daily business without some gossip spreading lies?"

Carlos was quick to latch on to that. "So he's a client?"

"I didn't say that."

"But that's what you meant." He sighed. "You need to get yourself a boyfriend, Yelena."

His sanctimoniousness rankled, tiny pinpricks stinging her skin. "Maybe *he's* my boyfriend, Carlos. Maybe he's decided to set me up as his bought-and-paid-for mistress and I'm going to dance naked for him every night. Whatever the reason, it's none of your damn business!"

She jammed her finger on the disconnect button, cloying heat choking her throat. But as she yanked the bathroom door open, she nearly ran smack-bang into Alex.

At the last second she sprang back, skillfully avoiding his steadying hands.

"Everything okay?"

"Fine." She gave him a belligerent look, straightened her T-shirt over her hips and tossed her head.

"Doesn't sound like it."

"It's Carlos." She brushed past him, too irritated to acknowledge the little zing as his body heat briefly enveloped her. "He's being an ass."

Yet as angry as she was, she could still feel Alex's presence close behind as they returned to the living room. "He's…" She threw her hands in the air before flopping down onto the sofa.

"Being Carlos?"

"Yeah."

When she fixed him with a considering look, he met it steadily.

"He thinks you and I…we…" She broke off, feeling the warmth on her cheeks. "I have no idea how he knew I was here."

The tiny stab of guilt hit Alex low. Of course he'd made sure Carlos knew. "Does it matter?"

"It does to him. What on earth did you do to him?"

His jaw tightened involuntarily. Yet his calm words belied

the fury simmering under the surface. "Maybe it's not all my fault."

"I didn't say it was." She frowned, glancing away. "But it's odd. Why would he think we're involved? He's never seen us together...I mean," she added with a flush, "*romantically*. Has he?"

"Not that I know of."

She went on, almost absently, "Sure, we've been to parties, official functions, but we've never been alone—"

"Except at the Christmas ball in July. In the kitchen."

The flush on her face remained, his slow smile aiding its presence. "And I've never been to your office or—" She broke off, eyes rounding. "I have. Once. And Carlos was there."

"When?"

She frowned. "It was September the first. Gabriela's birthday. I remember because she was running late and asked me to pick up the cake then double-check you'd left already. Your..." She paused, swallowing. "Your father turned up."

They both stared at each other. Alex needed no further reminder of that night: it was seared like a permanent scar on his heart. And like the flick of a switch, that hostile, fury-ridden confrontation came screaming back.

You've got a warped sense of what marriage means. Stay the hell away from her or by God I will—

You'll do what? William Rush had spat back. *This is my family*—mine! *No one's lacked for anything. No one would be anything if it weren't for me!*

And you've been destroying us for years, you selfish bastard!

He shook his head, refusing to let the black wave drag him down into that hellhole again. "Carlos was there?"

Yelena nodded slowly. "I saw him leave as I was getting the cake from the kitchen. After we—" her body prickled as she finished lamely "—were in your office."

Alex stared at her in silence, his mind ticking like an overheated engine.

If Carlos had been there...if he'd heard... Then this meant—

He was so sure he'd been right, so hell-bent on bundling the Valeros into one tainted basket that he'd failed to allow for one major flaw.

That Yelena hadn't blabbed to Carlos after all.

He sprang to his feet, realization sending licking flames of humility through his gut. "I have to go."

"Alex?"

He ignored her confused question. Instead he strode across the room, jerked the door open then walked out, refusing to look back.

Seven

Tuesday flew by in a flurry of meetings, phone calls and budget preparations. After liaising with Alex's press and banquet staff, she spent the night working late at the dining table in her suite, organizing, planning, checking then rechecking. The Rushes were first and foremost in her mind, from Alex's odd departure last night to her continued concern about Pam. As for Chelsea... When she'd dropped in with lunch, it was as if her cryptic admission had been erased from history. Instead, they chatted about movies, books and fashion, until work called and Yelena was again swamped.

On Wednesday morning as she booted up her laptop in her temporary office, her mobile phone rang.

It was Juan Valero.

"Hola, Papá."

"Yelena, Carlos told us about your new client."

"Told you what?" Yelena replied in Spanish, shoving her phone under her chin while reaching for a folder on the long desk.

The pause was significant enough for her to frown. Then her father said firmly, "It's Alexander Rush."

"And how would Carlos know?"

"Is it true?"

Yelena sighed and swiveled back to her laptop. She could never lie to her father. "Yes, but it's confidential. You can't say anything to anyone."

"I do not gossip, Yelena." She swallowed nervously. His stern rebuke made her feel nine years old all over again. "And is getting mixed up with that family a wise move?"

His condescending tone irked her. "It's my job, *Papá*."

She could feel the waves of displeasure thunder down the phone. "You are a Valero."

And you remind me every chance you get. "And..?"

"I do not appreciate your tone, Yelena," Juan snapped. "The man has been accused of murder."

"He was not charged."

"Nonetheless, it is not the sort of person—or family—I wish you to associate with."

Uncharacteristic rebellion bubbled up. "My boss decides my clients, not me."

"And what happens when you make partner? Will you get to decide then?"

She glanced up to see Chelsea at the door with a tentative smile, holding a tray. "Can we talk about this later? I have to go."

"Yelena—"

"*Papá,* I'm working."

His aggrieved sigh came down the line. "We will talk when you return home." And he hung up.

Yelena slowly placed her phone back on the desk.

"Breakfast?" Chelsea asked casually and slid the tray onto the conference table. "I didn't see you this morning and I checked—you didn't order room service." She quickly glanced around. "You know, this room *is* a bit spare. Needs more color."

Yelena tipped her head, considering. From Chelsea's overly nonchalant stance to the way her eyes darted, the teenager had more than interior decorating on her mind. "Something blue would be nice."

"And a comfy sofa, a few pillows…" Chelsea trailed off, arranging the cutlery before lifting the warming trays. "There's toast, coffee and fruit. If you don't like, I can always get Franco to make something more fancy…."

"When it comes to food, I'm not a 'fancy' kind of girl." Yelena smiled. "Toast and fruit is great."

They both tackled the food, munching contentedly in silence. After her second piece of toast, Yelena placed her cup of coffee on the table.

"Chelsea. Can we talk about what you said the other night? About your father?"

Chelsea flicked a quick glance at the closed door, her eyes running across the long glass wall to the offices beyond. Her chin went up a fraction. "What about it?"

Such bravado for one so young. Yelena warmed her hands on the cup and leaned forward with a smile. "You know, Gabriela told me you were friends. She used to call you 'Chelsea-bun.'"

Chelsea grinned. "Yeah."

"Between you and me, I think she liked you better than Alex." Yelena winked.

Chelsea laughed then, a sudden rusty sound that made Yelena think she didn't do enough of it.

Then suddenly her smile froze. "What do you mean, 'liked'?"

Yelena looked the confused girl straight in the eye. "I'm going to trust you with something. I've been asked not to announce it, but I think you should know. I'm sorry, Chelsea, but there's no way to put this gently. Gabriela...well, she died."

As Chelsea gaped, mouth wide open, Yelena leaned forward and took her hand.

"How? When...?" She finally managed to choke out, her eyes filling.

"In March. We were in Germany and she was taken to hospital. She'd lost a lot of blood and they just couldn't save her...." Yelena ducked her head as the wave of grief pulled at her legs, threatening to tug her under.

"So it was an accident? Car?"

Faced with the teenager's pooling tears, Yelena could only nod. *Forgive me for the little white lie,* she offered up. *But you know it's necessary.*

With a wrenching sob, Chelsea was suddenly in her arms. Together they held each other, Yelena holding back tears for the death of a sister she'd been forbidden to acknowledge, Chelsea crying for the loss of a friend.

Eventually Chelsea pulled away, swiping at her cheeks self-consciously. Yelena handed her a tissue and offered a smile. "I'm sorry for not telling you sooner."

"That's okay." Chelsea sat back down, her hands shoved between her knees as she leaned forward in her seat.

Yelena began to stack their plates, giving Chelsea time to compose herself.

"I miss her," Chelsea said suddenly.

Yelena nodded. "Yeah, I do, too."

"She... she was the only one I told stuff to."

Yelena paused, giving the girl her full attention. "Like what?"

"Stuff." Chelsea shrugged, her eyes going to Yelena's neat plate stack. She reached for her glass and stuck the straw in her mouth. "What I wanted to do with my life, the places I wanted to visit. She'd been to so many countries and had heaps of stories."

Yelena smiled. "She loved to travel. She used to brag she'd seen every country except Alaska and the Poles."

"Yeah." Chelsea returned the smile. "She was gorgeous but not in a bitchy way, you know? She always had time for me." She tipped her head, studying Yelena. "Like you."

Something warm and satisfying spread across Yelena's heart. "Thank you."

When Chelsea stiffened and glanced up, Yelena followed her eyes to the shadow beyond the glass wall. A second later Alex swung the door open with firm intent.

"It's nine-thirty," he said, glancing from one to the other from his position in the doorway.

"Sure is," Yelena answered, downing the last of her coffee before placing the cup on the tray.

"You've eaten?"

Yelena nodded to their empty plates. "Yep."

"Good."

Alex remained fixed to the spot, hands jammed in his pockets, his casual silence in direct contrast to the tension radiating from his stance. Yelena frowned.

"Did you need something?" she finally ventured.

Alex turned to Chelsea who was slurping her juice with purposeful intent. "Don't you have a class to go to?"

"Not yet."

A ghost of a frown creased his forehead. "Where's Mum?"

"Watching TV."

"What?"

"I dunno, something." Chelsea waved her hand.

"Why don't you go and see if she wants breakfast?"

"I think she's already—"

"Chelsea. Go."

"Fine." In a huff she grabbed up her bag, paused then with a pointed look at her brother, noisily slurped down the last of her juice.

"Go!"

"I'm going!" With a smile and nod at Yelena, Chelsea bounced from the room.

Yelena's mouth tweaked, only to waver when Alex gently closed the door behind him.

"How is your…" He paused then added, "Bella?"

"She's fine."

"Does she need anything?"

Yelena smiled. "Apart from food, sleep, a nappy change and brief entertainment? No. She's only five months old."

"Right."

Yelena tipped her head to the side. "You were what, fifteen when Chelsea was born?"

He nodded. "But I didn't see a lot of her. She was mostly with nannies and housekeepers."

"Your mum seems more like a 'get her hands dirty' kind of parent," Yelena ventured.

"Dad's idea. He was courting investors at the time and needed a wife on his arm."

"Oh." Another unfavorable mark against William Rush. Yelena couldn't imagine not being there for the feeding, the bathing, all the little changes and milestones that made parenthood a constant, wondrous delight.

Her thoughts must have given her away because Alex's brow raised in a slow question.

"Oh, nothing…"

"Tell me," Alex said, leaning against the edge of her desk.

"It's just…" She reached out to shuffle some papers into a neat pile, avoiding his eyes. "I know a lot of people who've gone from school, then uni, to some you-beaut job, focusing on climbing the corporate ladder. They work hard, they party harder, but they're still waiting for something to give their life meaning. A grand passion." She remained intent on rearranging her desk, this time slotting pens into a cup. "A baby is a life-changing experience. It opened up my heart in a new way." She finally glanced up, almost apologetically, as a faint flush spread across her cheeks. "But then, I imagine all mothers feel that way."

A thin film of self-disgust coated Alex's tongue. Quickly he swallowed it. What kind of jerk was he to make her feel embarrassed about that? "The good ones, at least."

She gave him a tiny smile then seemed to gather herself together. "So…do you want to see what I've been working on?"

With a firm nod, Alex pulled up a chair and sat. Thankfully she hadn't mentioned his abrupt departure Monday night and frankly, he'd spent ages trying to wrap his head around it all.

He'd been so damn sure of her involvement that he'd not stopped to think of the possibility of this mess just being Carlos's doing. That Yelena could actually be blameless hadn't factored in at all. So he'd spent yesterday getting things straight in his head, until he'd clicked online and read the late-edition papers.

A painful mix of fury and disgust had tightened his stomach. Another page of salacious lies about William Rush blinked onto his screen, this time from an "anonymous lover."

He'd felt like chucking the monitor across the room. Instead he'd downed one shot of top-notch bourbon, the burning alcohol a painful reminder why he never drank the stuff, before hurling the glass onto the patio where it shattered with a satisfying smash. Yet as he picked up the pieces, his thoughts turned not to Carlos, but to Yelena.

Christ, when had a decision—any decision—been this bloody difficult?

With Yelena now here, his plans half-complete, he realized he still needed her. As his PR person, yes, because she was damn good at what she did. And Pam and Chelsea seemed to like her. But now, as he gave her his full attention, a different kind of need began to filter in as the minutes ticked by. If it wasn't her "come here and smell me" scent twisting his insides, then it was the way she lit up as she got into her spiel. She gestured in typical European fashion, using her whole body to convey her message. When she smiled, her mouth made tiny dimples in her cheeks.

In the past he'd tried to make her smile as much as possible.

So the blame for the press leaks lay firmly at Carlos's feet. But she still had a child, one that wasn't his.

Did it twist his gut every time he thought about Yelena and some faceless guy in bed together? Hell, yes.

Why?

Because…because… He tightened his jaw and stared at the figures Yelena slid across the desk.

She's mine.

Fierce possessiveness snaked through his body, sending it into a craving, bittersweet ache. He still wanted her in his bed—that much hadn't changed.

"As you can see, the costs for decorations will be—" She ended up on a gasp as he reached for the papers and got her hand instead.

Their gazes collided and held. Her eyes rounded before those long lashes fluttered down, severing the moment when she withdrew.

For a perverse second, he craved something more. But then it was gone and amazingly, the loss saddened him.

After a moment's study of the papers, he said, "So let's hear the rest of your plan."

With a nervous swallow, Yelena began. "So after the party, your mother suggested focusing on the local community."

At his curious look, she continued, "She's got a deep love of this area and really wants to help the people, like setting up a scholarship program and donating to a few charities."

"And what about her work in Canberra? Won't that suffer if she's taking on more?"

"Alex…" She hesitated. "Did she not tell you?"

"Tell me what?"

With a flush, she said, "I thought Pam told you. Yesterday we talked and she—"

"Tell me what?"

Yelena frowned. "She's still officially donating to those charities. But she resigned from the boards."

His mouth flattened into a grim line. "I see."

"Pam *wanted* to resign. Alex, listen to me. She hated the politics and after those rumors started spreading, she—" She paused then said, "Look, I don't want to get in the middle of family issues here—"

"You're not. I told them both why you're here, which should make your job a lot easier."

Yelena knew this wasn't about the campaign. But she still nodded. "Thank you. But if we're all not on the same page—"

"I'm doing this for them," he said tightly.

"I know. But they may have differing opinions. Chelsea, for one, seems—" she paused, searching for the right word "—hostile. Why don't I organize a meeting so we can talk things over?"

At his inscrutable countenance, Yelena's heart crumbled a little. "I'm here to help you. All of you," she continued.

He pointed at the paper, shrugging off her concern. "And this?"

Yelena sighed then picked one page up. "A list of press we'll be alerting for the party, which will start around four p.m. and go on after sunset. We also need to work on the guest list. Pam's given me hers, so it's just up to you."

He barely glanced at the list before his eyes came back to her. "Have dinner with me."

She blinked, confused. "Sorry?"

"Have dinner with me."

"Why?"

"Why not?"

She leaned back in her chair. "I don't work after six."

"A baby sleeps, Yelena. A lot."

Yelena stared at him while he maintained composure with ridiculous ease. Her mind quickly flicked through the pros and cons of his invitation. The little morsels of information he'd shared about his family weren't enough. There were still too many questions. Surely she could spend one evening eating dinner to uncover more?

"Okay."

The half smile he gave her curled her toes and like Pavlov's dog, she smiled blindly back, heart racing.

"Excellent." He rose, taking her notes with him. "Wear jeans and be in the lobby at six-twenty."

"Wait—I thought we were eating in my room?"

That smile again, this time with a slightly decadent edge. "The fresh air will do you good. I'll organize Jasmine for Bella. Six-twenty."

When he was gone, Yelena realized too late that a smiling, charming Alexander Rush was way more worrisome than an angry, combative one.

Eight

Later that day, Yelena was in her suite working on her laptop while Chelsea sat cross-legged on her lounge room carpet.

"How long have you been dating my brother?"

Absently, Yelena looked up from her laptop. "What makes you think we're dating?"

"Oh, come on!" Chelsea rolled her eyes in mock derision and recrossed her legs. "You've both got that look about you—that 'I want to jump on you as soon as we're alone' vibe."

"Chelsea!" What the devil could she say without outright lying? But damn, the girl was intuitive, she had to give her that. "That's… that's…"

"None of my business?" Chelsea picked up a rattle and gently waved it in front of a gurgling Bella.

"Exactly." She managed to hide her grin behind her laptop. Then she closed it with a sigh and stood, giving her back a good stretch. "Now I have to go and have a shower."

"For dinner, huh?"

"Well, yeah."

"With Aaaaalex?" Chelsea winked, making kissy sounds.

"You…!"

Chelsea squealed and ducked as a small sofa pillow flew harmlessly past.

With a wide smile Yelena scooped up Bella and marched off down the hall. But when she emerged half an hour later, all primed and polished, the look Chelsea gave was frankly disapproving.

"What?" Yelena did a three-sixty, tweaking the drop-shoulder of her purple knitted sweater.

"What's with that tight hairdo?"

Yelena's hand went up to the French roll she'd painstakingly secured. "You don't like it?"

"No. Let your hair fall down but have the sides up. Go to the mirror and I'll show you."

The teenager sat her on a dining chair in front of the hallway mirror then flicked on the light.

"You're good at this," Yelena said as Chelsea began to deftly refix her long curls. "Ever thought of a career in fashion?"

"All the time."

"So why don't you?" Yelena asked.

She caught the glimmer in Chelsea's eyes just before she refocused on Yelena's hair. "Because it's complicated. Alex and I had a row the other night. I *am* good at tennis and a lot of money's gone into my training. And Alex and Mum—"

"Forget about what other people think for one second. What do *you* want to do?"

"I want…" Her voice drifted off then she added firmly, "To study fashion design. Maybe work at a magazine. There. You're done."

Yelena stood. "Then you should do that."

As they both stared at Yelena's reflection, Yelena could feel the mood take on a subtle change. And when she met

Chelsea's eyes through the mirror, she saw something flash across the girl's face.

"I need to tell you something...something personal."

"Okay." Yelena turned, giving the teen her full attention.

"It was my father... I..." Chelsea's eyes skittered away before coming back in sudden defiance. "I want to make a statement. A public statement. Can you help me write a press release?"

Yelena's brow furrowed. "About what?"

"I'm sick and tired of everyone making out like my father was some kind of living god."

The sudden venom in Chelsea's voice forced Yelena back a step. After a moment, she said slowly, "What did he do, Chelsea?"

Chelsea glanced to the door. When she spoke, it all tumbled out in a tight whisper. "He was a control freak. I mean, *major*. All of my friends were handpicked because of their parents. I played tennis because it was fun but then *he* decided I needed a coach and then it was four hours a day, every day. It sucked. He went mental when I said I wanted to do designing. And..." She petered off and glanced away. "He treated Mum like an idiot, always checking what she wore, who she saw. He'd start yelling over some stupid little thing, and she'd... I'd..." She flushed and glanced away, fiddling with the hem of her frayed T-shirt. "It'll take more than a few nasty articles to do him justice."

"Chelsea..." As the pieces in Yelena's head began to slowly click into place, a horrible thought occurred. "Do you have proof about his cheating?"

Here she looked uncomfortable. "No. But I wouldn't be surprised if he was."

"Have you talked to Alex about this?"

"No." She shook her head. "This is my problem. I didn't want to lump this on his plate, not with everything else that's been going on."

Yelena's mind began to toss. "I think—"

The bell to the front door chimed.

"That'll be Jasmine. Look, Chelsea," she said softly, placing her hands on the girl's shoulders. "I'd strongly suggest you talk to your mother about this first. Let her know how you feel and see if you can both come up with something together. Then we can talk it over with Alex, okay?"

Chelsea's blue eyes churned with all the intensity of a storm at sea. "Okay."

"Good. I want to help you."

Chelsea nodded then jerked her head to the door. "You'd better go. Alex is a bear when he's left waiting."

Yelena rolled her eyes and gave her a smile. "I know."

As Yelena stepped out from the swooshing glass entrance doors, the sight of Alex stopped her heart for a second.

Oh, mercy me. He was every woman's bad-boy fantasy in hard-core black leather—from the jacket that stretched across broad shoulders, down to tight pants that cupped a perfect behind and high-topped boots encasing long legs.

She grabbed her necklace and ran her thumb over the smooth glass. Pounding blood sped to her head, sending her skin into a full body flush. And when he glanced up from checking his watch and spotted her, the will-melting smile he gave made her want to run right into his arms and kiss him.

That just would not do.

Flustered, she glanced around, her eyes coming to rest on a shiny, sleek…

"Motorbike."

Alex's smile broadened and her breath hooked again. "Not just any motorbike… A Shinya Kimura. The man's a legend when it comes to customizing." He slowly ran his hand over the mirrored metal, taking his time to savor the polished surface.

Yelena swallowed, suppressing a small shiver at his unguarded raw joy.

"And it's the only way to see the Outback. Here." He tossed her a helmet from the seat then grabbed his.

Obediently she pulled it over her head then fiddled with the clip.

"Let me." With his warm fingers at her jaw she tried not to think about how eagerly her body reacted to him, how she secretly thrilled at the slightest contact.

While she stood there like a nervous teenager on a first date, he reached across the seat and produced a leather jacket. Slowly, with the deft intimacy of a familiar lover, he spread the jacket around her shoulders, waiting until she'd got it on before zipping it up.

In the cold, still night, she heard every single suggestive snick of those metal teeth snapping together, a signal for her blood to pump in earnest while she tried to control her runaway thoughts.

He slowly dragged the zipper up, the bright blue depths of his eyes sparking with humor… and something much more dangerous. Her hand jerked reflexively, seeking the comfort of her necklace before she realized what she was doing and forced it back down. His keen eyes didn't miss that, judging by the way his mouth tweaked into a smile.

Then suddenly he withdrew. "All done. Let's go."

Desperate to focus on something else, she stared at the bike and drew a slow, steady breath into her lungs.

"How do I get on?"

He grinned, threw a leg over the bike then glanced expectantly over his shoulder. "Like that."

Okay. With a nod she placed her hands on his shoulders, centered her weight then threw her leg over.

Thanks to the seat angle, she immediately slid forward and her crotch bumped firmly against his butt. She quickly wiggled back but Alex slapped her lightly on the thigh.

"Stop moving. You'll upset the balance."

He swiftly kick-started the engine and the bike leapt to life in one almighty roar.

"Hold on!" Alex yelled over the noise as the bike jumped forward with a gutsy growl. Yelena squealed, grabbed Alex's waist and they slowly made their way out onto the single road leading from Diamond Bay.

It was a strange and wonderful experience, her first time on a motorbike. The speed, the air streaming over her body, the absolute vulnerability of being out in the open, forced a laugh from her throat. As they flew along the road, she was swept up by exhilaration, her lips stretching in a wide smile. It was natural, automatic that she settle farther into the seat, wedging herself firmly up against Alex's wide back, his powerful leather-clad muscles in total control of the throbbing beast beneath them.

Yet as the minutes stretched and the road got more rugged as they sped towards Ayers Rock, one thing was becoming increasingly obvious. She was getting turned on.

At first she thought it was the throbbing metal beneath her butt, or maybe the way Alex's legs felt between her thighs, the heat from those hard muscles seeping through her jeans. It certainly didn't help that there were only thin layers of worn denim between her body and his. No, all those things did affect her, but it was every tiny bump in the tarmac that sent reverberating vibrations through her skin, stimulating her senses into overdrive.

After the second little surprise, she gave an inward groan and bit down on her lip. *Damn.* With her crotch wedged snugly up against Alex's backside, raw sensation shot up her body, arousal tingling at every tiny jolt.

By the time Alex slowed down, her mouth felt as if she'd indulged in a slightly rough, hour-long kissing session.

When they finally stopped, Yelena's legs wobbled as he helped her from the bike.

"It's a bit rough at first—you'll get used to it." He pulled off his helmet, a smile crinkling his eyes into wicked humor which only exacerbated her predicament further.

Get used to it? Did that mean he was planning on staying in her life? She removed her helmet and shook her hair out just before Alex grabbed her shoulders and pivoted her.

"What—?"

"Check that out."

With the setting sun at their backs, the sky had taken on a dusky blue-grey tinge, a smattering of cloud spreading across the sky like thin cobwebs. And smack-bang in the middle sat Ayers Rock, its burnt orange body seeming to swell and glow as the sun crept farther down.

Seconds edged into minutes as they both stood there, watching the sky deepen and darken, changing the Rock's orange into fiery red then eventually burnt amber.

Speechless, Yelena watched the light stretch farther and farther until finally, Ayers Rock became one massive, dark shadow on the horizon.

"Wow," she finally breathed.

"Yep. As stunning and unique as Diamond Falls is, I never get sick of seeing that." He put a hand at her back. "Shall we eat?"

He guided her towards glowing lights and they emerged from the scrub into a small, carpeted clearing surrounded by patio warmers. In surprised silence, Yelena saw a waiter put the final touches on a full dinner service, complete with white tablecloth and silver.

Oh, my. She glanced up at Alex who was wearing a satisfied smile, then back to the table, her fingers working the gold chain of her necklace.

Alex dismissed the waiter. The man nodded, stepped into a four-wheel drive—another fact she'd failed to register—and slowly drove away into the night.

The clearing gave off seductive heat and light, the air

rife with warm intimacy. When he pulled out her chair she murmured her thanks.

As he sat, Yelena reached for her water glass and took a gulp.

"Carbonara?" Alex offered a dish.

"Thank you." She took the bowl of pasta and spooned some on her plate. "So I talked with Kyle in accounts this afternoon, and I should have final costings tomorrow morning. Cathie, your press officer, has helped with the local side of things and together we're drafting a national release." She picked up her fork. "The sooner we announce it the better, then we can issue the invitations. Can you give me your list first thing tomorrow?"

"Sure."

Yelena blinked, put her fork down and reached for her wineglass. "Thanks again for letting Pam and Chelsea know why I was here."

He nodded, going back to his food. "I thought honesty was best."

Yelena felt a tiny pang and reached for a bread roll, deftly breaking it apart. "Yes." But after she popped the bread in her mouth, she added, "I've also drafted up a six-month plan to coincide with Diamond Falls' anniversary."

Alex slowly lifted his eyes to meet hers. "Can you do me a favor?"

"Yes?"

"Can we not spoil the view by talking about work tonight?"

"Oh." She'd psyched herself up to ask questions: now they all just fizzled on her tongue. "But—"

"Please."

Her skin tingled at that one small word. "Okay."

Perturbed, she concentrated on her food. "This is amazing!" She forked another piece, shoved it in then chewed, rolling her eyes. "I think I'm in love."

Alex chuckled. "Sorry. Franco's already taken."

Yelena gave a melodramatic sigh. "The good ones always are."

Their eyes met casually across the table, both smiling. But when the moment held longer than necessary, Yelena sensed the mood shift gears. This was more than just two people eating dinner. The darkness around them was absolute: it felt as if they were the last two people left on earth. And as Alex studied her over the top of his wineglass, those clear blue eyes slowly took on a darker hue in the dim light.

She quickly stabbed at the pasta.

"Slow down." She heard the humor in his voice. "The food's going nowhere."

"But it's so delicious."

"Speed isn't always best." He placed his fork slowly on the plate, giving her the full blast from his intense eyes. "It's better to savor everything—the taste, the texture—rather than dash through to the end. It can make the rewards so much more—" He paused for deliberate effect, those darkened eyes full of delight "—pleasurable."

She nearly choked. *Dammit.* She tried for a cool stare, but his roguish smile did vaguely illegal things to her body.

Smothering her panic, she dropped her eyes to her plate. Despite the hurt she'd caused him, despite their unrequited fling that had fizzled before it had even started, Alex's intention was crystal clear.

She looked him straight in the eyes. "Did you invite me to dinner to try and seduce me, Alex?"

Her directness didn't faze him. "Do you want me to?"

Her limbs became suddenly lethargic. "No," she lied.

"Why not?" His mouth curled.

Because I don't think I can get over you a second time. "Why would you want to?"

One dark eyebrow lifted. "Answering a question with a question, Yelena?"

She sighed, refolding her napkin to keep her hands occupied. "We hurt each other, Alex. Our past is complicated."

"Yes. But we're here. Now."

He rose with the fluid grace of a dancer, a powerful expanse of potent male. She had to crank her neck up to meet his eyes.

"I'm your PR manager." Nervous now, she, too, stood. But that didn't stop him from encroaching on her personal space.

"Does Bennett & Harper have some morality clause I don't know about?"

How the hell had he gotten so close? His familiar scent tightened her senses, sending subversive shivers over her skin. He smelt of leather, of passion and defiance and warmth. Of losing control. Of Alex.

"Morality clause…?" she choked out. "No."

When his fingers slid slowly between hers, linking them in a shockingly intimate touch, her senses jolted into overdrive.

"See?" He lifted their entwined fingers, his gaze full of secret knowledge. "We have something here."

"It doesn't mean it's right."

"Doesn't mean it's wrong, either."

"Alex…"

She heard the rumble in his throat, just as his eyes briefly closed. "Do you have any idea what my name on your lips does to me?"

And suddenly the time for talking was over.

Alex didn't waste a second on niceties—on the contrary, he took it as if her acquiescence was a given. As if it were his right. And in many ways it was. They'd already been as close as two people could be without actual consummation. And if she were honest with herself, Yelena had missed him. Missed the way his laugh engulfed her like warm flames. Missed his off-beat humor and flirty banter. Missed the feel of his skin against hers. Missed the sensual curve of his mouth and the way it made her want to lose herself, control be damned.

When she leaned in, mouth trembling, a bolt of triumph cleaved into Alex's brain. She wanted him—he'd *made* her want him. Yet in the next instant, white-hot desire saturated every sense, every muscle in his body. He growled, a sound that felt half wild, half uncontrollable, the way she'd always made him feel, and roughly pulled her up against his chest.

She made a small sound but didn't protest, which only fired him up even more. His mouth dipped down, ready to claim hers, but in the last moment, she shoved his chest, her palms hot, knowing she could feel his heart pounding through his shirt.

He stared into her dark eyes, their long lashes heavy with arousal. His blood pounded solidly, breath catching. Did she not want—?

"Let me."

The warm whisper skimming across his mouth did him in. All he wanted to do was rip off her clothes and take her on the ground, surrounded by this raw, primitive backdrop, yet he remained rock still, his groin throbbing with need.

She gently placed her hands at the back of his neck and slid her fingers up through his hair, murmuring appreciatively as she stroked his nape. And as his senses pitched, she pulled his head down.

Her lips brushed his for a second. Then another. She dragged in a breath, almost as if kissing him were somehow painful. But then her eyes opened and a smile spread across her entire face, a smile so full of sensual knowledge that he couldn't help but answer it with one of his own.

Because in the sweetness of her kiss, the pureness she'd given him, he didn't have a hope in hell of keeping his distance. Nothing short of a cyclone could stop him now.

As if sensing the thin line he teetered on, she kissed him again, this time with her eyes wide open, those chocolate-velvet depths reaching in, grabbing what was left of his control and yanking on it, hard.

Yelena felt as if every inch of her skin had completely exploded, that every touch, every smell, every taste was just too much to stand. His arms wrapped her tight up against him, his hard, throbbing maleness jamming into her belly with purposeful intent. The familiar smell of his skin engulfed her, every breath she took filling her up. And the taste…oh, his taste was something she'd always loved. She'd missed that. His mouth covered her bottom lip, gently sucking on the swell. He nibbled, he teased for long, sensual seconds. Then, finally he committed, capturing her mouth and twisting her head into a deep, heart-stopping kiss.

His tongue swept past her lips, teasing hers, encouraging her to respond. So she did, with all the pent-up passion and desire she'd locked away these past months.

Slowly, through the drugging waves of desire, she felt him turn her around and in the next second, the back of her thighs bumped up against the table. Groaning, Alex broke the kiss.

"I always wanted to do this."

And with a grin, he leaned in and cleared the table with one sweep of his arm.

The terrible crash of falling plates and dishes made her gasp, even as a giggle filled her throat.

"I can't wait," he added at her wide eyes.

Her skin flushed hot.

In one easy movement, he cupped her bottom and lifted her onto the table and they kissed again, this time with Alex jammed hard between her thighs. Dazed and drunk from his kisses, she barely felt him unsnap the buttons of her jeans, but when his fingers grazed inside to caress her warmth on the way down, she groaned, hot, demanding desire filling her limbs, her lungs.

He managed to peel both her jeans and knickers off and she gasped as her naked bottom made contact with the cold table. Then his hands were on her knees, caressing her skin beneath warm palms. She shivered.

"Cold?"

She shook her head and his wolfish grin shot her pulse sky-high. That's what she remembered, the way that devilish smile transformed his sculptured face into sin. Desire, so often cloaked in caution, now blazed from his azure eyes.

He studied her, watching her every expression, every tiny movement as his hands continued their excruciatingly slow journey upwards. They stroked her thighs, kneading the muscle beneath her hot skin. First outside, tracing every curve, then slowly, sensuously dipping in to the soft flesh of her inner thighs. When her body quivered in response he chuckled, but still she kept her eyes fixed on his, determined not to break first.

He raised one eyebrow, his look frankly seductive. *Just try it,* her expression said, even as her mouth teased upwards.

Suddenly he fell to his knees, eased her legs apart and the world stopped spinning.

He kissed her inner thigh, his hot breath stirring her curls and eliciting another shiver.

"Relax, Yelena, and enjoy it."

On trembling arms, she leaned back with a groan and gave herself up to the pleasure of pure sensation.

His mouth, warm and insistent, met the most intimate part of her and she jerked, gasping. She'd craved him before, needed his touch so desperately it had hurt. But now, as his tongue skillfully made love to her, every past desire faded into pale comparison.

"Alex…" She heard her half plea, half beg, but felt no shame. His tongue and mouth teased her into a frenzy, building her up with such ridiculous ease she had to bite down on her lip, to hold on to the climax that swelled so close to the surface.

Just when she thought she was doomed, she felt him ease back, his mouth placing gentle kisses along her inner thigh.

She gritted her teeth, groaning her frustration aloud.

He stroked her thighs, nuzzling his chin against her damp skin. "Come for me, Yelena."

All she could do was whimper her acquiescence, her mind whirling with a thousand colors and sensations. Yet she was acutely aware of Alex returning to her, of his skillful tongue as it dipped in and out of her core, his stubbled chin creating rough erotic friction as it rubbed against her hot, sensitive nub.

Her most secret scent surrounded Alex, filling every sense and stoking his lust until he could hardly think straight. Her thighs quivered, he felt her body charge with the sweet release even before he heard her small cry of pleasure.

His groin pressed excruciatingly hard against his fly and he gritted his teeth to force it under control, waiting until Yelena climaxed before he freed himself.

She did, loudly, almost triumphantly. Animal satisfaction charged though his veins, a grunt of victory on his lips. With a final kiss to that sweet flesh on her inner thigh, he swiftly stood and yanked down his jeans.

The picture she presented—leaning back on her elbows, gorgeous face an erotic picture of female satiation as her hair tumbled over one shoulder and down her back—was all it took. Needing no further encouragement, he quickly stepped between her legs, fumbled with the condom packet he'd pulled from his jacket, rolled it on then buried himself in her hot wetness.

Their breath came out in perfect unison, sweet pleasure echoing in the raw, still air.

Spots danced behind his eyes, forcing him to pause, to savor the exquisite, almost painful pleasure of her warmth closing around him. With gritted teeth he waited for control, barely registering that Yelena had removed her top and bra and now lay completely bare for him.

His eyes widened at the sight. Lush curves, defined waist,

breasts a man could lose himself in. He leaned forward, gathering her up and burying his face in the valley between those beautiful mounds. The deep breath he took spun his head.

"Lord, Yelena," he breathed into her skin. "If the world ended tonight, I'd die a happy man."

He felt the laughter rumble through her body, yet when his mouth latched on to one brown erect nipple, she gasped.

He grinned.

"You…" Yelena breathed, before longing obliterated her rebuke. His tongue was now intent on her hard nipple, flicking over and over until she began to squirm.

Inside, he tightened in response.

Oh… Slowly his eyes met hers, now navy with desire. His mouth curled into a smile, partially hidden by the curve of her breast, yet it still had the power to make her wet. Then he left that breast, crossing to the other with no great urgency while inside, she could feel everything build up again.

"Alex, please…"

"Settle," he crooned, placing a hand on her belly as if she was a horse ready to bolt, sending her impatience skyrocketing.

She jerked her hips, squeezing her inner muscles with a soft growl and was rewarded by his tight gasp. Unable to stop herself, she wrapped her arms around his neck, pulled him down and whispered something so outrageously erotic that it stunned even herself.

But it had the desired effect. His groan was pure animal, sending her desire off the charts. He began to move, deep, long thrusts that forced every breath to rush out on the down stroke while every inch of her skin sang with pleasure on the up.

Alex felt the familiar aching joy of orgasm blast him in one almighty wave, only seconds behind Yelena. Every muscle screamed for release as pleasure ripped through him, exploding. He heard a guttural groan in the air, knew it must be his, shocked yet primitively proud to be claiming this moment, this woman, as his.

She moved under him, slick and hot, her nipples pebbling as a cool breeze whispered between them. He reached out, an unsteady hand cupping one breast, warming the cooling flesh.

The moment hung, lengthened, the only sound their mingled breath as heart rates began to slow.

When she shivered, he withdrew, a soft murmur her only reaction.

His withdrawal left Yelena suddenly bereft, the cold air pricking her skin. She quickly reached for her clothes, hearing him do the same.

For some odd reason, her nerves jumped, and not in a good way. As she snapped on her jeans, she heard him flip out his phone, curtly directing his staff to clear away what was left of their meal. All the while, a silent strangeness sat between them. She wanted—needed—to say something more but the words just wouldn't form. She bent to zip up her boots. *Say something. Anything.* Yet the only sound was a lone dingo howling in the distance.

"Yelena."

"Please don't say anything to spoil it, Alex." She zipped up her jacket with stiff fingers, refusing to meet his eyes. She didn't have to see him to know he was frowning. She'd always been astute to his moods—especially irritation.

A moment passed before he said quietly, "Are you ready to go?"

She shoved her hands in her jean pockets and nodded, focusing on the bike and the dry dusty scrub surrounding them—everything but him.

They crunched through the grass and sand in silence. She took the helmet he proffered then swung her leg over the bike, covering a wince as her tender thighs screamed in protest.

As they drove back to Diamond Falls, Yelena allowed herself the guilty luxury of his warmth, his powerful body between her legs. Just like it had been, gloriously hard and naked, pleasuring her not more than ten minutes ago.

Thoughts whirled as the night tore past with cold, sharp fingers. Chemistry they had. But a future? Not when there was too much past between them, so many secrets that weren't hers to reveal.

You can't tell anyone. Not a single soul. For Bella's safety, for Yelena's, Gabriela had sworn her to secrecy. Which meant she couldn't tell Alex the truth. Ever.

She stared off into the night as tears welled then fell down her cheeks before the helmet's thick padding quickly absorbed them.

Nine

The next morning Pam, Alex and Yelena gathered around the conference table in Yelena's office.

Yelena had dressed conservatively in a pair of dark gray pants and a three-quarter-sleeved aqua silk shirt. She'd slicked her hair back, twisting it into an elaborate knot at the base of her neck. Yet every time Alex glanced at her, she might as well have been only wearing underwear the way her skin warmed. And then last night's memories quickly followed, causing every intimate part to tingle and leaving her with an uncomfortable feeling of longing.

Ahh. Last night.

When they'd returned to Diamond Bay, she'd eased off the bike before he'd barely killed the engine and offered a quick "Thank you for dinner" before practically fleeing to her room without a backwards glance.

Thank you for dinner? How lame was she?

Now she pointedly looked away, trying to ignore the

delicious curve of his bottom lip. Lips that had made her climax again and again…

More like, *thank you for rocking my world.*

"Do you want coffee, Yelena?"

She snapped her eyes up to Pam, who had a cup in hand.

"Thank you." She accepted with a smile and took a scalding sip.

Quickly she replaced the cup and drew her notepad forward.

"So I thought we could talk about where we're at with this campaign." She paused, looking at each one in turn before continuing. "We all know the press's direction these last few months. My aim is to turn that around."

"How can you make everyone forget what's been spread in the papers?" Alex asked, one eyebrow raised.

"I can't. We need to focus on the good stuff—charity and community works that will counteract all that gossip."

"You mean we need to suck up."

"No," she said firmly. "I don't want to do anything you'd be uncomfortable with. For example, Pam—" she smiled at Alex's mother "—I love your party idea. In fact, what do you think about calling it the 'Sunset Party'? We could use the gorgeous Outback sunset colors as our signature—red, yellow, dark blue, black—" she refused to falter when her eyes briefly met Alex's "—on decorations and invitations. I have an action plan we can work on together if you'd like."

Pam's face lit up. "I'd be happy to. I also thought we could hire out our boutique clothing for the locals who want to go all out. That way they can dress up but not think we're handing out charity."

Yelena smiled. "That's a great idea. So looking further along—in the next few months it will be slow but steady. One thing I want to address is interviews. Television only, because I can get final edit approval and unlike print, there's less room for misinterpretation. I have contacts with a few stations so I was going to push for *A Current Affair* and—"

"What would we say?" Alex interjected.

Yelena met his combative gaze but before she could answer he added, "Let me rephrase that—what do we *need* to say?"

Yelena leaned back in her chair. "The truth."

His face turned dark. "The public has the truth."

"Not in your own words, it doesn't."

When Alex opened his mouth, Pam interjected, "Yelena's right, Alex. You haven't said anything about—" she hesitated "—that night."

"Mum." Just like that, Alex's anger deflated. "Do you really want to dredge that up again?"

A meaningful look passed between them, one that brought a scowl to Alex's brow and lurched Yelena's burning curiosity into overdrive.

"Leave that with us," Alex finally said in a tone that indicated no further discussion. "What else do you have?"

"Alex." Yelena said firmly, linking her fingers together on the tabletop. "I've been working in PR ever since I left uni, nearly eight years ago. I've had a hand in hundreds of campaigns, from musicians, politicians, doctors and bankers Australia-wide."

"What—"

"Please, let me finish. You chose me because I'm damn good at my job. So can you please trust me to do it?"

She met his silent scrutiny head on, even as her mind suddenly flashed back to last night, to his warm, skillful fingers, his passion-riddled face, the decadent smile as he swooped down for another kiss.

Her skin flared, shocking her. She shook her head, desperate to refocus. "I know it's… difficult sometimes, to open up and reveal things you'd rather keep private. But I need to know you have confidence in me handling this campaign."

"I do," he replied without hesitation.

"So what is it? You're the client," she stressed, determined to cement that fact in her mind. "Do you think I'd do something without your approval?"

"No."

"Then trust me." She slid a list forward, one for each of them. "Here's what I'm going to focus on these next six months. Interviews, yes, but only with reporters I have a standing relationship with." She met Pam's eyes fleetingly. "I can trust these people to be fair and compassionate."

"Really."

Alex's snort of derision irritated her. "Yes. Believe it or not, there are some good guys out there." She nodded to the list and changed tack. "Besides the obvious interviews, there are a few nonofficial things that can subtly boost our profile without taking center stage—*Woman's Weekly* holds an annual Mother's Day shoot, featuring seven high-profile mothers and their children, for example."

Pam looked up and nodded. "I like that."

Encouraged, Yelena smiled.

"'An Australia Day event,'" Alex read. "'Guest spot on *Better Homes and Gardens*'…"

Yelena nodded. "With your solar energy and water recycling, Diamond Falls has an excellent green policy. The public loves the environmental angle, especially from a high-profile business. If you're willing, we can look at a 'give back to the earth' plan, where we can, say, support and fund the reintroduction of native wildlife that's under threat in the area."

"The Gouldian finch," Pam said quickly, naming the tiny, distinctive purple, yellow, green and blue birds. "It's endangered here, as are the golden bandicoot and the loggerhead turtle. I have details and Web sites with more information," she added. "And the Alice Springs Bird Festival runs mid-September, so I'd love to get involved in that somehow."

"I'm sure we can. Thanks, Pam." Instinctively, Yelena knew

she'd hit on something important, something that mattered to Alex's mother. Passion for a cause meant drive, which was always positive.

"'Chelsea fashion magazine intern'?" Alex read from the list.

"Yes. This one has an added bonus," Yelena said. "I know *Dolly*'s senior editor is planning a series of 'dream job' articles starting January, and 'fashion intern' is one of them. A photographer and reporter would follow her around for a day, taking snaps and letting readers know what she does." She looked over at Pam, adding, "Of course, I haven't mentioned this to Chelsea. It's just ideas at the moment and totally subject to approval, of course."

The moment of silence spread, until Pam said slowly, "I think Chelsea would love it."

"What about school?" Alex said.

"She's doing fine with tutors, Alex," Pam assured him.

"Her tennis?"

Pam gave him a long, meaningful look. "She's never wanted to pursue it professionally, darling. And now she has a chance to do something she's truly passionate about."

Alex paused, his expression unreadable. "We should talk about this later," he finally said.

"There's nothing to discuss. I've made up my mind."

Surprise flitted across his face before he shut it down. "Okay."

An odd feeling attached itself to Yelena's skin like remnants of a Band-Aid that refused to disappear even after you ripped the thing off. It continued to stick until their meeting broke up and she finally felt compelled to act.

"Alex? Can I talk with you a moment?"

He nodded, closed the door but remained standing. Nervous, she got to her feet then spent a few seconds silently reworking what she wanted to say in her head.

"I know what you're thinking," Alex finally said.

"Oh?"

"Yeah. And in reply, yes, it was good—no, great. And no, it doesn't have to change anything."

She blinked, startled. "That's not what I was—"

"Yelena, you don't owe me anything," he said shortly. "We haven't exactly promised each other fidelity. Hell," he snorted, a terrible self-derogatory sound. "Given our past, that'd be a stretch anyway."

What? Yelena frowned, her mind whirling with confusion until an awful clarity dawned. He was letting her off the hook for getting pregnant with another man. Worse, he was implying what they had hadn't been all that important anyway. Her heart thudded sickeningly as an awful thought reared up.

It made perfect sense from his perspective.

She swallowed that pain, that dreadful searing hurt he'd delivered with such worldly blasé. *Later. Later, when you're alone.* "Actually, that's not what I wanted to talk to you about. It's your mother."

A frown skittered across his brow. "Why?"

"Do you want to sit?"

"No."

She sighed. "Okay. Look, I think there's something going on with her…" She paused, searching for the right words. "Something she's not saying."

"Like what?"

"Well, it's more of a feeling, a sense I get when we talk." At Alex's narrowed eyes, she added, "For instance, she never mentions your father unless I bring him up. She's not overly affected by all the infidelity accusations. I know he was a brilliant businessman, a self-made man and most are absolute perfectionists."

"Your point?"

Boy, this wasn't any easier even now she'd verbalized it. "Did your parents have a good marriage? Was everything okay?"

He gave her a thorough going-over, eyes astute, hands resting on his hips. Finally he said coolly, "And how is this any of your business?"

She flushed. "I thought—"

"I hired you to do a job, Yelena, not psychoanalyze my family. I'd appreciate you sticking with that. Now if you don't mind, I have a phone conference."

Leaving her openmouthed and cheeks flushed, Alex turned and stalked out the door.

It was over, buried with William Rush. He could not—would not—dig about in the past. It didn't affect just him; it had repercussions for his entire family.

It was better this way, putting Yelena back in her rightful place as his PR consultant. Keeping her focused on her job providing positive spin.

Better, better, better. His feet echoed the chant as he strode down the hall, back to his office. So why did he feel like such a jerk?

He slammed his office door behind him, the sound shaking the walls, reverberating down the hall.

Amongst all the peripheral crap going on in his life, the one constant was his dark, burning need for that woman. Yes, Carlos had betrayed his trust and that would live with him until the day he died. But Yelena... Lord, she'd killed him when she'd disappeared. The one person he thought he could count on, the only one not involved in the media circus of his life and she'd not only wormed her way under his armor but had also taken his trust and ground it into the dirt.

He'd been mentally bereft.

He swung away from the door, towards the expansive view from crystal-clear windows.

His world had been black-and-white, until she'd returned and screaming color had crashed in. Yet he couldn't surrender that power again. He couldn't afford the devastation it would leave in its wake.

* * *

Yelena was grateful for the sudden frantic work load of the upcoming party—it meant she could claim to be legitimately busy and not think about what had transpired these last few days. And Alex must have felt the same way, judging by the way he pointedly avoided being alone with her.

Even though he'd declared their past a nonissue, Yelena could feel the ghosts dog her every moment from that point on. It made talking business awkward, it made every movement calculated so she didn't accidentally touch him. So incredibly exasperating when all she *wanted* to do was touch him.

Even as her efforts began to snowball into a solid campaign, she was still relieved when six o'clock rolled around and she could spend time with her daughter. Chelsea had taken to dropping by every night and Yelena gratefully welcomed the company and her obvious attentiveness to Bella. To her delight Pam turned up on Friday night and they all spent a pleasant evening watching television and eating dinner.

When Yelena's phone rang, she was midlaugh at something Chelsea had said. It was Jonathon, calling to approve her request to stay another week. But in the course of that brief exchange, Yelena sensed something was off. His next words confirmed it. When she hung up, her good mood evaporated.

"Problem?" Pam asked, her legs curled elegantly beneath her on the sofa.

"Just work. Can you keep an ear out for Bella? I need to see Alex about something."

Yelena grabbed her room card and strode out the door, oblivious to the look Pam and Chelsea exchanged as edginess began to swirl swiftly in her belly.

She knocked on Alex's door and after a moment it swung open. Before he could say a word, she swept past him then pivoted in the middle of the room, arms crossed.

"I just got a call from my boss," she started without preamble.

He scratched his chin, a harsh yet intimate sound in the warm room. "You're going to have to elaborate here."

"Did you tell him that we're romantically involved?"

"No."

"You sure?"

"Yelena, I've not spoken with the man for nearly a week."

He tipped his head, hands on his hips. It was then Yelena finally noticed his clothes…or rather, lack of them. His white shirt, unbuttoned and rumpled, teased open to reveal the curves and planes of a magnificent torso. Her eyes trailed slowly down, skimming over his chest to his stomach. His muscles were a work of finest sculpture, chiseled and touchable under warm, tanned skin, before tapering down to slim hips encased in black pants, belt suggestively unbuckled.

Too late she snapped her eyes up to his, the full body flush warming every inch of her skin.

"Finished looking?" His voice was husky, his eyes amused.

Her body hummed with energy, as if she'd stuck her finger in a light socket and the powerful force now thrashed to break free.

"I…" She paused, struggling for the upper hand. "So if it wasn't you, who?"

He shrugged. "Who else knows you're here?"

A spark of irritation nipped at the edges of desire. "My father. Carlos."

He didn't have to say a thing, his expression mirrored her thoughts. Carlos wouldn't. Her father, on the other hand, was Jonathon's squash partner.

Contrite and embarrassed, she broke eye contact. "I…I'm sorry. I may have jumped the gun."

"Not a problem."

She glanced back up and caught his smile at the worst possible moment. Now all she could think about were those curved lips nipping at her hot skin.

"Okay. Er…" She clasped her hands nervously in front of her body. "I'd better be—" she gestured one thumb over her shoulder, towards the door "—better be going."

"Okay."

Still she remained rooted to the spot, until Alex added helpfully, "Anything else?"

"Yes. No! No, I'll…" With a whoosh of breath she whirled to the door. *Estúpida. Surely you're not waiting for an invitation into his bed?*

She paused, her hand on the door handle, her back to him. Thanks to what would've undoubtedly been a skillful, off-the-cuff comment, her father had effectively undermined her and cast doubt on her abilities, reducing her to fifteen all over again, and with all the accompanying emotions of confusion, isolation and anger.

The same emotions Alex himself had dealt with on a daily basis since his father's death. Without her.

"I'm sorry, Alex."

"For what?"

She squeezed her eyes shut. "For not being there for you when your father died."

She paused, waiting, but his silence said it all. With a pained frown she cracked open the door, prepared to make a dignified exit.

It happened so suddenly she barely got out a squeak of surprise. One moment she was grasping the handle, the next Alex had slammed it shut, grabbed her arms and whirled her, pinning her up against the door.

He was in her personal space, close enough she could see the dark navy flecks in his eyes and the rough stubble on his strong chin, feel his warm breath brushing her cheek.

Then he kissed her, hard.

Their breath mingled, tongues tangling until her nipples pebbled in painful arousal beneath her shirt. His manhood pushed hard against her belly and when she shifted, his groan was a mix of vexation and desire.

She felt it, too, this fierce need that scorched like a fever under her skin, her willpower bending and swaying under its awesome power. Her mind tangled as she felt his hands under her shirt, slide up over her waist then her ribs, before he cupped her breasts.

His soft murmur of approval in her mouth fired her blood, sending aching shards of longing into her limbs, fanning across her body.

He fiddled with her bra clasp as they kept on kissing, and when her bra fell free, he bunched up her shirt and latched hot mouth on to one tight nipple.

"Alex…" A groan of pleasure ripped from deep within as her legs began to buckle.

"I have you," he murmured, his lips full of her flesh. It was true—his arms wrapped securely around her, the hard door at her back. His knee wedged between her legs, offering erotic support.

He was everywhere, in her senses, her mind, under her skin. In her blood. She took a breath and he was there. She opened her eyes and his face filled her vision. Her palms, shaking with passion, ran over his shoulders, until she cupped his nape, that special erotic area where his hair met vulnerable flesh.

It turned her on every time. She tunneled her fingers in his hair, gently pulling, a deep burst of satisfaction as she heard him grunt. Yet despite the raging desire in her blood and her desperation to have him inside her, she couldn't relinquish herself. Not tonight. Not now.

"Alex…" she whispered, desperate to ignore the shocks of pleasure as his tongue ran over her nipple, teasing and arousing it to painful erection. "I need to gooooooo…" Her plea ended on a groan as his hand dipped into her pants, his fingers quickly finding the damp sensitive nub of her arousal.

"Do you?" His teeth toyed with one rock-hard nipple, making her hiss.

"Your…mother and Chelsea….are….with—" his tiny strokes made her body jerk with pleasure; she squeezed her eyes shut, forcing her body to settle even as it screamed in joy "—Bella. We can't do this right now."

His hand stilled and Yelena breathed a sigh. Relief or disappointment? Right now, she had no idea.

Slowly, he lifted his head and Yelena nearly lost it then—the fire in his eyes still raged, bathing her in desperate yearning. His hand was still down the front of her pants, his fingers wedged intimately in her flesh, flesh that throbbed and ached beneath his touch.

"I need to go," she repeated breathlessly.

The moments ticked into seconds, long, apprehensive seconds that did nothing to clear the passion-fueled moment. Yet Alex finally gave in. In one slow, excruciating movement, he slid from her, the sensual glide of his fingers forcing her to swallow a frustrated groan.

Then the cool air rushed in. She opened her eyes just in time to see his jaw tighten before he turned away, tunneling fingers through his hair.

Abject disappointment warred with common sense. "Alex…"

"Don't." He got out hoarsely, his back still to her. "You need to go."

She blinked, still dazed. Then without another word she opened the door and finally escaped.

Alex whirled to the closed door, a deep scowl across his brow. Gently he thumped a clenched fist on his forehead, one hand on his hip. His groin throbbed, a painful reminder of what he'd had, what he still wanted. Yelena.

He muttered a few choice curses under his breath before

yanking his shirt free from his pants. This wasn't him, unable to figure out the simplest of problems. He'd had a mission—destroy Carlos's world by sleeping with his precious sister. But instead of triumph, bitterness tainted his every move, his every thought. Even when he thought about how amazing Yelena had felt in his arms, how mind-blowing it had been to finally taste her, to kiss her, to be inside her, a surge of guilt always followed.

Something he hadn't felt in a long, long time.

He'd used her in his revenge plan, even though he'd never been certain it'd work, even though he'd begun to believe she hadn't played a part in Carlos's lies.

The kicker was she had no idea how much of a bastard Carlos was.

The injustice of it burned like fire as he strode into the kitchen, wrenched open the fridge door and grabbed a beer. He scowled at nothing in particular, until his gaze landed on Yelena's file for the Sunset Party. He still hadn't given her his guest list—

It hit him like a bolt from heaven, immobilizing every muscle in his body. With a rush of breath that ended on a stunned grunt, he slammed a hand on the counter top.

If Yelena couldn't see the kind of person Carlos was, then it was up to him to *show* her. And he knew just the thing.

Ten

Saturday morning—the day of the party—slowly blended into early afternoon. After fussing over her hair, her makeup and her general nerves, Yelena walked into her lounge room for Chelsea's inspection.

"How do I look?"

Chelsea frowned, gently replacing Bella across her other shoulder. "As if you're about to chair a board meeting." The teenager looked fabulous in a sleek, dark blue halter neck, the empire waist slashed to reveal aqua-and-black satin that shimmered as she walked.

"What's wrong with this?" Yelena ran a hand down her red silk shirt then readjusted the waistband of the black wool pencil skirt.

"It's hardly a party dress, is it?"

"Well, I'm working."

"You're always working." Chelsea rolled her eyes. "It's a *party,* for heaven's sakes. You know—food, people, music?"

She sighed melodramatically. "Okay, you'd better let me look at what you've got."

In less than ten minutes, Chelsea declared every piece of clothing in Yelena's lineup unsuitable and was on the phone. Three minutes, to the dot, and the concierge was at her door with a special delivery.

"Open it," Chelsea commanded after she'd signed the slip and closed the door. To Yelena's surprise, a scorching-red dress unfurled beneath her hands.

"Go and try it on."

"I can't—"

"Yeah, you can," Chelsea countered firmly, hands on hips.

Yelena finally caved. "All right. Can you watch Bella?"

"Sure. And loosen up that hair!" Chelsea added as she went once more into the bedroom.

Yelena pulled on the delicious dress, the fabric pouring over her skin with silken cool fingers. She couldn't suppress a shiver of excitement as she stared at her reflection.

It was one of the most gorgeous gowns she'd ever seen. Stylish, dramatic and totally sexy. The strapless bodice hugged her figure to snug perfection, the sleek material emphasizing her waist and generous curves to flare past her hips into an elegant, floor-length train. A swathe of sheer red floated behind her, a flirty mermaid tail with tiny seeded crystals on the hem to add extra oomph when she walked.

There was a small knock on the door before Chelsea opened it a crack.

"Mum's here. Come on out and show—wow!" Chelsea's eyes widened. But her smile faltered when she came to Yelena's hair. "Hair down. Fluff it out."

"Yes, miss." Yelena grinned and reached for the pins holding it in place. It tumbled down, the soft whisper across her bare shoulders sending another shiver down her spine. "You know, Gabriela used to boss me about like that, too."

Sadness flittered across Chelsea's eyes before she smiled. "Well, she *did* have style." She eyed Yelena before adding, "And you have awesome hair—why on earth would you tie it up all the time?"

Yelena grinned at her though the mirror. "Try living with it."

"Pleeeease." Chelsea tweaked Yelena's curls into place, smoothed her own shiny, straight hair behind her ears then nodded at their reflections. "Okay. Let's go."

When Yelena swished into the lounge room, Alex stood there, talking in hushed whispers with Pam who was holding Bella. Alex and she had barely spent an hour together since that kiss. Yelena had been gratefully busy with the party preparations and via Chelsea, she'd gleaned that Alex was dealing with the day-to-day running of his father's businesses.

Yet when he glanced up, saw her and smiled, her normally iron composure just crumbled.

"You look gorgeous." His eyes told her much more, all of it definitely X-rated, judging by the glint in those jeweled depths.

"Thanks" was all she could choke out, more than aware of his sister and mother standing discreetly to the side, Chelsea attempting to fasten a simple gold necklace around Pam's neck as Bella gurgled.

"I didn't think a ball gown would've been on your packing list."

"The dress is yours, bro," Chelsea piped up, too focused on pretending not to listen to actually carry it off. "Lori at the boutique gave me a loaner."

Yelena met his eyes head-on, a small smile hovering over her lips as she shrugged.

"Nice," he murmured. But the timbre in that one word said so much more. Like, *I'd much prefer you out of it.*

Even as her body leaped in response, she gave him a steady

glare, telling him she knew exactly where his mind was at. He remained unfazed.

Just as Alex was about to offer his arm, Yelena took Bella from Pam.

"You're bringing her?" he asked, surprised.

Yelena shot him a cool look. "It's her first party. I have Jasmine coming over at six."

He eyed the gurgling baby, sitting comfortably on Yelena's hip. "Won't she—"

"What?"

"I don't know—throw up or something?"

Yelena laughed. "Maybe."

"What about your dress?"

"Then it'll get dirty."

Her smile stretched as the women shared the joke, one that made him feel uncomfortably male.

"Yelena's letting me show Bella off." Pam finally came to her son's rescue. "And after the wonderful job she's done, we can at least give her a dress."

"It's not that," he began, glancing at his mother. She was looking chic in a black pantsuit, a burnt-orange wrap around her shoulders. When she smiled, it was a real one, not those fake smiles that never reached her eyes, ones he'd seen her give way too often when his father was still alive.

They opened the door, Pam and Chelsea going first in a rush of excited whispers.

"My earrings!" Yelena said suddenly. Then to Alex, "Can you hold Bella?" and just like that, the baby was suddenly in his arms.

God, she was so tiny! He blinked, awkwardly clutching her to his chest like an oddly shaped piece of delicate china. Bella gurgled and gnawed on one fist, a thin line of drool slowly dripping from her mouth.

He shifted her minuscule, yellow-jumpsuited weight and studied her with a frown. Large, brown puppy-dog eyes fringed with thick lashes stared up from a round, cherubic face. Abundant, curly dark hair capped her head, her tiny mouth stretching into a wide grin, still full of baby fist and drool.

She was a miniature version of Yelena.

Something fluttered inside, making his breath catch, prompting a darker frown. Yet when Bella kept grinning at him and two tiny dimples appeared on the baby's cheeks, his heart skipped a beat.

The sight that greeted Yelena's return stopped her in her tracks, stuttering her breath. Alex cradled a tiny gurgling Bella in his powerful arms. And they were grinning at each other.

Oh, my Lord. The perfect picture sent a slice of yearning into her very soul, her heartbeat engulfing her heavy swallow. She blinked. *What am I supposed to do with that?*

"Alex?"

When his eyes swung to hers she nearly crumpled at the dazed expression there. A mixture of awe, delight… and something else, something she recognized but did not want to name because then she'd have to acknowledge it. And worse, deal with it.

Longing. Her conscience overrode common sense at the worst possible moment.

She dropped eye contact and reached for Bella. "Pam and Chelsea are waiting. Shall we go?"

But when he remained still, staring at her with Bella still in his arms, a spurt of panic erupted.

"Alex?" Yelena said softly.

Inscrutable eyes studied her, as if he wanted nothing more than to crawl into her mind and read her thoughts. She returned his gaze steadily, unblinkingly, even as her whole body inwardly trembled.

"She could have been ours."

No bitterness, no accusation. Yet the pure simplicity of his statement made every cell in her body weep.

Anguish threatened her composure: ruthlessly she choked it down. "I know."

He sighed, severing the moment as he firmly handed Bella over. "Let's go."

For a week, construction on two marquees had been underway, and now the results of everyone's hard work was clearly visible. Inside the main entrance, fake trees sparkled with tiny lights and a canopy of dark blue silk dotted with tiny diamantés gave a starry effect. A small pond and miniature waterfall had been built and, surrounding it sat massive toadstools with assorted fake bugs and critters as big as cats. Children squealed and shrieked and adults gasped as they discovered replicas of popular Aboriginal folklore creatures scattered amongst the scenes—a platypus in the pond, an emu grazing behind a tree. Koalas hid in the branches and kangaroos grazed lazily on the long painted scrub.

The back of this scene opened up to a huge, carpeted area, where long trestle tables were laden with a veritable feast, the local cuisine mixed in with Diamond Bay's offerings. Chelsea had dubbed this area the 'party tent,' where a bunch of local bands were setting up their equipment.

As Yelena watched the flow of guests arrive, she realized most of the small but fiercely strong community had turned up.

Which hopefully meant it was going to be a roaring success.

To her right, at the back of the marquee, her daughter commanded the attention of a handful of women. She chuckled, watching the way Chelsea kept on touching Bella's hand, how Pam gently patted her back. A baby had an amazing ability to bring out women's mothering instincts.

Most, that is, except Maria Valero's.

She blinked, burying that thought away. Now was not the time to dwell on things she couldn't change.

She glanced over at two reporters filming their segment

intros. The press was here; the guests were arriving. With a smile she watched a bunch of excited Aboriginal children run full tilt through the marquee, laughing as their squeals of delight filtered outside.

"Looks like it's going to be a hit."

She nearly jumped out of her skin as Alex's seductive breath washed over her shoulder.

She swiveled to meet his eyes. "You doubted my skills?"

His smile spread slowly, creasing his eyes in mischievous glee. "Not in the least."

As they exchanged a silent look she sensed a ground shift. As if something had changed in some deep, profound way.

"We're talking about the party, right?" she said slowly, her eyes flitting back towards the arriving throng.

"Of course."

She avoided his gaze, nervously pressing one hand to her abdomen before flicking a long curl over her shoulder. It obviously proved too much of a temptation because Alex retrieved it, twirling it around his finger in deep concentration.

The look in his bright blue eyes made her knees buckle. "You'd…" She swallowed and tried again. "You'd better go and attend to your guests."

His mouth spread into a grin. Then to her astonishment he took her hand, kissed it and bowed low like a gallant courtier. "Of course. I'll be back."

Yelena watched him go, smiling as guests continued to arrive. Pam mingled with natural ease, talking to employees and their families, local business owners, even Yelena's contacts from Sydney and Canberra.

She spotted Chelsea shyly chatting to the waiter who had caught her eye a few days ago and her smile widened.

Then a broad figure cut through the crowd and that smile froze in place.

"Carlos!"

* * *

From his vantage point across the room, Alex watched his enemy greet Yelena with a smile and a hug. Yelena's obvious joy at her brother's presence sliced Alex's insides. But his veins iced over when he caught Carlos's complacent smirk, a look that said he knew and fully accepted his sister's worship as his God-given right.

Yelena's eyes sought his, yet he met her curiosity with a raised eyebrow and a shrug. The grateful smile she shot him dug in the knife just a little more.

She won't thank you after tonight.

Swallowing that bitter pill, he grimly reconnoitered and moved forward.

"What are you doing here?"

He heard Yelena's happy exclamation then saw her brother's mouth curve. Yet those dark eyes remained wide and alert. "Is that any way to talk to one of your guests, *cigüeñita?*"

Her smile faltered. The nickname "little stork" had annoyed her ever since tenth grade, but her irritation only amused Carlos.

"I got an invite in the mail. I would've expected at least a phone call," Carlos said casually as she grabbed him a drink from a passing waiter. The gentle yet obvious rebuke wrinkled Yelena's brow.

He took a gulp of his drink, gagged then choked it down. "What the—?"

"Iced tea. Yandurruh is an alcohol-free community."

"Great. Another reason why I hate the Outback."

That was Alex's cue. He stepped up behind them. "We have a fully stocked bar at Diamond Bay if you prefer, Carlos."

"Alex." Carlos slowly turned and they both went through the motions of shaking hands.

Yelena glanced from one man to the other, studying them closely. They were both tall and strikingly good-looking. But where Carlos had that Antonio Banderas, swarthy-romantic-screen-idol look, Alex's appeal was infinitely more subtle. From his short-cropped hair to the strong, stubbled jaw and piercing blue eyes, his appearance reminded her of powers barely leashed, of treacherous waters lurking beneath his cool, controlled exterior.

Seeing them together was palpably uncomfortable to watch, like witnessing two rival politicians exchange pleasantries just before they ripped each other to shreds.

"I'd kill for a real drink," Carlos said gruffly as they broke the handshake.

Yelena winced at his word choice, noticing the dark clouds passing over Alex's face.

"I'll show you the way," she said quickly, linking her arm in his. As they walked away, she chanced a backwards glance.

Pam and Chelsea had joined Alex and as she watched, Alex's gaze landed on Bella.

His mouth curled up, his finger going out to stroke the baby's soft cheek.

Carlos frowned down at her. "You all right?"

She nodded, releasing her tight grip on his arm. He glanced back and his frown deepened.

They silently made their way through the night until they reached the security gate that signaled the perimeter of Diamond Bay property. Yelena keyed open the gate and led Carlos through.

"Nice place," Carlos mused as they followed the path through the lush vegetation. "Must've cost billions to develop."

Yelena ground to a halt, forcing Carlos to stop, too. "Tell me what happened, Carlos."

"About…?"

"Between you and Alex. You were business partners. You were *friends*. And now—"

"What's *he* said?" Carlos efficiently flicked a small leaf from his sharp collar.

"Nothing. He refuses to talk about it."

"I'm not surprised."

"What's that supposed to mean?"

Carlos raised one perfect eyebrow before turning back to the path. With a growl of annoyance, Yelena followed.

"Well, look who his father is—a man who went from poverty to topping Australia's rich list. Of course he's not going to tell you he screwed up."

They finally reached the sweeping courtyard of Merlot, Diamond Bay's most popular wine bar.

Yelena grabbed his sleeve, bringing him to a halt. "What do you mean, 'screwed up'?"

Carlos sighed and crossed his arms. "Sprint Travel isn't doing well."

What? Why hadn't Alex told her? "How? Management? Capital? Advertising?"

"Lots of things I won't get into." *It's over your head so don't worry about it,* his look said. Yelena's eyebrows ratcheted up at the barely veiled insult. "I'll have to take it to the courts."

"You're going to *fight* him for the company?"

"I'm surprised you don't know this, considering all you're doing for him." His expression tightened before quickly smoothing out. "I have no choice," he added matter-of-factly. "Sprint Travel can't survive with Alex Rush at the helm." He gave her arm a pat for good measure. "And Alex will do anything to get the upper hand with the business. Including—" he dropped his gaze, unable to meet her eyes "—using you to get to me."

"What's that supposed to mean?"

Carlos gave her a hurt look. "I'm just looking out for you, Yelena. I've dealt with men like Alex before. He'll stop at nothing to get what they want. Now, are you coming in for a drink?"

She shook her head slowly, then watched Carlos shrug, pity and regret on his handsome face. That couldn't be right.

Alex wasn't like that. And he wouldn't withhold that kind of information.

The realization that this was much bigger than she'd first thought lay like fiery leaden chains across her chest. It followed her as she left Carlos and went back to the party, dogged her steps as she put on her happy face and mingled with the guests while she looked for Alex.

She found him in front of a camera, being interviewed for a national news channel. On first glance he appeared relaxed and confident with one hand in his pocket, one gesturing as he talked. Yet even from this distance she could tell he was out of his comfort zone: the rigid jaw and shoulders, for one. The small tight lines around his mouth. Even his casual, wide-legged stance. The body language in all his press footage said the same thing: "I'd rather be somewhere else."

"...one final question, Mr. Rush," the female presenter was saying. "How are you coping now, nine months on from your acquittal of your father's death?"

Every muscle in his body appeared to stiffen. His hands clenched, eyes narrowing to forbidding slits.

Yelena stepped forward. "Hello, Val. You *do* know a person can't be acquitted for something they were never charged with?" She casually glanced around. "I thought Mark was on this piece."

Val Marchetta shrugged her thin shoulders and tilted her head, an affected gesture meant to encourage confidences. "They sent me instead. Fancy seeing you here, Yelena." The icy smile mirrored in her wide, perfectly made-up eyes.

"Yes. Excuse me," she said, smiling politely. "Alex, could I see you for a moment?"

She took his arm, smiled again at the now-frowning Val then firmly led him away.

"You didn't have to rescue me," he said tightly as they kept on walking.

"Just think of it as preempting a possible awkward moment."

She threw a brief glance back over her shoulder. "And when Val puts the pieces together, our business relationship will no longer be private."

Alex shrugged. "It had to happen eventually."

They were finally outside, pausing in a corner where brief shadows gently merged, cooling the early evening. The dozen questions teetering on her tongue all dissolved into a soft murmur of surprise when Alex swiftly pulled her into his arms and kissed her.

Purpose immediately melted into divine pleasure. His hands held her face, trapping her mouth in a sensual prison and with a half sigh, half groan, she kissed him back.

For minutes they indulged in the simple, erotic pleasure of sharing mouths and tongues, oblivious to the party in full swing inside, to the people walking and mingling not two meters away. Minutes in which Yelena forgot what she'd marched over to say, forgot her exchange with Carlos…hell, she even forgot her name at one point.

When Alex finally broke the kiss, they were both breathless and heavy eyed.

"Do you want to leave?" he asked, voice husky.

"I can't."

"I didn't ask if you could. I asked if you wanted to."

More than you know. "Alex, I'm working. Did you talk to the press—the *other* press?" she added.

He sighed. "I did. So did Pam."

"No hiccups? Everything's going smoothly?"

"From what I can see." But at her look, he paused. "Except..?"

"Carlos."

"Ahh." Slowly he released her and took a step back, shoving his hands into his pockets.

"Did you invite him?"

"Yes."

"Why?"

To show you how manipulative and selfish he is. "Because I know how much he means to you."

The look on her face was inscrutable. "He's been making accusations."

"About?"

"Sprint Travel's on the rocks."

"It is," he said slowly.

She sucked in a breath. "You're paying a small fortune for B&H to represent you and you fail to tell me this? Are you crazy? Or do you really not care what I'm trying to do here?"

Alex's expression tightened. "It's complicated."

"Oh, how I wish people would stop telling me that! This is why you and Carlos had a falling out, right?"

"Yes."

"But—" she crossed her arms "—that's not all."

Alex seesawed between two truths while his gut pitched. He wanted her to *see* the real Carlos, not just tell her. Why should she believe him over her flesh-and-blood brother?

"It's—"

"Complicated. Right."

This was not going well.

"If you could just give me some time to—"

"Was the other night just a way to get back at my brother?"

He had to hand it to her, she had style. She delivered that question so calmly she could've been inquiring about the weather. Impassive face, straight back. Yet through the businesslike façade, Alex knew he'd hurt her.

Damn. "Yelena." He moved to take her hand but she just stepped back, one eyebrow raised. He squelched a frown, guilty as hell. "That night, it was just you and me. I was thinking of nothing else, had no ulterior motive except pleasure. Yours and mine."

He'd never wanted someone to believe him more at this

moment. Even after all those months of speculation and repeated interrogation by the cops, Yelena's belief meant everything right now.

"You didn't answer my question."

For one stupid, insane moment it was revenge. Not now. He couldn't meet her eyes, couldn't bear to see the hurt in those wide depths. A disgusted murmur echoed in his throat, self-loathing rising up to choke him.

As the silence and growing distance thundered between them, the cheerful sounds of the party breezed by on the cooling air, paradoxically highlighting the moment with almost vulgar emphasis.

His tongue refused to work, words sticking inside his mouth. Yet at her raised eyebrow, he finally settled on "I didn't mean to hurt you."

"Really?" she got out, her frosty look now glacial. "Wow. Imagine if you tried."

"Yelena—"

"Don't, Alex. I can't…" She shook her head firmly. "I need to feed Bella and put her to bed."

Then she was gone.

Eleven

On swift, urgent feet, Yelena clicked into the main marquee, yet just as she was about to enter, a jagged sob caught her throat.

Mortified, she quickly stepped back, swallowing that horrible vulnerability down. *You can't cry. Not here, not now.*

Sheer willpower forced back the tears, sent steel into her composure and determination into every muscle. With a quick toss of her head she stepped inside.

It took under a minute to find her daughter, the center of attention in a bunch of cooing women. Despite her swirling thoughts, Yelena managed a smile. Pam had Bella cradled securely over her shoulder, doing that familiar, slow step-sway dance every mother did to comfort a baby.

She moved forward.

"It's getting close to six—time to feed Bella," she said, careful to ensure Pam knew she was there before putting a hand on the woman's shoulder.

Pam turned and smiled. "I hope you're coming back to the party."

Yelena nodded. "I'll see how it goes. The staff seem to have things under control."

A movement caught her eye and Yelena glanced across. Alex stood at the exit.

Their eyes met and despite the horrible truth she now knew, Yelena felt every nerve in her body charge.

"Yelena?"

"Mmm?"

"I can take Bella if you want."

Yelena took a deep breath and refocused on Pam. "I'm sorry?"

The older woman was smiling in a way that Yelena couldn't fail to interpret. "I can go and put Bella down if you want to—that is, I mean…"

Now they were both embarrassed. "No, that's okay," Yelena assured her, her skin flushing with guilt. "She's been a bit fussy. Unfamiliar surroundings, I think."

She gently extricated Bella with a smile then made her way outside.

Alex was nowhere to be seen. Yelena sighed. *Relieved? Or disappointed?*

Both. She keyed open the security gate and soon the gardens engulfed her.

With a shiver, she quickly made her way down the winding path, lush foliage and the sounds of dusk whispering around her. The afternoon heat had eased off as the ritual preparation for sunset began. Thanks to enthusiastic discussions with Pam, she recognized a flock of rare Princess parrots noisily roosting in River Red Gums, then farther on, more busy bird chatter in the spinifex grass. The trees and plants were abundant, providing coverage for not only the bird population but also various reptiles she'd spotted most mornings soaking up the sun on her patio.

Lost in the sights and sounds, she started when she rounded the curve and Carlos emerged from the opposite direction.

She gave him a smile, too tired to make sure she meant it. "Having a good time?"

She waited while he lazily took a drag of his cigarette before blowing smoke into the air.

Her smile dropped as she pointedly coughed then repositioned Bella on her other shoulder.

"Not as much as you are, apparently."

Her mouth thinned but she said nothing.

"He denied trying to take Sprint Travel then," Carlos said flatly.

"I didn't ask him."

"Oh, right. Too busy, were you?"

She sniffed, catching the scent of scotch on his breath, but clamped her mouth shut, smiling politely as she made way for a passing couple.

"The man isn't fit to run a charity raffle," Carlos said, grinding the cigarette beneath his toe. "And you're cheapening yourself hanging around him."

Her breath came in sharp. "What?"

"Just look at his family. His father grew up in Bankstown, for starters," he scoffed.

"So did Paul Keating, Australia's twenty-fourth prime minister. What does living in Sydney's western suburbs prove?"

Carlos sighed. "Breeding, Yelena. William Rush cheated on his wife. Then he dies in mysterious circumstances and Alex gets off scot-free. And from what I'm hearing, Rush Airlines' business practices weren't exactly aboveboard."

Yelena shook her head. "That's the first I'm hearing of it."

"Well." Carlos glanced past her, his smile hinting at condescension. "I have sources. If you stood to inherit a billion-dollar company and knew it was going down the gurgler, wouldn't you be a little pissed off?"

"I'm not going to validate that by answering."

He swung his gaze back to her, eyes blazing. "You're a Valero. What you do is public business and reflects on everyone, especially Papá. I think he'd have something to say about what is going on here."

A cold shard iced over her heart. "Carlos…"

"And for heaven's sakes, Yelena, fix your hair! It looks like you've just tumbled from his bed."

Yelena automatically put her hand to her head as he glanced about again.

Then she stilled. Slowly, she let her hand fall.

Carlos's narrowed eyes caught that. "I thought at least *you'd* have a little restraint. I knew Gabriela was a bad influence."

She sucked in a breath. "Do not say *one* word against our sister." Now she just itched to slap him. But frankly, she wouldn't give him the satisfaction of seeing her lose control.

"Well, what would you call it? First, thanks to her we end up in this god-awful, ass-end-of-the-world country! Then she becomes a discount store *model*—" he spat out the word like others would say "prostitute" "—then she calls and you drop everything to bum around Europe for months on end. God knows what you both ended up doing over there."

"Remember, she died, Carlos," Yelena choked out.

His eyes barely rested on Bella before he glanced away. "And you end up with a bastard child."

The air crackled with rising tension and Yelena tried to shove her way through it. But his bitter expression, one that went beyond mere anger and disappointment, forced a terrible thought into her brain.

"And you'll never forgive me for that, will you?" she said slowly. His impatient gesture told her what he thought of that ridiculous thought. But gradually, clarity began to dawn. "Here, hold your niece."

"Hey!" Carlos took a step back, hands up, and in that moment, Yelena saw a brief flash of disgust twist across his face. It shattered something inside her, propelling a bitter acrid burn into her throat.

"Oh, my God," she whispered fiercely. "You can't even hold her, can you?"

Carlos plastered on a tight smile, nodding politely as a woman walked past.

"What are you talking about?" he finally hissed.

"You've never once picked her up, talked to her, engaged with her. She's a *baby,* Carlos. And just because I don't have a husband does not give you the right to—"

"To what?" he spat, the venom pitched low and hard as he grabbed Yelena's arm. "We are Valeros, descended from Spanish royalty! *Dios,* the irony from you, a public relations expert." He dropped her arm with a snort of disgust. "Did you think for one second how this looks for our father? Our mother? You're not only flaunting that child but you're also sleeping with a convict, a man who killed his father!"

"He did not kill anyone!" Yelena countered, gently patting Bella as she stirred.

"Oh, and you were there, were you?"

"Yes, I was."

Triumph leaked from her voice: she felt it empower every muscle, every bone as she lifted her chin.

Carlos stepped back, a dark frown contorting his face. "You weren't."

"Alex was with me at the time his father died. Let it go, Carlos."

He looked so stunned that for one second, Yelena almost took pity on him. Yet she knew, really knew, how he felt about her and Bella and she just couldn't forgive him for that.

Carlos might be family, but so was Bella. She glanced

down at her sleeping baby, cupping her warm head with one trembling hand. Carlos not only treated her presence like dirt under his triple-stitched, imported Spanish shoes but now this… this.. disgusting revelation.

All that history had been stripped away, reduced to nothing but bitter ashes. Carlos had done that.

"I don't want to argue, Carlos," she muttered, exhaustion and loss engulfing her.

"Then don't." He gave her a tight look. "I'm going back to the bar."

Yelena watched him stalk off without a word, her heart aching. Carlos was her brother. Her charming, funny, smart brother, her champion, her protector. She'd worshipped him. He was her flesh and blood. He and Gabriela were family, more than her absent parents ever were.

When had it all gone sour?

On quick footsteps she got to her suite, smiled at the waiting Jasmine then keyed them both in. She prepared the formula then went into the bedroom, settling in the comfy rocking chair and positioned Bella in her arms.

As Bella fed, the insistent pounding that had settled in the middle of her forehead slowly began to ease. Yet she refused to think about what had just happened, not until she'd settled the baby. Instead she sighed, releasing the tension from her tight shoulders, let the moment calm her limbs and relax her body as she watched Bella feed.

Too soon, the formula was gone and Bella's eyes had fluttered closed. After a moment, Yelena rose then gently tucked her into the crib. Staring down at that sweet, innocent face, her heart tightened just a little more.

Carlos's disapproval had always been there, she acknowledged as her hand rested gently on Bella's rising chest. After moving to Australia, Gabriela had curbed her rebellion into small localized ones. Hair, makeup, wardrobe and boyfriends were the main points of contention. And when she'd reached eighteen, her brief fling with modeling had earned her enough money to move out.

Despite the years in between, guilt still burned.

What Gabriela didn't know was the more waves she caused, the more Yelena deliberately smoothed them. Controlling her environment, bringing order into her disorganized world, like Alex had said.

With one last look at her now-sleeping daughter, she crept from the room.

"Going back to the party?" Jasmine asked, glancing up from the book she'd been reading.

Yelena nodded, unable to force out pleasantries. Swiftly she picked up her purse and quietly left.

She couldn't let it go like this.

A myriad of conflicting emotions dogged every step as she walked down the shadowed path, twisting and turning inside. It hurt, damn, it hurt. It was her *brother,* the same man who'd said all those awful things, shown her a terrible side she'd never witnessed before.

But if she gave up on Carlos, she'd have no one left.

That appalling thought quickened her pace and soon the path widened out into Merlot's raised courtyard, the low sun and spreading shadows highlighting her brother drinking deep from a glass, his back to her as he glared at the elaborate water feature in the center of the patio.

Carlos. Just as she was about to call out, Alex emerged from the bar.

She shrunk back, instead taking the fork in the path that led down a gentle slope until the marble wall grew taller and taller, eventually hiding her from view. The cool stone against her shoulder goose-bumped her flesh and she suppressed a shiver.

"What the hell do you want?" she heard Carlos growl directly above her head.

"You're drunk, Carlos."

Carlos snorted. "And you're a murderous son of a bitch who's screwing my sister."

Yelena's hand went to her mouth, stifling the gasp. She glanced up but unless she took a step back, revealing her hiding place, she could see nothing but the wrought-iron railing topping the marbled wall.

"Wrong on the first one," Alex murmured, sounding way too calm. "But on the second…" The pause was long and deliberate. "What's it to you if I was?"

Something smashed close to her feet, the bitter smell of scotch assailing her nostrils a second later. "I'll kill you."

"Careful. I might think you actually mean it."

"I don't give second warnings, Alex."

Thick apprehension swirled as Yelena frowned, holding her breath.

"And I'm sure that's been enough to scare the others into silence," Alex finally said. "But it won't work with me. Not now. We both know who's been feeding those stories about my father to the press. Stories that have no basis in truth, I might add."

Carlos remained silent.

"You're itching to say it, aren't you?" Alex sounded almost amused. "So why don't I save you the trouble? You overheard a private conversation between me and my father, assumed he was cheating then used it to fuel a publicity headache, one you're hoping will sway Sprint Travel in your favor." He paused, then added almost regretfully, "Why do you hate me so much?"

Yelena could feel the heavy tension in the air. It wasn't hard to imagine Carlos's flaming glare, radiating pure fury. She'd been the recipient of that look already.

"You were the son of the great and powerful William Rush, adored by millions, the talented heir to a bloody saint." A loud crack signaled Carlos had slammed his palm on the stone wall.

"Nothing was ever handed to me on a plate. *I* had to work for it."

"So did I."

Carlos reeled off a blistering curse in Spanish, making Yelena's ears burn. "That's a crock. Nothing ever came hard to you."

"So that's what this is about—jealousy?"

"It's about getting just reward," Carlos threw back. "I've put every penny into Sprint and unlike you, I don't have an airline company and a billion-dollar resort to fall back on if it goes bust. You gave no thought to the consequences when the cops started questioning you, did you? No consideration for our partnership deal. You could've just said, 'No, I didn't do it.' Instead you hid behind a lawyer and clammed up."

"I didn't kill him, Carlos."

"I don't really care," Carlos sneered. "Our business plummeted because of you, which breaches our partnership agreement."

"And that justifies what you're doing now?"

"I'm doing what I have to to save Sprint and my reputation."

"What the hell does that mean?"

Yelena couldn't bear it any longer. She eased along the high wall until it began to dip. Just above eye level she snuck a glance over the top.

Both men were squared off, bodies rigid. Yet where the thunderous look on Carlos's face was painfully familiar, Alex seemed almost…calm. Confident, even.

"My solicitor assures me the courts will be in my favor," Carlos said now.

"Not after they know you've been slandering my family in the press." Alex placed his hands on his hips. "You'll stop this vendetta. Now."

"What vendetta?"

"Don't play dumb. We both know what you've been doing."

Carlos snorted. "Fine. But only if you hand over Sprint. And stay away from Yelena."

A raw moan of dismay rumbled in her throat but she managed to swallow it. Her hands, she noticed, clutched damp fistfuls of red satin and quickly she released her grip, furtively smoothing out the skirt.

"No."

Alex's cold response rang clearly across the courtyard, breathing life into Yelena's stiff form, warmth into her cooling limbs.

"You've got no proof," Carlos hissed. "And with a few well-chosen words in Yelena's ear, she'll drop you and your account quicker than last week's leftovers."

"She won't believe you."

"But I'm her brother. The only person she trusts. She'll believe me."

Although she couldn't read Alex's expression, his tense shoulders and angled jaw at Carlos's smug words spoke volumes.

"What Yelena and I do is none of your business, Carlos."

"Like hell it's not!" Carlos's fists tightened. "You've dragged her down to your level and I should—"

"Do not threaten me, Valero." Alex stepped into the light, his face a mask of angry impatience and dark shadow. "You can try your luck right here, right now, but I've taken on guys twice your size before and won. In fact—" his chin lifted, a tight smile stretching his lips "—go right ahead. I'm just itching to punch that pretty face of yours."

In deathly silence, Yelena watched the standoff, heart thundering, every limb and muscle alert with horrible anticipation.

Then, after interminably long seconds, Carlos slowly stepped back.

Alex shoved his hands in his pockets. "Ultimatums only work if you're holding all the cards, Carlos."

"What's that supposed to mean?"

"It means you lose. I have your threats on tape. I have proof you were talking to the press. And pretty soon I'll have proof you were stealing not only from Sprint but others, too. And more importantly, I have Yelena. Don't try it," he added tightly as Carlos rocked on his feet. "I will take you down."

Carlos's face twisted into a furious mask of rage but Alex kept going. "Keep talking to the press and you'll see how much mud sticks."

Finally Alex turned and headed across the courtyard, to the path that led back to the party. At the last minute he paused, glancing back. "You need to leave now. I'll have security drive you to the airstrip."

A stream of curses followed him as he disappeared, before Carlos turned on his heel and stalked inside.

Yelena slipped back, the lengthening shadows enveloping her. With racing heart, she placed her palms on the smooth stone, taking relief from the cold, unyielding surface against her burning skin.

This changed everything.

A few seconds passed before her body craved movement, her mind solitude. It was no surprise she ended up at the most secluded area of the resort.

The grotto was private and intimate, a small rock pool surrounded by an impressive array of trees and strategically placed slabs of granite to form a miniature version of Diamond Falls' waterfall.

She sat in a deck chair, the gentle rustle of material whispering around her legs. The bubbling, lapping water, coupled with the hypnotic ripples shimmering across the illuminated surface slowly edged into her consciousness, gently prying loose her fervent thoughts. Gradually the noise in her head eased off, leaving her with unanswered questions.

Since when had Carlos become so vindictive? How could her brother willingly set out to destroy a family? He'd never even met Pam and Chelsea.

The crystalline waters held no answer. A gentle breeze rushed through the trees, bringing with it the faraway noise of the party. Moments later, a bunch of jovial partygoers interrupted her reverie. As they laughed and joked, clumsily stripping off their formal wear, Yelena rose.

"Hey! Come and join us in the pool!"

The cute guy was grinning as he paused midstrip but Yelena shook her head with a smile. "No thanks."

Amidst their calls of disappointment, Yelena threw them an apologetic smile before clicking open the pool gate.

She kept on walking until the path stopped. Startled she glanced up, to the very last suite, which stood alone and apart from the others. Her eyes ran over the brickwork, the fancy tiled patio with its top-shelf furniture and drawn curtains.

Such perfection and beauty. Yet she wondered if the occupants would come up quite so well under scrutiny.

With a heavy sigh she turned.

"Yelena?"

She whirled, her eyes seeking the figure in the long shadows, fear pounding her heart.

A tiny click and warm light flooded the path. Alex's broad shape filled the doorway, one arm leaning against the sliding door. "Are you okay?"

Fate. She rocked on her toes, eager to leave yet unable to. Her granite resolve crumbled like dust on the wind, erased by what she'd overheard. The inexplicable urge to move surged through her then suddenly she was taking one step forward, one step, then another. "No. No, I'm not."

When he opened his arms it seemed perfectly natural to step into them. And then the tears came.

Somehow he managed to steer her inside, close the door then seat them both on his couch. And still she clung to him, savoring the feel of this huge, muscular man, taking comfort in his protective arms.

That's how he made her feel. Protected. As if he could fix anything for her.

"What happened?" he finally asked when she eventually pulled back.

Feeling a little foolish now, she dipped her head from scrutiny, quickly wiping at her cheeks. He couldn't fix this. It was something she had to get through all by herself.

"Carlos and I... we had a falling out."

"I see."

She glanced up. His expression remained neutral, waiting for her to continue.

"He..." She hesitated as everything came flooding back. "He still blames Gabriela for...well, everything. And he certainly hates me for Bella. I...I heard you both in the courtyard."

"Heard what?"

"Everything—Carlos's lies, his threats, his..."

The anguish on her face made Alex's heart ache. He reached for her hand, linking her fingers in his. "I'm sorry."

"So am I. For not seeing what he was really like sooner." When she brought those dark watery eyes up to meet his, he was a goner.

"You couldn't know," he managed to get out.

"But I should have. I should have—"

"Don't." He cupped her cheek, a sudden intimacy that shocked her into silence. This is what he had wanted, for her to see the depth of Carlos's nature, yet the victory rang hollow in the face of Yelena's pain.

Despite her tears his body reacted on an elemental level, a primitive level. Me, man. You, woman.

My woman. He'd had her once, and the urge to have her again surged through him. The guilty forbidden pleasure only heightened his need, a need far beyond his control.

A dark and terrible shard broke off inside him, disappearing into the murky waters of his past to be lost forever. In its place something sparked, something warm and hopeful.

Something that made him want things he had no right to.

She searched his face, looking for what, he didn't know. Compassion? Humanity? Whatever it was, her scrutiny undid him, unraveled the last of the control he'd been clinging onto.

When he leaned forward and kissed her, she let him, her sigh of acceptance sweet in his mouth. Her lips tasted of salt and warmth and Alex explored every inch of that flesh, from the generous swell of her bottom lip to the wide corners that would spread in mischievous abandon when she laughed.

He felt the desperate urge to hear her laugh again.

But right now, laughter was the last thing on his mind. Instead he eased her back into his soft leather couch, his hands full of her hair, his lips on her throat and his senses reeling from her sensual scent.

She shifted her weight, allowing him to settle more firmly between her legs. His manhood was already hard and throbbing and when it bumped up against her thigh, his breath rushed out on a groan.

"The floor," she got out beneath his mouth, eyes heavy with arousal.

He needed no further direction. As if she were no lighter than a doll, he scooped her up and deposited her on the carpet.

Yelena stared up at him as he made short work of his shirt, his tie already long gone. The appreciative sigh rumbled deep in her throat as he kneeled before her, purposeful intent glowing in his darkened eyes. Reaching out, she swept a hand over that broad chest, her fingers teasing from one nipple to the other.

His sharp breath made her chuckle.

Then she let her fingers trail down over his abdomen,

savoring the beautiful eroticism of those bumpy ridges, the warm yet iron-hard muscle beneath, until she got to his belt buckle.

She chanced a glance, absorbing the raw desire in his face before slowly trailing her palm down, over the large bulge of his erection.

"Lord, Yelena…" ended on a groan as she quickly unbuckled, unzipped and dragged his pants down.

He was a large man in every area. Her hand wrapped around his silken heat, quivering when he groaned again. The power she held, the power she commanded, was amazingly humble. It filled her to the brim, spilling over as she slowly bent her head.

She heard him mutter an oath as she slid him past her lips, his fingers tightening in her hair, gently urging her on. Even as the deep pulse between her legs rocketed, she took time to savor his every taste, every smell, until finally her mouth settled at the base of his groin and she murmured a satisfied sigh.

She breathed deep, filling her lungs with his pure, musky male scent, loving the way it excited her.

"Yelena…"

He was a man on the edge and losing control, his guttural command ripped from deep within. Wasting no more time, she moved, her mouth working him, loving him while his hands rested possessively on her head, guiding her pace.

It was an act so raw, so shockingly primal, loving him with her mouth. But it was also absolutely perfect. To hear his harsh breath, to feel his pounding heart, knowing she was the one giving him so much pleasure, thrilled her every single nerve.

She had the power to control a man, this man who exuded such palpable command. It numbed her thoughts. She couldn't think, she could only feel. His tight hard butt beneath her palms, the damp arousal sweating from his skin. His granite-hard erection in her mouth.

She felt his muscles quiver and in the next second, he pulled free. "Stop."

"But I haven't—"

"Sweetheart," he choked out, gently pushing her down to the floor. "I need to be inside you."

She melted right there and then, bonelessly sinking back into the plush carpet. But after he bunched her skirts around her waist, his hand searched to no avail.

Yelena grinned, twisting sideways. "Try the zipper."

They both chuckled as Alex dragged the zipper down. But amusement swiftly fled when the dress parted from her body and like Venus released from the sea, she lay bare for his inspection.

He took a deep, staggering breath. "God, you're stunning."

The raw look that passed over his face floored her, empowered her. She placed her hands behind her head, smiling, unashamedly teasing him in her black high cut G-string. "Why, thank you, kind sir."

Then he lowered his head and her smile ended as a gasp. Strong teeth teased her nipple, rolling the hard bud around his mouth, creating sudden hot friction between her legs.

He spent what felt like ages cupping the generous swell of her breasts, licking the valley between, teasing both nipples with his thumbs until she was panting, ready to explode.

"Alex, please…" She felt no shame in begging, letting him know she needed him inside her, making love to her.

And he was there, his hands spreading her thighs wide.

She held her breath, waiting, waiting. When he entered her, swift and hard, she cried out in joy.

Alex paused, heart pounding in his throat. "Did I hurt you?"

Her mouth curved into an erotic smile, her eyes fluttering

open. She could kill him with that look, all dark and wide with arousal. Then she wrapped those long legs around his waist, angling down. "No" came her breathless reply as she arched her back. "Not at all."

Her perfect neck called to him; he placed hot kisses across the length of it as she moved again, inviting him to continue.

He eagerly reared to meet her. She was so tight, so wet. He moved first in gentle strokes, then as he felt her passion begin to swiftly build, he switched to hard, almost rough thrusts. She murmured her satisfaction, meeting him all the way, tilting her hips so he could go deeper, harder.

Yelena was filled to the brim with sensory overload. He rocked her hips, grasped her bottom with skillful hands, filling her totally, completely. She felt like she could do anything, be anyone in this one moment. She was at one with him, an essential part of two halves that fit perfectly together, deep in the throes of some powerful, amazing force.

Alex's hot breath bathed her, his mouth devoured hers on the down thrust, then up again as he continued.

She was…it was…

Her eyes sprang wide, every sensitive inch of her skin throbbing, tingling with breathless climax.

She heard Alex groan as with one last thrust he emptied into her.

Oh, how she loved him.

Twelve

Yelena floated back down to earth slowly with a satisfied smile on her face, her entire body throbbing with pleasure.

With his full weight completely covering her, their flesh slick and wet, she took a deep breath. He was as necessary to her as air.

"You look pleased with yourself."

She opened her eyes into Alex's smiling ones, wicked with humor. Where their bodies joined, she could still feel him inside, intimate and hot.

She tightened her legs around him with a slow grin. "I am."

"You should be."

He rolled, taking her with him so she was on top. And when she pulled back, his hands went to her breasts, cradling the generous curves in both palms.

"You are beautiful."

She tilted her head. "So are you."

"It's official, then."

They laughed, two lovers sharing a deeply private moment. But as the seconds lengthened, Yelena's grin slowly sobered.

"Alex."

"Mmm?" He was still on her breasts, seemingly fascinated by the way her nipples pebbled beneath his thumbs.

She dragged in a sharp breath. How could she be so quickly aroused again, so soon?

"Alex. We didn't use protection."

His hands stilled, his eyes flying to hers. "Are you...?"

She felt the flush spread from belly to scalp. "I'm healthy. I've—" *Loved you for years.* She pulled in a breath before adding, "I'm fine."

"So am I."

He reached up, took her head between his hands and dragged her down for a kiss.

It wasn't a kiss full of lust and longing. It wasn't designed to arouse or command like so many others they'd shared before. Instead it was tender, soft. Loving. Yet more than the others, it made Yelena's blood pump faster, her lungs swell, her heart sing.

She let herself get swept away on the moment, let her mind take her to a place where she and Alex were together, where Bella completed their perfect family and they all lived happily ever after.

Yet she could only indulge in the fantasy for so long because slowly, her head began to fill with questions and doubts, ones that became too loud to ignore.

"Alex?"

"Mmm?" He'd moved down to her throat, his hands still holding her in place. She groaned as her body responded with sluggish delight.

She wanted to tell him her deepest secrets right then, let him know exactly how she felt. Yet fear robbed her of courage.

Alex put a high price on the truth. Would he want her after he knew she'd been lying all along?

"Was Carlos right? Did you hire me to get back at him?"

Her questions had the desired effect: his questing hands stilled, his head angling back to take her in.

"Do you really want me to answer that?"

Abruptly she withdrew, backing up against the couch, pillow clutched to her chest. "Which means yes."

Alex's thoughts tangled at the look on her face. "You know Bennett & Harper are the best in the business. That you are exceptional at what you do." He held up a hand at her impatient frown. "And yes, I did start out angry and desperate to cause Carlos damage. But then—"

"Then, what?"

"I didn't want to anymore."

Her brow wrinkled. "You didn't want to sleep with me?"

Lord, she undid him. "I didn't want Carlos to be the reason," he explained, taking her hand. When he brought it to his lips, her eyes widened. "There's never been a moment I've not wanted to make love to you, Yelena."

He watched her face relax, her eyes go liquid. Then she blinked and shook herself.

"You used me," she said flatly.

Her eyes, so dark and expressive, wounded him to the core. He could dredge up excuses but shame humbled him. He nodded. "I know. And I'm sorry."

She studied him for another moment before her chin tipped up. "Why did you invite Carlos tonight?"

"Because I needed you to see him for who he really is."

"You couldn't just tell me?" But even as the words left her mouth Yelena realized how stupid she sounded. She wouldn't have believed him. Not then. But now…

"And he's been going to the papers."

His chest tightened but he forced himself to relax. "Yes."

Yelena stared past his shoulder to the opposite wall in silence.

"I'll get my proof. About everything."

The silence stretched again until Alex said gently, "Look, Yelena, I know he's your brother but—"

"You've got to understand something about Carlos," she said firmly, bring her eyes back to his. "His reputation, his... his..." She struggled for the words, hand accentuating her dilemma. "His obsession with being who he is and what that stands for is the only thing he cares about. You know what it was like at school—no one touched the Valero girls. It was flattering having an overprotective brother. Gabriela hated it but had no choice, given what had happened back home. And when I got older, it became..."

"Stifling."

She nodded. "It was never about me. It was about him and his perfect reputation."

"Yelena..."

"He's never held Bella, not once." Her breath caught, a dead giveaway to her distress. "He never even asks about her."

She finally sees how Carlos really is. Alex wanted to pump his fist in the air, shout out his victory, but triumph was tempered by the obvious pain that shone in her eyes.

Then Yelena said, "So what Carlos heard...what I heard. Your father *wasn't* having an affair?"

His heart paused. "No."

"Then what were you arguing about?"

"Nothing important."

He rose in one fluid movement, so abrupt Yelena involuntarily gasped.

"Alex...?"

"I'm telling you to leave it, Yelena."

She paused. It was his voice, all rawness and jagged angles, a stark contrast to the smooth way he pulled on his pants.

He was damaged. Oh, not on the outside, because Alex

Rush had perfected a polished façade of control and restraint as necessary to his survival as breathing. No, it was something deeper, something missing.

She knew him. *Really* knew him, and not in the casual-date way Gabriela had cheerfully described before Yelena had cut her off, red-faced. And not in the "my business partner, Alex Rush" Carlos had bragged about.

Was she the only one who could see into his heart, see the cloying demons that touched his soul, ones she knew came from his picture-perfect home, ones he refused to address?

"I won't leave it," she said firmly. "Please tell me, Alex."

He rounded on her so suddenly, with such fury blazing from his eyes that she jumped.

"I said, leave it! Just because we had sex does not give you carte blanche to my entire life!"

She felt the slap as surely as palm meeting skin. Blood fled from her face, the dark truth a hard lump in her chest.

"So I'm just good enough to sleep with, is that it?"

Disgust hit Alex's stomach the exact moment shock distorted her features. He took one step back, dropped his eyes to the floor with a growl. It was done. He couldn't undo it now. *Way to go, mate.* The slow, victory clap of his conscience rang hollow in his ears. *You've been looking for a way to push her away and now you've found it.*

"I think I should go." She reached for her dress, a flush staining those high cheekbones.

He groaned. "Yelena, you don't have to—"

She shot him a look as she fumbled with her clothing, finally dragging the dress over those beautiful curves. "I'm flying home tomorrow, remember? I need to focus on your campaign."

Yelena grabbed her shoes then hurried to the door, silence dogging her retreat. Yet as she cracked the door open, she forced herself to glance back.

Alex had picked up the remote control and was flicking

through the channels, his bare back so painfully straight that her hands ached to touch him, to help ease the tension bunched along those beautiful shoulders.

Her throat tightened, choking whatever breath she had left.

"You need to think about this situation with Carlos and Sprint Travel. If you fight him for it, it'll hit the papers. It could turn ugly and overshadow what we're trying to achieve here."

The efficiently spare nod, along with a gruff "I will" was her only acknowledgment.

Pain sliced her heart but she managed to hold it together until she walked out, closing the door behind with an inaudible click.

Yelena paused in the corridor, the subdued lights throwing her shadow across the pristine white walls. Gently she placed a hand on the door.

"I love you."

She wanted to shout it loud instead of whispering into the empty silence. She loved Alex Rush.

Slowly she dragged herself down the hall, muscles aching with delicious exertion, shoes dangling from her fingers, the hem of her dress bunched in her hand.

She understood Alex better than he thought she did. He was an exceedingly proud man, one who did not take attacks on his family lying down.

She finally made it to her door and fumbled in her purse for the keycard. A wave of guilt lapped at her heels as she softly made her way inside. Alex wouldn't lie about Carlos. Not about something this important. And she'd heard it with her own ears. Her brother was behind those awful rumors, not only trying to destroy Alex's reputation, but also Pam's and Chelsea's in the process. Three innocent people.

And then there was her own bombshell. How would Alex take that?

She gently woke Jasmine, who'd fallen asleep on her couch, then took a quick shower. As the smell of Alex washed from her body, her mind went into overdrive, senses inundated as she recalled every second, every passionate moment of their lovemaking.

She loved him.

For another hour she lay awake in her enormous bed, the feather quilt bunched about her waist as she tossed and turned.

A tiny cry permeated the silence and Yelena rose with relief, padded into Bella's room and scooped her up in her arms.

In the semidarkness she gently jogged the hungry baby, cooing softly as she took the bottle from the fridge, heated it then settled on the sofa.

"Is it wrong that I don't want to tell him, Bella?" she whispered softly as the baby fed. "I promised Gabriela I'd keep our secret and keep you safe…" She trailed off, her fingers tightening around the bottle. She recalled Alex's fury, his pain, when he'd first seen Bella on the plane.

"He still thinks you're mine." And as much as she desperately wished Bella was hers in every sense, she knew the lie would eventually come between them. Not right now, not in the first flush of desire and lust. No, it'd be later, when the bonds of trust were again strong between them.

That is, if there *was* a later. Alex was desperate to push her away. And right now, she had the awful feeling it would be easier—and safer—if she let him.

After her restless night, Yelena was determined to focus on work the next morning before the midday flight took her back to reality. But instead of going to her makeshift office where the chance of running into Alex was high, she made a detour for Ruby's.

Breakfast and coffee, she reasoned. Plus the added bonus of people watching in case her thoughts wandered.

She needn't have worried—when she clicked on to the morning's papers to check last night's coverage, one small article caught her eye. Quickly she read, a deep frown forming. According to the reporter's skillful prose that skirted the edges of truth, she and Alex were deep in the throes of a secret affair.

"Yelena, do you have a minute?"

Yelena blinked up from her laptop screen to Pamela Rush, who stood next to her booth, eyes hidden behind large sunglasses. Her fingers played with the plaited belt at her waist, telling Yelena something was off.

With a reassuring smile, she clicked the laptop closed.

"Sure. Take a seat." She nodded to the vacant spot opposite, then gestured to a waiter. "Would you like a drink?"

"Iced tea, please," Pam said automatically, giving the waiter a smile as she removed her glasses.

Yelena waited patiently as Pam carefully folded her sunglasses on the table, then recentered the coaster. Finally, the older woman linked her fingers and glanced out to the entertainment area, to the view of the semicrowded pool beyond.

"A lovely day for a swim."

"Mmm. Did you stay long last night?"

Pam smiled. "About ten. The bands were still going when I left. And Chelsea looked to be having a good time."

Yelena nodded, smiling back.

A brief pause, then Pam said, "You're leaving today."

"Yes." Yelena nodded. "Now that we've started the ball rolling I need to get a team together, start organizing details for the anniversary, plus put a few feelers out for some one-on-one interviews."

Pam looked surprised. "Alex has agreed to it?"

"Last night was a start. I'm working on it," Yelena added with a rueful smile.

"Ah." Pam paused, her fingers going to a thin, elegant diamond ring on her left hand, methodically turning it around and around. "Chelsea and you have been getting along well."

"She's a great kid."

Pam nodded. "Thank you. She's been so angry for so long—I suggested therapy but she balked at that. Which would be fine except she wasn't talking to anyone, me and Alex included. I'm grateful she's had someone to open up to. Which is what brings me here." She petered off and took a breath. "I need you to organize an interview."

Yelena eased back in her seat. "For you?"

Pam nodded, her gaze direct. Those dark blue depths contained a multitude of feelings—pride, honesty. And fear.

"Does Alex know?"

"No. He'd just try and talk me out of it." Her face turned stormy. "I love him, Yelena, but he always takes on too much responsibility for this family. He's always has been my little protector, ever since he was a boy." Her smile was bittersweet, speaking of pain long buried. "No, this is for me, Yelena. I need to do this."

Impulsively Yelena reached across the table and placed her hand on Pam's, looking her straight in the eye. "Okay."

Pam nodded, her relieved sigh coming out in a rush. "Thank you."

Yelena withdrew to make a note in her diary. "And the other thing?"

At the sudden silence Yelena glanced up. Pam's fingers were linked together on the table top.

"How is your gorgeous baby?"

Yelena smiled. "Sleeping at the moment. Pam…"

"Yelena." Pam's hand shot out to cover Yelena's, her fingers suddenly cold despite the warmth of the morning. "I'm sorry. I need to ask you something."

"Yes?"

"It's a personal question. I'm sorry," she repeated and quickly pulled her hand back. "But it's been eating at me ever since you arrived and, well…"

"Pam," Yelena said slowly. "Whatever it is, I'll try my best to answer it."

Her face flushing, Pam said, "I have to know. Is your… I mean…" Her gaze dropped to the table as she finally whispered, "Before all this. Did you and Alex…were you…?"

Yelena sat back in her chair. "Did Alex and I ever date?"

"Sort of." Pam's face flushed deeper. "Were you and he ever…intimate?"

With a tangled tongue, Yelena stared at the deeply mortified woman. The silence lasted until the waiter brought their drinks and moved on to the next table.

"No," Yelena finally managed as she grabbed the cold, tall glass. "Can I ask why you want to know?"

The woman's shoulders sagged. "Thank you for being honest. It's obviously just my eyes playing tricks. Ever since I saw that sweet little baby of yours, well…" She gave a little laugh, wavy with embarrassment. "Bella is the spitting image of Alex and Chelsea at that age—same nose, same chin. And you and Alex do have some chemistry—" She quickly cut herself off with a faltering smile. "Put it down to my eagerness at wanting to be a grandma. Well…" She rose from her seat, palming her glass. "I should let you get back to work. Thank you."

Yelena watched Pam go, her brow furrowed. Odd. Very odd. As if Bella would be—

A terrible, ridiculous thought crashed in, leaving her gasping as the world suddenly tilted on its access. Everything—her brain, her breath, her very heartbeat—came to a screeching sickening halt.

Oh, no. Oh, no, no, no. Gabriela hadn't… She would have told her.

There was no way on earth her baby sister had lain in that small hospital, bleeding to death after she'd given birth, using the last breath in her body to *lie* to her. Which could only mean one possible thing—Gabriela hadn't known who Bella's father was.

With jerky movements, she flipped open her diary, back to last year's calendar. Her finger shakily traced the dates, skipping backwards as she counted.

Alex and Gabriela had been dating on and off since May. She paused on July then tapped her finger thoughtfully. Too many things had happened that month—Gabriela returning from Madrid, the embassy ball. Alex kissing her.

Her heart bottomed out, leaving a terrible numbness in its wake.

What was she supposed to do now?

Thirteen

Emotionally exhausted, Yelena was unfazed when her family's official chauffeur greeted her arrival at Canberra airport. She got into her father's car and strapped Bella in, resigned silence accompanying the drive to the Valero residence.

The car drove along Morshead Drive, then left onto the King's Avenue Bridge that took her over Lake Burley Griffin. As they headed towards Capital Hill and Parliament House, Yelena watched the steady flow of traffic. Soon the change of landscape told her they were in Yarralumla. The affluent suburb was populated by foreign diplomats, politicians and various families of Canberra's super rich, and it showed—from the neat gardens, the subtle and not-so-subtle homes, even the streets themselves. Meticulous and groomed, that's what the area reflected.

When the car drew to a halt in the long curving driveway, Yelena finally broke from her apathy. A Valero summons meant only one thing—displeasure.

She got out of the car, shouldering Bella as she studied what had had once been her home. She still loved the look of those white rendered walls, terra-cotta tiles and clean, smooth angles that made up the seven-bedroomed, two-storied house. And as always, the gardens were superbly groomed, the windows sparkling.

But it had always been her parents' house, never hers. This thought was confirmed when she stepped into the living area, an aura of "look, don't touch" permeating every square inch from its high ceiling to its timber floor and period features.

On the beautiful antique couch sat her perfectly groomed mother, legs crossed elegantly at the ankles, skirt demurely covering her knees. Her father stood behind, dark and towering, a scowl on his autocratic face. To the left, Carlos leaned against the polished bar, a glass of amber liquid cradled in his hand.

"What is this, an intervention?" Yelena joked lamely, even as her grip tightened on Bella.

A servant came forward, hovering expectantly. Yelena frowned.

"Let Julie settle the baby," Juan commanded.

Yelena blinked. "Why?"

"Because we need to talk."

"So talk." Yelena glared at the unfortunate Julie, who had flushed deep red.

"Dios." Juan sighed and waved the servant away. "Fine. I don't need to remind you, Yelena, that I am not happy with your continued association with Alexander Rush."

Her eyes flicked to Carlos. He met her gaze head-on as he slowly took a sip from his glass.

"It not only impacts on you," Juan continued sternly. "It affects everyone in this family."

"How?"

"People talk, Yelena," Maria said tightly. "Your father—

this family—has a reputation to uphold in this community. Rumors and malicious gossip can damage it irreparably."

"The same way the ones circulating about William Rush's affair are destroying his family?"

It wasn't her mother's reaction she was after, although Maria's moue of distaste was satisfying. No, she carefully watched Carlos' eyes narrow, a second before his expression smoothed out.

"Yes," Juan said. "The longer you continue associating with the Rushes, the more damage it will cause."

Yelena sighed, her hand automatically going to Bella's back as she felt the baby stir. She was tired, so very tired of these mind games. The burden of respectability and family honor weighed heavily on her shoulders, dragging her down, warring with her own sense of right.

"I'm sorry if you feel that way, Papá. But Bennett & Harper signed a contract—"

"Then get out of it. No one's indispensible—surely you can hand the job over to someone else?"

His unconscious insult slapped her firmly in the face and she felt her cheeks color. "No, Papá. Even if I wanted out— which I don't—I have a promotion riding on this."

Juan's eyes narrowed. "I did not *ask* you to withdraw, Yelena."

Chagrin welled up, chasing away her fatigue. "So your wishes are more important than my career, my life?"

"We are talking about the Valero name," Carlos said curtly. "About our public reputation, our—"

"Oh, how I am sick to death of hearing that!" she hissed. "Especially from you, someone who claims diplomatic immunity every time he gets a speeding ticket."

"Yelena," Juan rumbled ominously.

"You held the 'reputation' card over Gabriela's head for years and where did that get her?"

"Yelena!" Maria and Juan echoed in unison.

"She's dead. And still you're so ashamed of her you refuse to let people know. Despite everything she did, despite how disappointed you were, I *loved* her." Her voice cracked then, a sob tearing at her throat. Bella let out a grumble, sensitive to her mother's distress and Yelena immediately started rubbing her back.

"Of course you did. We all did," Carlos said quickly.

Surprised, Yelena stared at him, until Maria added, "But she was also uncontrollable and selfish." Her mother's mouth thinned, a red-lipsticked slash of displeasure. "Even when we moved here, she was still the same reckless girl. I *know* you saw that."

"When she was *sixteen*," Yelena said, exasperated. "So she dropped out of school, modeled for a few chain-store catalogs. But she quit modeling, she had a regular job. She wanted to move on from her past but you all just wouldn't let her."

"That is enough, Yelena!" Juan thundered, making everyone jump. A second later, Bella let out a mighty wail.

Yes, it was enough. Yelena shifted Bella to her other shoulder, patting her firmly through the warm layers. "It suited you all to keep her tied to her past mistakes, to use her as an example. But she deserved better. She was my *sister*. And if this is the way you treat people in this family, then I don't want to be a part of it anymore."

Every face in the room displayed their own version of total and utter shock and for long seconds, triumph spiked Yelena's blood. A short-lived triumph when mortification quickly flushed her burning cheeks.

She turned on her heel, stalked out the living room and down the hallway, her clipped footsteps echoing on the polished slate.

With a hefty wrench she pulled the front door open and the blast of cold air hit her hot face.

What have you done?

Panic crept in, spreading its insidious tentacles of doubt

and uncertainty, but for the first time she kept right on going, down the steps and across the driveway, to the car that still waited.

You've done it. You're free. Instead of the crushing sense of loss she'd expected from this moment, relief mingling with tentative joy lifted her heart.

She patted Bella, warm and comforting against her chest. She was well and truly alone now. Yes, there was fear of the unknown, but she'd overcome that before. She'd do it again.

"Yelena!"

She whipped her head around to see Carlos slowly jogging to catch up to her. When he stopped, his small smile oozed nervous contrition. "Look, I think I owe you an apology."

Her heart gave a small cautious jump. "For what?"

"For what happened on Saturday night. I'd had a few drinks and things just got a little…heated."

Yelena let the silence flow around them. Despite the half-hearted apology, the pain of his rejection still throbbed under the surface.

"So I'm sorry, okay? Okay?"

His smile spread wider, one eyebrow curving up as he tilted his head in that charismatic way she'd seen a thousand times before. But now, after everything she'd seen and heard, she was immune. Instead of giving him an answering smile, she forced her expression to remain impassive.

"Here, let me get this." He opened the car door and stepped aside.

What does he want? The thought lingered as she bent to strap Bella in the baby capsule.

"So…you're still seeing him?"

Her body stiffened but she kept on with her task. "He's my client."

When she straightened, Carlos had shoved his hands in his pockets, staring down at his feet.

A perfect picture of reluctant gossip. *Oh, come on.* It was all Yelena could do not to roll her eyes. Instead she scowled, which only seemed to appease Carlos.

"Then you should know he called this morning and threatened me."

Threatened? That wasn't Alex's style but she was way too tired to tell Carlos that. "And why are you telling me this?"

"Because I need your help."

She slowly leaned against the doorframe. "How?"

He paused for effect. If she didn't know any better she'd peg him as reluctant, even embarrassed. But she did know him, all too well.

"I was thinking—and I know this is a lot to ask, and I wouldn't normally do this—"

"Carlos…"

His irritation showed in the brief downward turn of his mouth. "If you could have a word with him, maybe convince him not to—"

The sharp inward sound of Yelena's horrified breath silenced him.

"No."

Carlos's expression tightened. "So you'd let this stupid vendetta go to court? How is this going to impact on us? Our parents? Your campaign?" He added in a moment of inspiration.

With cool deliberation, she got in the car, slid down the window then closed the door with a firm clunk.

"Carlos," she said slowly as she slid her sunglasses into place. "Let me say this once and once only. I heard you and Alex by the pool on Saturday night. As much as you're my brother and I love you, I will not—cannot—trust you. You've hurt too many people, including me, for us to ever be okay again."

As she turned to clip herself in, Carlos slapped a hand on the window frame, making her jump.

"So you're choosing *him* over your own family?"

She sighed. Surely her heart couldn't break anymore, not when she knew the full extent of Carlos's malice? Yet a tiny piece still cracked, reminding her of the brother she'd once blindly adored.

"Yes, I am."

His stunned expression gave her no satisfaction as she powered up the window. As the car drove away for the very last time, she knew where she had to be—with people who needed her love and support, who'd been damaged terribly by the actions of someone she'd loved. She needed to help make amends.

And slowly, the pain in her heart began to retreat.

Fourteen

It was Tuesday. Yelena had been gone nearly two days. Two long, arduous, maddening days, days full of work, of papers and files and copious amounts of coffee.

Days without Yelena.

Despite the constant influx of people and the work load, Diamond Bay seemed empty somehow. With his mother and Chelsea on a shopping trip in Sydney and Yelena gone, the gaping hole was even more obvious.

It was so not like him to be this unfocused, this distracted. A handful of times he'd glanced up at his office door, certain Yelena was about to walk in with that mesmerizing hip sway that sucked him in every time.

But she wouldn't. He'd seen to that.

So he'd punished himself by playing every encounter over in his head until, as the early morning sun began to blaze over the horizon, he'd jumped on his bike and zoomed off.

Now he'd been on the road for an hour but still the grueling heat couldn't wipe Yelena from his mind.

He drove, mile after mile of red dust, the hard, throbbing machine between his thighs and the gutsy roar of the engine in his ears as he burned up the road, on his way somewhere, anywhere that didn't have a memory of her, her mouth and that hot lush skin he'd possessed so completely.

With the sun blazing high in the sky, he finally paused for a breather. The desert heat hit him full force as he yanked off his helmet, tarmac hot beneath his boots, searing up through his leathers as he swiped the beaded sweat from his forehead.

No matter how far he rode he couldn't outrun *her*. Their last night together spun dizzyingly in his head, forcing him to focus on the one thing he wanted to forget.

With a curse he hurled his helmet, scowling as it hit the ground in a shower of red dust.

And in that moment, something deep and yearning inside him cracked wide open. It made him want things, things that only Yelena could give him.

He recalled the feel of the hot, sweet body beneath his, how she'd welcomed him inside with almost frantic desire in her dark eyes. She'd tasted like always—sexy skin, want barely restrained. She'd looked amazing, from the wild cloud of hair spilling over lush breasts, to the way her waist indented and flared into sinfully curvy hips.

His groin tightened painfully with the memories. Of dipping his tongue into her belly button before dragging his mouth across that perfect belly, the skin hot and reactive to his touch...

A perfect belly.

He paused with a frown. Perfect belly, perfect hips, perfect breasts.

He snapped in a sharp breath, mind racing backwards. He hadn't just been swept up in the moment. Her skin *was* perfect.

No stretch marks, no C-section scar.

Realization instantaneously heated into rage, and rage into

fiery knives of pain, tiny pinpricks stabbing into every muscle, every nerve.

She'd lied to him.

He was on the bike in less than a second, racing back to Diamond Bay, to Yelena.

To the truth.

He stormed into the resort like the hounds of hell themselves were snapping at his heels, uncaring of the stares, the whispers left in his wake. His jerking strides devoured the long hallway and when he slapped his hand on Yelena's office door, it crashed back on its hinges with a satisfying crack.

Nostrils flared, blood thumping, he took in the empty room at first with fury, then dawning realization.

She's gone, you fool.

He gave a groan before viciously unzipping his jacket and pulling out his phone. He palmed it, poised to dial, but an e-mail reminder flashed on the screen and his whole body stilled.

Re: Pamela Rush interview

All his veins felt as if they'd suddenly frozen, leaving him unable to even breathe. Then panic quickly rushed in, forcing his heart rate up, tightening his lungs. With a few taps he was reading an e-mail from a Leah Jackson at Bennett & Harper.

It was confidential, obviously sent to him by mistake. As fury mounted, he scanned down, finally getting to the original exchange between Yelena and the show's producer.

Thanks for fitting us in on Tuesday, Rita, Yelena had written. *My client is anxious for the public to hear her story and I'm sure you'll agree it's a powerful one. I appreciate you giving us approval over final cut and I'm positive there will be no major problems with this.*

He slumped in the chair, his pounding heartbeat a deep echo in his brain. Then in the next second, he dialed the office phone.

"It's Alex Rush. Organize a car and have the airstrip fire up my plane. I'll be leaving for Canberra in twenty minutes."

Yelena stood behind the lighting stand, watching the makeup girl dust Pam's face with powder. "Are you sure you want me here?" she asked for the third time.

Pam smiled. "You've made all this possible, Yelena. Why wouldn't I want you here?"

Chelsea stood beside Yelena, giving her hand a reassuring squeeze. She'd taken her suggestion and talked to her mother all right, and it had resulted in a full-blown report for *Morning Grace,* Australia's most-watched current affairs/breakfast show. So here they were, in Pam's sun room in the Canberra "mausoleum" house. Masses of afternoon light streamed through the glass walls, falling squarely on Pam, seated alone on the comfortable couch.

Guilt swept Yelena's conscience. Alex was her client, he was the one who'd signed the contract, the one who was paying Bennett & Harper. No matter how much she knew Pam needed to do this, Alex would accuse her of going behind his back. And he'd be right. Yet she was human. Pam had a right to let the public know the real truth, even if it did mean losing Alex's trust in the process. At least he'd be cleared once and for all for his father's death.

Admit it. You're afraid. Afraid that you'll reveal everything to him with one look from those all-seeing blue eyes.

And that would mean losing control of everything she'd worked so hard for since Gabriela died.

She glanced at Pam, who was studying her with disturbing thoroughness. "We couldn't wait," Yelena added. "It was either now if we wanted to make tomorrow's show, or wait another two months."

"I know. It's time," Pam said softly, her troubled blue eyes stormy as the makeup girl finally finished. "I need to speak out, especially with that thing in today's paper."

Yelena flushed, knowing Carlos was probably behind the two-part article scheduled to hit Sydney's *Daily Mirror* come Monday. She'd got a heads-up barely twenty-four hours before, the promo ad screaming from the front page with voyeuristic glee.

"I need to let people know the truth," Pam said softly, her eyes going to Chelsea. Suddenly her face, so elegant and refined, crumpled. "I love you, sweetheart."

"I love you too, Mum," Chelsea choked out. Her fingers tightened around Yelena's and Yelena squeezed back.

Here were two amazing women, facing their demons and speaking out to the world. Their strength and courage floored Yelena, her throat tight as she choked back tears.

Her head was one big mess, what with Alex, Carlos, the upcoming exposé and now Pam's interview. And sitting back in her little apartment, burning a hole in her briefcase, lay the means to possibly shatter her future: forms for the DNA test that would prove or disprove this ridiculous suspicion regarding Bella's paternity.

If Alex wasn't the father then what would be the point of revealing she'd lied before the results proved it either way? Yet short of stealing his hair or bodily fluids, how could she get a DNA sample *without* telling him?

She'd wrestled with her conscience at Diamond Bay until her call to Channel Five had provided a convenient escape. But now, with everything crowding in on her, she couldn't stop her mind from going there.

You love him. He needs to be told.

She glanced up as Grace Callahan settled in the chair opposite Pam, fixed on a mike then nodded to the segment producer.

The producer called for quiet, said, "And…go!" and they were off.

"Pamela Rush, can you start from the beginning and tell us

why you decided to do this interview after all these months of silence?"

When Yelena felt Chelsea's fingers tighten in hers, she gave the teenager a reassuring smile. An awful sadness weighted her heart, creating a pall over what should have been a triumphant moment for her career, for Pam and Chelsea and the truth.

If these two women could take control and put things right, why couldn't she?

It was close to five o'clock before the crew packed up.

"What's going to happen to Mum now?"

Chelsea had been picking at her fingernails for the last ten minutes, her face fraught with concern. "Will she go to jail?"

Yelena met Pam's look. The older woman nodded.

"We don't know. George says it depends on what the police want to do," Yelena said, deferring the situation to their newly hired criminal lawyer. "Your mother did provide a false statement."

"But there are also mitigating circumstances," Pam added as Chelsea's expression turned fearful. "I've arranged to go into the station and make a formal statement tomorrow morning."

"But she could be arrested," Chelsea said.

Pam nodded slowly. "It's possible, yes."

Chelsea clutched her mother's hand, her fingers firm as her chin went up.

"Don't worry, Chelsea." Yelena smiled bravely even as her heart constricted. "We'll work this out. And George is one of the best. We're going to try our hardest to ensure your mother doesn't spend any time in jail. I'll be there for you both."

After a few tear-ridden hugs, Yelena finally left, giving both Pam's and Chelsea's hands another reassuring squeeze and murmuring positive reassurances.

It took twenty minutes to drive out of affluent Yarralumla

until finally hitting the Commonwealth Bridge, another five until she wound her way around Canberra's multiple roundabouts before turning the corner to her city apartment complex.

She was going to do her damnedest to ensure the Rushes were not punished further, which meant putting a stop to those slanderous articles. And *that* meant dealing with Carlos.

A dark blue Mercedes sat directly in front of her building, a familiar figure standing ramrod straight by the passenger door. Her breath sped out. Even at this distance, she could see Alex's tension bristle from every muscle in his broad, commanding body.

She pulled into the basement car park, heart in her throat, dread freezing her fingers as she took the key from the ignition. When she got out and turned, he was right there, hands on his hips, face tight with barely leashed emotion.

"Alex! What—what are you doing here?" She readjusted the bundle of files she held, a poor barrier of protection.

With a dark scowl he shoved his phone under her nose. Blinking, she took a step back, but not before she recognized the e-mail on the screen.

Her heart bottomed out and she winced.

With a furious question in his eyes, he yanked his phone back. "Get in the car, Yelena."

"Why?"

"Would you prefer we do this out in the open?" His voice bounced off the cement pylons, echoing in the cavernous silence as his eyes skimmed the car park. "Or upstairs in front of your *daughter?*"

Yelena's stomach clenched. She nodded, swinging open the door of her shiny BMW then closing it firmly.

After he got in the passenger side she expected unleashed fury, a blast of accusations and demands. After the crazy day she'd had, she was fully prepared to accept whatever he threw at her. Yet he just glared at her, blue eyes slowly picking her apart with ruthless efficiency.

She fidgeted, first with her necklace, then with the edges of the files she still clutched.

"You went ahead with an interview after I'd specifically told you not to." He finally got out. "Why?"

"Because it was Pam's choice, Alex."

"This is *not* what I hired you for."

"But it's what she wanted."

She could see his jaw working as he fought to bring his emotions under control. His eyes, now flashing with bitterness, held something else, something odd and infinitely more scary. "So instead of letting me know, I have to find out via e-mail?"

"That was a mistake—"

"Oh, and that makes it all better." His face contorted into harsh planes, freezing her out. "Do not presume" came his tight reply, "to know anything about what's happened in my life, Yelena."

"How can I, when you don't tell me?" She took a deep breath. *He's vulnerable and angry, lashing out.* "I was there at Pam's interview. I know your father controlled every aspect of your family's lives. I know he hit Pam regularly. I know he hit you until *you* were old enough to fight back." She paused, remembering Pam's stiff, heartrending recollection. "You never left home because you were scared he'd start on Chelsea—"

"Stop."

She ignored the dangerous warning. "That night in your office. You were talking about your father leaving your *mother* alone, weren't you?"

"I said, stop!"

His deafening command made her flinch, the venom washing over her like some horrid stain. With eyes wide and muscles taut, she stared, until the furious lines on his face suddenly melted into anguish, then horror.

"Yelena, I…" He lifted a hand then quickly dropped it, revulsion reflected in his eyes. "I didn't mean to… I'd never lay a finger on you, you know that."

She took a breath, then another, her whole body humming. "I know."

"He never touched Chelsea," he choked out, his face contorted. "She adored him. And I covered for that bastard because I didn't want to shatter her illusions."

Just like yours were. She could have wept then but one look at his face, his strong, implacable face tinged with self-disgust and she dared not.

"Chelsea knew, Alex. She'd seen it happen a month before his death," she said softly. Shock stiffened his body, just before the pain poured in, pain that wrenched at her own heart.

"That night we were together…when I came home…" He dragged a hand over his face, raw emotion carved into every line, every muscle.

"Tell me, Alex. Tell me what happened."

"I don't know!" He banged his fists softly on the dashboard. "I came home and he was in the pool. And Mum…"

"She didn't fall asleep watching television like she told the police."

Still he said nothing, just stared out the window, a faraway look on his face. Yelena placed a tentative hand on his leg, a gesture aimed at soothing, consoling. Yet it was like touching fire-forged steel.

"Alex. You're not alone in this. I want to be here for you."

His head snapped up so quickly she jumped.

"How can you when you lied to me?" His jaw tightened, eyes narrowing. "When you *still* lie."

"I…"

"You let me believe Bella was yours."

She faced his disappointment, small and still with the burden of guilt he'd unexpectedly laid on her. "How did you know?"

"No scars or stretch marks."

"I see." She sighed.

"Is that all you have to say?"

She shot him a fierce look. "She *is* mine, Alex, in all the ways that count. My name is on her birth certificate. I raised her, I love her."

"But you are not her natural mother."

Her heart ripped from her chest, sending a screaming ache into her brain. "No."

"Whose is she?" He paused, considering her as a beat passed. Then his face contorted with realization. "Gabriela's."

"Yes." One word yet she could barely get it out.

"So why didn't you tell me?"

She felt sudden tears well in her eyes before she quickly blinked them away. "Because Gabriela made me promise before she died. That night I left you, the night your father died…" When she dragged her eyes up to his, his frozen look broke her heart a little more. "Gabriela was involved with Salvatore Vitto."

He frowned. "The Spanish drug lord?"

She nodded. "Gabriela had no idea—they'd been on and off since they'd met a few years back, at some agency party in Madrid." She couldn't meet his eyes, knowing her distaste for Gabriella's multi-boyfriend habit was not the issue right now. "When she returned in June she found out and broke it off, which was when he abducted her. She…" She swallowed. "She called me on the run and I met her at the airport. To make sure we weren't followed, we crisscrossed Europe for weeks. Then we ended up in Germany."

The horror of those few months flooded back, sending her hands trembling. She clasped her fingers firmly together and placed them in her lap.

"Bella was born on the eighteenth of March, one week before her due date, in a small German hospital with Gabriela registered as me. In order for the dates to fit my pregnancy, I had to claim she was two months premature when I applied for her passport. You can't fly with premie babies so I had to wait until May to return home." She took a breath then continued, "Vitto is a vicious, ruthless man. Gabriela had no doubt he'd kill her and take Bella if he ever found out."

A small, strangled sound. When she looked up, she thought she saw something more on his face, a small crack in that perfect shield of composure he showed to the world.

"Why didn't you come home before Bella was born?"

"Vitto had Gabriela's passport. We couldn't risk getting a new one in Spain, not when he had government officials in his pocket. When we finally got to the Australian embassy in Germany, we'd been anonymous and trouble free for a month. By that time Gabriela was showing and didn't want to come home. I tried talking her around but you know how stubborn she could be."

Despite the gravity of the moment, he gave a brief, spare smile and a curt nod.

"And you could imagine my parents' reaction if she came back pregnant and unwed." Well-worn frustration sparked, stiffening her posture. "My father and Carlos, demanding to know who the father was, horrified the Valero name was again tarnished. My mother, mortified and disgraced in front of all her social peers. My God—all the questions, the accusations, the yelling, on and on and on." She tightened her grip on the files and pain sliced her fingers. "Of course, I was the shining example of all things good and proper. I cannot remember one single lecture to Gabriela when her exploits weren't followed with 'why can't you be more like your sister?' She made out like it didn't matter, but the comparison killed me every time."

She stared out the windscreen, too afraid to meet his eyes, to see that familiar icy shield shutting her out.

"And yet you willingly posed as an unwed single mother."

"I had to protect Bella. A blemish on my sterling reputation was a small price to pay for her life."

This was it. This was the moment. She took a deep cleansing breath. She was afraid, of course—willingly sacrificing control went against everything she'd struggled for since Gabriela had died. She'd had to be strong, strong for Bella, strong for her dead sister.

Yet as she finally looked up into Alex's eyes, that strength began to bend like a tree caught in a hurricane.

"Alex? I need to tell you something else."

A dry laugh, full of tight irony, emerged from his lips. "Oh, please. Be my guest."

"Upstairs."

He glanced towards the elevator bank, then back to her. Yelena nodded. It was time for her, too.

Fifteen

In her living room, amongst the well-loved collection of books, antiques and modern comfy furniture, he paced. He reminded Yelena of Canberra Zoo's tigers—majestic, proud yet ultimately aggravated with containment.

She approached him slowly. "Did you and Gabriela ever sleep together?"

He stopped dead in his tracks. "What kind of question is—"

"Please, Alex. I need to know."

His frown became darker. "Once. At the Christmas in July ball. It was after our kiss. You'd shot me down, I got drunk and she was there…"

She knew the moment he trailed off. He paled.

"You think Bella is mine?"

"I assumed Vito was the father. And from her actions, so did Gabriela. She never even mentioned you and her…" Yelena felt her cheeks warm as she broke off. "But the dates fit. And your mother mentioned a resemblance to you and Chelsea when you were babies."

He stepped back so quickly it left Yelena breathless. Then he spun, one hand on his hip, one diving into his hair.

She struggled in silence as he began pacing again. She heard him groan as he whirled then suddenly slammed his fists on kitchen counter. They made a terrible hollow sound, one that stabbed straight into her heart.

"I can have a DNA test back in as little as ten days," she said softly. His hands braced wide on the cold, marble surface, head dipped as her every nerve ending teetered on a thin tightrope, waiting for him to say something. She'd done the right thing. So why did it feel as if she'd ripped her world apart?

When the knock on her door came, they both jumped.

Melanie stood on the doorstep, holding Bella. "I thought I heard you come in and…" She trailed off as she spotted Alex.

Yelena ignored the question in her eyes, instead cupping Bella's warm head with a smile. "Could you give me some time, Mel? I'm in the middle of a situation here."

"You okay?" Yelena's nod only brought forth a frown. "Are you—"

"I'm fine," Yelena said softly. "Half an hour, okay?"

"Okay."

After her neighbor left, Yelena gently closed the door and turned back to Alex. He had his back to her, studying her photo array on the armoire.

Curious, she moved closer.

He held a silver frame with a picture of a smiling Bella in a pink romper suit.

She glanced up at him, expecting a scowl. But what she saw flipped her heart in her chest, making her breath stumble.

"I thought she'd killed him."

Confusion fuzzed her brain. It took a moment to realize he was talking about his parents.

"Alex." She reached for his hand, her fingers enveloping his. "Pam did it for you, to clear you once and for all. She found him floating in the pool at eleven-fifteen p.m. From the autopsy report, his time of death was eleven-twenty."

"So if she'd called an ambulance, he'd still be alive," Alex said softly.

"Maybe. It's hard to say."

"I thought…"

"That she'd pushed him into the pool?"

He nodded, staring at the picture of Bella before putting it back.

"And you were covering for her with your silence."

He didn't respond, just pulled his hand free and sat heavily on her sofa.

"Alex. Your mother's going in to make an official statement tomorrow and we have a top criminal lawyer on the case. But what she really needs is your support."

When he looked up, the bleak look in his eyes squeezed the breath from her chest.

"Of course."

The desperate urge to throw her arms around him, to soothe his pain until he was her old Alex, the laughing, teasing man who'd flirted with abandon and made love to her with wild passion, swamped every muscle in her body.

"Alex…" She paused, the words hovering on her tongue. But the longer the silence lengthened, the more fear took over. Instead, she said, "Do you want to do the DNA test? To make sure that Bella…" She flushed as he looked up. "Of course, I'll completely understand if you choose not to."

He quickly stood, an oddly graceful movement for such a big man. "Yelena. Do you honestly think I could live with myself not knowing?"

The raw honesty blazing from his bright eyes humbled her. "I thought maybe…"

"That I'd ignore my own child?"

The horrible truth slammed into her full force. She may be Bella's mother on paper but if Alex wanted to fight for custody, blood would win out every time.

"What?" Alex frowned as he watched Yelena's face drain of all color. "Yelena?"

She shoved her hair back, flicking it off her neck with an efficient sweep. With hands on hips, she looked him straight in the eye, the cool expression belying her compressed lips, the worry lines creasing her brow. "What?"

Clarity dawned, softening his expression. "I'm not going to take Bella from you."

Her eyes sparked. "No, you're not."

A small involuntary smile escaped him. He'd no doubt she would fight him with every breath in her body. That was his Yelena.

His heart soared then, forcing his body into a familiar thrum, even as his grin made her frown. It just amused him more.

"I love you."

From the frozen look on her face, he'd stunned her. Hell, he'd stunned *himself.* He hadn't meant to own up to it right here, right now, but somewhere in these last few minutes he realized he'd be a coward if he didn't.

Yet she whirled away, arms crossed, head bowed as if seeking divine guidance. The silence grew—an uncomfortable, expectant silence that gnawed at his control. He'd said it and all he'd gotten was a big fat nothing.

Finally, with her back still to him, she broke it.

"Don't, Alex. My brother is trying to destroy your family and—"

"This has nothing to do with Carlos."

She spun back around, her dark eyes riddled with skepticism.

It wounded him, knowing he'd put that look there. He said, "I called him this morning and offered him a deal. He could buy me out in exchange for me not charging him with slander."

"And?"

Alex raised one eyebrow. "He took it. With a few choice curses."

She said nothing, just considered his words in wary silence.

"Can we stop talking about your brother now?" he finally said. "This *really* isn't about him. I…" He paused, cleared his throat, straightened his shoulders and took his first ever leap of faith.

Gently capturing her wrists, he waited until she looked up. When their gazes met, his heart began to thump in earnest. Moment of truth.

"This is about you and me. You're fierce, loyal and passionate." He cupped her cheek, her soft, warm skin heating his palm. "My mother and Chelsea adore you. You were more than just a hired consultant—you were their friend."

"I still am," she choked out, blinking. To his surprise, Alex felt his eyes well in response. Dammit! Here he was in one of the most important moments of his life and he was about to stuff it up by *crying?*

He took a breath, wrestling for control. When he finally had it, he grasped both her arms and drew her closer. Tension tingled beneath his fingers, telling him her entire body was ready for flight. Her dark eyes held a stark vulnerability that touched him deep in his soul, called out to every primitive male instinct to protect her, keep her from pain and harm.

He'd willingly lay down his life for this woman.

"Yelena. I love being with you, love making love to you." He paused, alarmed to see a tear track slowly down her cheek. "I'd love to wake up with you every moment of my life. I love you." He brushed his thumb across her cheek, catching that tear in the silence.

With taut nerves and held breath, he waited. Finally, Yelena looked up through big, watery eyes, her mouth stretched into a wide, traffic-stopping smile. His heart stopped.

Yelena took a breath, a deep, jagged breath that felt like the first true one she'd taken in a long, long time. He looked so concerned, studying her with those bright blue eyes that held so much emotion, so much passion that she felt she'd explode with joy.

"Yes," she managed to say. "I love you, too."

When he cupped her face, her breath stuttered to a halt, her world shrinking to this one room, this one moment.

"I've loved you from the first moment I set eyes on you, Yelena Valero."

Love, hope and desire all surged up, threatening to choke her. But in the next instant his mouth came down on hers and joyous, life-giving breath filled her lungs.

Her lips parted beneath his, taking everything he offered with unabashed pleasure. It was more than she'd ever expected, had ever hoped.

Her desire ramped up as his mouth and tongue slowly explored hers, her breath and blood racing through her body, matching the joy in her heart.

"Please," came her breathy plea. "Please, Alex."

He cut her off with another kiss, just to feel her tremble beneath him. Then he cupped one generous breast, his fingers curling around the soft flesh, and deep male possessiveness surged up.

"Yelena, do you have any idea what you're doing to me?"

"Yes." Her satisfied smile sent his blood boiling, made his groin so hard he was amazed he didn't lose it right then.

He fumbled with her skirt, bunching it up around her waist as she went for his belt buckle. When the zipper slid down and her hand closed around him, the world seemed to stop spinning.

"Yelena," he managed to get out, his breath hoarse with

need. He needn't have said a thing—she stepped from her shoes, and pulled off her pantyhose in record time, then went down to the sofa, pulling him with her.

They kissed again, at first languorous, then more urgent, before Alex quickly stood and tugged off his pants, then pushed her down into the soft cushions.

Quickly he nudged her legs apart with his knee. She spread them willingly. He paused above her, weight straining on his arms as he stamped her passionate features in his brain. Bruised full lips, flushed high cheekbones, eyes black with desire. And that mass of curly dark hair, spread across the floor.

Then he thrust and she gasped, her eyes springing open before pleasure closed them again.

"Alex," she murmured, wrapping her arms around his neck, his name on her lips rocketing his need.

Together they moved, a slow, sensual motion that gradually surged and built until they were both slick with sweat, panting for release.

With her frantic breath in his ear, Alex gathered her up and rolled, and suddenly she was on top and he was deeper than he'd ever been.

She let out a gasp, her thighs tightening around his waist before quickly finding his rhythm. His hands grabbed her waist, rocking her back and forth. He was entranced by the look of utter pleasure on her face as she rode him.

A deep groan ripped him apart, pleasure afire in every muscle, every nerve. She kept the pace, her teeth biting down on her swollen bottom lip, her rapturous expression urging him on until he finally leapt over the edge.

Yelena collapsed on his chest, sweet satisfaction thrumming as their sweat and heat mingled. And as their breath heaved, the aftershocks hit, reverberating through her body, trembling every muscle.

Her cheek rested on his chest, his pounding heart in her

ear, the echoing beat still throbbing between her legs. When his arms tightened around her, blatantly possessive but still deeply satisfying, she took in a deep breath, their earthy scent of lovemaking filling her senses.

All hers.

They lay there as their heartbeats gradually returned to normal, until the sounds from the outside world began to filter in—the faraway hum and beep of traffic, the gentle whir from her fridge.

After a few moments Yelena reluctantly rolled onto her back with a satisfied sigh.

A deep laugh of realization rumbled in Alex's chest.

At her quizzical look, he grinned. "One day, my love," he said, placing a tender kiss on her forehead, "promise me we'll actually make it to a bed."

Yelena smiled back at him, her heart tight with happiness.

His mouth met hers in a laugh. "Deal."

Epilogue

Two weeks later Yelena propped her head up on her elbow, dragging the bed sheet up over her breasts with a satisfied sigh.

"That had to be the best lunch break ever."

In her bed Alex lay beside her on his back, sweaty and replete from their furious lovemaking. He laughed, a deep joyful sound that prompted her to join in. When their laughter finally faded, she placed a hand on his chest. The hot, tempered skin over corded muscle felt delicious. And it was all hers.

From their pile of clothes on the floor came a muffled ringtone.

"Yours," Yelena said, then after a confused pause, "and mine?"

"Sounds like it," Alex said, throwing off the sheet before getting to his feet. Yelena's mouth went dry. Her gaze brushed over his wide shoulders, down the smooth muscular back, tapering waist and beautifully curved buttocks before ending at the pair of extremely masculine legs.

A glorious sight indeed.

"You gonna get that?" Alex said, plucking the phone out of his jacket.

"Mmm-hmm."

"Yelena." The exasperation in his glance was tempered with mischief. "Your phone."

With a sigh, she pulled the sheet around her, left the warm bed and rummaged through her clothes on the floor.

"Hello?"

When she hung up, Alex was sat on the edge of her bed, a pair of cotton boxers spoiling her view. But the wide grin on his face compensated for all that.

"That was Mum. The Director of Public Prosecutions is willing to make a deal."

Her heart swelled as she padded over to him, tossing her phone on the bed. "Really? What's going to happen?"

His hands shot out, grabbing the front of her sheet. Slowly he pulled and she ended up wedged between his powerful thighs. "Her attorney's going to explain everything tomorrow but the bottom line is no jail time. The DPP is reluctant to try such a high-profile case that involves long-term spousal abuse."

The flinch barely reached his eyes but Yelena still saw it. She gently cupped his rough face in her hands. "That's wonderful. I'm so happy for her. And for you."

She leaned down. His lips were warm and pliant, meeting hers eagerly, and slowly they explored each other, soft flesh testing and tasting, breath merging as the kiss lengthened then deepened.

When his tongue tangled with hers, her blood went from languid lethargy to full boil. She'd never get enough of this, this glorious heat that only Alex seemed to arouse.

His arms encircled her waist, hands questing, and soon the sheet fell in a pool at her feet. Rough palms met her bottom and he gave an appreciative murmur.

"Alex?" she got out as his lips moved from her mouth to her neck.

"Mmm?"

"Don't you want to know about my call?"

Alex pulled her sharply up against him and was rewarded with her sudden gasp, one that eased into a groan as he leaned in and slid his mouth over one nipple.

He grinned against her silken skin. "Not really."

"It was—" he nipped at the hard pebbled nub and she gasped "—Jonathon."

He muttered something unintelligible, his mouth full of hot flesh. As the blood sped through every vein, stirring his manhood, he swept his palms over the twin globes of her butt.

Beautiful, just beautiful. And she was all his.

"I quit."

"Okay." He left her bottom, making his way up over her hips, the gentle indentation of her waist, her torso until—

She pulled back, his face firmly in her hands. "Specifically I quit your campaign."

He frowned, embers of desire burning the edges of his concentration. "What? Why?"

"Because a partner who sleeps with the clientele isn't the right image for Bennett & Harper."

"They didn't approve." His hands fell.

"No. So I quit."

He blinked, confused by her wide grin. "But you wanted that promotion."

Her expression softened. "But I want you more. And I actually like the idea of being my own boss."

His arms snaked back around her waist. "Say that again."

"I said, I'm going to start my own PR co—"

He pulled and she crashed into his chest, her hands

instinctively going out to temper the fall. But he quickly rolled and suddenly she was under him on the bed.

"And I want you."

Her mouth tweaked in impish delight. "So you'd better do something now you've got me."

Alex kissed her until they were both flustered and aroused, until his body screamed for release and his blood echoed loud and fast in his ears. He groaned when she took his earlobe between her teeth, gently nibbling.

Then Yelena said, "And one more thing. It arrived today."

She heard his breath snag. She didn't need to elaborate: reaching over to pull the large envelope from her night stand was explanation enough.

She repositioned the sheet around her body, took a cross-legged seat on the bed and offered the envelope. "Do you want to open it?"

He stared at her, his expression jumbled. Slowly he nodded, took the envelope, ripped it open and unfolded the contents in silence. Yelena fiddled with her necklace, chewing on her bottom lip as he read.

"Well?" she said after a moment. "What does it say?"

"Hang on."

She waited a few more impatient seconds. "Well?"

Shocked, Alex looked up, eyes wide as everything ground to a whirling halt. "Bella is mine."

Joy and amazement bubbled up in Alex's chest, widening his mouth, making his face ache with a broad grin. How many times had he wished he could rewind time, change the past? Yet for all those hollow wishes, everything from his roller-coaster life had brought him to this one amazing moment.

"So you're happy," she said slowly.

His joyous shout startled her, making him laugh. "Yelena, love, I am thrilled beyond words."

He grabbed her and planted a deep, warm kiss on her

mouth, his breath quickening when she responded without hesitation.

Then he pulled back, brushed the hair from her eyes. "I love you, Yelena."

"And I love you."

"You know what would make this moment perfect?"

Her dark eyes practically twinkled. "Food?"

"No." He chuckled. "I was thinking more along the lines of 'let's get married' but I guess I could go a burger or—"

"Are you serious?" Her eyes rounded in a way that made his groin tighten in excited expectancy.

He grinned. "Yeah, I'm actually pretty hungry."

"Alex!" She thumped him on the shoulder, way too soft to do any kind of damage. Then she continued, more soberly. "My brother was out to ruin you. My family staged an intervention, remember?"

He cupped her cheek in his palm, savoring the feel of her soft, warm flesh in his. "And I am stunned and humbled that you chose me."

"It wasn't difficult." And, Yelena realized as she gazed into his eyes, it was the truth. Since their ultimatum, the Valeros had at first tried to lay down the law, alternately threatening then cajoling. At her impassive silence, they'd grudgingly agreed to announce Gabriela's death if she'd reconsider her stance. Yelena had thanked them and offered to write the release but on everything else she refused to bend.

Alex was all she'd ever wanted.

"So isn't it about time you became part of my family?"

The pure, unadulterated love radiating from him choked the very breath from her lungs. Was it possible to have too much joy?

Slowly she leaned forward, kissed him gently on the lips.

"I love you, Alex. I'd marry you tomorrow if we could."

He grabbed her, his murmur of triumph warm against her mouth. "I'm sure we can work something out."

As desire swiftly rushed in, Yelena realized that throughout every trial she'd faced, every hardship, fantasies still came true. And then all thought fled as Alex proceeded to show her a few of his own.

* * * * *

2 in 1
GREAT
VALUE

THE MILLIONAIRE MEETS HIS MATCH by Kate Carlilse

Adam Duke's mother plans to marry him off. And when his desirable assistant, Trish James, hints she wants more than just a business relationship, alarm bells go off…

DANTE'S TEMPORARY FIANCÉE by Day Leclaire

Rafe Dante's family paraded women in front of him. Until Rafe hired sweet Larkin Thatcher to be his fake fiancée…

HIS CONVENIENT VIRGIN BRIDE by Barbara Dunlop

Just weeks after their roll in the hay, virgin Stephanie Ryder was expecting his baby. Now millionaire Alec Creighton's proposing…

SEDUCTION ON THE CEO'S TERMS by Charlene Sands

Frustrated that her boss was judging her by her looks, Ali had a reverse makeover. Ironically, as a plain-Jane, she *really* caught the wealthy bachelor's eye.

VIRGIN PRINCESS, TYCOON'S TEMPTATION by Michelle Celmer

Garrett Sutherland wanted his biggest claim to fame to be the seduction of Princess Louisa—the infamous virgin princess.

THE SECRET CHILD & THE COWBOY CEO by Janice Maynard

Trent Sinclair had never forgiven Bryn Matthews and her lies. But Bryn had returned…with a child he could not deny was pure Sinclair.

On sale from 17th June 2011
Don't miss out!

*Available at WHSmith, Tesco, ASDA, Eason
and all good bookshops*

www.millsandboon.co.uk

0611/

MILLS & BOON®

are proud to present

June 2011
Ordinary Girl in a Tiara
by Jessica Hart
from Mills & Boon® Riva™

Caro Cartwright's had enough of romance – she's after a quiet life. Until an old school friend begs her to stage a gossip-worthy royal diversion! Reluctantly, Caro prepares to masquerade as a European prince's latest squeeze…

Available 3rd June 2011

July 2011
Lady Drusilla's Road to Ruin
by Christine Merrill
from Mills & Boon® Historical

Considered a spinster, Lady Drusilla Rudney has only one role in life: to chaperon her sister. So when her flighty sibling elopes, Dru employs the help of a fellow travelling companion, ex-army captain John Hendricks, who looks harmless enough…

Available 1st July 2011

Tell us what you think!

millsandboon.co.uk/community
facebook.com/romancehq
twitter.com/millsandboonuk

BAD BLOOD

A POWERFUL
DYNASTY,
WHERE SECRETS
AND SCANDAL
NEVER SLEEP!

VOLUME 1 – 15th April 2011
TORTURED RAKE
by Sarah Morgan

VOLUME 2 – 6th May 2011
SHAMELESS PLAYBOY
by Caitlin Crews

VOLUME 3 – 20th May 2011
RESTLESS BILLIONAIRE
by Abby Green

VOLUME 4 – 3rd June 2011
FEARLESS MAVERICK
by Robyn Grady

8 VOLUMES IN ALL TO COLLECT!

www.millsandboon.co.uk

Polo, players & passion

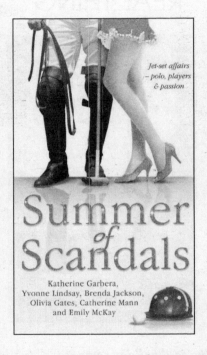

The polo season—the rich mingle, passions run hot and scandals surface...

Available 1st July 2011

www.millsandboon.co.uk

SIZZLING HOLIDAY FLING...OR THE REAL THING?

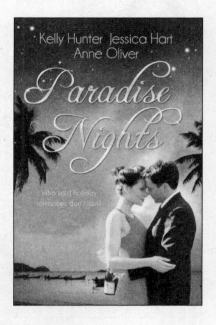

Who said holiday romances didn't last?
As the sun sets the seduction begins...
Who can resist the baddest of boys?

Available 1st July 2011

www.millsandboon.co.uk

FREE BOOK
AND A SURPRISE GIFT

We would like to take this opportunity to thank you for reading this Mills & Boon® book by offering you the chance to take a specially selected book from the Desire™ 2-in-1 series absolutely FREE! We're also making this offer to introduce you to the benefits of the Mills & Boon® Book Club™—

- **FREE home delivery**
- **FREE gifts and competitions**
- **FREE monthly Newsletter**
- **Exclusive Mills & Boon Book Club offers**
- **Books available before they're in the shops**

Accepting this FREE book and gift places you under no obligation to buy, you may cancel at any time, even after receiving your free book. Simply complete your details below and return the entire page to the address below. You don't even need a stamp!

YES Please send me a free Desire 2-in-1 book and a surprise gift. I understand that unless you hear from me, I will receive 2 superb new 2-in-1 books every month for just £5.30 each, postage and packing free. I am under no obligation to purchase any books and may cancel my subscription at any time. The free book and gift will be mine to keep in any case.

Ms/Mrs/Miss/Mr _____ Initials _____

_____

Surname _____

Address _____

_____

_____ Postcode _____

E-mail_____

Send this whole page to: Mills & Boon Book Club, Free Book Offer, FREEPOST NAT 10298, Richmond, TW9 1BR.